ABSORPTION

Also by John Meaney from Gollancz:

Bone Song
Dark Blood

ABSORPTION

RAGNAROK TRILOGY

Book 1

JOHN MEANEY

GOLLANCZ
LONDON

First published in Great Britain in 2010 by Gollancz
An imprint of the Orion Publishing Group
Orion House, 5 Upper St Martin's Lane, London WC2H 9EA
An Hachette UK Company

A CIP catalogue record for this book is available from the British Library

ISBN 978 0 575 08533 6 (Cased)
ISBN 978 0 575 08532 9 (Trade Paperback)

1 3 5 7 9 10 8 6 4 2

Typeset by Input Data Services Ltd,
Bridgwater, Somerset

Printed in Great Britain by
Clays Ltd, St Ives plc

www.johnmeaney.com
www.orionbooks.co.uk

A note on Norse names:

In English, the letter combination *th* has two pronunciations – compare 'this'll' (as in *this'll be good*) with 'thistle'.

The following names have a hard *th* as in 'this' or 'other': Óthinn, Heithrún.

These names have a soft *th* as in 'thistle' or 'thing': Thórr, Thórrvaldr.

PROLOGUE

Asleep, a man of living crystal lies on a silver bier. Can it be possible to truly sleep with eyelids so clear, so transparent? Yet he does, he and the crystalline woman nearby. Her bier is silver too, inscribed with angular scarlet runes glowing softly in vacuum.

Is that a twitch of the man's fingertip?

Around them stands a hall of glass and sapphire hung with shields, some of battered leather while others look unused. All bear runes that glimmer red.

The man's face wrinkles – highlights rippling through pliable crystal – and he rocks his head, rolls a little to one side, then sees the woman. Pushing himself up, he swings his legs to sit sideways on the bier.

—*You're so beautiful, and I know you.*

They are words without sound, for there is no air in here. Oddly, it makes no difference to the way he feels, chest swelling as if inhaling vacuum, fluids moving inside his complex body, his mind coming alive. The woman's name does not matter for now, and neither does his own. Soon, he will know all he needs to know.

Scarlet runes are glowing brighter now.

Down to the floor – he feels its temperature through crystalline soles, hears nothing save the internal sounds of his body – and finds it easy to stand, to walk, to look around. There is an archway, and he walks towards it, through it; and he finds a larger hall, star-shaped with nine pointed annexes. Near the ceiling, a constellation of nineteen dots of sapphire light is shining.

Each annexe leads to a hall with polished biers. The nearest, a place of silver and emerald, contains another crystalline man, while above him floats an array of twenty-three shining lights, all of them green, like burning copper.

He remembers burning, and oxygen, and being alive in normal flesh.

Then he staggers, with this memory:

Floating in space, surrounded by a billion blazing suns. Tumbling, he sees what he was meant to see: like a needle thrust by gods through the galactic core, a jet one thousand lightyears in extent, its brightness a soundless resonance in his mind, a scream of fear amid magnificence, because this should not *be here.*

This is the work of Darkness.

As he rotates, the abomination slides out of sight, and he can remember what he should be feeling: awe and joyous humility, for he is the tiniest fragment of awareness at the galaxy's heart, living for an eyeblink, no more; so how important can humanity's welfare be?

But then the galactic jet is visible once more, and this time he feels anger, because humans may be insignificant to the cosmic history but not to ourselves, and the betrayers deserve to die, while we do what we can against the Darkness.

There is a spear on the wall nearby, and he takes it down to use as a staff. The runes along its shaft flare brightly at his touch. He stands for a while, leaning on the weapon, letting the emotions from his flash of memory diminish. Soon he will deal with things much better.

From one annexe, a corridor leads away, long and straight, ending in a patch of blackness that draws him. He begins to walk, first with the spear's support, then with a growing feeling of aliveness. Shifting his grip, he continues with the weapon held horizontally beside his thigh, feeling secure. In this place, there is no danger.

He comes out on a rune-carved balcony of stone, and stares at a black star-strewn sky above a landscape of grey and sharp black shadows, a chiaroscuro of lunar wilderness, because this is indeed the moon that orbits Earth, the world that gave birth to humanity but not to him, not directly.

Beneath the clouds of that living world, bands of crimson and silver shine more brightly than oceanic blue. What they signify, he does not know.

—Hello my love.

The words are inside his head. Smiling, he turns to see the crystalline woman.

—My beautiful Gavi.

—Is that my name?

He reaches out, his clear hand grasping hers.

—I am sure it is. If you remember mine, let me know.

They stand looking out at the surface for some unknown time.

—How long have we slept?

It is a fair question. He is about to tell her that he does not know when something causes his gaze to drift to a familiar constellation. Three distinct stars form a row.

—See Orion's belt. What colour is the central star?

—It seems . . . red. Does that mean something?

If he waits long enough, she'll remember the answer by herself. He tells her anyway.

—It means a million years have passed.

Her fingers squeeze his.

—So much time.

They stare at the banded Earth, sharing wonder, not knowing why they are here. Then words sound inside them, delivered by a feminine voice they respond to, a voice of command.

—You remember what we've always known to do. Observe what the enemy does, deduce what the enemy intends, and then prevent it.

It is the awakened woman, Gavi, who responds:

—And now we fight the Darkness?

—Now we fight.

From the lunar night, like the All-Father's eye, the

homeworld of humanity regards them, as it swirls with cloud, banded with silver and crimson, changed in ways they cannot know. The crystalline man raises his spear, saluting Earth.

And then, in soundless vacuum, he laughs.

ONE

FULGOR, 2603 AD

Roger rolled straight out of bed, to his feet. According to his old school's neurokinaesthetics teacher, this was typical acrophobic behaviour; but all he knew was it felt good to be alive, particularly today, because this was freedom. It was also scary: tomorrow, aged eighteen Standard, he would wake up in a new room, his parents far away.

His physical wake-up routine was complex, moving his limbs through clover-leaf patterns, rolling on the floor, neither dance nor yoga nor fighting yet with elements of all. It had been a while since anyone had bullied him; but he remembered the humiliation.

Slapping a glob of pine-scented smartgel on his chest, he walked around the room, touching each wall in turn, tapping the orange quickglass bed with his foot, saying farewell. As the gel wriggled across his skin, cleansing and exfoliating, he checked the tu-ring on his middle finger. Above it, a tiny real-image holo ninja sprang into being, holding a scroll that spread out into an old-style FourSpeak lattice, listing the templates stored inside: his favourite holodramas, his furniture design – if he wanted his new room to look like this one, then it would – and his clothing, all his artefacts besides childhood toys. Those, he was leaving here.

All the information he needed was in his tu-ring. He was packed, ready to go.

After pulling on a suit of clothing, he tuned the fabric to dark-blue edged with yellow, and hardened the slippers' soles, suitable for outdoor walking. Then he tapped his tu-ring, and pointed at the quickglass bed, subvocalizing a command.

The orange quickglass shivered, grew viscous, and melted into the floor, absorbing the smartfabric duvet. Some people changed their living environment daily; but his room's configuration remained static in normal times. Dissolving the bed was a gesture, marking a transition.

An adult at last.

He went down to breakfast. Mum smiled at him, waving a bowl of peach rice.

'You need to fuel up. Big day, isn't it?'

'I guess so, Aged Parents. Dad, are we going in to the city together?'

But his father's eyes were solid white, the smartlenses opaque, lasing images against his retinas. Even over breakfast, he was hard at work.

'Carl, have words with your upstart son, why don't you.'

'Sure.' Dad's smartlenses cleared. 'Plasma. Negentropy. Custard. How am I doing?'

His eyes looked grey now. That was no more the truth than white opacity had been.

'You're confused,' said Roger. 'I can beat you this morning.'

'Suicide chess, seven dimensions. Most negative points in two minutes to win.'

In 2- or 3-D, it was a fast game, offering pieces to the opponent to take, the objective being to get rid of your pieces as quickly as possible. Given a vulnerable opposing piece, you had to take it; but if there were several, you got to choose, and that was part of the art. Seven dimensions could slow the game right down, or cause cataclysmic high-speed reversals, depending on the game-flow.

'Deal.'

Mum said nothing as they worked on virtual boards visible only to them, Roger flinging around his yellow pieces with subvocalized instructions, failing to hold back the onslaught of red attackers he was bound to take, unable to avoid the tide dissolving before him.

When the game popped out of existence, Mum put a bowl of rice in front of Roger.

'He'll take you in to Lucis City anyway, never mind.'

Roger looked at Dad, and they both shook their heads.

'Mum, you're a genius.'

Part of the game had been to mask their body language. Without access to their shared virtual holo, Mum should have been unable to work out who won – though the odds were against Roger.

'I try to keep up with my favourite son,' she said.

'You know I'm your *only* son.'

'That's right, isn't it? Fair enough.'

Dad smiled. The banter was familiar.

'But there's no such thing as—'

'—a fair fight,' Roger and Mum said together.

'Keep that in mind' – Dad smiled with one side of his mouth – 'in the big, bad world.'

Mum let out a breath.

'I'll remember.' Roger blinked, misting his smartlenses. 'I— Whew. Is it time we got going?'

'You haven't finished your—'

'I don't think I can. When I get there, I'll eat. Promise.'

'You're not too big to get a clip around the ear.'

'No.' Roger smiled at her. 'And I never will be.'

Dad's hand clapped his shoulder.

'Spoken like a man.'

'Goodbye, Mum,' said Roger.

The aircab ascended in a spiral, the house and its blue surrounding flagstones diminishing below. In the Conjoined Calderae to the north, giant silver guardian fish leaped from dark waters, hunting pterashrikes. Overhead, stretched a lime-green sky with golden-cream clouds.

They passed over a scree slope leading to the nearest hypozone. Far from its natural habitat, a purple native slimegel followed a slick track, moving by laminar flow, sheets of tissue looping like caterpillar tracks. Once out of poisonous oxygen, it would split apart to form a fast-moving herd of fist-sized blobbers.

'That's a big one,' said Roger. 'Near to budding.'

He meant generating a sub-organism, a daughter herd.

'How can you tell?' Dad touched his shoulder. 'You belong here, son, in a way I never will.'

A tight claw of tension squeezed Roger's torso.

Then why don't you let me leave?

Because there were other places he could venture, far beyond Lucis City, beyond the world of Fulgor, even beyond the universe. But this was a hired aircab, and for all of Dad's capabilities, the stakes were too high to discuss confidential matters here. If he'd wanted to raise the subject, he should have done so at home.

That was what he thought. But what Dad did next surprised him.

'Let's talk openly.'

'But—'

'This aircab is, well, special. We're protected here.'

Beneath them, a valley was filled with striped fog, a moving tiger-skin configuration of purple and green, forming a Turing pattern: emergent properties from simple chemistry.

'How protected?'

'This much.' Dad reached up and dabbed at his eyes, removing his smartlenses. 'See?'

Freed of disguise, his natural eyes were obsidian, without surrounding whites. Black upon black, dark as space.

'You can't be serious.' Roger reached up to his own smartlenses, then stopped. 'I can't.'

'That's a good inhibition to have, son.'

'While I'm among ordinary humans, you mean.'

'Yes. You *do* belong here, Roger. I meant that.'

'And Labyrinth? Isn't that where I was born?'

Dad looked away as if checking the sky, but if they weren't shielded from SatScan then they wouldn't be speaking like this.

'Maybe I've been wrong.'

Roger tried to work out the right words to say, some persuasive rhetoric that would change Dad's mind all the way. Nothing occurred to him.

'You've had to live with secrets your whole life,' said Dad. 'We even wore smartlenses around you at home when you were a baby.'

'I know.' Meaning, he'd heard the stories before. 'I don't remember that, or the time in nursery that you had to mindwipe the teacher.'

'It was a very selective amnesia,' said Dad. 'And you only betrayed yourself once.'

'Betrayed you, you mean.'

There was a tightness in Roger's voice that he hadn't intended, a roughness of accusation.

'It's important, what we do here. But there's something I've forgotten to tell you, son.'

'What's that?'

'The most important things in my life are you and your mother.'

Such simple words. There was a directness in those jet-black eyes that Roger could not withstand. Then he rubbed his face and made himself smile.

'What about your other lover?'

'My–? Ah. Well. *Her.*'

'She'll take you any place you like, any time. Doesn't it make you want to fly away from Fulgor, away from everything?'

Dad's answer was filled with surprising vulnerability.

'You'll never know how much.'

Neither said anything as Dad replaced his smartlenses and his normal expression, settled back in the seat, and closed his eyes, pretending to work.

They alighted on the edge of a piazza, in the shadow of an aqueduct. Dad paid the aircab, the fare a simple four-dimensional money matrix in the two-hundred-dimensional phase space of Fulgidi finance. Occasionally Mum or Dad complained about the complexity of buying or selling, especially if any Luculenti were involved; but Roger had never known anything different.

The cab ascended into the green sky, looped behind a grandiose quickglass tower, and was gone. This week's architectural fashion favoured trompe-l'oeil illusions, and many of the two dozen towers in sight looked translucent or oddly shaped, including several that were formed from 'impossible' polygons, or appeared to be. Skywalks hung among the towers like necklaces, sparkling where the sunlight struck.

'You're mediating some kind of deal?' Roger said.

'Uh-huh. The more sophisticated Fulgidi merchants become, the more resourcefully they find ways to disagree with each other.'

'I never thought of that.'

'So often they fail to negotiate because their plans are just so twisty and complex.'

There was something different in Dad's tone, as if talking to an equal. Or perhaps that was some kind of wishful thinking.

'You've got to go straight away?'

'I'm afraid so. I want to catch some of them before the meeting starts. How long have you got to wait?'

'Another forty-seven minutes.' Roger knew the answer automatically. 'I thought I might buy myself some jantrasta, maybe some chocolate.'

'Chocolate.'

'Some new thing from Earth.'

'Wasn't that the name of an old programming language? Anyway, have a good first day.'

They hugged.

'Thanks, Dad.'

As Dad walked away, he reformatted his clothes so that a pale-grey cloak hung from his shoulders. He walked towards a sheer ceramic pillar, support for an aqueduct, then brushed past a steel buttress. Only Roger saw what happened next.

Dad's hand disappeared *inside* the solid-looking steel, came out in a fist, then tucked inside his cloak. Out in the open like this, SatScan would normally notice such a manoeuvre – but an attenuated tingling in his nerves told Roger that Dad had deployed a smartmiasma to make subtle optical shifts in light travelling upward.

It was called a dead-letter drop, and his parents had taught him the basics and the variations years ago; while the technique itself was centuries old. Tried and true, was how Dad described it.

For even espionage has its traditions.

TWO

EARTH, 777 AD

Ice covered the upper slopes, reflecting cold orange dawn. Above, circled two black ravens. On a wide irregular ledge, Ulfr crouched, spear in one hand, his other fist inside Brandr's leather collar, tight against the war-hound's bunched and trembling muscles.

Their prey, so magnificent, so handsome, paused beneath their ledge, perhaps hearing the beating of hunters' hearts, or sensing their breath upon the air. Antlers raised as nostrils flared, chestnut eyes widening, searching for the source of unease.

Ulfr's thumb rubbed the true-aim rune that Eira had inscribed upon his spear-shaft. The gesture brought back the memory of chanting, and the altered perceptions that came with the ritual. Now, the stag seemed to grow huge in his vision while the landscape faded. Life-blood beat in the long artery in the neck: Ulfr could see the pulse.

Soon it would be time.

But a raven cawed overhead, causing the stag to jerk upward and catch sight of Ulfr, the whites of its eyes showing as it jumped back; and there was nothing Ulfr could do but fling everything into the moment. He slammed the spear downward in a throw of power, not finesse. Then he was launching himself, springing from rock to rock, while Brandr flowed past him, cutting off the route to the forest.

Clenching and unclenching the big buttock muscles, dark hooves arcing, fastened spear bobbing from its side, the stag ran, clattering across stony ground, swishing through gorse and heather, fleeing the hunters, Ulfr and Brandr, sprinting in its wake.

The stag kicked out but Brandr dodged.

'To me,' called Ulfr.

Brandr loped back, then trotted alongside Ulfr as he dropped the pace. Ahead was a desolate, beautiful stretch of heathland and ice, and the stag might continue for hours yet, perhaps until the day's end. The hunt was about to become a test of endurance, more suited to a youthful warrior than to his hound; and Ulfr would have to make sure that he kept track of Brandr's fitness. Many times he had run with Brandr across his shoulders.

They immersed themselves in running.

Eira sometimes said the Norns weave fate at varying speeds, and the present slowed into a single, elongated moment as the pale sun rose to its midday height. All was movement, breath from the working of torso and arms, warmth in the legs' big muscles, the feeling that he could run forever; while Brandr kept pace.

At some point, the spear sucked free of the wound, and the blood-streaked stag ran on, faster for a while. Ulfr dipped to retrieve the weapon, slowing for a moment, before resuming the rhythm of the chase, heartbeat and footsteps in time with the chanting in his head, the mesmeric hunting song he memorized as a child of five, some twelve summers ago.

He was smiling and Brandr's teeth were bared, hunters together, doing what they were born to do, bound by love, sharing joy in the toughness of the moment.

It was late afternoon when the stag failed to clear a rock, stumbled and went down. It lay on its side, kicking, saliva frothing at the sides of its small mouth, eyes wide as Ulfr leaned over, one fist against his chest as he uttered the words of Thórr's blessing. So clear and dark and insightful, those eyes—

Now.

—that seemed to fill with mist, like the surface of a lake at dawn, while the final breath was hoarse, drawn out, lasting beyond the final kick of limbs.

'Thank you,' said Ulfr. 'You honour us with the treasure of your gift.'

His knife-blade was of bronze, and it sliced deep and fast, so that slick hotness bathed his hand, blood steaming in the still-cool air, as he cut the liver free. He sliced it into nine pieces, tossed two to Brandr and bit into one, thanking his prey for the warm life it gave him. Blood trickled down his chin, and he wiped it.

Afterwards he made a dry heather fire using flint and iron, wrapped the remaining liver pieces in mud and put them to cook. Returning to the stag's body, he unwound cords from his waist – cured sinews from the bear he slew last winter with Hallsteinn's help – and bound its legs together.

Then he sat with knees drawn up by the fire, one arm hugging Brandr close, sharing warmth while the liver cooked; and the carcass of its former owner stared with lifeless eyes.

Night was a grey-black cavern, clouds like shrouds obscuring the stars, and the moon's glow was dull. Ulfr passed the village boundary, the dead stag heavy on his shoulders, Brandr trotting at his side. Ahead, the long halls were cast into silhouette by orange-lit smoke from the fire-pit that lay beyond. There was a thunk of axe-head in wood, then another, followed by sarcastic laughter. Ulfr wondered who was winning the competition, who was losing, and how much they had bet.

Then a moan resonated through the night and he stopped, the carcass pressing against the back of his neck. He squatted down to shrug the weight off, almost springing into the air with release as he stood once more, freed of the burden.

Brandr snarled.

'With me,' said Ulfr.

Was that a raven's shadow passing overhead through night-time clouds?

'Me next,' he heard. It sounded like Tófi's voice, followed by: 'Good aim.'

This time there was a definite cry.

'You whimper like a girl.' That growl could only come from Thórrvaldr, bear-like warrior and the village's weaponsmith. 'Your manhood's next. I like to aim for small targets.'

'That's too small even for you,' said someone.

What in the name of Niflheim was happening? Ulfr circled his shoulders, trying to loosen the bands of pain, and tossed his spear from one hand to the other. Then he strode past the single men's living-hall and halted, taking in the firelit drama that was worse than he had feared.

Jarl, his friend and Eira's brother, stood bound to the hall's doorpost by leather ropes, his shoulder split apart, jagged white-grey bones soaked in sopping red, gashes and wounds across his torso and bare thighs, a leather gag in his mouth, the terror of Hel in his eyes.

An axe sailed end-over-end through the air and smacked into Jarl's stomach, burying its iron head, splitting his liver. Ulfr thought back to the stag, then pushed the memory aside.

'What's going on?' he called.

Behind the men he knew, a cloaked man pulled down the brim of his hat, and slipped back into shadow. Then a tall warrior with long moustaches and braided hair stepped in front of Ulfr. It took a moment to recognize him: Skári, who had gone a-viking as far as Hibernia, normally emotionless, his expression odd and twisted in the firelight.

'Young Jarl,' he said, 'took himself a lover. Over the mountain, as if that would stop us finding out.'

'A lover?'

'But not a girl, see? This one pokes *men*. How disgusting is that?'

'I don't—' This made no sense. 'Stop now.'

'Too late for that. Too late for shit-dick here.'

Another axe, another *thunk* – a butcher's sound – and a

gagged scream from Jarl, eyes wide as he stared at Ulfr, then nothing as he slumped, head down.

Too late for life.

Jarl was suffering but there was no healer who could deal with such wounds, except perhaps in the old stories, not in the hard reality of the Middle World.

'I'm sorry,' said Ulfr.

He took two paces forward as he threw.

So sorry, my friend.

The spear cracked through ribs, ripped the heart apart and pierced the wooden post. Death was immediate. Ulfr thumped his fist against his chest, then raised it, offering the sign of Thórr's hammer to the disembodied shade.

Soon enough, poor Jarl would begin his journey to Niflheim and the kingdom of Hel.

I've killed Eira's brother.

How could poor Jarl, no matter how far he strayed from warrior ways, deserve this? Even some of the gods – the darker gods – were shapeshifters and gender-changers: Óthinn as much as Loki, the All-Father and the Trickster, both evil as much as good, ruthless and tricky. Was it any wonder that some men followed those ways instead of the bluff, straightforward lives of ordinary warriors, the children of Thórr?

The village's foremost archer, Ivárr, was approaching with bow in hand. He looked at Jarl, then at Ulfr, and nodded.

'No one deserves that,' he said. 'Well done.'

'But you didn't try to stop them.'

'What, fight the whole village? Defy the chief's orders?'

Everything was awful.

'Folkvar ordered this?'

'Yes, or so they said.' Ivárr moved his chin to indicate Thórrvaldr and Snorri. 'They were at a feast with the poet, and someone said what Jarl had been up to. I'd been outside to piss, and when I went back in for another mead—Anyway. They'd already hammered Jarl to the ground.'

'Feasting with the poet? *Jarl's* the poet. Or was.'

'I mean the other one. He—The other one.'

Lines of puzzlement deepened on faces all around: Ivárr and Snorri, Hávarthr and Ormr, Vermundr and Steinn and Thórvalldr, glancing at each other or down at the ground, puzzling something out.

Far off in the distance, disturbing chords of music sounded: *da, da-dum, da-da-da-dum, da-da.*

'Do you hear that?' Ulfr knew as he formed the words that they were pointless. 'Never mind.'

He would ask Eira. She would know what the music meant. Except ... except she had a slain brother to mourn, riven by axes and killed by his spear, and how could this have happened?

'We were ensorcelled,' said Ivárr. 'Does everyone agree?'

There were both shakes and nods of the head, and many frowns.

'I guess.' Thórrvaldr inhaled, expanding his barrel chest, then blew out. 'Maybe we were.'

'So who was this poet?' said Ulfr.

'Poet?'

'I thought there was—Ivárr, you said the feast was for a poet, yes?'

'I don't ... know.'

Ulfr looked from warrior to warrior, seeing only confusion.

'Whatever happened, it's fading.'

'Um.' Steinn rubbed his face. 'What's going on?'

'Nothing now.'

Then Steinn jumped back, blood fading from his cheeks, raising his hand to point at Jarl's bloodied corpse.

'Gods, what is this?'

'You don't remember?'

'What—? No. I had a dream that we killed him. But we couldn't have, because ... because ...'

While the others grew horrified at their own thoughts, Ulfr stepped forward and wrenched his spear free. A dreadful hiss sounded – could Jarl be alive? – but it was gases from the corpse, no more. His shade was already gone.

With his knife, Ulfr cut the body down and laid it straight upon the ground. Poor Jarl.

'So where has Eira got to?'

'She, um ... Folkvar ordered Ári to watch over her.' Thórvarr shrugged his huge shoulders. 'He wanted to keep her safe.'

Thórvarr's gaze kept sliding away from Jarl's corpse, then slowly returning.

'In the *volvas*' hut?'

'Uh, yes.'

Unwiped spear in hand, Brandr at his side, Ulfr walked away. Let the others deal with the body. How was he going to explain that his weapon had ended her brother's life? Inside himself, he searched for any feeling of blood-thrill as he remembered the throwing of the spear, any sign of the same ensorcelment that had affected the others. But all he could find was a deep, desperate sorrow and a need to end Jarl's suffering, nothing more. Surely Eira would accept that.

Then he was at the entrance to the hut, once shared by Eira and her teacher; but old Nessa had died last summer, leaving Eira the only *volva* – priestess and seeress – in this or the neighbouring valleys. The man standing guard, Ári, looked blank-faced, and his eyes were making continuous rapid blinks. Ulfr had a good idea what that meant.

'Is Eira inside?'

'Y-yes.'

'Never mind. I'll look anyhow.'

Inside, the hut smelled of herbs and incense. Runes, both painted and carved, formed lines along the ashwood beams. Of course there was no Eira. Poor Ári was entranced, and there could be just one reason; but Eira was too late to prevent Jarl's death.

At my hand.

But Chief Folkvar had given the orders. What an angry *volva* might do to a miscreant warrior-chief was unthinkable. If she blamed him—

'Sorry.' He brushed past Ári, exiting fast. 'Relax.'

Ári had gone for his sword – he'd probably forgotten Ulfr was inside – but stopped, perhaps because it was Ulfr and not Eira running from the hut.

Inside the main hall, Folkvar was frozen in his wooden chair, one arm upraised and stiff, while Eira – her copper hair incandescent in the torchlight – stood with tightened fists, tears shining on her suffering face. In a rage she could make Folkvar forget his name or experience paralysis in arms or legs. Once, old Nessa had caused Folkvar's predecessor to go blind for nine days, as punishment for letting a young cattle-thief go free. The chief had not known the thief was a rapist too.

All of the tribe's women were fierce, but the *volva*s, seeress-priestesses, were something more.

'Don't do it,' said Ulfr.

'Jarl is dead.'

'I know.'

'By Freyja . . .' She stared at his spear's bloodied point. '*You.*'

'He was suffering when I found him.'

'Truth.'

'Yes.'

She turned back to Folkvar, slipped her fingertips down his eyelids, then touched the back of his upraised wrist.

'As your spirit lowers your hand, good Folkvar, you slip deeper and deeper into normal sleep, and when you awaken later you will remember all the visiting poet said and did, and be able to tell me free of any ensorcelling effects he left behind as you sink deeper now.'

Folkvar's hand touched his thigh and his chin lowered, his breathing grew easy, and the softest of snores arose.

'He was ensorcelled,' she said, 'but you were not. I'm sorry, Ulfr.'

'But Jarl's pain was—'

'You told the truth. Let me do the same.'

'So you see me as your brother's killer.'

'I'm sorry.'

There was more to it than that, or she would have struck him down with whatever punishment she'd had in mind for Folkvar. But however much she knew that he had granted Jarl a kind of mercy, she also saw the killing thrust inside her mind, and could not forgive him for it.

At least that was how he understood her words.

When he came to – he hadn't realized he was drifting into sleep – he and Folkvar were still in the hall, and Brandr was sitting on the rushes beside him, but Eira was gone.

Stígr wept for the beautiful boy he had killed. Seated on a hard rock, staff in hand, he sobbed, while his ravens circled in the darkness above. If only they would leave him alone.

But he knew, by the burning of his left eye – the eye that was missing, that did not exist – that however the darkness chose to manifest, however far it sometimes seemed to drift away, it was bound to him, and he to it, forever.

Sweet Jarl, with lips so soft.

On a mouth that was cold and hardened now, soon to be food for worms, unless the villagers chose an honourable burning.

As he stood, though it was already night, shadows seemed to curl around him, swirling and embracing. Pulling his hat low, gathering his cape, he took a step forward, then another and another, moving as if in dream – call it nightmare – and when his mind cleared, he was at the top of a moonlit slope, looking down upon a village. This would be several days removed by normal walking from the place where Jarl had lived beneath Chief Folkvar's rule.

One less poet in the world could never be a good thing, but the shadows had spoken and Stígr could only hear and do what they commanded.

It had been so long since things were otherwise.

Another village. Perhaps I can stay longer this time.

Sometimes there were periods of ease, of silence from the voices. He was due another sojourn, a time to recuperate.

Here, someone had posted night-time sentinels – he could sense their hiding-places – and even with his protection, descending to the village would be a risk. In the morning, he would make himself known.

And take advantage once more.

He forced that thought behind him, then sank down to the ground, curled up inside his rough cloak, and pulled down his hat to cover his face, denying the sight of the ravens that circled still, high above in the night.

THREE

FULGOR, 2603 AD

Sumptuous in cream and gold, the hollow sphere was decorated in the neo-baroque mode, and it could accommodate three hundred floating people for a dance or choral evening. At the centre, Rashella Stargonier floated, her skin sparkling with maggel, her gown and cape fluttering in a simulated breeze, while symphonic music played, composed on the fly by a part of her mind, performed by the house system, reflecting and elaborating her mood, intensifying her focus during meditation.

Her Lupus Festival celebrations would be complex, taking her guests through subtle changes in emotional state as they passed along the rooms and halls of Mansion Stargonier, the dinner and cognitive entertainments a statement of expertise to surpass even last year's success. It was taking considerable time to plan, for while – as a Luculenta – she could form in-Skein corporate empires in a matter of seconds, her guests would be Luculenti too. That meant an evening's extravaganza required coordination on a timescale of deciseconds, backed by femtoscopic technology.

She was having fun.

From a peripheral channel of awareness, a cascading windchime sounded.

'Hello,' she said, slowing to ordinary human speech.

The holo sharpened into rich colours, real-image rather than virtual, depicting a bearded man's head and shoulders some five times life-size. The communication channel was in Skein, but only in what Luculenti called Periphery among themselves: simple protocols for simple folk, unenhanced Fulgidi and other humans.

'Please excuse the interruption,' said Greg Ranulph in magnification.

Had she wanted, Rashella could have read every emotion from the degree of tumescence in his lips, the lividity of his facial skin, the dilation and saccades – flickering search patterns – of his eyes. But Ranulph was only her gardener, and whatever *he* thought of his part-time position here – with his doctorates in biomath and ecoform engineering – she considered him a temporary adjunct to the house system's expertise in landscaping and garden management.

Still, her parents raised her to be nice to the hired help.

'You're a welcome diversion, Greg. Have you sent down the borers yet?'

'Just about to, ma'am.'

So what wasn't he telling her?

'Er, I *did* try a first probe,' he went on. 'Just inside the western boundary.'

'And the result was?'

'It's secreting symteria just fine.'

For anyone who wanted a designer ecosystem that combined organisms native to two worlds, symteria seeding was a necessary early step, allowing hybrids access to microlife that combined both biochemistries. From the tension and release in Ranulph's voice, this wasn't where the problem lay.

'What about the borer-probe itself?'

'It, er, made its own mind up about where to go. But it settled eventually, eight metres down.'

The borers were an expensive model – and their control systems were designed and grown by a company Rashella had inherited from her father, its ownership buried so deep in layers of corporate aggregation and trading proxies that Ranulph could not know it.

'I'll be right there.'

'You mean in person?' There was unconscious joy and surprise in the widening of his eyes. 'Physically?'

'That's what I mean.'

Although if she'd anticipated this response, she might have worked in Skein. Could he really find her attractive as well as overwhelming?

Never mind. He could never be more than an employee, for her passion and cognitive powers would burn someone like him: think snowflake, dropped inside a nova.

She cut the comm channel, ran a fingertip along the nine golden studs that arced across her brow, then spread her hands.

Floating forward, she rode the mag-field toward huge golden petals that furled back on themselves, revealing the corridor beyond. There, as her feet touched the patterned carpet, it began to flow, carrying her along. In alcoves stood disparate works of art – bronze sculptures from every Molsin sky-city, a living sand-picture shipped from Sereflex, song-motes from Nulapeiron – forming nested subtle themes. Wanting the exertion, she began to walk, while allowing the carpet to continue flowing, adding to her speed.

A linear gradient of exotic fragrance was replaced by an interwoven series of blossom scents and animal musks from seven worlds, far beyond a professional parfumier to appreciate, not without upraise to Luculentus capabilities.

Entering a vast white-and-glass atrium, she commanded the flow to stop. Then she gestured, and a helix of carpet and quickglass grew upwards, spiralling toward the transparent roof. Just for a moment, she went deep inside herself, accessing low-level interface services the way an élite meditation-trained athlete might deconstruct the minute muscle activations involved in striking a ball or flipping a somersault.

<<cmdIF::Carbud.Manufactory.getInstance(here.alt+33)>>

Then she was standing on the quickglass helix and it was bearing her upward, spiralling toward the great ceiling that was already softening and pulling apart to allow her exit. At the spiral's tip, some thirty-three metres above ground, a bud was swelling, morphing into her favoured car design, open-topped with room for only one. She glided up the spiral stalk and allowed the quickglass to deposit her inside the carbud, then relaxed as the seat reconfigured, holding her perfectly.

Other ways of travelling were faster; few were as stylish.

Sailing high over blue lawns and purple topiary where whistling songmoths tended drooping scarlet flowers, the carbud carried her smoothly, finally curving down, past a grove of orange novabeeches, and touched the soft ground. The carbud shivered then melted as she walked clear.

Ranulph was standing at the edge of a long drop, almost a cliff. In one hand, he held a stubby silver trident, a symterial manufactory used to inject mutant colonies into the borers. His attention was on a drone, hovering some way below.

'It's about level with the rogue borer,' he said. 'The others are inserting fine.'

His tu-ring generated a real-image holo of surprising crispness in the sunlight. It was a simple 3-D diagram, topped with a miniature translucent sward representing the ground they stood on, while below shone jagged yellow streaks like lightning, showing the paths the borers had taken. Their descent depended on soil structure, as they sought to optimize the upward growth patterns of symteria colonies, forming the controlled foundation of a new hybrid ecosystem throughout the mansion's grounds.

There was something half-hearted about Ranulph's attempt to direct her attention toward the borers that were working successfully. Perhaps it was because he knew that his subterfuge could not work against a Luculenta. At any rate, he was not worth psychophysiological probing – being nice to the hired help had limits.

'I'm glad the equipment mostly works. Here, let me take that.' The holo now shone above her outstretched hand, generated by the house system and magnified by an invisible smartmiasma. 'Thank you.'

This was rude, snatching data from his tu-ring and causing it to power down, but she no longer cared. The borer in question had followed a strange trajectory because it was trying to avoid some obstacle whose nature did not register in the normal parameters. The device had detected *something*, without being able to tell what it was.

Now given the capabilities of the borer's control system, whose design Rashella had total access to, this obstacle was an interesting mystery in what had been a normal day. Whatever she was about to find, she did not need her gardener's help to unearth it.

'Minor errors aside,' she said, 'your work is mostly impressive, and I'm awarding you a bonus.'

'Really? Well, um, thank you.'

At her summons, a bronze aircar lifted from the south wing and headed this way.

'And while you're at home, you can think about planning the eastern expansion. I might shift my attention to the rainbow fungus maze for a while.'

'Home? Er ... Sure.' He looked down at the trident in his hand. 'Thanks.'

The maze would be vulnerable to shifts in the soil's microbial population. It would give Ranulph the kind of problem he liked to work on, with no need for him to be here while he worked the calculations.

Can it be what I think?

A host of voices in her head provided answers while rainbow-hued phase spaces and equations danced in her mind's eye. The borer's inbuilt scan system was wide-ranging, and the one thing that might disturb its perceptions was a transparency toward scanning, a failure of resonance.

A null-gel capsule, buried on my property?

No one made or used them nowadays – for one thing, the legal penalties were severe – but occasional historical relics turned up, wrapped in gel designed to hide the contents from scan technology. And the thing was, about one hundred standard years before, this area had been witness to some very strange events.

Could there really be an artefact from that period, right here in her mansion's grounds?

*

Like giant horizontal saucers dangling from a quickglass tree, circular balconies overhung a plaza near the centre of campus. Roger leaned against a balustrade, staring down. He had dealt with his acrophobic fear at an early age, but there was still an edge of vertigo, and a part of his mind that wondered how it would feel if he jumped.

Whatever the sensation, it would last about two seconds, his last perception ever, unless the flagstones below could soften themselves in time. He wondered how alert the embedded systems were.

'Are you Roger Blackstone?'

'Uh-huh.'

'I'm Rick Mbuli.' Dark skin, wide smile. 'We're the group, then?'

'So far.'

They touched right fists and bowed, all very formal.

'The others probably went to the house first. Have you seen it yet?'

'No. You?'

'Thought I'd wait till later. Bet the girls take the best rooms.'

'More than likely. There's seven of us, right?'

'Yeah, and our tutor is Dr Helsen. You talked to her?'

'No,' said Roger. 'What's she like?'

'Interesting.'

A circular blue table rose on a short stalk, budded by the balcony floor. Seven stools morphed into being, and Rick sat down. He gestured, and a goblet grew from the table, sparkling liquid swirling inside.

'Can I get you anything?' He broke off the goblet and sipped. 'Mm, nice.'

'Not yet, thanks.' Roger pointed to a group of three young women ascending the central stalk by flowdisk. 'They're coming this way.'

'I wonder which one's scheduled for upraise.'

'Upraise? But a Luculenta in the group—'

'Don't tell anyone I said that. And until it happens, she's just one of us, right?'

'I guess.'

The trio approached, their leader pale with white-blond hair, another thin and young-looking, her hair striped in black and cobalt blue, and a heavier girl with downcast gaze.

'I'm Stef,' said the blonde. 'She's Trudi and she's Gella, short for Angela.'

'And I'm Rick, short for Ricardo Mbuli. Hi.'

'Roger.'

'Well, good.' Stef seated herself first, then waited for everyone else to settle. 'Has Petra Helsen appeared yet?'

'Is that what you call Dr Helsen?' asked Rick. 'And citrolas all round, does that suit everyone?'

Roger and Trudi nodded, while Stef gave a movement of her lips that was both acceptance and dismissal. Amused, Roger played a mnemonic game that Dad had taught him, exaggerating everyone's features in his mind while adding their names and keywords. *Haughty* was emblazoned on his mental image of Stef.

'My father studied with her, I believe,' said Stef.

Did that mean they were students together, or that Dr Helsen had taught her father? Roger was about to ask when a faint musical chord stopped him. Then it was gone, and he had no idea why it had caught his attention, or why his stomach had felt curdled, just for a moment.

'He was under her, your daddy?' said Rick. 'She seems the kind of person who'd like to be on top, right enough.'

Stef's chin went down and one eyebrow went up.

You're braver than me, Rick Mbuli.

Roger took a swig of sweet citrola, filling his mouth with cold effervescence, letting his tongue absorb the taste before—

'If you love me, you'll swallow,' said Rick.

And Roger's head jerked forward, drink spurting through both nostrils, spraying down. Then he began to laugh, at himself and at the three girls' shocked faces; and in a moment everyone was laughing – Stef included – while he was convulsing with it, tears down his face.

'I guess that settles your orientation,' Rick went on. 'Sadly enough.'

That seemed just as funny, and laughter took hold again.

'Shit. I need to wipe myself down,' said Roger.

'I like to leave 'em wet and sticky.'

'Somebody save me.'

He pushed back from the table, crossed to the balustrade, and leaned against it, still chuckling as he rubbed his face. Someone was saying something behind him, but there was a flicker off the edge of his vision, and a repetition of that strange musical chord followed by another, a cold vibration along his back. He turned his head from side to side, not quite catching the dark movement that was just beyond what he could see.

Suddenly he zeroed in. Across the plaza, by a settled bronze aircar, two people were talking. One was a bearded man, holding a foreshortened silver trident in one hand; the other was a slender woman, blond hair tied back. Around them, *darkness* was twisting.

He triple-blinked his smartlenses, zooming in, but the darkness failed to magnify while the faces grew clearer. Shadows rotated at right angles to everything. This was no optical effect, but something different. And from the casual-looking passers-by around the plaza, it was something only he could see.

'You okay, Roger?'

'Sure.' He rubbed his face, blinking his lenses back to normal. 'I think I've recovered.'

Except his old vertigo was back, powerful now, accompanied by the sense of music playing in his bones: *da, da-dum, da-da-da-dum, da-da.*

Then, from the other side of the plaza, the blonde woman turned to stare straight at him. Even without magnification, he could tell.

'Oh,' said Rick. 'Is that Dr Helsen over there?'

'Where?'

But Rick meant the blonde woman.

It's like the outdoor nightmares.

Twice when he was young, he'd seen dark shadows like this, both times in public places with Mum. She'd wanted to take him to see neuromedics, despite the risk of revealing his true nature; but Dad had talked calmly on both occasions, questioning him and then reassuring Mum there was nothing wrong, that it was a child's active imagination, nothing more.

'I've seen the same kind of thing myself,' he had said. 'Though maybe not as strongly.'

Now, replaying the old memory, Roger decided that Dad had told the truth, but that what it meant was different from Mum's interpretation.

It's something real.

He rubbed down his clothes as the fabric cleansed itself, then returned to the table. Rick and the three girls stared at him for a moment, then Stef said: 'So what's Petra Helsen like, Rick?'

'She's a little different,' said Rick. 'That's all I can say.'

Roger tapped the table, ordering himself a fresh citrola, confused by the images twisting in his head.

In the great airy atrium, a newly extruded quickglass table held Rashella's find: a slick black cylinder the size of her forearm, still speckled with soil. She stood there regarding it, her clothing cycling through many colours, reflecting her indecision. For her, hesitation was unusual, therefore a worry in itself.

She tuned her gown to black, ordered her thumbnail to razor sharpness, and slit through the null-gel coating. Revealed, the cached object was a silvery cylinder, looking too big for what it surely was.

'They put things like *this* inside themselves?'

Several drones entered the atrium, directed by the house system that was unused to hearing Rashella speak rhetorically aloud.

'It's okay,' she said, sticking with ordinary speech. 'I just can't believe what my ancestors went through.'

Touching the golden studs on her forehead, she called up a mental schematic, a virtual holo displaying the plexnodes webbed throughout her body. They were part of her nervous system, as much as the natural organic brain and neural cords, the ganglia and synapses, and the receptors of all the major organs, the orchestra that played the peptide symphony of human emotions.

Imagine having to extend your brain with clunky plexcores embedded in your body ... but that was what the oldtime Luculenti had to do.

This cylinder was inert ... but once powered up, what inchoate fragments of thoughts and feelings and memories might it possess? She reached forward, then stopped herself and pulled back. And flinched, feeling or hearing a wisp of sound.

'Why not?'

She whirled, trying to locate the whisper's source, seeing nothing save the drones that awaited her command.

'This is stupid.'

With her thumb, she pushed the null-gel back in place. Perhaps a hundred years ago, when it was fresh, the material would have sealed up; but now the slit remained, revealing a sliver of plexcore.

'You want to try,' came the whisper that was not there.

'Shut up.'

The drones backed away as she stalked from the atrium, gown whirling, odd patterns spilling across the fabric as her concentration wavered.

'Just leave me alone.'

She commanded the carpet beneath her feet to carry her, then ordered it to flow faster, then faster again, until she was speeding along the east wing's main corridor, artwork a blur on either side.

'You know you do.'

The whispers followed her.

'No. This is stupid.'

She raised her hand, and the carpet stopped flowing. Then she turned, faced the way she had come, and ordered it to carry her back toward the atrium.

For she was Luculenta Rashella Stargonier, and this was her home, where she was always in charge, and the most intimidating thing around was herself.

So what harm could an old plexcore do? Just how twisted and dangerous could its stored thoughts be?

She stopped a metre from the null-gel capsule, and stared at it.

FOUR

EARTH, 1926 AD

So here she was, in this long neo-Renaissance hall, beneath balconies forming galleries on either side. Black ironwork, globular white lights, a gleaming floor: everything polished and strong, suiting such a place of learning, for this was the Erdgenössische Technische Hochschule, where only a few decades before, Einstein himself had been a student. Now she, Gavriela Wolf, was here as an undergraduate to follow the same ambition: to determine how the universe worked, for the sheer joy of discovery.

This morning she had sent a letter to her parents, whose little shop in Sendlingerstrasse, in the heart of Munich, had been just around the corner from Einstein's childhood home. It was only five years since the Wolf family relocated to Berlin.

Dear Mutti and Vati,

Zürich is such a pretty town, like our old München but with the broad flat lake, and such icy mountains all around. The trams, too, are cheerful as they wind their way up and down the cobbled streets. You would like to take your Sunday promenade here by the Zürichsee!

The road up from river level had been a steep climb, but those same trams she had written about were expensive, and the Polybahn funicular from Central would have been an extravagance. Still she had enjoyed the walk, listening to people greet each other with a gruff Schweizerdeutsch *Grüezi!*, smelling fresh-cooked Berliner doughnuts from a bakery, breathing cool air blown in off the glacial lake.

Two men in long brown work coats, one with mop in hand,

were standing at the edge of the flow of students, watching them. It was like laminar flow in a river: moving fastest in the centre, diminishing to zero velocity at the edges. Except that these were people, not water molecules, and perhaps they could tell her where she was supposed to go.

'Excuse me, please. Could you tell me where Lecture Theatre 3 is?'

'Ah, with the thunder and lightning machine. The big metal lollipop.'

The incomplete sentences sounded rude, but perhaps her Hochdeutsch sensibilities were not appropriate. On the other hand, while the man might be uncertain about her Jewishness, her gender was undeniable. It was an attitude she had hoped not to find, not here.

'Do you refer, sir, to a Van de Graaff generator that might be used for electrostatic investigations?'

The older man smiled.

'She's got you there. Sorry, miss, but my young colleague is unfamiliar with the name of the apparatus. Are you attending Herr Professor Möller's lecture?'

'Yes, that's right.'

'Then it will be our pleasure to help you, in order that you might get there on time.'

There was nothing unusual in the answer's precision – the use of the subjunctive was an everyday courtesy – but in contrast to the younger man's abruptness, it was reassuring. She nodded, memorizing the directions, and was gently formal in her thanks.

Two minutes later, she was settling herself among thirty young men in a lecture theatre that smelled of beeswax and chalk. She made no attempt to introduce herself; none of the men tried to talk to her. Since she was joining late, three weeks into the semester, the others would already have made acquaintance with each other.

No matter. She was here to learn.

In front was a bench, currently supporting the upright metal lollipop – not a bad description, really – that was the Van de Graaff generator. The vertical shaft contained a drive belt, and friction inside the metal sphere on top would generate an electrostatic charge of some considerable – and dangerous – magnitude.

Had Einstein sat in this room, or even in this seat?

My life is amazing. I'm so lucky.

She was poor only in her lack of money. The opportunities before her, and the family love behind her, were treasures that she had done little to deserve, however hard she worked. Neither her mother nor any of her earlier ancestors could have dreamt of being here, in Zürich's finest centre of scientific learning.

Sunlight like pale honey shone through clear panes, highlighting the random dance of dust in the air, the Brownian motion that Einstein had shown confirmed the existence of atoms.

Professor Möller was broad-shouldered, with a large beard, a far-receded hairline but with a mass of fine grey-white hair, worn shoulder-length. He looked like the leonine illustrations in the Conan Doyle books that Gavriela enjoyed so much: Professor Challenger, scientist and adventurer.

Now, as the very real Professor Möller commenced his lecture, his gaze passed across the rows of faces, lingering on Gavriela no longer than on anyone else, as if unsurprised to find a young woman among his students. Nor did he look surprised when a door opened at the rear of the lecture theatre, and more people filed in, filling all the empty places behind the original twenty-seven students. Surely such lateness was a discourtesy? And could there really be this many first-year undergraduates? Some of them looked old enough to be faculty.

A young man with curly hair leaned towards her.

'You're in luck. This is no ordinary lecture.'

'Oh. It's my first day.'

'I thought so, but that's not the reason you didn't know

about this. I've been talking to some of the older students.'

That did not make complete sense; but most of the other first-years were looking as puzzled as she felt. So what was going on?

'So, I wonder,' mused Professor Möller from the front, 'how many of you know what a Faraday cage might be?'

At this, some two-thirds of the room erupted in cheers, wolf-whistles and applause, more like a beer hall than a staid lecture theatre, while the first-years mostly looked surprised. Then two men in brown work coats – the pair that Gavriela had encountered in the hall – came in, bearing a big greasy-looking slab between them. They placed it down on the parquet floor next to the demonstration bench.

'This is made of wax,' said Professor Möller, 'which, as you know, is a poor conductor of electrical current. At least, I hope I have that right.'

More cheers and laughter. Around Gavriela, some of the first-years were smiling, still puzzled but picking up the festive ambience. She thought of it as a form of resonance.

Then the two men left and returned with a smaller wax block, plus a large wire basket, at least a metre and a half tall: the kind of thing you might find in a park, convenient for visitors who had rubbish to dispose of. Its purpose here was beginning to dawn on Gavriela – surely the Herr Professor could not be serious?

He was starting up the Van de Graaff generator, so whatever the point of the preparations, everyone would soon find out. Then he beckoned forward one of the students: a burly, muscular fellow who stripped off his jacket at the Herr Professor's request and rolled up his shirt sleeves. His revealed forearms were thick and strong-looking, his waistcoat snug around a barrel chest.

'That's Florian Horst,' whispered the curly-headed student. 'He served in the Army, so I guess the Herr Professor considers him trustworthy.'

'Oh. I'm Gavriela Wolf.'

'And my name is Lucas Krause. I'm honoured to meet you, Fräulein.'

Seated, he gave a small bow as they shook hands. Meanwhile the burly man, Horst, was hefting the big wire basket – to him it appeared feather-light – then putting it down and nodding to Professor Möller.

The Van de Graaff groaned and growled as it ran. The metal sphere on top was large, and Gavriela wondered what kind of potential it might reach. Ten thousand volts, a hundred thousand? It was possible to reach five million volts.

With Horst's assistance, Professor Möller climbed atop the wax slab and steadied himself. Then he nodded, and Horst stepped back.

As the professor's fingertips touched the metal sphere of the Van de Graaff, everyone – first-years included – raised a great cheer and applauded. Around his head, his long hair drifted upward and spread out in a nimbus, each individual hair repelling the others, for they were similarly charged, as was the whole of Professor Möller's body. And without the insulation of the wax slab, the potential would connect to earth, causing a fatal current to flow.

'You may be wondering,' he said, 'just how I feel today. Well, I'm—'

Two-thirds of the students roared: '—feeling very positive!'

Everyone cheered.

Then Horst was carrying out his true task, raising the cylindrical wire basket, standing on the small wax block, and helping to lower the basket around Professor Möller, encasing him. As he did so, the hairs on the professor's head drooped, no longer repelling each other, for the free electrons in the wire basket drifted under the electrical force, until all charges were balanced, cancelling out.

Around Gavriela, the applause reached a crescendo, but she could only sit there, blinking with tears. You could read in a book that there could be no electrostatic field inside a conductor, but *this* was what made it real, brought understanding to life, in a way that demonstrated the courage as well as the perspicacity of science.

She was stunned and honoured to be here in this moment. And it was so different from the stilted atmosphere of the German schools she had attended.

Horst helped Professor Möller to remove the wastebasket Faraday cage – the professor's hair once more spreading out, forming fine radii – and then to shut down the demonstration, the Van de Graaff generator whining, its drive belt shuddering, as it came to a halt.

Then the professor supplied a surprising addendum. Pointing to the blackboard that showed Coulomb's equation for electrostatic forces – like gravity, an inverse square law – he held position like an actor on the brink of soliloquy.

'This is such a simple equation, is it not? You might think of it as a consequence of geometry, since a sphere's surface area grows with the square of its radius. If we spread a constant amount of *stuff* across a growing area, its concentration must be diluted by the same factor.'

Then he pointed to a sextet of equations, all partial differentials – the operator symbol looked like Old Norse – relating electric and magnetic fields.

'And for electrodynamics, we will expect to master Maxwell's equations, as our older students doubtless have engraved on their memories.'

A few rueful smiles and chuckles came from the rear of the lecture theatre.

'But you will be pleased to learn, however necessary such mastery might be, *there is no such thing as a magnetic field*.'

To Gavriela, who had played with magnets aged six and been fascinated ever since, this was news.

'Or rather,' continued Professor Möller, 'we can show that Herr Doktor Einstein's theory can replicate all magnetic effects as a relativistic correction to Coulomb potential on moving charges. By changing our viewpoint, we can see that it is *all* electricity, not a mixture of two forces, and that the unitary force is subject to the alterations of spacetime geometry that you may have heard of.'

And the man who had changed everyone's worldview had been right here, alternating between wondrous daydreams and furious, intent studying of his physics books, always on a quest, heading for the truth that lay beneath the surface of illusion.

'Let me add that it is perfectly fine for you all to look puzzled. If you have seen distraught expressions upon my colleagues' faces or my own in recent days, it is because we have been struggling to understand another second-order equation, one derived by Herr Professor Schrödinger, and we do not yet know how to change viewpoint in order to accommodate it.

'We seek to assimilate what is known, yet the frontiers of science are at the unknown, and that is where we must work, like archaeologists chipping away stone, revealing the knowledge beneath. Good day, ladies and gentlemen.'

There might have been applause, beyond the surf-like waves of sound inside her head; and there might have been movement at the edge of her vision, as the professor and other students left; but she was inside herself, almost paralysed by the combined wonders of what she had seen and the images shining in her mind, blossoming from the professor's words.

Such a wonderful time to be alive in!

In the evening, she walked the steep, cobbled, twisting alleys of the Altstadt, the old town, enjoying the cool rain that fell. Her room at Frau Pflügers' house was comfortable enough, and in future she would surely spend most of her time studying there, but for tonight she wanted to explore. Then she found herself descending to open ground leading down to the river, while to her right rose one of the many old churches. No one else appeared to be here.

'—you shithead!'

The vehement coarseness was unexpected, and so was what happened next: a swirling group of young men, spilling out from behind a stone wall, grappling and striking each other, grunting with effort and hatred. Then the mêlée split into two groups who glared, and finally backed off, with focused stares and wiping of faces, ready for the trouble to begin again.

Gavriela was trembling, too scared to make herself conspicuous by moving. But the young men were retreating now, each group in a different direction, and soon they had disappeared along separate alleys, and were gone.

Had one group worn yarmulkes: black skullcaps clipped to their hair?

But it was the strange twisting of the blackness in shadowed alleyways that—

Optical illusion.

Vision was a physical phenomenon, optical and electrical within the brain. Stress might deform one's ability to perceive geometry.

Because I was scared.

Surely this was not the peaceful Zürich she had heard about? But now it was quiet, so perhaps trouble visited seldom, and the reputation for law-abiding calm was deserved. This *was* a cultured city.

So she walked toward the bright lights of Bahnhofstrasse, thinking that among the elegant shops everything would be peaceful. But as she passed a café, three young women, around her own age but expensively dressed, came out onto the cobblestones, laughing.

'—dance the Charleston as well as Peter, darlings.'

'Is that the horizontal Charleston you're referring to?'

'Elke, sweetheart. What are you implying?'

'Only that—Oh, hello.'

'Er,' said Gavriela. 'Good evening.'

'Are you on your own, dear?'

'Well, I was . . . Um. Yes.'

'So why don't you join us for a coffee, or perhaps a cheerful Glühwein?'

Conscious of her purse's few coins and notes, Gavriela shook her head.

'I'm sorry, and it's very kind of you, but I don't think I can.'

'Not even if Petra here does the paying? And I'm Inge, and this is Elke.'

'I need to arise early to study.'

'You're a schoolteacher?'

'No, a student at the ETH. A physics student.'

'At the Poly? You must be very bright.' Inge pointed at the others. 'Elke paints, Petra reads everything, and I'm a haberdasher.'

'You must come with us,' said Petra. 'Please.'

'Now, look.' Inge held up one hand. 'Here's why we need you. Petra believes that a rocket could fly to the moon, because she's been reading fantasies by Jules Verne.'

'Honestly, Inge—'

'But my encyclopaedia directly states that a rocket cannot fly in space because *there is no air for it to push against.* So how can you argue against that?'

Gavriela looked from one face to the next.

'Maybe one glass of Glühwein,' she said.

Not so far away, where the small town of Berchtesgaden crouched amid Bavarian forest, a small feverish man was alone in his room, surrounded by dark, insanely energetic paintings, the product of his own hand and strange imaginings. The more recent were like design sketches: gleaming cities, fluttering banners, romantic uniforms of black and scarlet.

But words held the true power, the magic he had tapped into while the faceless bourgeoisie had tried to silence him, to lock him away in prison. And not just written words: as he stood before the mirror, eyes glaring, he rehearsed his mesmeric language, his visions of a warrior future, deeply aware of the magnetic hold he could have upon the mob. For they would act as if they had a single mind – he had studied the works of Gustav Lebon on mass psychology, and understood the weapon those books had given him – and if a mind could be unified, it could be controlled.

I am become the darkness.

Sweat poured from his skin as he gesticulated, imagining the visions that floated above a multitude, the spellbinding directives of his voice. Scattered around him like flowers on the floor were sheets of newspaper and printed notices, all related to him, the one who would master destiny, while in the background a compelling nine-note sequence played, product of a non-existent military band.

One of his most dangerous rivals had turned to become a disciple, his adulation apparent in the new article lying here, in the *Völkischer Beobachter.*

This was what young Göbbels had written, exhorting his comrades to bow to their rightful leader, *'with the manly, unbroken pride of the ancient Norsemen who stand upright before their Germanic feudal lord.'*

And why would they not? For Göbbels was only acknowledging what had to happen, that: *'He is the instrument of the Divine Will that shapes history with fresh, creative passion.'*

Artist, visionary and orator.

I am become myself.

Time passed in a manner beyond ordinary experience, until someone tapped at the door.

'Supper is ready, Herr Hitler.'

He expelled a breath.

'You may come in.'

FIVE

FULGOR, 2603 AD

Watching Dr Helsen ascend from the plaza and draw near to the saucer-shaped balcony, Roger felt his skin tremble, like a membrane stretched across a drum. Helsen was a hard-faced woman, and she was staring at him. His fellow students still had not noticed her.

They jumped as her voice issued from the circular tabletop.

'I'm Dr Helsen, and you can address me thus or simply as Doctor.'

A female student trailed her: pale and slender, coppery hair and turquoise eyes, taller than Roger

'This is Alisha Spalding,' continued Helsen, speaking normally instead of through the system, as she indicated the pale young woman. 'She's in your group. And you're the Blackstone boy, is that right?'

'Uh, yes, ma'am. Doctor.'

'You weren't startled by my voice' – the location switched again – *'as it came from here, inside the table.'*

'I saw you approaching.'

'Psychosocial skills are based on sensory acuity, but they're only a small part of what we work on here.'

Stef's mouth twisted to one side.

'On the other hand,' Helsen went on,' we need to be careful as we interpret expressions, because *derisory amusement* might not be what you intend to convey, Stephanie Thrawle. Particularly since I have full access to your cognitive skills logs. Surely condescension can emanate only from perceived superiority.'

'Sorry, Dr Helsen.'

'I'm sure you can be. Now let's have a look at the Cyclone Lab. Quadruple blink, everyone.'

Roger did as she commanded, and the visual environment shifted, an indoor scene replacing the outdoor reality, with the six students' relative positions unaltered. The illusion was visual and auditory – no sense of touch – with the image lased in to his smartlenses and the sound focused from the real surroundings, including presumably the quickglass table.

Helsen herself was no longer visible. Roger wondered what she might be up to.

'Nice,' said Rick, turning inside the illusion.

They were in a steel-and-amber artificial cavern, where the air billowed in glowing greens and blues, revealing the currents as they flowed and twisted around morph-capable obstacles. It was a realtime image of an actual laboratory, designed to investigate the flow of fluids – gases and plasmas included – and of devices designed to funnel currents or to navigate inside them. Right now, a flock of quickglass songbirds was trying to find stability, wings continually altering as they tried to hang in place against the flow.

Beside them, a sheaf of holo equations denoted the design parameters of the birds, along with status values of the tremendous airflow.

'They look accurate enough.' Alisha pointed at the equations, then nodded toward the hovering birds. 'Don't you think, Roger?'

So she knew his name. But he was thinking more about the unseen Helsen in reality, and what she might be up to while none of them could see her.

Then he gave a snort, trying to dismiss his fear with humour. Alisha turned away, her face growing stony.

Shit. I messed that up.

Stef had read through the equations slowly. Now she looked up at the quickglass birds and shrugged.

'Look at that growing turbulence. Their performance is unpredictable.'

'Maybe that's the point,' said Rick. 'Well done, Stef.'

'There's no need to be sarcastic.'

'I'm serious, really. Maybe that's why we're looking at all this, so we can work out that the equations are insufficient for the whatyoumaycallit, the context. Is that right, Dr Helsen?'

The last question he called out while turning around on the spot, not knowing where she might be located in reality.

'Four of the birds are about to lose control,' said Alisha.

'You can't know that.' Rick stared up at them. 'All thirteen are practically identical.'

'And the lead bird will break up in five seconds from ... now.'

'Come off it. There's no way you can—'

At the front of the flock, the leading bird began to shiver in the turbulence, caught by some kind of resonance, and then it was liquefying as it shook apart and spattered in the bucking wind, destroyed. Four others, wings flapping in vain, lost their ability to keep their beaks pointed into the growing gale, and the air picked them up and flung them against pillars and walls, shattering their vitrified forms. The remaining eight birds reconfigured, fighting to keep position in the flow.

'Nicely done, Alisha,' said Helsen. 'Everybody, quadruple blink again.'

They did so, falling out of illusion, back into reality, standing on the saucer-shaped balcony. Around them were the other balconies on stalks, and below was the blue plaza, nearly deserted. Helsen was standing where she had been, her attention on Alisha.

'Would you write up your thinking for the others to follow, please?'

'Sure, Dr Helsen.'

'Good. What I'd like all of you to do is construct a critique of the Founding Charter's Assumption 17. Of course you'll have done it years ago in school; what I'm looking for is an in-depth revisiting based on the knowledge you have gained since then.'

Alisha was frowning, and Roger took a moment to wonder why. The appearance of turbulence and other phase transitions in the Cyclone Lab just now – perhaps there had been a reason for Helsen's showing them that, a hint in how to approach their analysis of Assumption 17: *A surveilled society is a safe society.*

'For the rest of the afternoon,' continued Helsen, 'I'd like you to construct a simulation of an Earth city from the 1920s. Choose the city now, among yourselves.'

Then she turned away and stared across the plaza, either lost in thought or deep in Skein – as deep as an ordinary human could go, at any rate.

Rick gestured a real-image holo into being: an Earth globe floating above the tabletop.

'Shanghai,' he said. 'An interesting mix of influences, with representatives of all the global powers of later centuries there. Plus lots of sex and violence.'

'What about Paris?' Stef pointed at the globe and a glowing spot appeared. 'Centre of fashion and philosophy, what more could you want?'

Trudi's smartlenses went opaque as she immersed herself in data, then cleared.

'Chicago would be better, Rick, if you're after bloody violence.'

'No, Shanghai. I mean, come on—'

Alisha's voice was authoritative: 'I nominate Roger to choose.'

'Excuse me?'

'Seconded,' said Trudi, as Angela nodded.

Rick opened his mouth, but Alisha tilted her head toward Helsen and said: 'A quick decision is in order, don't you think?'

'Then I agree.' Rick grinned. 'So I'm not going to suggest you *choose Shanghai now,* Roger.'

'I'm glad you're not suggesting that.' Roger took control of the holo globe, expanding it and bringing it closer. 'All right, let's see.'

As he ran his hand across the surface, major cities flared, their names revealed in glowing white script: *Budapest, Constantinople, Harare*. Then he moved back up to western Europe, and his forefinger hovered over Berlin.

'Is that your choice?' said Rick.

'Maybe.' Then Roger's hand drifted and he pressed down, pointing with forefinger and hooked thumb, the standard selection gesture. 'This one.'

The city name glowed scarlet – *Zürich* – before fading back to white.

'We've chosen, Dr Helsen,' said Alisha.

'Good.' Helsen turned, her smartlenses opaque, then clearing. 'So you've chosen Zürich, Mr Blackstone.'

'Uh, yes, Doctor.'

'I wonder you didn't select Berlin.'

He tried to control his flinch, but a microgesture motion at the corner of Helsen's mouth implied that she had read him perfectly. But why did it matter? Thinking back, he could not identify any covert commands in her earlier dialogue, unlike Rick with his deliberately obvious instruction regarding Shanghai. So how could she know that Berlin had tempted him? He didn't even know why it had seemed to pull at his hand.

It wasn't as if Earth history was even a favourite subject. He had studied it only because he had to.

Something seemed to shift beyond the edge of his vision, and he tried not to yell. Again, there was – perhaps – the tiniest twitch of Helsen's mouth.

Have I failed a test? Or passed one?

Sour fear rose inside him. And now Alisha was staring. It was bad enough being psyched out by one person, but did they have to gang up on him?

'I'll see you in my teaching room tomorrow morning,' said Helsen. 'Seven fifteen, everyone.'

'Yes, Doctor.'

'Doctor.'

'Ma'am . . . Uh, Doctor.'

Helsen was the first to leave, descending the quickglass stalk on a single-person flowdisk. Then the others drifted away, while Roger remained staring down at the plaza. He watched as Helsen reached ground level and walked away.

Just as she turned out of sight, black shards flickered in the air, twisted impossibly and were gone.

Is this *a test?*

But why would he feel such revulsion? This made no sense. Maybe Dad could explain – but he was facilitating those negotiations today, and besides, the point of going to college instead of studying virtually was to gain some adult independence, to strengthen the psychosocial skills that would let him make a career in the competitive world around him.

Except I'm not like other people.

He didn't even know what he was. Perhaps he—

'Interesting choice, Roger.'

He jumped.

'Uh, Alisha. Um, thanks for having confidence in me.'

'What do you mean?'

'Voting for me to choose, of course.'

'You thought that was a compliment, picking the quiet one?'

'I – don't know.'

'That's interesting.'

She broke eye contact, then walked toward the nearest flowdisk without a glance back at him. He could only stand watching as she descended, then walked off in the opposite direction to Helsen. The other students were already gone, including Rick, who had seemed so sociable.

'So this is going well,' he said to the empty balcony.

Then the tabletop spoke up.

'The bill for seven drinks is outstanding. Do you wish to pay now?'

He sighed.

'All right,' he said.

In the evening, Rick suggested they play cops and robbers.

'Excuse me?' said Stef. 'Are you serious?'

'When you can't tell the difference between avatars and in-scenario characters, it can be sort of fun.'

'Then we should've chosen Chicago,' said Trudi. 'Shouldn't you, Roger?'

'I have no idea. My brain is dead.'

'So you need some stimulation.' Rick looked around the group. 'Agreed?'

Around them the walls glowed soft pastels, while couches and chairs to individual taste had morphed from the floor. This was the communal lounge of their house, and their work on the Zürich simulation was finished. At least, none of them wanted to do any more.

'Why not?' said Stef.

Within two minutes, all six of them were standing in their own forms in a cobbled street on a foggy winter afternoon, their surroundings lit by hissing gaslamps. There were pedestrians – men in frock coats, women in bustling dresses that covered their ankles – none of whom saw the students. Some of the passers-by were speaking, their words translated but their tonality rendered with historical accuracy, along with their speed of movement.

'They're so *slow,*' said Trudi. 'The way they walk, and especially the way they talk. Do you think the records are really correct?'

'After verification by twenty-two independent and loosely dependent methods,' answered Alisha, 'the analyses are trustworthy enough.'

Rick looked at Roger and raised an eyebrow. Clearly the group's Luculenta-to-be was Alisha. Her expression was tightening, no doubt understanding their silent communication and not liking it.

'Why don't you three' – her gesture passed across Rick, Roger and Trude – 'commit some crime, while Stef, Angela and I take you down?'

'That's hardly specific,' said Rick. '*Some* crime?'

'Anything you like, anywhere in the city. To escape, to

achieve game over, you need to get on board a train – any train – at the Hauptbahnhof or one of the minor stations. That's how you *hypothetically* might win, while our goal is to arrest you. It's not like you're going to be hard to catch.'

'But—'

'So we'll decamp and let you plan. Ten minutes long enough?'

Rick mouthed the word *decamp*.

Trudi spoke up. 'It sure is.'

'Then we'll leave you to it.'

At that, Alisha, Angela and Stef disappeared. They might remain close in reality, but they would now be in some other part of the simulation, perhaps in whatever passed for Police HQ. Roger wished he'd spent more time on the city's geography, but he'd been working on persona templates for the city's virtual inhabitants, and two of the generics had crashed with paracognitive failures that took ages to debug.

This was a city where banks proliferated, and soon Trudi and Rick – more aware than Roger of the simulation's topography – had picked a branch of the Greater Helvetian to rob. Part of the game was to don avatars that would remain for the duration. Soon all three of them were portly gentlemen with extravagant moustaches and silk waistcoats beneath their frock coats, and revolvers weighing down their pockets.

'And switch,' said Rick.

They were standing in front of the Rathaus, the city hall, which stood on the river's edge. The waters of the Limmat were black. This time of year, it was often frozen over.

'This way.' Rick led, followed by Trudi.

Roger enjoyed the uphill walk as they climbed a narrow road formed with large irregular stones too large to be called cobbles. The grey stone buildings on either side looked old, some perhaps dating back to the Middle Ages. In reality, the gradient was a product of a morphing, flowing quickglass floor, and the image of the buildings was lased in to his smartlenses.

Antisound would ensure that the two teams could not hear each other.

Then they were entering the gloomy bank branch.

The robbery itself was exciting but straightforward, as the three of them produced revolvers and threatened staff, who obeyed their instructions and handed over the bags of cash. The money-bags felt tangible and heavy, the effect produced by their clothing – their sleeves had elongated to form gloves – responding to magnetic induction that tugged downward in a high-fidelity simulation. Within minutes of stumbling from the building, Rick and Trudi were puffing, while Roger could already feel his forearms burning from the weight.

Struggling uphill past the cathedral-like Frauenkirche, they became aware of police whistles behind them. Rick grinned.

'The game is afoot, gentlemen. Excuse me, Trudi.'

'You're excused.' Her feminine voice issued from her overweight male avatar. 'I don't think I can move any faster, though.'

'Me neither. How about you, Roger?'

'It's tough.'

Passers-by were pointing at them as they hurried.

'We should've stolen diamonds,' gasped Rick. 'Would've weighed practically nothing.'

'*Now* you think of it,' said Trudi.

There was a rattle of trams from up ahead, then more police whistles.

'Crap. They're closing in.'

Roger caught a glimpse of dark uniforms, just as Rick and Trudi staggered left into a narrow cross-street. Then he stopped, a second before Rick did likewise.

'Shit,' muttered Rick. 'It's a dead end.'

Nicely played, Alisha.

She must have worked out where they were fleeing, and held back from the sounding the whistles until herding them here. Now they were trapped.

'We go into one of the shops,' said Trudi. 'Try to get out through the back.'

'No.' Roger hefted his money bags. 'This way.'

He pushed the pace into a near sprint. Behind him, Rick and Trudi muttered. Beyond a buttress he hauled left, into a tiny space between two buildings.

'Huh,' said Rick.

Then they were following a narrow lane parallel to the street. Unable to hold bags out to the side, they had to move awkwardly. Soon Roger's shoulders were filled with pain, and he was finding it hard to breathe. Behind him, Rick and Trudi were struggling.

But after a time the sound of whistles diminished, and then they were following a descending route down a wider road where trams clanged along shining tracks.

'There,' said Roger. 'That's Alisha.'

He pointed to a thin man in civilian clothes standing down on the bridge across the Limmat. The Alisha-avatar – no doubt a senior police officer – was facing away from them, and he pulled the other two behind a tram stop just before the avatar turned. After a few seconds, Roger peeked out, and when the time was right he led the other two across the street.

Then they circled around the magnificent Hauptbahnhof, and jumped down on to the tracks. No one cried out or whistled as they stumbled towards an empty train. Roger pulled open a carriage door and threw the money-bags inside. Then he boosted Trudi up the step and through the door, followed by Rick.

Ten seconds later, he was inside as well and pulling the door shut.

'Nice work,' said Rick. 'Game over.'

Everything shimmered around them. Roger closed his eyes, then opened them to see the lounge in their student house, while he, Rick and Trudi were sitting on quickglass seats extruded by the floor. Alisha, Angela and Stef were standing, facing in various directions. They turned.

'Well played,' said Alisha. 'Considering our team had the greater knowledge of the city's layout, you dodged us far more easily than expected.'

'You call that easy?' Rick was rubbing his arms and shoulders. 'My God, it was painful.'

Trudi gestured. 'It was Roger who found a hidden alleyway. And spotted you, Alisha, outside the station.'

'You saw through my avatar?'

'Uh . . . Yeah,' said Roger.

'Interesting.' Alisha blinked several times. 'I'm looking at your escape route now. How did you know that alley was there? The road appeared to be a dead end.'

'It was instinct.'

Alisha looked at him. 'If you say so.'

So how did *I know?*

He tried to blank his expression, but could not tell if he succeeded. Then Stef was ordering the room to serve daistral, and everyone got busy with refreshing themselves, while Alisha continued to glance at him, and he grew increasingly puzzled by his own ability to navigate the hidden byways of 1920s Zürich, a simulation of a period he had never studied, on a world he had never visited.

Correction: an *historically accurate* simulation, verified by twenty-two different methods, according to Alisha. And she was a near-Luculenta, therefore impossible to beat in a game situation, or so he would have thought.

SIX

EARTH-CLASS EXPLORATORY EM-0036, 2146 AD

Rekka Chandri woke from delta-coma with a headache. All around, the rest of the pre-contact team seemed fresh-eyed, their voices energetic as they sat up on couches and greeted each other. They were in a spartan cargo hold that made no attempt to emulate a comfortable passenger lounge. Nor was there any greeting from the unseen Pilot who had navigated them through mu-space to here.

But she was offworld, in orbit around a new planet for the first time.

'Hey, Rekka,' called Mary Stelanko, the team leader. 'Are you okay?'

The others were checking holo displays, conversation suspended, ensuring their equipment was intact. Acting professional: maybe Rekka ought to do the same.

'Sure,' she said. 'I'll just check my autofact has survived.'

Tapping a display into being, she ran a status check, then powered down the kit.

'All right.' Mary clapped her hands together. 'I'm not going to tell you to be careful down there, just as there's no way I'm going to threaten you with dire consequences if you make contact—'

'I'm glad you're not telling us that,' said Lucy Chiang, to laughter.

'—or with even worse penalties if you do make accidental contact and not do it right, because I expect professionalism at all times.'

Amid catcalls, Ralph Antero said: 'You sure you got the right team, Mary? Professionals? Us?'

'Whoop it up now, because down on the surface you'll be all alone and quiet as mice. All right, everyone?'

'Were mice quiet?' asked Lucy.

'I thought you had to click them,' said Ralph. 'But history was never my subject.'

Mary smiled, relaxing her shoulders, holding her hands at hip height, palms down. The room quietened.

'Be careful, be watchful, be safe.'

'You got it, boss.'

'Let's get to the drop-bugs.'

Penrose tiles fluttered back as a bulkhead dissolved like leaves in a wind. Beyond lay an array of one-person capsules, dark-grey and glossy, ready to launch.

Oh God, I'm scared.

Then Mary's hand pressed upon her shoulder, and she stepped forward, heading for her drop-bug.

Soon she would be on a new world, fending for herself, observing.

As Sharp walked alongside Father he was excited, almost dancing. For Father's presence was formidable: broad shoulders and dark fur, square jaw, massive spreading antlers. Few Mint City dwellers emitted such a sense of presence. Smooth-foreheaded women glanced from beneath their veils, their amber eyes widening in horizontal slits, unconsciously reacting.

Some day Sharp would have antlers of his own. That notion brought strange feelings whirling inside him.

Then they were in the market square. Such a bustle of individuals! A thousand folk from dozens of castes thronged the temporary booths and huts and stalls, their scents an overwhelming kaleidoscope of exotic and pungent fragrances. The place was so crowded, you could almost hear the people.

Father's tunic was his best: shining white, edged with brocade, decorated with overlapping triangles to denote the Geometers Caste. By chance, a group of Mint City Geometers was passing before them, their tunics less formal, attending to everyday business. Seeing Father, they paused; but Father, as a visitor from an outlying borough, waved them on. They bowed, antlers dipping, then continued past.

With the ceremony forthcoming, Father must be drenched with urgency; yet his manners were perfect. Sharp felt so very proud.

Beyond the square, they took a shadowed alleyway. From last year's visit, he remembered that this was a shortcut to the Forum. He hurried, matching Father's quickening pace. From a doorway he caught a faint scent, stale and embarrassing: one of the house daughters had illicitly entertained a young warrior here, perhaps one of the City Guard. Father strode on, perhaps not noticing.

~Dad? Are you . . . scared?

The answering scent was strong and reassuring.

~Everything will be fine. With my son here, how could it not be?

Coming out into sunlight, they crossed Central Plaza, a circular expanse paved with shards of turquoise and white. A few merchants and household ladies were walking here, no one else. Sharp opened his mouth, belatedly noticing the aftertaste of Father's reply, the involuntary fear he had tried to mask.

Then they were at the broad steps leading up to the Forum.

Bannermen fell in to either side, accompanying them as they climbed. Scarlet-and-gold banners flapped in the breeze. The smell of oil rose from leather scabbards and the polished blades they enclosed. Once inside the shaded atrium, where wall-mounted plants scented cooler air, the bannermen moved away. All around were alcoves with odour-absorbing hangings, set there for confidential conversations between lobbyists and councillors. Sharp held his breath out of politeness.

Two servants hurried past with covered meal-pots, and Father emitted faint amusement. Not one to make fun of lower castes, he was probably thinking of yesterday morning as all four of them – Mother and Bittersweet in the cart, Sharp and

Father walking alongside – came into sight of the city walls.

Because to one side, in a village with open courtyards, a poor family had been eating their vegetables in full sight of anyone who happened to pass by. To Sharp it had been disgusting; but Bittersweet, young brat that she was, had jumped around on the cart, pointing and making fun. It took Mother to stop her, with a frigid declaration that poverty was nothing to joke about.

Bittersweet could be such a pain, but part of Sharp wished she could be here too, to drink in the scents and sights of the Mint City Forum, to see the straight-backed bureaucrats and officials who—

~Tang, you are summoned.

Father lowered his head.

~I respond, Councillors.

They entered the so-called Sphere Chamber, in fact a hemispherical space decorated in a melange of colours and scents, an overpowering design. Here – in the white marble chair that rose like a throne in the centre – was where Father would prove his worth, demonstrating the maturity of his professional and intellectual life, to finally become a first-class citizen.

Sunlight made the marble chair glow.

In the encircling gloom, only a handful of Council Elders sat, though the circular bench-seats could contain up to two hundred councillors if necessary. Two of the Elders appeared to be asleep, chins on chests and their white-edged antlers drooping.

An attendant made a gesture, and Sharp stood still while Father continued along a soft blue strip of carpet. At the white chair he turned to the Elders and waited.

Meanwhile, another attendant led Sharp to the public gallery where he could sit. A silver-furred maiden at the bench's far end looked at him, amber eyes widening. Then she pulled up her veil and tugged her robe's cowl forward.

Sharp's hearts gave synchronized thumps.

A tall male entered the chamber, his sleeveless robes and

brocaded headgear imposing, his antlers broad and lined with age, his long arms patterned with whorls of heavy scarring. This was the Chief Librarian; he was trailed by four acolytes who bore silk-wrapped instruments in their gloved hands.

Father took his place on the marble chair. His big chest rose and fell, his breathing controlled, holding in all scent.

Addressing the Elders and Father, the Chief Librarian delivered a soft common-language sermon that powerfully evoked racial memories of life on the pre-civilized plains, followed by the painful evolution of culture and intelligence. Sharp's eyelids drooped. Then he forced himself to inhale and sit up, before checking the cowled maiden.

Her attention was on Father, not on him, but never mind. Father's success would extend to cover his family, and today was going to be spectacular – Sharp was sure of it.

Many times he had watched as Architects and Engineers created intricate clay models from Father's designs, etched in solidified sand. At night, Father used the larger sandpit behind the house to track the movement of stars. The neighbours considered him brilliant, ignoring the darkness of his fur that proclaimed him an immigrant, child of a northern tribe.

Among the villagers, Father was the first immigrant of his generation invited by the Council to Share his knowledge here in Mint City. Sometimes Sharp dreamed of years to come, when he himself was adult and Father was a City Elder. Perhaps it might happen for real.

Bronze glinted.

The lead acolyte took care unwrapping his sickle, then used both hands to pass it to the Chief Librarian, who bowed before accepting the sacred instrument.

Father's face was clenched in stone-like, impassive hardness, as the shining blade swept high—

This was it!

—before the Chief Librarian sliced downward, separating a sliver of flesh from Father's shoulder. Did the Librarian wince? Then the other acolytes were there, one using tongs to transfer the sliced flesh to his partner's bronze platter, while the last acolyte used his unwrapped goblet to capture some of Father's thick, dark blood.

Not the slightest scent of pain hung in the air.

Sharp was incandescent with pride as he watched the Chief Librarian lead the acolytes, with their wonderful offering, to the waiting City Elders. First, they stopped before the Prime Elder, who picked up the fleshy sliver between the thumbs of his right hand, raised it to his mouth, hesitated, then popped it in—

Truly, this was the pinnacle of Sharp's life.

—before spitting Father's flesh on to the floor.

~No!

Sharp could not contain his fragrant exclamation, but *that was his Father's meat* lying on the flagstone, rejected.

The Chief Librarian's face was crinkled with revulsion. Then he blanked his expression and stood in place, trembling. But the offering on the floor was an accusation that no politeness could mask.

This was awful. What made it worse was the way they gave Father a second chance: the Vice-Prime Elder took the goblet, held it steady, then tried to take a taste.

But the bitterness was too much. Shuddering, he handed the goblet back to the acolyte, who bowed.

No one could look at Father.

To an aroma of disgust – that was the maiden at the other end of the bench – Father rose from the marble chair and walked to the exit. Helpless, Sharp took his place behind him.

But that damning indictment remained on the floor, raw and accusing, for they were both, father and son, bitter immigrants in a land of sweetness, interlopers who could never share their deepest learning with their neighbours, outsiders forever.

It was evening when they reached the hostel at the city's edge. Once inside the foyer, Sharp pretended an urgent need to visit the eating-room. All he wanted was to lock himself away in private, insulated from the stench of shame as Father tried to explain his failure to Mother and Bittersweet.

But when Father went up to the room, Sharp wandered outside and took the outer stairs to the roof garden. There he sat on a low wall as darkness fell and the night-blossoms opened in a symphony of cool fragrance. It was beautiful here. Silver stars grew brighter as the sky became black. So peaceful, so far from the sourness that had ruined his life today.

A green light burst into being, tiny but clear, and drifted down toward a distant range of hills. As it neared the ground – or appeared to – it shot off horizontally before finally coming to land. This was like nothing he had ever seen or smelled.

Could the green light be alive?

Frightened, he pulled himself up and headed for the steps. The rooftop seemed to sway, but that was illusion. He used the inner staircase, and found the corridor where their room was situated. Faint-scented candles lit the way.

He stopped, tried the handles, and slowly opened the door.

Bittersweet was asleep on her couch, a faint trace of milk and blood around her mouth, left over from her evening lesson with Mother. The brat was always a quick learner. Neither Mother nor Father remained in sight: they were inside the canopied bed, with the drapes drawn.

Should he waken Father?

He opened his mouth, but then an acid question rose inside: who was Father to spread the knowledge of what anyone, especially his son, had seen?

The thought accompanied him all the way down to the basement level of the hotel, where the kitchen and pantry were located. No one was around to smell him open a discreet cupboard, filch a thick sack, and fill it with vegetables. This was a time to be practical, ignoring niceties.

A nauseating thought: if things got bad, he would have to survive on vegetation in the wild. At least he would be alone in his embarrassment.

Finally he reached the hotel lobby – ducking back and holding in his scents as a duty clerk passed by – and went through to the night outside. He hitched the sack over his shoulder.

Any direction would serve, for his intention was to escape this place, to flee from his family's shame. Perhaps that strange green light was nothing; or perhaps it marked someplace to go, the illusion of a goal when everything else in his life had rotted away to foulness.

He walked into the night.

Rekka's hands were shaking as she planted the microwards, marking the perimeter of her camp. Soon a ragged ellipse of protective devices was in place, each spiked into the ground, making no sound but responding when her infostrand – worn bracelet-wise around her wrist – polled them one by one.

She wished she'd landed on the bright side of the terminator line, with hours to go before darkness fell. But here she was, trying to set up her first offworld campsite at night-time, telling herself there was no need to be scared, finding it hard.

Her infostrand gave a soft chime. The scanners had swept inside the perimeter, deep into the soil, detecting nothing dangerous. Now the microwards would turn their senses outward, guarding her.

Finally she powered up her biofact, having dragged the heavy device to the centre of her camp. Already in place was an evolver framework ready to create her beeswarm; as soon as the initialisation completed, she invoked the factory marrows, watched the progress displays for the first dozen instantiations, then closed down the holo, leaving the process running.

She held a breath, then slowly, slowly released it. Mind and body as one: thoughts as neurochemical events; emotions as neuropeptide flows; 'reality' a magnificent neural construct, the illusion known as *maya*, since every image she saw 'out there' was constructed in her head, whether she was imagining or remembering or looking at her campsite now: the image appeared to be all around her, but it was built by the collaboration between her visual and entorhinal cortexes. Or perhaps all this conscious thought was a form of internal chatter – a form of fear – that she needed to let go of.

Calm down, Rekka, girl.

Another slow breath.

Relax, relax, relax.

She had practised yoga for years, but this was different from sitting on a mat in a warm room with her friends, or working *asana*s in her study-bedroom at McGill.

Relax.

Several of her grad school friends had been extreme-sport adrenaline junkies; but she was quiet Rekka Chandri, shy and absorbed in her studies, almost reclusive. How she had got from there to here, via UNSA's fast-track programme, seemed unreal. And now she was on a world so new to humankind that it was known by a numeric code, not yet named.

Climbing into her padded sleeping-suit, she wondered whether she would be able to sleep here. Differing gravity, an odd but pleasing quality to the air – her unconscious mind had not yet accepted them as normal, so it was likely to keep dragging her senses back to alertness.

'Lights out,' she whispered.

All artificial illumination faded as she settled back on the ground. Overhead was magnificence: black sky swirling with clear white stars, the arcing bridge of the Milky Way.

I am the alien here.

She turned on her side, but could not close her eyes. Except that she must have, because at some point she came awake, and pre-dawn was painting the sky deep-green, while fractal branches were silhouetted against the backdrop. And inside the shadows, she seemed to glimpse a pair of amber eyes: some trick of the light.

Then she shot up to a sitting position because *the eyes had blinked*, then the shape moved, not branches after all – maybe antlers? – and it was gone, the creature, noisily retreating into the undergrowth and out of sight.

She began to shake.

SEVEN

FULGOR, 2603 AD

Almost oblivious to the flowshaft he was descending, Carl Blackstone wondered how he could have grown old enough to have a son who had left home. This would be Roger's first morning waking up in his new place; yet it seemed such a short time ago that Carl himself had entered the Academy in Labyrinth as a newbie trainee, while meeting Miranda still lay in the future, and the thought of parenthood was inconceivable.

Entering the conference centre's lobby, he saw seven visitors rising from their seats. It was time to focus his attention outwards. He had already checked the meeting room upstairs and configured it the way he wanted – as facilitator, he had control of all morphing, apart from minor adjustments for comfort.

'I'm Neliptha Braun,' said one of the women, who had been sitting apart from the others. 'And you must be Mr Blackstone.'

She was holding out her hand to shake: a custom from certain Earth regions, marking her out as an offworlder.

'I'm honoured,' said Carl. 'Let me introduce you to the others. This is Dr Latitia Lakos. How're you doing, Latitia?'

'Wonderful, Carl. Ms Braun, how delightful.'

'Call me Neliptha.'

The Earthwoman had caught on quickly, noting the use of first names. That boded well for the negotiations, as her employers, Norwest Seattleton First Banking, were best placed to provide Earthside financing for the proposed business, importing from Fulgor.

A bulky shaven-headed man approached, offering his hand to Neliptha.

'And I'm Xavier Spalding. Please call me Xavier.'

'From Mercantile Metatrade? I'm surprised you came in person, sir, instead of delegating. It's a pleasure to meet you.'

'I'm always interested to meet someone from NWSB.'

Carl introduced the other five – the trio from Lucis Traders Agg., led by Vermundrs Overne, plus Jiang-Shan Cho and Treena Cassell, independent venture capitalists and entrepeneurs in their own right. Then they all walked as a group to a flowshaft that carried them up some hundred metres to the floor that Carl had booked. Prismatic quickglass shifted, brightening and changing colour, as they walked through to the great room that overlooked, on every side, the shining towers and viaducts of Lucis City.

He began by outlining the objectives of the meeting as he understood them, and received minor clarification from Treena and Vermundrs while the others nodded. Then it was time for him to disengage, encouraging the others to speak in turn. For now, he needed only ensure that everyone received sufficient time to speak, which in the early stages was easy enough among professionals, though later it might prove challenging.

Soon there was an inevitable descent into detail. Carl followed, only because he would later have to be able to bring everybody up to an overview level where they could agree common goals, because while focusing on the trees, agreement is almost impossible; while everyone can agree on what is important to the forest. Managing this transition between high and low level was an important part of his job today.

Luculenti would have thrashed out an agreement in seconds, but Fulgidi businessfolk with every enhancement short of upraise moved far more slowly. As Carl had told Roger, they used their upgraded cognitive skills to find creative ways to disagree or challenge each other as much as to formulate agreements. But those agreements, once made, were rigorous and watertight, the transition from meeting-minutes to legal contract scarcely more than a formality.

The morning passed with few surprises. By the session's end, the import-export financing and corporate structures were agreed, Carl had wrapped up the meeting, and lunch was a celebration of completion instead of the working break it might have been.

'Good work,' Treena told him. 'I didn't think we were all going to walk away happy, but you turned it around.'

Xavier watched them but did not approach.

I didn't figure you for shy.

In fact, Carl had been impressed by the low-key strength of the man. If anyone had achieved their goals today, it had been Xavier Spalding.

'I've got the afternoon free,' Treena went on. 'We could spend it in Tranquillity Park, if you like.'

'Love to, but I've so much work on at the moment.'

'And a wife at home. Never mind. Give my love to Miranda.'

'I thought for a moment you wanted to give it to me.'

'Naughty, naughty, darling. But you are so right.'

She drifted away. Carl was about to head over to Xavier, but his tu-ring chimed, indicating a private call. He double-blinked his smartlenses, and Miranda's face appeared in his vision.

'Hello, sweetheart. Are you carrying on this afternoon?'

'No,' he subvocalized. 'We wrapped the whole thing up already.'

'So you're coming straight home?'

'Maybe not. I know Treena Cassell wants to talk to me about something.'

'She'd better stick to talking only, Carl Blackstone.'

'Yes, ma'am.'

'See you later.'

'Later.'

The image cleared.

I didn't lie to her.

But neither had he told her about already rejecting Treena.

There are risks worth taking, and risks that aren't.

The thing was, what he was about to do in secret was one thing, but the habit of lying to everyone about everything was a dangerous temptation in his profession. You had to erect layer upon layer of false personae to move through the everyday world; but Miranda deserved better than that.

Perhaps if she had known him earlier, at the time of his most public shame – when he was only three years older than Roger was now – she would understand the temptation he was giving into.

The year was 2580 Earth-equivalent, and he was one among a hundred and seventy-three Pilot Candidates filling the silver waiting-hall. Most were newly graduated from Academy training, but that was literally academic: the real test was almost upon them. That was why the whole group was shit-scared.

Clothing played a part, indicating preference. Carl wore pure black like the majority, as if determined to gain a ship. Commander Gould had insisted on it.

But I'm going to fail.

Others wore yellow, green or red patches: those who wanted to live on a planet (usually because they were raised on a realspace world among ordinary humans); those who wanted to remain in Labyrinth, shipless; and those who professed no ambition but to accept judgement.

It's going to be awful.

For a second, he fantasized about faking sudden illness. But the local scan nodes would check him over without even contacting MedCentral; and besides, half the Pilot Candidates looked ready to throw up.

'Look at chickenshit Anderson.' Riley, bluff and square-jawed, gestured towards a candidate with scarlet epaulettes. 'Accepting judgement, my ass. He doesn't deserve a ship, no way, and he knows it.'

'Who can know what will happen?' Soo Lin looked calm. 'Perhaps acceptance is wise.'

'Yeah? So how come you're wearing black, my friend?'

'I know who I am.'

'And you know you're going to fly, cos you is a *Pilot,* right? Exactly my point. Even Blackstone agrees, don't you, pal?'

'Er, sure,' said Carl.

'You could be more positive.'

'It's just—'

But then Lianna was walking towards them. Riley fell silent. Most of the males nearby were looking.

'Are we all supporting each other?' Her voice was gentle in the way a whip is soft. 'So where is Eleanor? Who's watching out for her?'

From the tearful conversations of the past few days, Eleanor's confidence was lower than anyone's, her stress levels higher.

'Come on, guys.' Lianna, as she turned around, looked lean and very fit. 'Can't anyone see her?'

She was the fastest runner in their year, but dismissed all compliments on her athleticism, respecting only academic achievement. Around her, the air was only faintly amber, the distortions from Euclidean reality scarcely apparent.

They might almost have been in realspace, instead of an annexe of Hilbert Hall in the heart of Labyrinth.

No pressure, making this a public ceremony.

If only he had remained on Molsin, or some other human world. Some of those young Pilots never even came here, believing that Labyrinth and the rest of mu-space held nothing for them. They might be wrong, but at least they would avoid the humiliation about to be inflicted on him.

A message reverberated through their minds.

=Pilot Candidates, make ready.=

Soundless, it thrummed inside them.

=Fifteen minutes remain in which to compose yourselves.=

Riley rubbed his face.

'Another fifteen shitting minutes. I want my ship *now.*'

But the shakiness in his voice was obvious, and the words finished with a rising note tending toward a squeak. When Lianna put her hand on his shoulder, he blushed.

Carl blinked. She was his best friend, sort of, with long conversations and him treating her as an equal. It was only at night, alone, that he had dreamed other kinds of thought, but the thing was that none of them could come true, not with his impending humiliation.

And she was the instructors' favourite, destined for a proud future, already favoured with access to certain restricted sections of the Logos Library. Meanwhile he was the quirky one with odd views, so often out of step with his classmates, self-sufficient and possibly too stubborn.

'Oh,' said Lianna. 'There's Eleanor. Come on, you three.'

Riley and Soo Lin followed her, with Carl trailing. But he was the first to stop, realizing what Eleanor was up to. By the time the others reached her, the air around Eleanor was filled with sliding shards of glass-like nothingness, spiralling through rotations that could not occur in realspace.

'So she's impatient,' said Riley. 'Do we blame her?'

Now only a shivering distortion remained, as Eleanor was outside normal timeflow, sidestepping the least-action geodesic, experiencing the tense remaining minutes in a few subjective seconds.

Riley looked envious. Carl wished he'd thought of Eleanor's ruse himself; but he didn't think he could summon the concentration, not now.

So they passed the remaining time in the normal way, with nervous murmurs here and there among the waiting candidates. Finally, Eleanor rotated back into normal timeflow and smiled at her friends.

'Hey,' she said. 'Was I the only one to—?'

=Pilot Candidates, move out.=

'I think you were,' answered Lianna. 'And we're jealous as hell.'

'That makes me feel better.'

Jostling, they lined up four abreast, before the massive sealed archway. Then the great doors began to open, furling back into a myriad polygons, revealing a shining walkway that led down to the magnificence of Borges Boulevard: the most notable thoroughfare in Labyrinth, contained within the city bounds yet infinite in length.

Then they began to walk out, all one hundred and seventy-three of them, every one of them scared. Even the downramp, short though it was, felt infinite as they descended its length and finally, in formation, stood on the boulevard proper, gleaming sidewalks and rails on either side, and then a drop, for Borges Boulevard ran on mountain-high buttresses in this part of the city. Far overhead, the city's ceiling was a complex mosaic of dwellings and the city's own physical self; while off to one side floated several tiers of spectator seats, currently occupied by several thousand Pilots who had specifically arranged their schedules so they could be in Labyrinth at this time.

As if Graduation were not intrinsically bad enough, the Pilot Candidates were beneath the gaze of those who had passed the test with ease.

How do they feel?

Perhaps the mature Pilots did not really see their younger counterparts. Possibly what happened inside their heads was merely vivid memory, as their minds took them back to their own triumphs, to the nova-burst of elation when they met their ships for the first time. For these were the true winners: the Pilots who lived for voyaging.

I can't do this.

But of course he had to.

Beside him, Lianna's face was shining with pride and excitement, her obsidian black-on-black eyes filled with the certainty that today was going to be the most notable day of her life.

Mine too.

Not in the same way, however.

Fuck it.

Sickness was building up inside him. However much he had trembled and dreaded this moment earlier, being in the moment was so much worse.

Then the massed Pilot Candidates began to walk on, heading toward judgement, to the end of their cosy years in Labyrinth, the beginning of real adulthood.

Not long now.

Call it a walk of shame.

There was a rhythm to their walk, as the candidates marched in time – *left, right, left, right, fail-ure, fail-ure* – while the tiers of watching Pilots hovered over them, and the worst thing was – *Gods, no* – the observers included Carl's parents, though he had begged them to stay away.

A watery haze of shame and stress filled his vision. Hadn't Dad already apologized for his commitments in the Halberg Nebula, and Mum for being with him on board?

I can't endure it.

Could he simply break formation and run?

No, I can't.

'Relax.' Lianna had fallen in step beside him. 'You'll be all right.'

'I don't think so.'

'Yes, you will.'

He could have argued but that would be stupid. Everything hurt. Commander Gould was a monster, forcing him to go through this.

After an unreckonable time spent marching on that gleaming surface, they exited Borges Boulevard, and descended to a wide platform that overlooked a bluish chasm. On the far side was the cliff-like Great Shield, an outer wall of Ascension Annexe.

Along the titanic wall, scallop shapes were arranged in rows, each a doorway that was tiny-looking from here, but in reality huge.

=Make ready.=

They spread out along the platform, all hundred and seventy-three of them, separated by psychological more than physical distance: they were each on their own.

For this was it: Graduation.

He remembered his childhood on Molsin, the wonder of its sky-cities and the harshness of its underworld and acid seas, followed by the youthful return to his birthplace. Rediscovering Labyrinth had been a joy. And then the growing sense of purpose, the learning and the internalization of discipline, the notion of his destiny in life. A cascade of memories tumbled through him, making him want to cry.

This is impossible.

High up on the Great Shield, one of the scallop-doors moved.

Too late. I can't run now.

Graduation was starting, and he would simply have to endure. All he could do was watch as a white frosty ribbon-path extended from the scallop-door like a vast serpent, snaking its way through the air toward the platform, toward him and the other waiting candidates.

It touched, and shivered into stillness.

=Pilot Candidate Ruís Alfredo, step forward.=

A slight-looking candidate advanced a pace, stopped, then continued to the platform's edge where the ribbon-path began.

=Rise and be judged.=

One more step and he was on the path. Though it remained in place as a bridge, its surface began to flow, carrying Alfredo over the beautiful abyss – the Labyrinthine structures far below were a marvel – upward to the Great Shield, high up where the scallop-door was retracting.

Off to one side, a huge holo grew, displaying Alfredo's progress for the watching Pilots, showing him in close-up. They could see the fear and wonder on his face as he stepped through the opened door, entered a great pale hangar, then froze below the beautiful thing that hung there.

The ship was luscious purple and rich cobalt blue, and its lines were strong; but no one applauded yet.

Tiny beneath the ship, Alfredo advanced. Finally he reached up to touch her hull – her under-surface hung close – with tentative fingers.

The ship's hull shivered, and Alfredo bowed his head.

Then a carry-tendril snaked down, wrapped around his waist, and bore him upwards, all the way to the top of the ship, where it lowered him through the dorsal opening, into the Pilot's cabin, on to the control couch he was born to occupy.

Finally the tendril retracted and the dorsal hatch sealed up.

And now the Pilots cheered, their applause washing through the serene abyssal space, echoing in the cool air, while on the Great Shield the scallop-door lowered into place. There was another way out of the pale hangar, and the big holo displayed it now.

The new ship turned in place and began to fly along a blue-lined tunnel that passed all the way through Ascension Annexe. Everyone grew quiet.

Then, when the ship burst out from the city and into golden mu-space, everybody roared. This maiden flight was a triumph, as Alfredo took his ship on a soaring trajectory towards a crimson nebula. It glimmered against a speckled backdrop of black fractal stars, like coal carved into snowflakes.

Soon the holo faded to transparency, waiting to come to life again. One hundred and seventy-two candidates breathed out, trying to keep calm. Some were weeping. Alfredo's ship was a good one, his flight a fine start to Graduation.

=Step forward, Pilot Candidate Adam Kirellin.=

The first ribbon-path was gone. Another grew, this time from low down on the Great Shield.

=Rise and be judged.=

It carried Kirellin to the waiting hangar, where his vessel was long and bronze, ringed with lustrous green. When he touched the hull, he tipped his head back and laughed; the sound reverberated from the holo display, accompanied by cheering and clapping from the massed Pilots. The ship took Kirellin inside; within a minute they had burst out of Labyrinth, aimed at a black star, and flown.

=Pilot Candidate Helena Tchal, step forward.=

Carl did not know her. She was wearing a brown tunic with yellow panels, and when her ribbon-path bore her to a hangar that stood empty, no one was surprised.

=No ship. This candidate has a different path to follow.=

There was a smaller platform off to the right, and the ribbon-path carried her to it. Soon there would be other losers to keep her company.

Whatever her alleged preference – yellow for a realspace world – she hung her head. Carl thought she might be weeping.

I wish I wasn't wearing black.

Or perhaps clothing would make no difference to his forthcoming humiliation.

=Step forward, Pilot Candidate Riley O'Mara.=

Carl muttered: 'Good luck.'

Riley's shoulders looked tense as he advanced onto his ribbon-path. He let it carry him to an opening hangar, where a polished bronze-and-steel vessel awaited him.

In the holo, his tears were shining, even as he grinned.

Why am I here?

Good for Riley, but it hurt so much to watch him fly from the floating city into golden void. Another triumph, another contrast to Carl's own situation.

Somehow, he remained standing while thirty-one more candidates – he counted – rode on ribbon-paths to hangars, twenty-nine of them containing bright new ships. The other two joined Tchal on the losers' platform.

=Pilot Candidate Carl Blackstone, step forward.=

The ribbon-path sparkled beneath him. Blood-rush washed in his ears. Somehow he remained upright as the flow carried him out over a bluish haze, buildings and piazzas far below, a wealth of architectural constructs within the more-than-city that was Labyrinth. All of it magnificent, usually awe-inspiring; but today it seemed to mock him.

His teeth bit into his lower lip as the flow decelerated, nearing the Great Shield. Ahead, a scallop-door was edging inside, retracting.

Revealing an empty bay.

This is so awful.

The feeling was even worse than he had expected: from his tightened forehead, a sickening downward rush of nausea, a spinning sensation though his feet did not move. The watching Pilots were a blur of tiny featureless faces, splotches of colour.

=No ship. This candidate has a different path to follow.=

Awful, awful, awful.

Standing with Tchal and the other shipless candidates, Carl kept his head down, shaking and trying not to puke. He looked up only twice: once when Soo Lin gained his ship – bronze-and-turquoise with bold curves – and again when Lianna rose for judgement.

In the holo, her face was radiant. He had always known she was special, and here was the proof: her ship was of sweeping silver, a teardrop with eight narrow fins, gleaming and unusual. When she launched into golden mu-space, her first destination was the Mandelbrot Nebula, the boldest of choices for a maiden flight.

The cheering lasted long after the holo faded.

On the losers' platform, Carl Blackstone wept.

EIGHT

EARTH, 1926 AD

Vodka, borscht and a black cigarette to follow – what could be better? Dmitri Shtemenko leaned back in the hardwood chair and scanned his fellow denizens of the café. Narrow, hard faces, some with spreading beards like his own. He himself was nineteen but looked thirty-five in his reflection, the window turned into a black mirror by the night outside. There were times when he felt ninety-nine.

He sucked smoke, glad he was alive.

'You want more borscht, comrade?' called the burly woman behind the counter.

'No thanks, Ivana.'

Half of the people here knew what he did for a living – so much for secrecy. But it could be useful, and he often acted on the information his neighbours gave him.

One of the things Ivana and her husband Mikhail knew about Dmitri was his dislike of meat, though if fatty gobbets of beef or horse were the only thing available, he would force them down, fighting not to vomit. The proprietors may have had theories about this dislike; they made no attempt to verify by asking.

Things could be hard enough here in Moscow. In the countryside, well, perhaps some of the older men here, with the long hard faces, had seen the same kinds of thing he had. Laughter was something that belonged to childhood, far behind him now.

'This is the one.' It was Leonid from the market, brushing past Dmitri on the way to refill his vodka glass at the counter. 'Grey coat, coming in now.'

Dmitri slowly lowered his chin, an unobtrusive acknowledgement. Then Leonid was talking to Ivana, and Dmitri's attention, apparently on his own glass, refocused on the door.

The thin man who entered had a long grey coat, as Leonid had said. It was torn and stained with coal and oil, no surprise for a railway worker. His name was Vadim Sergeiev, and he did not look like a criminal. In fact he looked worn out; but Dmitri had no intention of feeling sympathy.

He watched while Sergeiev drank the one glass of vodka he was here for, before buttoning his coat back up and checking his woollen hat. Then he went back out into the night; and after a few moments, Dmitri followed.

Outside, snow was accumulating. In the morning, young women (for there was no unemployment in the great Soviet state) would use square boards on sticks – looking like placards for the kind of demonstration the downtrodden proletariat occasionally organized in imperialist regimes like England – as snow-shovels, clearing away the deep drifts, for pedestrians and also for the occasional official car that might use one of the broad roads.

Up ahead, at the entrance to the Metro system, Vadim Sergeiev met up with two men – they had been smoking to keep warm – and all three continued walking. Down below, the Metro station was like a palace, its walls marble and spotless, its intricate chandeliers gleaming, a symbol of the immense wealth that future citizens would all enjoy, generations not yet born, after many decades of rational planning, mobilizing the resources of the state.

It was quite a walk to the men's destination, the above-ground railway station, but perhaps they did not have money to spare for the Metro fare. Neither did Dmitri, but in his case he had ways to ride for free.

None of them appeared security conscious. Perhaps they were too weary to check behind them; perhaps they were too stupid. In any case, Dmitri pressed inward with both arms as he walked, not patting his pockets, but feeling with his inner wrists the hardness inside each coat pocket. The trio up ahead might be amateurs; he was not.

Despite the darkness, the cold and the snow, there were others trekking along the streets. It was only when they neared the station and headed around the back, towards the marshalling yards, that Dmitri had to be careful. Now he moved from shadow to shadow, glad that the snow was fresh and therefore silent as he walked.

Finally, they were standing next to a tarpaulin-covered pile, itself caked in snow. Railway sleepers, waiting to be laid beneath tracks. From what Dmitri had learned, this was where he had expected them to be; the surprise was the fourth man who joined them, bulkier than the others, a departure from the rail-thin norm of Muscovites. Of Russians in general, really.

'Ten roubles,' the newcomer said. 'Is that really the price you think you can get?'

'Everything's so scarce.' This was Vadim Sergeiev. 'These things are valuable.'

He pointed at the pile of sleepers.

Thank you. That was all I needed.

Dmitri broke cover, reaching inside his coat and pulling out his wallet.

'Stay exactly where you are, comrades.'

'No—'

'Stand *still*. I'm State Security, and I have reinforcements with me.'

'But—'

'Stay exactly as you are, Vadim Sergeiev.'

That caused a whimper in response. When State Security knew your name, there was rarely a pleasant outcome.

'Oh, Jesus,' murmured one of the others.

'I really don't like Christians,' said Dmitri. 'So you keep your bastard prayers to yourself.'

But the big man, the stranger, spoke in a deep, easy voice.

'Good evening, *gospadin* Shtemenko. It is nice to meet you at last.'

So. *Gospadin* instead of *tovarisch; mister* instead of *comrade.*

'Cosmopolitanism,' said Dmitri, 'is a crime against the state.'

'You think I deserve the firing-squad for good manners? For offering politeness?'

'Perhaps.'

'I think your mother would not have approved of your attitude to the Church. Perhaps even you, Lieutenant Shtemenko, could learn to accommodate the needs of others.'

My mother!

And then, because the man's words were intended to invoke uncoordinated rage, Dmitri went cold and emotionless. This would be a professional criminal, with excellent information, therefore highly placed.

Dmitri gestured towards the railway sleepers with his chin.

'Stealing the people's property. This hardly accommodates their needs.'

'And such selfishness' – the voice was almost gentle – 'did not exist in your village?'

Dmitri ignored this.

'As you said, Vadim Sergeiev, the railway property is valuable because of the economic scissors.'

It was often in *Pravda* and *Izvestiya* these days, both newspapers – the *Truth* and the *News* – reporting the current twin trends of high and increasing prices for manufactured goods and raw materials against low, falling prices for the simple goods that the proletariat were trying to sell. The graphs looked like open scissors, sure enough.

From his left pocket, Dmitri drew a pair of black, heavy, battered scissors.

'Um.' The big man looked surprised. Then his face tensed. 'You *don't* have reinforcements. That's why I'm willing to talk. I'm Alexei Krymov and I—'

Dmitri pulled his revolver from his right-hand pocket.

'Reinforcements,' he said.

The name of Krymov was familiar. He was big-time, and an arrest would be spectacular. On the other hand, any bribe he might offer would be substantial.

'Put that weapon away, Lieutenant.'

'You should not have mentioned *her*.' Dmitri meant his mother. 'You are a bad person, *tovarisch* Krymov.'

The revolver bucked, simultaneously with the crash of sound. Krymov dropped like a stack of dead sticks.

'Please, sir—' Vadim Sergeiev was on his knees in the snow, tears on his face. 'My son wrote an essay on Darwinism at school, that's why he's in trouble and I need the money to, to ease his way ...'

'To bribe a teacher?'

Contradicting Lysenkoism meant turning against a doctrine beloved of Josef Stalin, the genetic basis for the agricultural plans designed to bring food to an ever-hungrier people.

'Technically, but my son's ideas could produce actual crops that—'

Again, the crash and the recoil came together.

'It's only a few years,' said Dmitri to the two cowering survivors, 'since we were a feudal society that was almost fully illiterate. Within a decade, fifty per cent of the proletariat will be able to read and write.'

'Yes, comrade.'

'We agree,' said the other. 'We didn't mean to go up against the state. It was just that we were hungry and—'

Two more bangs, one bullet each. Two more corpses splayed and tangled on the snow.

'Freedom of the people,' said Dmitri, 'is inevitable.'

Then he pocketed his revolver, and transferred the heavy scissors to his right hand.

'Scissor economics,' he added.

Only dead things were here, piles of bone and cooling meat, no longer bearing minds to appreciate his humour.

He took the little finger of each left hand, leaning down to force the blades through bone, then put all four trophies in his pocket along with the scissors. From their wallets he took the dead men's money – pitifully little, apart from Krymov – not from greed but because whoever found the bodies would rob them anyway, so why should he not benefit?

After all, he was the one who had just carried out his part in purifying the proletariat, was he not?

That's right.

His internal voice mocked him, while far off in the distance he could hear a nine-note sequence that sometimes haunted him, particularly when he remembered the village and his fifteenth birthday; and if that bastard Krymov weren't already dead, Dmitri would shoot him now, because no one should mention his mother, no one should even know.

He fired again, and the Krymov-thing's coat leaped; the dead meat inside did not.

Wasting bullets.

And causing noise. Moving back into shadow, he made his away across the tracks, away from the station proper. He would take a roundabout route home, checking behind him all the way – he was a professional, unlike those idiots – and check that no one was inside his rooms before putting his four treasures in the secret part of his pantry, along with the others.

Not that he was intending to eat them, though they were stored so close to food.

Mother.

That was a thought to push away, to force from his mind.

No.

But sometimes – like now, when the dark shadows twisted in their diabolic ways, off beyond the edge of his vision – the other voices came back too, the voices of traumatized innocence remembering the before-times.

Mother, and the taste like bacon.

Whimpering, he pushed on. Snow was falling heavily now,

hiding his tracks, cold on his face, because he could not be crying. That had been leached from him four years before, when hell descended on a starving world.

Most of the village had perished, and there had been no food, no other food; and those who survived shared the secret they could never talk about, not among themselves and never to strangers.

He had never eaten her fingers. It seemed important to remember that.

I'm sorry.

All around in the night, snow caked Moscow's grand old buildings, creating beauty.

At the same time in Zürich, Gavriela was trying to insert her front-door key into the lock. It took several iterations of zeroing in by feel, and then she had success – except that, as she pushed the door, it rattled but did not open. Solid bolts were in place.

Frau Pflügers has locked me out.

Thanks to the Glühwein, Gavriela wasn't thinking clearly. *That* was clear. Or maybe it wasn't, maybe the world had grown fuzzy while she wasn't looking, because you never knew what happened out of your—

'My dear girl.' Frau Pflügers, old-fashioned oil lamp in hand, was standing there. 'I thought you were in bed, or I'd never have locked up.'

'I met some people.'

'Come in, come in. So, were there young gentlemen present?'

'Oh, no.'

'Did it sound as if I was criticizing?' Frau Pflügers slid the bolts home. 'Never mind. Were you making new friends?'

'Actually, I think I was.'

Inge, Elke and Petra. They were excellent company; but they lived life in a way Gavriela could not afford to keep up with.

'Then we'll celebrate with some nice hot chocolate in the kitchen, before you go to bed.'

'I couldn't ask you to—'

'The range is still hot, and I'd appreciate the company.'

'In that case, thank you.'

Out back, Gavriela stood and watched as Frau Pflügers heated a saucepan of milk. Gavriela found herself fascinated with the looping currents inside the liquid, the columns of steam that rose then broke apart: a gentle form of turbulence. Then she realized Frau Pflügers was watching her, smiling.

'You look fascinated, Fräulein Wolf, like a two-year old. Oh, I'm saying it badly, because that sounds like an insult, but' – Frau Pflügers paused to stir the milk with a wooden spoon – 'it's a grown-up innocence, if that makes sense.'

'It does to me. There's so much to see everywhere, if people only look.'

'Hmm. You know, there were women students when I was a girl; but I didn't know it then.'

'Oh. Would you have liked to go to the ETH, Frau Pflügers?'

'It was the Polytechnik in those days.'

'People still call it the Poly. If you'd gone, what would you have studied?'

'I don't know, dear.' Frau Pflügers stared up to her right. 'I can't see myself as a scientist, more an arts type.'

'Paintings or books?'

'Do you have to choose between them?'

'I don't see why.'

The milk was coming to the boil. From a saucer, Frau Pflügers scraped dark flakes of chocolate into the saucepan, and stirred.

'We all do the best we can,' she said. 'I'd like to believe that. Even Faust, in the end . . . Do you read Goethe?'

'Of course, Frau Pflügers. And he was quite the scientist, too. Not a sufficient mathematician, or he would not have opposed Newton's optics' – Gavriela saw Frau Pflügers' gaze shift, and realized she was assuming specialist knowledge – 'but he foreshadowed Darwin's work. He studied *everything*.'

'Wouldn't that be wonderful?' Frau Pflügers poured two cups, then handed one over. 'You know what Napoleon said about Goethe, after they met at Erfurt?'

'Oh, yes.'

The two women clinked their cups of hot chocolate together.

'*Voilà un homme,*' they said in time.

Gavriela lay back on the clean-smelling pillow, staring at grey shadows, while the room seemed over and over to rotate by degrees, reset to normal, then rotate once more. She felt pleasantly dizzy lying there, supported by a soft, enveloping mattress.

But when she closed her eyes, she tumbled back to a memory of earlier that evening, before her meeting with Inge and Elke and Petra, back to the confusing, awful fight she had seen in the Altstadt, two groups of young men brawling, and the twisting of blackness-within-darkness, accompanied by grating discordant music unheard at the time: *da, da-dum, da-da-da-dum, da-da.*

Youths scrapping at night meant little; but something lay behind their actions, something awful.

The enemy.

It seemed a weird thought to generate.

The Darkness.

She slid away from horror, into sleep.

When she awoke it was inside a dream, but the contradiction seemed natural. Looking down, she saw her body formed of crystal – intricately organic and pliable, a bluish transparency – draped in a transparent garment, and felt no panic.

She was standing in a high hall, before a long glass table around which nine empty throne-like chairs were placed. Was anybody here?

—Hello?

How strange to speak without expelling air. Not needing to breathe, she attempted inhalation anyway, feeling her diaphragm move with no inrush of any atmosphere.

Perhaps the strangest thing of all was her acceptance.

Shields hung on the wall, some ancient-looking, others new. Carved into the leather were dull angular runes. They caught her attention oddly, then seemed to slip away.

Another crystalline woman entered.

She was tall and slender, haughtiness and wisdom combined; or perhaps that was an illusion caused by her transparency. Her clear eyes, like finest glass, focused on Gavriela.

—I bid you warm welcome, Gavriela Wolf.

So the regal woman knew her name. It seemed all of a piece with this place, so exotic and yet so natural. Here was the strangest dislocation in Gavriela's life; yet it also felt like coming home.

—How did I get here?

—Truly, you are not *here. Not yet.*

The explanation was inconsistent; still she embraced it as reasonable.

—Then why *am I here, or seem to be?*

—To prepare. We all need to prepare.

She looked around the glass-and-sapphire hall. It was archaic, modern and futuristic, all at once.

—So there are others?

—I am Kenna.

The regal stare was intense, glistening and filled with power.

—And you're the leader.

She realized that she hadn't asked a question, but stated it as fact.

—Yes, Gavriela.

—And the others?

The woman, Kenna, raised her transparent hand, inside which clear sinews and blood vessels (carrying transparent blood) were visible.

—You're the first.

Then Kenna's fingertips descended, causing Gavriela's eyes

to close; and even though her eyelids were clear, soft darkness closed in. Then the dream folded up inside her, wrapped itself in warm amnesia, to hide snugly in her mind.

Waiting for the time when it could creep back to awareness.

NINE

FULGOR, 2603 AD

Carl left the conference centre on foot. As he walked, his smartfabric suit reconfigured to extend a cloak from his shoulders. Others, dressed as formally, were crossing the blue plaza, entering or leaving via one of the glowing ellipses set among the flagstones.

To his left, three men rose out of an ellipse and walked off. Carl's tu-ring signalled that the shaft was vacant, so he stepped on to the glowing surface in their place.

His downward motion through flowgel felt slow; but that was only his impatience. Then he was in a great vault, descending on a thread of viscous gel to the floor. A spiderweb of narrow black tracks littered the ground in all directions; on the web, one- and five-person speedcapsules were in motion.

Beckoning the nearest vehicle, he waited for it to approach, then – while its shell was still opening – jumped inside. It sealed up, then moved along the route he selected, flicking among the other capsules before shooting into a tunnel that ran beneath Quiller Park and continued all the way to Lithrana Province.

I shouldn't do this.

Miranda wasn't expecting him home soon. What he'd implied was a meeting with the predatory Treena; the truth was somewhat different, and far more compelling.

If only I could keep away.

At the far end of Quiller, the tunnel veered north. Soon he was amid the active volcanoes of Pyrol Landing, where the capsule's motion had to slow, as the tunnel twisted to avoid the magma chambers. That was where the shadow-code took over, hiding the details of the capsule's deceleration, broadcasting false data that failed to show its opening shell or the way its solitary passenger tumbled out.

Sealing up, it continued on its way, accelerating once more.

Such a moronic risk.

If someone found a reason to stop the capsule and inspect it, the difference between the official logs and its empty interior would cause an immediate investigation to swing into action. Peacekeepers would descend – on Miranda and Roger – and all would be finished, all because his massive self-control was a fake, because there were times that temptation could not be fought, only surrendered to.

Stupid.

His cloak changed colour to blend with the rock. After a moment, a small door dissolved and he stepped into the narrow tunnel he had prepared so many years before. So foolish to risk everything, and not just his own well-being.

But it was remembered public shame, from twenty-three standard years ago in Labyrinth – not the imminent slaking of desire – that filled his mind as he squeezed along the narrow shaft.

The losers' platform had not been the worst thing.

After Graduation proper, there had been a party: a noisy maelstrom of energetic music and triumphant fun, because one hundred and nineteen additions to the fleet meant benefits to humanity and the joy, for those young Pilots, of public vindication for their work and daring, and a declaration of purpose for the rest of their lives. However far they flew, in whichever universe – mu-space or realspace – they were part of a community that publicly acknowledged them, treasuring their contribution.

Somewhere, his parents were among the Pilots greeting and congratulating their new peers. He could avoid them, for the main ballroom was dominated by the younger folk, while the others remained near the doors. But sooner or later he would have to face Lianna; and finally she saw him.

'Oh, Carl.' Her triangular features looked sad. 'We'll still be ... friends.'

'Sure. You'll be in the smartest ship ever, flitting across the galaxy, while I'll be– Shit.'

It wasn't supposed to go this badly.

'I'm sorry,' he went on. 'The thing is, you did so well. So really well.'

Her sadness drew back, as her smile became pure pleasure.

'Isn't she beautiful?'

'One terrific ship. Lots of people are talking about her.'

'Yes ... Look, I have to go see Commodore Durana. See you later?'

'*Daredevil* Durana?'

'The very one. And *she* wants to talk to *me*, is that possible?'

'Of course it is. You're brilliant.'

Her fingertips, when she touched his face, felt like miniature novas.

'You're a good friend, Carl Blackstone.'

'Thank you.'

But she withdrew her fingers too quickly.

'Whatever you end up doing, good luck.'

She despises me.

'All right.'

She flowed away from him, so graceful as she moved among their dancing, celebrating friends – former friends, in his case – and smiled back once. Then happy people swept past, shouting a party song, bedecked with streamers, and his contact with Lianna was gone.

No: it had disappeared earlier, before she had even gained her ship. It had happened the moment those words sealed Carl Blackstone's fate in public consciousness.

=No ship. This candidate has a different path to follow.=

They would reverberate forever inside him.

Across the room, he glimpsed Soo Lin and Riley, glasses in hand. Perhaps they would be easier to talk to. But no. That was not the way it was going to go. Not today.

Depression was a laxness in the trapezius muscles atop his shoulders, heaviness pulling down his chin, slouching to squeeze stress-juice inside: cortisol and neuropeptides springing from glands, washing through every organ. Feeling bad is a complicated process, not a state.

Shit. Shit. Shit.

He found a quiet exit and used it.

Now he waited in the Logos Library, sitting in a study-carrel, elbows on desk and head in hands, ignoring the infocrystals that promised so much knowledge, wishing instead that he could forget all of his life, or at least today.

No. He needed to take control.

Breathe in. Then out.

The simplicity of inhale-exhale was all he needed to focus on. Over and over, to simply breathe, to get in touch with his inner awareness. To forget the stress – the look in Lianna's eyes as she turned away – to push all that aside.

To attempt calm.

Forget today.

Because everything was new. He had to focus on himself, to gather his resources, because—

=It is time.=

He looked up.

'I know.'

The Logos Library being infinite in complexity, he was able to locate an obscure corridor to leave by. A quiet route allowed him to bypass the great Borges Boulevard, travel beneath the Great Shield, and enter the Ascension Annexe from below.

There was a bronze door that crinkled up like tissue, allowing him to pass, before it reformed with adamantine hardness; a screen of pure light, washed through with sapphire and emeralds; and a dozen other barriers, each capable of obliterating him or passively obstructing; while scan fields passed through him, invoking sensations like itching deep inside.

Finally, he was in a blank ovoid vault with no apparent exits. A chair budded from the floor and rose, but he ignored it.

So this is it.

His face felt like sand exposed by retreating tides. Every feeling inside was fresh and strange.

'I'm ready.'

An oval of wallspace melted away. A blocky figure entered: shaven head, heavy shoulders, rolled up-sleeves revealing muscled forearms. Eyes of jet, naturally.

'So how do you feel, Pilot Candidate?'

'Surviving, sir.'

'You suffered the celebration party.'

'I did.' He thought of Lianna, the look in her eye, the quick withdrawal of her hand. 'It was bad, but I felt no desire to explain myself. I was too busy making myself feel depressed.'

'Good.'

Carl looked away, then turned his attention back to Commander Gould.

'Sir? Was it chance that my parents were here? They weren't supposed to be.'

'Perhaps not.'

That was ambiguous, but the purpose of Carl's question had been to demonstrate his perceptiveness, his awareness of manipulation; the answer was not relevant.

'The real ordeal,' continued the commander, 'is right now.'

To Carl's left, the wall shimmered, transformed into a concave lattice of blazing white miniature stars, and then dissolved. Beyond lay a pale-blue hangar.

While floating inside it—

Oh my God.

—hung a ship such as he had never seen: a black dart with scarlet edging, smaller than other vessels but with immense power, dynamically unstable, so it could tumble and manoeuvre with swift agility, and with devastating weaponry installed.

You're beautiful.

For the first time he understood somnambulism, as his body walked forward without conscious control, his mind in awe, not daring to think this was real.

Yes.

You're—

I am. And you are Carl Blackstone, Pilot.

He would have hung his head and wept; but her beauty captivated him.

'You can take her out now, son.' Commander Gould's hand touched his shoulder. 'Even though the city is full of people.'

Carl glanced at the hangar walls.

=You will be unobserved.=

The commander smiled.

'The city has spoken, Pilot Blackstone. She'll provide you with a covert exit and cover outside.'

'Sir . . . Thank you.'

And if ever a ship had stealth capabilities, it was this one.

'Enjoy your victory, Carl. A solitary victory, of course. That's the nature of the beast.'

'I know.'

'That's why we chose you. Why you chose yourself. You can push yourself to win without spectators or boasting, suffer defeat in obscurity, endure whatever you have to in public.'

'Sir.'

'Because that's what it means to be a spy.'

Carl reached up to touch his ship – his magnificent, powerful, lovely ship – ready for her to take him inside in their moment of triumph.

A very private triumph.

Now, over two decades later, he felt the same resonating thrill as he walked along a polished black glass floor and came out into a vast natural cavern. A bubble of triple quickglass layers separated him from the empty vault; that was a good thing.

When she burst into being, a thunderclap of displaced air crashed among the rocks, and then she was hanging there: black, scarlet-edged and powerful. Such a tremendous ship.

I've missed you.

It was impossible to tell which of them originated the thought.

'At last.'

The quickglass shield dissolved; and then he was rushing to her, unable to hold back, needing both the intimate communion and the chance to immerse himself in mu-space, for a too-brief time.

TEN

EARTH, 777 AD

Dawn was a tattered cloak across the sky, grey and torn with nascent thunderclouds. Beneath Stígr's body, the chill ground sucked warmth from him, as if underworld spirits of deep Niflheim drank from his lifeforce. Unpleasant wakefulness goaded him into standing.

A skeletal, leafless tree stood nearby. From its bonelike branches, two dark ravens watched. At the familiar sight, his empty left eye-socket, beneath the patch, crawled and itched.

'You are a stranger here.' A woman's voice came from some distance behind him. 'Are you alone?'

Something shifted as he turned. A quick peripheral glance showed him the expected: a tree unoccupied, bare of corvine watchers. Then he was regarding a grey-haired woman whose cloak was wrapped around her body, against the wind.

'My name is Stígr,' he told her. 'Poet and wanderer, is what I am.'

'Then you'll visit our stead, and grant us an epic, if you will.'

Her tone was peaceful, and it took a few seconds to perceive the source of her security: two warriors in shadow, spears in hand.

'I am called Alfsigr,' the woman continued. 'And these are two of my sons, Alvíss and Meili.'

Stígr touched the brim of his soft hat as he bowed.

'My honour, sirs.'

Poets were supposed to see more deeply into the world, to catch sight of things that others missed. If that were true, then how could three people so easily walk up on him? He was fortunate that they were friendly.

Staff in hand, he walked with them to the village. His face was smiling, for part of him enjoyed meeting new people, and lived for the warmth of making friends; yet he felt a haunted tension around his single eye, courtesy of his other half, the part that responded to darkness when it called.

Inside the main hall, by firelight, he divested himself of hat, stave and cloak. From some of the villagers, a hiss sounded. A one-eyed wanderer: that resonated with the old tales in a way that could be disturbing.

'I am Stígr,' he said. 'And I am a very ordinary poet, I'm afraid.'

'*Is he Othinn?*' whispered a child's voice.

Stígr was able to chuckle, and then he clasped his hands together before the flames, casting a birdlike shadow on the wall.

'I *do* have a raven. You see?'

The little boy groaned, and several adults laughed.

'Perhaps your verse is better than your shadowplay, good poet.' A heavy-shouldered man, his beard hanging in twin braids, grinned at Stígr. 'In any case, avail yourself of mead and solid food.'

'My thanks, chieftain.'

'I'm Gulbrandr. A spinner of tales is always welcome, though we have young Hildr here' – he pointed to a girl of perhaps seven – 'who creates many a fanciful yarn to explain her unfinished chores.'

Stígr bowed to her, and men and women laughed again. This was a friendly hall.

If only they knew what I really am.

But he was weak, and would accept their openness, and pray to whatever part of the light remained that he would spare them, that he would not be called upon to wreak evil in this place.

Someone placed a horn cup in his hand, and filled it from a leather bag with sweet, heavy mead. Roast meat was emitting a wonderful odour.

Then he noticed the large collection of weapons by the threshold, and bundles of supplies tied with leather cords.

'There's a Thing occurring soon,' murmured Gulbrandr. 'Perhaps you know of it. Many chieftains will be there, even the Rus.'

'I . . . did not know, sir. Do you gather for a reason?'

'As chieftains,' Gulbrandr said ambiguously, 'it is our clans' welfare we consider above all.'

Stígr looked around the hall, at the easy gestures and smiles, hearing the murmur of jokes and ironic boasting, and from one corner the sound of young warriors battling with riddles instead of arms.

'Yours is a fine clan, with marvellous people,' he said.

Several days' journey away (as an ordinary wanderer might travel), in a single men's hall, a large warrior farted without waking up. Beside Ulfr, Brandr stirred, ears twitching once: the warhound could come alert in an eyeblink, as Ulfr knew from experience, but tonight there was no need. Ulfr himself was keeping watch, though not from choice: he simply could not sleep.

In his mind's eye, reflections from the spirit world were clear: poor Jarl's bloodied features, his dead stare accusing, against a backdrop of Niflheim, the black realm of Hel.

Almost as bad was his memory of Eira's expression, her knowing that Jarl's death was a mercy, but unable to forgive him for it. He felt so weary.

'It wasn't you,' said Jarl.

The dead spirit's voice was clear, perhaps because Ulfr's eyes had drooped shut.

'You died at my hand, warrior.'

'You ended what another started.'

Had there been ensorcelment? Or had some temporary madness controlled the others for a time?

'I'm sorry, my friend.'

'Not all the dark ones are in Svartalfheim, good Ulfr. Some wander the Middle World and wreak their foulness.'

'Tell me of the—'

But he started awake then, and the hall was filled with ordinary shadows that did not speak, while the only sound was snoring – from warhounds as well as men – and then another long, plaintive fart that on some other night would have made him chuckle.

Stígr sang his saga, choosing the spine-tingling tale of Fenrir's binding, beginning with a description of the dark god Loki, Father of Lies – evil and good, trickster and warrior, shape-shifter and gender-changer, so disturbing to ordinary men and women – and Loki's three monstrous children: Hel, destined to rule the shades in Niflheim, realm of the dead; the loathsome serpent Jormungand; and the master-wolf Fenrir, destined to kill Óthinn the All-Father during the final days.

Fenrir, the gods bound by trickery with unbreakable cords, in what was supposed to be a demonstration of the wolf's vast strength. To guarantee his own safety, Fenrir agreed to the binding only if one of the gods, the bright Aesir or Vanir, placed a hand in his, Fenrir's mouth.

The war-god Tyr, bravest of the brave, put his right hand – his sword-hand – between Fenrir's fangs, knowing that at the moment of binding those jaws would chomp down on his wrist and sever the hand forever.

As Stígr sang of Tyr's handsomeness and courage, he noticed a young woman with red hair and fire-bright eyes who regarded him with absorption. He subtly altered his voice, directing the greater warmth of his tones toward her.

In truth, his spellbinding song captivated everyone – there were shivers and gasps at the right places, as he foreshadowed and then related the horrors – but for himself, the true awfulness was not in the dread entities he described nor the sacrifice of the war-god's hand. For the saga, in order to place Loki's children high in the hierarchy of evil, foretold events that had not occurred; and so it was the place to describe those dread sisters, Fate, Being and Necessity: the Norns who guide destiny.

After the saga was done and the cheering was over, it was natural that he should find a quiet corner in which to talk with the woman who was so fascinated by him. Her name was Anya, she was little Hildr's sister, and she was neither married nor betrothed.

'You've seen so much,' she said. 'I wish you could show me, with your magical words, all of the Middle World.'

'I can show you, sweet Anya, but yours is the truest magic of all. The magic of touch.'

In the night, he held her. Wrapped in their cloaks, they made quiet love, softly gasping and shuddering when they came. Finally, she kissed him and slipped away, for little Hildr could not sleep without her older sister beside her. Not since their parents' death some months before.

He fell asleep and dreamed of axes, blades bright as they whirled in firelight, flying toward their bound victim, the warrior-youth Jarl with lips as sweet as Anya's, with skin almost as soft, his need as great.

But then his dreamscape shifted and he moaned, for everything that followed was exactly true.

As the dream began he had two eyes.

There was blood on his hands and sleeves as he staggered along soft ground. Heathland, clad in dull greens and purples, beneath a sky swept with greys and reds and violet: harsh, cold and beautiful. Behind him were strewn the corpses whose death he had caused.

With words.

Only with words. That was the magic and the horror of it.

How did I do that?

For he had found the inspiration in himself, the ability to subtly alter his tone and mark out certain words, to create the effects on warriors' and warrior-women's minds that he had desired, as if he had painted a scene and brought it to life, using only voice. It had been so easy to intensify jealous fantasies, to bring forth molten rage and make it spill over, and then back away from the swirling madness of blades and fists and teeth, and a well-remembered hammer crashing down and down, again and again, spattered with brains and blood.

But everyone had died, even the hammer-wielder, in a fury of mutual stab and thrust, of hack and smash, which only Stígr escaped.

He was a journeyman poet, but he had never dreamed of doing that: of the inspiration and the horror, the part of him that was in awed ecstasy, and the part that howled inside.

For an unknown time, he stumbled along that cold magnificent landscape, until he found himself on the cusp of an ice-patched dell, where on the far side a solitary ash-tree grew.

'Are you the World-Tree?' he whispered. 'Can you be Yggdrasill in truth?'

Perhaps it was a manifestation of the true world-joiner that ran through all three realms, a small shoot springing from the greater reality, so that one who could travel its length might leave the middle world and climb to the gods' realm in Asgard, or join the dark and the dead in Niflheim.

Before the tree stood a simple well, a few broken stones ringing a hole of blackness.

'No.' His voice was hoarse. 'It cannot be his. Not Mimir's.'

Surely this was ordinary, a well built by men who had moved on or died away, nothing more.

Not his.

Stígr was a wanderer, yes, but that was all he was. Wanderer and poet, singer of sagas, master of words, keeper of memories. It was a blasphemy to think of anything else, of the other who wandered the middle world and sought wisdom regardless of the price.

The painful, bloody price.

No. Don't ask this.

A sacrifice, offered with determination, garnished with suffering.

I will not.

But still his feet stumbled down toward the well's black centre, where he stopped.

'Please . . .'

His right thumb, crooked and tensed, rose toward his face. Sinews trembled as he fought the movement, warring against himself; but the motion was inexorable. Slowly, slowly, his hand ascended, growing large to dominate his sight, then touched his nose, the bridge of his nose—

Please. Please, no.

—with his thumbnail scratching into the skin, sliding left, into the eye socket and down, to the inner corner of his eye—

'NO!'

—and pressed in with enormous strength, pushed inside, slickness coating his thumb as he ripped outward, a slick pop as it came free and half his world went dark forever.

Sweet All-Father, no.

But he had done it, as he had been commanded.

'Why me? Why *me?*'

He sobbed with pain, hating himself. Then his dagger was in his hand and he made the final severance, cutting it free, changing his world for always.

The worst part was afterward, when it was too late to revert to his previous life, and he could not fight the motion of his hand again, this time as it held out his eyeball over the well – white, bloodied, glistening – and let it drop.

His eye fell forever into darkness.

Pain raging in his head, he could hardly see with his remaining eye, as he strained to focus through blood-mist on the ash-tree, where it stood in silent observation. So this was the first agony, not the last ordeal.

His tunic was belted at the waist with braided leather cords. Hands shaking as if palsied, he undid the cords, unravelling them. Then he carried them to the foot of the ash-tree, tears flooding down his right cheek, blood and fluid down his left.

Climbing the tree was torture.

When did it happen?

Twice he slipped, formed his hands into desperate hooks, and found a grip, tearing his skin. No matter: the ascent was everything.

When did the darkness take me?

His early childhood was happy. He thought he remembered that, through the roaring chaos of present pain. Or perhaps all his memories were false, and all of his existence was this: pure and bloody agony.

Two loops, with sufficient play, he placed around a branch. This was going to be it.

The other sacrifice.

For the eye, given to Mimir, was not enough. Nine days and nine nights: that was what the ordeal demanded. He knew it now, and felt the tiniest of respite from pain with the knowledge of giving in, accepting what was happening.

Turning outward, back against the trunk, he slipped one wrist inside a loop to his left, then the other to his right. Arched back, he could not maintain the pressure for long. Slowly, he worked his heels down the trunk, aware that a sudden slip now would wrench both arms from his sockets, dislocating them, and causing him to strangle as his damaged shoulders squeezed his neck.

For now, his body cruciform, he hung in place, his every sinew etched in pain.

By my own will.

If not his, then whose?

Or is *it mine? Why are you making me do this?*

When the wind rose, its passage through the tree was a metallic rustle that quickly magnified and then became lost in the tidal howl that grew up all around, and when the lightning flashed he felt no surprise.

The storm banged and growled, twisted, and tore the world away.

*

There was light in the world when something pushed him into wakefulness—

'Stígr? My sweet?'

—but for a moment he was back there, at the beginning and at the end, nine days and nine nights, as he hung there ever closer to nothingness yet unable to die, wishing for cessation but knowing that it held a price, did knowledge, a price that every wandering poet should be prepared to pay, a tribute of pain, a toast of blood, a meal of eye-flesh, a sacrifice—

'It's morning, and you should wake.'

—and at the end of the ninth night, the storm that had been ever-present grew stronger and stronger, black clouds rotating overhead, opening up the storm centre, and then it happened, because that was the moment—

'Stígr?'

—when *the sky looked at him*, and he was lost.

Her name was Anya and they had shared their bodies last night but this was agony, the remembrance and the reality of it, and the sweep of present momentary time – Being, the Norn whose true name was Skuld – was eclipsed by the past collapsing on him, the knowledge that darkness was omnipotent and he was nothing, the most terrified of thralls, no more than that.

Rubbing his face, he came into more ordinary wakefulness. There was a wetness on his left cheek, below the dirty eye-patch he wore. He sucked in his breath as Anya gently pulled the patch upward; then she shuddered and lowered it back.

Perhaps she had expected to see a covered eye, not this pink-red madness that sometimes wept clear fluid, nothing like tears.

'I'm sorry,' he told her.

'I . . . I need to return to Hildr.'

But she paused and looked at him, and for a moment she appeared as enthralled as last night, when he felt his power upon him but no destructive imperative, so he could use his words to beguile for romance, for simple lust.

In this moment, he could change her mind, commit himself to her and her to him.

'Then go,' he said. 'Do it now.'

She pulled away, trying not to sob, and then broke into a half-run, back toward the hall. He stared with his single, unwise eye. For that was part of what he had learned, during his nine-day crucifixion.

Pain is the eye of wisdom.

A socket full of never-healing rawness, that was the portal to reality, the lens of darkness.

All I deserve.

Perhaps Anya would find goodness; he himself already had his painful reward.

Almost as if the Norns knew what they were doing.

ELEVEN

FULGOR, 2603 AD

Carl rode the one-person speedcapsule back along the tunnel beneath Quiller Park, exited via the cavernous underground terminus, and rose to the surface in a flowgel column. When he stepped off the elliptical upper surface on to the plaza, he was scanning the environment only because that was natural for someone with his training.

He was energized because of his time in mu-space with *her*, his ship; but he was still careful, and there had been no signs during the return journey of anything untoward. The speed-capsule had been the same one he rode out in, with no sign of having been opened or deepscanned: he had left telltales on board, femtoscopic flakes that would have informed him of peacekeeper inspection.

A shaven-headed man was walking toward him. Xavier Spalding, from the meeting earlier. Behind Xavier rose the quickglass conference centre, the tower morphing with glacial slowness as it cycled through a variety of impressive but conservative forms, taking days to change from one to another.

Carl had not expected anyone else from the meeting to still be here. He wondered what Xavier's objective was.

A discrete off-Skein discussion? Or something more?

Xavier was smiling.

'How nice to run into you again, Carl.'

They touched fists formally.

'Likewise, Xavier. Are you pleased with today's outcome?'

'Surely. And I was hoping you'd come back here.'

'I was just wandering as I worked in Skein.'

'So you could have been physically anywhere, and I could

have just called you, of course. But since you'd booked an aircab pickup for twenty minutes from now, it seemed likely you'd return here.'

'How could you know that?'

He did not like this. Covertly, he clicked his tongue and curled his left big toe. Warmth in both forefingers indicated that his tu-rings' major defensive systems had responded, coming online and polling the surroundings for danger.

Nothing so far.

'I've got many controlling interests,' said Xavier. 'Including the cab company and other transport providers. Your itinerary is confidential, as is every passenger's.'

'Uh-huh. So why meet in person, all the same?'

'For the same reason we hold trade talks in reality, when they're important. We're brachiating primates, Mr Blackstone, with large brains, that's all. Tactile and sociable.'

That, and ordinary Fulgidi felt safer off Skein when Luculenti were involved in negotiations, since the élite had full control of that environment. It was a habit they carried into other interactions, with purely ordinary people.

'And of course,' Xavier went on, 'it's why virtual education isn't good enough, and why we send our sociable children to real colleges and multiversities.'

Carl smiled, made his voice sound natural, and said: 'Funny thing, my son Roger has just started in Lucis Multi.'

'Obviously I knew that, Carl, while *you've* not realized that my daughter Alisha is in Roger's study group. I'm hoping they'll become friends. As might you and I, let me add.'

'Friendships and alliances are good things.'

'My daughter is . . . particularly astute,' began Xavier.

There was something in his voice, the tension of mixed emotions. Something worth following up, once this encounter was over.

'She's noticed that their primary tutor, Dr Petra Helsen,' Xavier added, 'has some unusual behaviour patterns. Not off the scale, you understand.'

Around them on the plaza, a few scattered travellers were passing by. No one was paying attention. Talking this way was more low-key than inside a privacy field of whirling diamond dust. Still, they were in the open, perhaps subject to SatScan surveillance right now.

'So she's an academic,' said Carl. 'Some of my tutors were a little odd.'

'And that was—?'

'A long time ago. Are you worried by this Helsen person, Xavier?'

'She's displayed some odd reactions toward your Roger.'

'In what way?'

'Look, Alisha's trained in observing minutiae, just as you are, Carl.'

Obviously he meant his daughter was reading body language cues and verbal patterns, including tonality. Put it another way: Helsen was giving Roger funny looks.

But Carl was not dismissing such observations.

'We all learn psycholinguistics, don't we?'

'Right, and it's interesting,' said Xavier, 'to find someone as skilled as you are. We'd never have reached agreement this morning, not so quickly and with such good feeling, without some very slick elicitation and guidance from yourself.'

There was still no reaction from Carl's tu-rings. If this was the prelude to physical action, perhaps a snatch squad about to drop from the sky, then Xavier was taking his time in issuing the command.

Does he know about me?

Perhaps the man was thinking like a businessperson, no more than that.

'At any rate,' Xavier went on, 'I think Alisha likes your son. So that makes us allies, doesn't it?'

'I guess it does.'

'Then' – Xavier reached out a fist – 'I'll see you soon.'

'All right.'

They touched fists once more, then Xavier went to stand on an ellipse. He nodded, then sank out of sight.

All around, the plaza looked normal.

So does he know I'm a Pilot agent-in-place? Or am I just a business contact?

Carl became aware of the smile he was making.

An interesting problem.

As always, the stakes were serious because Miranda and Roger were as liable to peacekeeper arrest as he was. But Xavier Spalding was an interesting man, and whether as ally or opponent – well, that was the challenge, wasn't it?

He stood there until the aircab descended. Knowing it was owned by a possible enemy, he scanned its systems before boarding, finding nothing.

'Take me home,' he said.

After the morning tutorial, Roger felt weak and dispirited. Old Hatchet-Face Helsen had been scathing about their construction of virtual characters in the simulated 1920s Zürich; only Alisha had received praise, for the depth of historical accuracy in the city architecture.

Once out in the corridor, he headed for a flowdisk that would carry him to the rooftop, someplace where he could think alone about this morning's work. There was something that nagged at him below the conscious level. There had been perhaps the minutest of dark flickerings around Dr Helsen – that strange phenomenon again – but mostly things had been normal, if you counted intellectual bullying as normality.

As he stepped on the disk, another person joined him.

'Can I come up with you?' asked Alisha.

'I . . . guess so.'

She gave the command – by subvocalization, he assumed – without betraying the tiniest of motions. Then the disk was rising, and in a few seconds they were on the open rooftop. Roger stared across the quickglass campus towers, aware that Alisha's attention was on him.

'What are you thinking?' he asked her. 'No, sorry . . . We don't know each other well enough for questions like that.'

'That's right. Did your teachers use *mindreading* as a pejorative term? Meaning that you make assumptions about other folk's intentions and thoughts by interpreting their actions.'

'Some people use the word that way.'

'And you know how, when someone visualizes an image that's purely mental, even without holo, their eyes focus on very definite locations in space.'

Roger let out his breath.

'It's the entorhinal cortex in here' – he pointed at his own head – 'whose spatiotemporal grid creates the geometry of mental images, and I knew that when I was ten years old, so thanks for asking.'

'I didn't mean—'

'Luculenti aren't as superior as they think. There are people with skills no Luculentus could—'

He stopped himself.

What am I doing?

Did he want to reveal his Pilot nature? Did he want his parents arrested?

'I'm not a Luculenta yet.' Alisha's face was always pale; now it was white. 'I'm not one or the other. And Luculenti are still human, in case you haven't noticed.'

'All right. Shit. I'm sorry.'

'I have plexnode interfaces, if you're interested.' She pulled back her sleeves. 'Webbed inside my skin all over, but without processing nodes. I'm open to all Skein protocols, far beyond the subset most people use.'

'That's not my business.' He felt unsettled by her sharing this. 'Look, I wasn't trying to offend you.'

'But it's like swimming in an ocean with blinkers on, feeling massive predatory shapes moving below you but unable to make them out, to understand what's happening. It's like being two years old and overwhelmed by the world, and it's making me insane.'

Moving by intuition, he stepped closer and put his hand on her shoulder.

'You see things in Skein, but can't make sense of them.'

'Perception is computation, and I know that you know that, Roger. I'm not trying to belittle you.'

'Right.' He used his tu-ring to tune his clothing to black. 'This fabric is reflecting more light, up here on the roof, than a white object would indoors. But you perceive it as black because of computation in the visual cortex, comparing it to the background average.'

'That's it exactly. In Skein, I can perceive the rawness of things, just as a retina perceives frequency and intensity, but I can't experience even basic *qualia*, like the sensation of colour.'

'So it's frustrating.'

At some point, he had become aware of just how beautiful she was.

'Look,' he went on, 'every Luculentus before upraise must have felt the—'

'We were discussing you,' she said. 'And the way Dr Helsen looks at you.'

'Uh . . . We were?'

'Well' – her smile was intensely cute – 'that's what I was leading up to, anyhow. I'd already noticed the way she reacted to you. Hadn't you felt a paranoid notion that she was out to get you?'

'Yeah, and I notice she likes you. Your architectural reconstruction was *splendid*, as I recall.'

'But she's reacting to something you do, or hadn't you noticed?'

Roger blinked, suddenly feeling like a neophyte swimmer who's only just realized how far they are from the shallow end.

'What kind of thing?'

'I don't know what you're thinking,' she murmured, 'but I know *how* you're doing it.'

It was an old saying from those who knew how to perceive the signals of body language, to distinguish visualization from internal dialogue and other modalities by throat tension, locus of voice, eye motion, fullness of lip and skin lividity.

'So tell me.'

'You're seeing something around her, something that causes you to feel dizzy and repulsed. Your body language is screaming it.'

'Um, maybe.'

'You want to tell me about it, Roger?'

He stepped back from her.

'No,' he said. 'I'm sorry, but I don't.'

Her expression closed in.

Shit. Now what have I done?

Then she gave a tiny nod, walked back to the flowdisk, and descended into the building. Now Roger was alone on the rooftop, just as he had wanted in the first place.

Except now he felt badly, wondering just how much of an idiot his education and his undeveloped Pilot's abilities had led him to become.

She had not dared to move the thing.

Rashella Stargonier, having pretended to focus her attention on everyday affairs, to work and to sleep – all of this subterfuge-against-self being most un-Luculenta-like – finally returned to the atrium where she had left it on the glass tabletop.

The null-gel capsule, and the shining old plexcore it held inside.

I need someone to talk to.

It was Greg Ranulph, her ecologist-gardener, who had unknowingly caused her to find the buried capsule. But he was an ordinary Fulgidus: the hired help, his doctorates meaning little, certainly not a confidant.

This being a potentially valuable find, maybe she ought not talk to another of her own kind. Or perhaps that was disingenuous: another Luculentus or Luculenta was competition. The only person she wanted to talk to right now was herself.

And there were several ways of doing that, undreamt of by the plebs.

<<cmdIf::self.clone(Clone.level1)>>

Beyond the table stood another of her, with an equally ironic smile.

'Instantiation,' said Rashella2, 'is different from being born.'

'I'll bet,' Rashella answered. 'So, you know what I want to talk about.'

Her counterpart existed purely in Skein, her image holo, with no material body to touch.

'You should report the plexcore to the authorities.' Rashella2 smiled wider. 'And yes, we both know what *should* means.'

The artefact was not strictly her private property, regardless of its being cached in the grounds she owned.

'But I might receive kudos if I did make it public.'

'And acknowledge the little man, Ranulph?'

'Maybe.'

Then Rashella2 grew still – not like a breathing human, but frozen – in the virtual equivalent of contemplation.

'Do you remember something I don't?' asked the original.

Between her and the virtual clone there were differences. There had to be, for Rashella2 was an instantiation whose lifetime could be measured in minutes, yet she remained helpful to her progenitrix.

'There's nothing conclusive. But I wonder about the little man's intentions.'

Implying that Ranulph had ulterior motives here?

'You want to provide me with a full stochastic graph of that?'

'What's the point? You're going to open the capsule anyway.'

Rashella looked at Rashella2, and considered debating the point. Instead, she nodded to the surrounding house, and immediately the black nul-gel material began to disintegrate into black floating dust, pulverized by masers. Rashella2 smiled with one side of her mouth.

Then the dust swept away. Remaining in place was the shining silver cylinder that had once formed part of a Luculentus nervous system, a plexcore that extended the organic brain. It was so heavy and large. Rashella's plexnodes were tiny, webbed throughout her body, and she normally thought about them only as often as she mused on the mitochondria that powered each of her cells, like those of every other Earth-derived animal in the universe.

'It must be a hundred years old,' said Rashella2.

'I can use backwards-compatible protocols.'

'So you *are* going to interface with it.' Rashella2 stared up, then allowed a flock of tiny shapes to form around her head. 'My netSprites cannot identify the likely owner, but they can deduce that there is legally secure data related to this whole area. Historic data. At too high a security level for me to even identify it.'

'I'm glad I instantiated you, darling.'

'And I have your propensity for talking to myself, so thanks from me. It's been the highlight of my existence.'

'Yes.'

'Yes.'

Sadness made both their voices heavy, their words somehow viscous.

'I'll be going now,' said Rashella2.

'I—'

'Good luck.'

Rashella2 dissolved into a virtual blizzard of shards and facets that whipped and rotated through the air and out of existence. Her constituent code would be scattered and absorbed in Skein, as a human's atoms spill into the universe on death.

'So,' said the original. 'Time for that interface.'

She stared at the shining cylinder.

```
<<cmdIf::Devices.register(here + fwd(2), new Watcher(
{init(){handshake(getProtocol())}})>>
```

Somewhere – all around, or deep inside her: she could not

tell – a hot glow intensified, a growl became like thunder, and the whole world became a maelstrom of stomach-dropping vertigo and whirling sensations, a tornado of chaos.

Just for a second, spinning fragments of light tried to coagulate, to reform; and a broken, jagged outline of Rashella2's hand reached out toward her creator, virtual cracked lips attempted to cry a warning; but then the blizzard hit and Rashella2 was gone, dissolved in Skein forever.

The real Rashella spun then toppled to the polished floor.

Blackness.

Except, perhaps, for the distant part of her awareness that tracked the progress of her house drones, who slid from their wall-caches and drew near, then stopped, trembling where they stood, unable to come closer.

As her universe became a howl of madness.

TWELVE

EARTH-CLASS EXPLORATORY EM-0036, 2146 AD

Sharp retreated into cover, but not far, sure that the fragrant bushes would hide him.

He had seen the creature, and remembered every detail: clothed (therefore intelligent), slim and tiny, no antlers, and only a single thumb on each hand. It had made a campsite of sorts, with shining objects that looked crafted. Nothing in his memory indicated that his ancestors had ever come across such a thing.

And it was alone. Could it be an outcast, a casteless one like himself?

Casteless.

So it was time to confront that thought. He had run away, placed himself beyond friends, beyond codes of conduct. Thinking that, he felt his childhood drop away. His northern nomadic forebears had survived; and so would he.

Strangely without fear, he stood straight up, and headed back directly to the interloper's camp.

The creature rose, its head reaching barely halfway up Sharp's chest. Yes, those coverings were clothing for sure. As the creature's mouth moved, Sharp's interior ear detected faint sound, not unpleasant.

From a shining box, several small insects took flight, and joined their fellows who were hovering above the creature. Were they under its thrall somehow?

Sharp broadcast his name, pointing at himself with all four thumbs.

Then he waited.

Possibly the creature's face wrinkled. It took a step back.

Perhaps it was sick; perhaps it needed time to think. Then suddenly it leaped to the shining box that had produced the insects, and began to gesture at it, using intricate flickering finger movements, while its mouth worked.

Patterns of light shone above the box. Sharp drew closer. Then a blast of scent made him stumble backward.

~SHARP!

The box had emitted his name. Astounding. It meant the creature could communicate, or might learn to, and that was the answer to everything.

His answering scent was simple, the fragrance of happiness.

For here was his opportunity. Casteless and untouchable, he might yet taste knowledge far beyond the long-digested traditions of the Council Elders. The power of novelty was his.

The thought made him salivate profusely.

For Rekka, the alien was a brooding ursine presence with watchful amber eyes. It wore a short sleeveless robe, hood thrown back. Seated, its head was level with hers when she stood. It kept still, not because of her beeswarm flying overhead – the alien probably did not understand how dangerous they were – but because it understood her fear, and wanted to reassure her.

At least, that was how she interpreted its posture and gestures. But how anthropomorphic could her thinking be? This planet's lifeforms approximated the division between animal and plant kingdoms; and many animal species had a close analogue of spines and jointed limbs, along with bilateral symmetry. In the context of xenoevolution, that made this world almost identical to Earth.

Still, this alien's cells bore no DNA – of course – so however Earthlike it looked, she had fundamentally more in common with a centipede or jellyfish, even a fungus.

Except that intelligence is an emergent property, arising from many kinds of substrate.

And I'm the alien here.

Light rain, softer than tears, began to fall. Rekka wiped drops from her forehead, then slowly approached the creature and touched its cheek. Damp fur over hard bone. Then it took her hand in its double-thumbed grip, turned it palm-up, and gave a soft, darting lick, its tongue rasping. She closed her eyes, shuddering, remembering MacDuff: her adoptive parents' collie, shaking himself indoors after a rainy walk.

Finally, she opened her eyes and backed away, then returned to her biofact. Light-headed, she worked on the displayed codeframes, evolving aggregates and subtypes, initiating two evolution threads. Soon she would be able to transmit to ... Whiff, she would call him in her journal. Arbitrarily, she had decided the creature was male.

I've made first contact.

She hadn't sought it out; but now it had happened, she needed to work properly. Permanent comms with the rest of the team were forbidden – ever since the disaster of Watson's World, where thousands of enraged creatures, their nervous systems enflamed by radio-wavelength energy, had fallen on the exploratory team – and her reports would be zipblips, delivered nightly, their duration a matter of picoseconds.

For the rest of the day she worked, taking no breaks, save for several quick trips behind the bushes to her latrine. Her progress was incredible, and by nightfall she had the beginnings of conversation in place.

'Rekka,' Whiff told her, his voice emanating from the biofact's speakers. 'Sit.'

And she did, obeying the command.

'Whiff? Stand.'

So Whiff did as she asked, rising from his stool.

Success.

This was more than a day's work, and she had yet to report on it. Her stomach growled. For hours she had been pushing herself; now it was time to eat. On Earth, sharing food with any animal builds trust; but her biochemistry was too different to allow her to share with Whiff.

She went to her ration pack and extracted a container of vegetable masala, wondering if the mild curry might smell enticing to Whiff. After thumbing the pad, she waited five seconds, then peeled back the top. Steam rose as she detached the spoon, and the fragrance was—

Whiff lurched to his feet.

Shit. What's wrong?

Then he stumbled out of the camp, into the undergrowth and darkness.

'Hell's teeth.'

She took a few seconds to direct some of her beeswarm to sweep the surroundings, looking for Whiff. As an explorer she might be a neo, but when it came to coding, she could practically make a biofact sit up and beg. Her bees were smart, and sure to find him.

The masala smelled wonderful, so she tucked in.

Later that night, she lay on the ground in her sleeping suit, watching an arc of small holos: viewlogs from her bees. In the images, Whiff was squatting, hunched as he chewed on raw vegetables, his body language furtive.

Don't anthropomorphise.

But perhaps she was reading him correctly, and there was some imperative – cultural, medical, aesthetic – that made him eat alone.

In the morning, he would be back. Somehow she knew.

When she flicked the holos out of existence, only the vault of stars in black sky remained, the vastness of the universe cradling all its fragile creatures for the precious seconds of their lives. A feeling of awe carried her into sleep.

Sharp remembered Bittersweet's childish antics, making fun of poor untouchables eating their vegetables in the open. He'd been embarrassed by his little sister then. Now he realized there was a lesson in the memory – he should think of the fragile creature as intelligent but uneducated, aware but uncivilized.

And so he returned to its – possibly to *her* – campsite. As for her name, it approximated to Sweetash, an internal contradiction that become more pleasing the longer he considered it.

With the aid of the shining device, they tried to extend their range of linguistic understanding ... and spent the whole day struggling. Finally, they made a leap in abstraction, moving beyond names, from *Sweetash* and *Sharp* to *you* and *I*.

Two words in a day. It would take a long time to learn the art of conversation at that rate.

Sweetash did not eat in front of him, perhaps understanding her mistake. When evening fell, he retreated to his own spot out in the undergrowth, and after eating, he curled up, trembling in the cold. His sleep was strange and disjointed.

On the third night, he slept inside Sweetash's camp, within the ring of protective devices, wrapped in a cloak that warmed from inside itself. Everything was strange, so different from his village where a thousand subtle scents told him, at any time of day, of others' presence, of how he should behave.

And there was another kind of onrushing pang inside him, triggered perhaps by the stress of being here.

But the strangest thing of all was Sweetash's conjuring box, the shining case that could do more than create intelligent insects and broadcast scents. For one thing, it could display disembodied pictures – moving pictures – hanging in the air. The colours were not quite right – perhaps to accommodate Sweetash's small, unslitted eyes – but he knew what the images were: pictures from inside the little insects' minds. He figured that from seeing himself and Sweetash, inside one of the pictures, from the viewpoint of an insect that was hovering overhead.

She controlled them, did Sweetash, directing her insects to observe Sharp's people as they lived their ordinary lives.

But then they ventured further, and showed such sights!

Some images came from parts of Mint City he had never seen – several sequences came from the Librarians' Enclave, he was sure of it – and then from cities far away, places he could never hope to visit.

Yet it was the ordinary domestic scenes that fascinated Sweetash most. And her reaction to seeing a mother teach her children – the young ones taking delicate nips, their faces smudged with maternal blood – was extraordinary: Sweetash stumbled away, crouched over, and spilled the contents of her stomach on the ground.

Some kind of ritual of her own?

Over the next few days, when they weren't extending their vocabulary through the device, Sharp and Sweetash watched these scenes of life together, including several Sharings, the expressions of triumphant pain so different from Father's awful experience. Then it was back among Librarians, watching them work with sand-frames, making little patterned marks Sharp did not understand. And then there was a Convocation, with Librarians from far away, such a mix of fur coloration that he could not understand how they could Share knowledge at all. Except that, in what looked like Sharing ceremonies, no blades were produced. Instead, sand-frames or patterned clay were passed around in lieu of flesh.

Sharp grew bored and poked around the camp. But Sweetash remained fascinated, and finally the implications were obvious. Librarians' writing was arcane, a thin approximation of knowledge, a faint taste of true learning's richness – but it allowed communication between strangers whose flesh might be mutually unpalatable.

He returned to the display and hunkered down beside Sweetash. Together, they continued to observe.

All was blood and pain.

Rekka found herself haunted by so many of the images she watched. Her own genetic mother had tried to kill her – there was so little she knew of India and the Changeling Plague, so much her adoptive parents would never tell – and at first the cruelty inside families here reminded her of childhood nightmares. But then she realized how much the parents suffered for the sake of love, and in that moment her view of Whiff and his people underwent a permanent change.

Nevertheless, several of her watchful bees remained hovering overhead, laden with toxins deadly to any native form.

For exercise, they took long rambles along the ridges and escarpments, sometimes venturing to village boundaries, never inside. Rekka trusted Whiff to keep them downwind, unnoticed.

After a time, she amended her log. Now attuned to the subtleties of scent, she renamed her friend 'Sharp'.

Staying close to him on their excursions, she could appreciate the play of muscles beneath his dark fur that rippled in the wind. Sometimes she stroked his arm as they walked. And it seemed to her that two dark buds on his forehead were growing bigger by the day.

Soon he would be sprouting antlers. For Sharp's people, puberty looked to be a rapid procedure.

Her beeswarm kept busy, observing the native people who knew written language, the bees' femtoscopic spectrometers analysing airborne molecules on the scene, allowing her to cross-reference between scent and script.

Few of her wilder speculations made it into the zipblips she transmitted at night. She received only short acknowledgements from Mary Stelanko, as team leader; there was no communication with the rest of the team. None of the others had made contact, but they had plenty of observational data, much of it downloaded into Rekka's biofact.

For practical purposes, she was alone with Sharp.

It was fifty days into the project when, late on a warm afternoon, she found herself staring at Sharp's strong body and flushing all over. Local male and female forms were astoundingly analogous to Earth's, and her watching bees had long confirmed Sharp's maleness. Perhaps some form of mutual gratification could be—

No.

Whimpering, pushing back her desire, she crawled into her padded sleeping-suit and pulled up the mask, sealing herself inside, insulated from the world. With longing eyes, she watched Sharp continue at his lessons – he was teaching himself to write script – but finally he wandered off to eat alone.

She rolled over, stripping off the suit, and crawled on hands and knees to the biofact. It took her ages, struggling to concentrate, to fabricate a large pad of what looked like wild cotton, from which she took two small pinches, and inserted one inside each nostril.

There. Now she could be in Sharp's vicinity without her hormones going wild.

One hundred and thirty days into the project, Sharp was seated on a carbon-fibre stool, allowing Rekka to rub soothing cream around the base of his antlers. They were spreading fractals, still itching, but already proclaiming his status: he was an adult now.

~That feels good.

Around his neck he wore a circlet or torc given him by Sweetash, whose auditory name (as much he could decipher, at a volume that made her wince) was *Rekka*. The torc responded to his scent and to Rekka's air-vibration language.

Her reply, translated, rose from the torc:

~You're done now, Sharp.

She was picking up the brush for his fur, but he raised his hand, thumbs spread wide.

~No. Your turn for pleasure.

Rekka made the facial expression of amusement.

~All right.

They changed places. With Rekka on the stool, he began to knead her back.

~Soon, your travelling vessel will arrive, not so?

~That's right.

~You'll return home, to the smell of your parents.

She moved beneath his grip, then relaxed.

His intuition told him there was something here, in her memory of family and parents. But it would be complicated, and he only had a flavour of her culture – so much remained unknowable.

And now, there was something he had to ask.

~Will you take me with you, Rekka?

There was a long scentless interlude, then:

~Yes, my friend.

He leaned forward, closing his teeth gently on her ear.

Four nights before the pick-up, Sharp jogged slowly away from the camp. A handful of Rekka's bees flew overhead, almost invisible.

He jogged through the night, finally reaching farmland, and laid up in fragrant shrubbery until darkness. Finally, lungs burning, he reached the outskirts of the village he called home. Slowly, trying not to emit his exhaustion, he walked to his parents' house.

There was a small courtyard at the back. He stood for a while, seeing Father's silhouette against the drapes. Father! He wanted to go in, but it was impossible.

Then movement occurred at another window.

~Sharp?

~Bittersweet!

His sister's lithe form slipped over the windowsill. They hugged mightily.

~Mother and Father. How are they?

Bittersweet tipped her face back, eyes widening at the sight of Sharp's antlers. Then she looked down.

~Father . . . hasn't worked much since you went away. We searched for so long . . .

~I can't come back yet, little sister. But soon, when I know enough, they'll never be able to cast us out.

He stopped, then sniffed. There were strangers nearby.

Bittersweet smelled them, too.

~Proctors, from the City Guard. There are stories of lights in the hills, strange creatures . . .

Over the courtyard wall, bobbing outlines told of bannermen, armed with halberds.

~I'm sorry, dear Bittersweet. Be strong.

Her reply was redolent with concern, but he was already moving, exiting alongside the house, on to the street, hidden from the bannermen. He began to jog, and after a while accelerated as an alarm scent floated behind him.

All his hearts were thumping as he ran for cover.

But finally he was into the wilderness, scratched by thorns as he went deep into the overpowering fragrance of sourscrub trees, masked from his pursuers.

Midnight, two days later.

Clasping hands, Rekka and Sharp stood in the centre of their former camp, biofact and equipment cases at their feet. Only a few bees remained to circle overhead.

Her bracelet beeped just as Sharp sniffed.

'Shit.'

It was one of the few scents she could understand without translation.

'Proctors?'

'Yes.' His voice came from the bracelet. 'Many of them.'

She could hear the bannermen now, heading this way.

I don't want to use the bees.

But then a shuttle was descending from the sky, and a male Pilot's voice came from Rekka's bracelet.

'So you've got company with you. You know there's a hell of a lot more on the way.'

He would be in his ship, controlling the shuttle from orbit.

'My friend here is coming with me.'

'Shit.'

Beside Rekka, Sharp moved his shoulders in amusement.

'We have a universal code.'

But the shuttle was hovering, its hatch unopened.

'Are you invoking Prime Contact protocols? Or do you want me to pretend this is a non-sentient specimen you're taking back?'

'Please . . .'

It touched down, opening to reveal a small, blue-lit cabin, with no one inside.

'Don't worry. I could give a rat's ass what the bureaucrats think. And those armed buggers are speeding up, so why don't you hurry now?'

Sharp slung the equipment inside, then Rekka got in and he followed. The hatch slid shut as they were rising. Rekka expected the clang of thrown spears or fired bolts, but there was nothing as the shuttle rose fast.

Soon they were at high altitude.

'Hold on to that handle, Sharp.'

'All right.' His big arm was around her. 'Why?'

'There's something called freefall I forgot to mention.'

Seconds later, they were experiencing just that.

THIRTEEN

FULGOR, 2603 AD

Pulling herself back to awareness was hard. As Rashella opened her eyes, three of her house drones drew closer, then stopped. She looked at them.

They whipped away in reverse, bolting back to their wall-caches.

<<audio: I summoned medical aid.>>

On Luculentus modalities, she received the house system's communication.

<<visual: a flying ambulance, its green hull strobing>>

She checked inside herself for pain or injury.

'I'm fine' – she used ordinary speech – 'so cancel, please.'

'Perhaps,' the house answered, 'since they are already close, they can check—'

'Tell them to go home.'

'If you insist, ma'am. However—'

Rashella frowned.

<<cmdIF::Assistance.getInstance().invoke(self.getCache( ))>>

From deep inside herself, she simulated biometric data – a false memory all the way down to the biochemical level – and transmitted the results via house surveillance to the incoming ambulance. Fake telemetry poured into the house sensors.

'Emergency call-out cancelled, ma'am. My apologies for panicking.'

The house memory now contained the fake data, indicating blood pressure anomalies, but nothing beyond either its own or Rashella's abilities to fix.

'You've done a fine job, House.'

'Ma'am.'

At the far side of the atrium, a faint outline swirled, like autumn leaves in a twisting wind. An echo of Rashella2.

'Have to . . . warn . . .'

With a sneer and a gesture, Rashella dispersed the struggling code fragments, pulled them apart all the way down to raw trinary, and set every trit to *mu*, to neither-nor.

'You saw nothing, House.'

'Ma'am?'

She wiped its caches for the last thirty seconds, substituting harmless extrapolations of the previous few minutes' surveillance.

I was Rafael.

It wasn't supposed to be like this. Like pulling one instrument out of an orchestra, memories of a single plexcore should be incoherent fragments – particularly for an individual as unusual as the late, murderous Luculentus Rafael Garcia de la Vega, dead for one hundred years. And he had subsumed so many other Luculentus personalities, absorbing them into his vast plexcore network, trembling on the brink of transcendence, when a single human felled him . . . with the aid of Pilots.

'Pilots,' she said out loud.

The ones who had killed her – killed Rafael – would be long dead themselves. She considered this for nearly a thousand milliseconds, a long time for a Luculenta.

Lowering her head, she closed her eyes and immersed herself in Skein. So much data about the past was invisible, but she instantiated a flock of netSprites and netAngels to help, scouring the query-reefs, helping her to interpolate and extrapolate, to form a strong guess about what ordinary Luculenti knew, and what the peacekeepers were likely to suspect.

Pretty much nothing, was her estimate. They had buried the old knowledge too deeply.

So she did a thing to please herself, to create an ironic footnote in history, should Skein survive her intentions. Accessing the legal functions, she changed her name.

She was now Rafaella, not Rashella, Stargonier.

'I'm hungry,' she said.

A holo menu grew to one side, displayed by the house system, but offering only food. How could the poor thing understand what she really needed? There had only ever been one other person such as she was now.

And Rafaella was *not* going to meet Rafael's sudden, violent fate.

Hungry . . .

Inside Lucis City, with so many people, she could find what she needed. Of course there were surveilling systems in every building, in the smartmaterial of the ground, and in the open from SatScan. That made it all the easier to get away with it, for someone of her capabilities. Peacekeepers would believe the data, believing it incorruptible.

She walked across the atrium and gestured an opening in the outer wall. Outside was the blue lawn, shimmering beneath a creamy sun in a dark avocado sky. Any of her aircars could get her to the city in twenty minutes.

High in the sky, a clear shape was soaring. She wore no smartlenses – that was so plebeian – but could still magnify the image, by accessing the house surveillance and by using coherent sound, emitted by vibrating smartmotes, to alter the refractive index of the air overhead, forming a lens.

A lone man rode in the clear hull. Gliding for fun, high above the grounds of Mansion Stargonier.

She pinged him. A Luculentus.

So hungry.

There he was, a Luculentus, élite of the élite, his mind enhanced with plexnodes: faster, more powerful than an un-enhanced human . . . and succulent prey for Rafaella Stargonier, trembling on the brink of her first, panting with the knowledge of another kind of virginity she was about to lose.

While the other party knew nothing of his imminent transition.

Daniel Deighton was not born a Luculentus. Nor had he belonged to a family who aspired to upraise for their son.

His mother Liva had been poor, raised in old Schaum Crescent on the Tarquil Coast. She met his father on a trip into a hypozone, one of the receding areas of natural ecology that continued to shrink before the encroaching, centuries-old terraforming.

Shadow Folk of various clans and clades still lived there, needing respmasks to breathe outside their homes – very traditional, a dying way of life. Oz Deighton was one of them: slimeherder and biochemist, thirty Standard Years old when he met Liva. He loved the outdoor freedom, even in a region where to breathe unmasked meant lung-searing death. Yet he gave it up to marry an urbanite who could never thrive amid native ecology.

Oz and Liva opened a small store in Caltrop Pentagon, on the outskirts of Lucis City. They worked hard. Daniel was born during the first year of their marriage; and many of his earliest memories involved crawling around the shop floor, playing with bright toys, sitting in shafts of sunlight that fell through skylights.

What happened was, one of the store's customers, a Fulgidus merchant trader who shipped goods via the Pilot's Guild to a dozen human-occupied worlds but remembered his own humble beginnings, saw just how bright the young boy was. He recommended the mindware enhancements that first allowed Daniel to excel at his schooling.

Richer Fulgidi often did everything they could to assist their children, sometimes pushing them too far in their familial ambition. There was no talk of hothousing Daniel that way; still, his parents loved it when he won a literary prize aged fifteen for his essay on cognitive changes during the twenty-second century.

His thesis was that writing changed the way people thought. In old two-dimensional writing, ideographic languages were written vertically, alphabetic languages with vowels were written left to right, while those without vowels, such as Hebrew and Arabic (the missing sounds filled in via the reader's interpretation) were written right to left. And the neurology was different too, like the additional right-hemisphere processing required to contextualise missing vowels.

And in the late twenty-first century, with the advent of FourSpeak holoscript for both Anglic and Web Mand'rin, the beginnings of modern cognition were evident. He traced current trends, with a diversion on new departures, such as the high-response triconic writing of the mysterious world called Nulapeiron.

On the third day of Lupus Festival, the family attended the Lucis Literary Congress where Daniel received his award, a crystal statuette. Afterwards, his parents drank far too much jantrasta-laced champagne. In the aircab home, their singing had been loud, off-key but harmonious in the ways that truly mattered.

That night, while they slept in their apartment above the store, thieves broke in.

Oz and Liva were giggling as they staggered downstairs to investigate the noise, asking each other who had let the cat in – a joke, since they had no pets. Perhaps the last sound they heard was each other's laughter; or perhaps it was the hum of vibroblades in the seconds before death.

It was Daniel who found them later, never knowing what had woken him up, for he had slept through everything else.

The therapist who helped him afterward was a Luculentus. The bills were paid by the Fulgidus merchant trader who had first recommended mindware for the young Daniel. The man was kind, and though he had no wish to enlarge his own family, he helped with Daniel's finances and education, guiding him.

Neither of the thieves-turned-murderers was caught. A smartatom mist and strategic scanwipes were all they needed to evade surveillance.

Pride and vengeance drove Daniel to study hard, to become ambitious, and when he applied to the Via Lucis Institute for upraise, he passed every test. One year later, he was a Luculentus.

Aged fifteen, he had written about old FourSpeak, whose name partly derived from the ability of some people to think four-dimensionally given strong three-dimensional constructs to work with, such as model hypercubes. Now, entering his third decade, his expertise became mathematical fields whose understanding required the many-dimensional and multi-modal cognition that only a full Luculentus, at home with every capability Skein offered, could comprehend. Esoteric, strongly-coloured figures in hypergeometrical spaces were just part of it – a person had to *feel* the momentum and intensity as it varied through the figures, and taste the rightness of his logic.

Peacekeeper Intelligence was always interested in bright people.

He trained with others like him, but only himself and his friend Keinosuke graduated to counterintelligence, thanks to their abilities in analysing surveilled behaviour patterns. Their first joint mission of importance had been against the Siganthian embassy; soon, everything the opposition cell was learning consisted of material devised by Fulgor's peace-keepers.

Daniel also found time for twelve auxiliary careers – he was a Luculentus, after all. The least kudos but a whimsical satisfaction attached to his poetry. Perhaps he was least successful in his relationships with Luculentae.

Lately, his netSprites had been working on new determinants of suspect behaviour. One of the possible targets was an ecologist called Greg Ranulph, whose behaviour patterns *might* be consistent with conspiracy – betraying interest in Lucis Multi's security, hiring equipment off Skein that might be used for infiltrating secure systems. Daniel was keeping the investigation wholly private, because he was testing new algorithms that might prove wrong.

Using the quickglass glider had been a whim. He had been too sedentary of late, and he was curious as to why Ranulph spent so much time on the Stargonier estate. From the owner's viewpoint, an ecologist was required to work on symbiosis between DNA- and ZNA-based lifeforms, the native ZNA being a triplet of cooperating substances, not a single compound.

But some of Ranulph's trips to the estate had been flagged as furtive, and *possibly* suspicious, by Daniel's netSprites.

For now, he was enjoying the gliding.

High above the grounds of Mansion Stargonier, he gazed down, simultaneously noting in Skein that the owner's name was now Rafaella, a legal amendment. Still, here he was in a quickglass glider, so who was he to challenge whimsy? She could call herself anything she—

From a patio below, a tiny figure – surely the Luculenta in question – was looking up at him. Perhaps he should initiate comms.

But then low-level messages – such as he had never experienced since training – flared through his awareness.

<<microcode subsurface breach>>

<<danger danger danger>>

<<interface tunnelling exception>>

<<violation is maximal>>

He needed to react.

<<fightbackfightbackfightback>>

And then he realized —

Vampire code!

—was ravening through his deep defences, a monstrous

violation, but his plexweb was swinging into action, because such code existed a century ago and femtoscopic inoculation had been laid down inside him, but *the code was fast* and evolving new stratagems, while he did everything he could to hold it back.

A challenge, on her first kill!

Rashella's plexweb fought to enhance the vampire code inside her. Deep within were factory-marrows and ecologies of code entities containing ware-organs, cells, components, and finally objects, all goal-directed and adaptive. Her thoughtware was on the offensive.

Her target's name was Daniel Deighton – she now knew – and his defences were fast, peacekeeper-fast, their battle accelerating on a timescale of femtoseconds. Their thoughtware warriors combined the rigour of symbolic logic with the power of evolution, in a blindingly swift arms race. Then a 303rd-generation descendant of Rafael de la Vega's original code burst through the latest versions of Daniel's defences.

Got you.

Vampire code ravened through barriers, spread like wildfire down paranerve channels, tearing and ripping, copying and plundering, taking the quantum state of Daniel's mind and copying it back to Rafaella's cache, to the waiting, hungry buffer, heisenberging the original brain-plus-plexweb into oblivion.

Daniel's mouth opened to scream. Then he slumped inside the quickglass cockpit.

Nothing human was here now, only dead meat, already beginning its slide into biochemical chaos, the dissolution from pattern to randomness, the transition known as death.

Rafaella clenched her fists, thrumming with victory, her vampire code – already improved – shining in her awareness, the conqueror in a battle that had last four hundred and two milliseconds.

You're the first, dearest Daniel.

Overhead, the quickglass glider, with its carrion cargo that no longer cared, continued its flight.

FOURTEEN

EARTH, 1926 AD

Migraines, and the hints of memories of dreams. For the past week or longer, Gavriela had been finding it hard to focus during lectures. Or perhaps that was partly due to Lucas Krause's habit of sitting near her, his intent look so compelling.

Today, as Professor Hartmann wrote on the blackboard, her mind drifted from thoughts of electrons and current flow, remembering the strangest thing, a being of crystal who could move and talk and—

'Fräulein Wolf?'

'Um, excuse me, Herr Professor.'

'And your explanation, please?'

His diagram showed a curving track of varying width. Inside the chalked track were small circles containing minus signs – electrons, obviously – while off to one side was an equation, $I = dq/dt$, defining electric current as the rate of flow of charge.

'Er . . .' She struggled to reconstruct his half-heard original question. 'You want to know how current can be constant everywhere in a circuit, even with a twisted wire, squeezing electrons closer together in tight turns, farther apart elsewhere.'

'So you heard what I asked, but I have not yet heard your answer.'

There were rueful looks around her – sympathy from her fellow students, none of whom looked to have a solution. But when she stared back at the diagram, it came to life inside her mind, a moving picture of jostling pearls inside a curved pipe, and the answer *felt* so obvious, but she could not put it into words.

She gestured with her hands.

'The closer the electrons get the more they, um, push against each other – inverse-square repulsion – so they have to spread out. It balances the curvature exactly, and the, um, well ... It's *obvious*, isn't it? But I just can't, um ...'

Then Professor Hartmann did an unusual thing.

He gave a broad, happy smile.

'So you *are* a physicist, Fräulein Wolf. You feel exactly what's going on. All we need do is add some conversational skills – a minor matter – and you will do very well. Excellent.'

Lucas winked at her.

Afterwards, she went off to study by herself, but every few minutes she found herself looking up from her book, and seeing not the library but a transparent woman whose name was Kenna, while other tangled images fell through her awareness, too fast to interpret.

In the evening, she went to play cards with Petra, Inge and Elke. It was Elke's apartment, and she owned a card table covered with green baize. Their stakes were matchsticks, and often they would place all the cards face-down, suspending the game in order to chat.

'Are they giving you a hard time, Gavi?' asked Petra. 'I mean the professors.'

'Oh, no. Today Professor Hartmann picked on me, but he knew that I knew the answer, while no one else did. At least I think he knew. He's quite a sweet old man.'

'Picking on you is sweet, huh? Well, good for you.'

'And there's no boy in class distracting you?' asked Elke.

'Um ...'

'Tell us his name,' said Inge. 'And how he's hurt you.'

'Hurt me? What do you mean?'

'You've not been yourself.' Petra patted her hand. 'We've noticed, haven't we, girls?'

'Oh.' Gavriela blinked, feeling black pressure over one eye. 'It's the headaches and the, um, the dreams. Lucas hasn't ... We're just acquaintances, really.'

Her friends looked at each other.

Then Inge said: 'There's a family friend visiting from Vienna, and he's rather famous. Do you really have bad dreams that upset you, dearest Gavi?'

'Just . . . recently.'

Gavriela's right hand, still holding her cards, began to tremble. It was awful, because she could not control the motion. So she put down the cards and placed both hands in her lap, squeezing them together, using pain to fight back the shaking.

'You're very pale,' said Petra.

'I'm sorry.'

'You need to see him, the Herr Doktor.' Inge touched Gavriela's upper arm. 'My family has a good relationship with him. Some of his ideas are deliciously racy, but—Never mind. My mother will make the arrangements.'

'No, sorry. I can't afford—'

'Excuse me, but I said my family will arrange everything. There will be no charge.'

Gavriela swallowed salt tears.

'Thank you.'

She needed help. Suddenly it was obvious.

'Thanks . . .'

Then she was crying, and the worst part of it was, she had no idea exactly why.

Two days later, she knocked on a front door, and a short maid opened it.

'Good morning,' said the maid. 'Are you Fräulein Wolf, please?'

'Um, yes. Your employer's daughter, Inge Scholl, arranged for—'

'So, please come in. Herr Doktor Freud is expecting you.'

The maid showed her to a small drawing-room, the cupboards decorated with Delft plates and jugs. There were two high-backed armchairs, one of them occupied. The man rose, and shook her hand, sniffing a little.

'You must be Fräulein Wolf?'

The voice was higher than expected, and his eyes were bright with energy.

'Yes, and I'm pleased to meet you, Herr Doktor.'

Several minutes later, they were seated – he at a reassuring angle, rather than facing her straight on – and she was telling him about the shards of remembered dreams.

Then she paused.

'Transparent people?' Doktor Freud prompted.

'I know it sounds crazy, wide awake in the everyday world. It's as if the dreams are trying to break through. And there's pain inside my head.'

'Such small derangements, or *neuroses* as I prefer to call them, are perfectly common, dear Fräulein. I notice you've not mentioned your father.'

'Papa? No, he's got nothing to do with it. There's a crystalline woman, a stranger whose name I almost know, and sometimes hints of a young man ... No. I just don't know.'

'Hmm.'

'Sorry.'

After a few silent moments, Doktor Freud nodded.

'With your permission, it is time to try something different. Just one moment.' He stood and crossed to the drapes, then pulled them closed, leaving a slit of daylight. 'Yes, this will do nicely.'

There was a glass paperweight on a shelf, and he manoeuvred it until it sparkled, catching the sunlight.

'Now focus only on the brightness, that's right, Fräulein, and now your vision begins to defocus as you relax, so deeply relaxing now' – at some point his voice had slowed to an odd cadence, rising and falling in unusual ways, like waves – 'as you go deeper and deeper inside your unconscious mind, where you can tell me clearly what you see.'

The room looked odd as her eyelids flickered, then she was

in a dreamlike state, understanding she could move if she wanted to, yet feeling so odd, with no desire to do anything but remain like this, in a stillness beyond sleep.

A hand – the Herr Doktor's – took her wrist and raised it, then let go. Her arm remained suspended, catatonic with no sensation of gravity.

'And the part of you controlling dreams,' came his odd voice, 'as I address you now, the Id, can relate in every detail what you see.'

'Yes . . .' came a tiny voice from Gavriela's mouth.

'As you agree to do that now.'

She sank inside her dream.

There is a leafy avenue. A young man escorts her – his suit has oddly wide lapels, and his tie is a long strip, not a bow – and then he stops, removing his hat.

'There they are, ma'am. You want I should introduce you?'

The language is . . . for a moment, she's not sure. It's her second tongue, that's all she knows. Her escort is indicating two gentlemen farther along the sidewalk, strolling this way.

'No need, thank you. The professor and I are old friends.'

'You know Professor Einstein?'

The young man's voice is hushed.

'Why else would they have asked you to take me here?'

'I thought—'

'I'm not familiar with Princeton, that's all.'

'Then, um . . . Do you want me to wait for you?'

'You've been kind, but there's no need.'

'Um . . . Okay.'

After a trembling moment, the young man – with an awed glance back at the approaching figures – is on his way.

Overhead is a plane. Automobiles are parked along the street, bulbous and closed in, their design strange; and yet she accepts it all.

'Gavi.' Professor Einstein's moustache is greyer than before, but his eyes still sparkle.

She trembles as she kisses his cheek.

'Kurt,' continues Einstein, 'allow me to make introductions. Herr Professor Gödel, meet Fräulein Doktor Wolf.'

Of course they are speaking German now, so comforting.

'We're discussing the existence or otherwise of time,' adds Einstein.

'In the context of entropy?' asks Gavriela.

Gödel raises his eyebrows; Einstein grins.

'A lifeline,' says Gödel, 'is a fixed geodesic in a four-dimensioned continuum.'

'There are six million murdered Jews,' she says, 'that you can't have a conversation with now.'

Einstein half-smiles, as if he expected this.

'I beg your pardon,' Gavriela adds. 'I feel so stuck in the past at times.'

Gödel opens his mouth to speak, but the world is spinning away, is gone.

In the gloom, Herr Doktor Freud leaned closer.

'Back into the dream, that's right, as you go back—'

'I don't . . .'

'—more deeply now.'

The wheelchair responds to a tiny gesture of her fingertip. It's just as well, for she's capable of little else. Whining softly, the motor engages and carries her closer to the desktop, then stops.

Her skin is old and blotched with brown, her hands fragile memories of youth.

'Tell me,' she whispers.

'Sure, Gran. See here?' The bearded man is pointing at a glass pane containing a picture, like a cinema screen, but the glowing picture is in focused colour. 'There's the event.'

Three scarlet dots shine in a starfield.

'Finally,' she whispers.

'What do you mean, finally?' asks the young man.

'Never mind.'

Beneath the screen, a simple folded card bears the label: Property of Project HEIMDALL. Please leave running.

'No.' This is a woman's voice from behind her, not friendly. 'I'd like to know. What did you mean by that, Dr Wolf?'

Gavriela causes her wheelchair to rotate on the spot.

Surrounding the young woman are flickers of darkness, and her eyes are hard.

'I've led a long life,' says Gavriela.

Turning away from the inevitable has never been her style.

Like a bubble spiralling up inside a brook, Gavriela returned to wakefulness. She blinked several times at Doktor Freud.

'I don't know what you did, Herr Doktor, but I feel marvellous.'

'You remember nothing?'

'Not a thing. Should I?'

'Um . . . No, that is fine. So thank you for coming, Fräulein.'

'Are we done?'

'If you feel good, then we are.'

'Oh. Thank you so much, again.'

She almost floated out of the house, seen out by the maid. Once out on the street, she walked in a way that felt like dancing, unable to stop smiling.

It would be several hours before she regained a more normal emotional state.

Freud stared for a long time at his rough session notes. Then he carried the loose pages to the burning coal grate, dropped them atop the coals, and used the poker to rake the fire. Smoke rose from crinkling paper as it curled into black charcoal, an echo of the phenomenon his patient had described – twisting blackness – an hallucination not unknown to him.

He pulled out a handkerchief that was monogrammed *SF* – a present from a buxom client who reminded him of his mother – then dabbed his forehead.

Finally, he sat down at the table, opened a notebook, unscrewed his fountain-pen, and began to write.

Returning to my previous experimentation with the techniques of Monsieur Mesmer, I successfully induced in Fräulein S a state of deep trance. In this state she was able to recount her dreams, in a detailed and entirely unconscious manner, remembering nothing on waking.

As to the nature of her

He paused, used blotting paper to dry what he had written so far, and read over the words.

'No.'

After tearing the page from his notebook, he dropped it onto the fire, sending it to charcoal oblivion.

Back at the table, he began again.

April 1st 1926.

Today, as a result of a session with Fräulein S, I have made the decision to abandon the techniques of Mesmerism, which I feel are inappropriate in the process of exploring and comprehending delusional neuroses.

He stopped. After a dab with blotting paper, he closed the notebook up and resealed his pen. From his waistcoat he took a small pill-box, opened it, and regarded the white powder within. Then he shook his head, and put the pill-box away.

Getting up quickly, he left the drawing-room, ignored the maid looking at him in the hallway, and went upstairs to the bedroom where he was staying.

His host, Herr Scholl, had given him a present earlier. Now, he had to look at it again.

Unwrapped, the painting was on his bed. The artist was young, unknown to Freud, but the man's psyche was dark: that much, anyone could tell from the swirl of shadows and deep reds. As he stared, he thought he heard a distant echo of discordant notes: *da, da-dum, da-da-da-dum, da-da.*

'I will *not* share my client's delusion.'

The painting was surely not flickering. That was impossible.

'I refuse to.'

Biting his lip, he hefted the painting, and carried it downstairs. In the hallway he stopped to address the maid.

'Under no circumstances,' he said, 'tell Herr Scholl what you see here.'

The maid stared at the painting, then quickly made the sign of the cross.

'You have my word, sir.'

They stared at each other; then Freud nodded.

'Very well.'

He carried it into the drawing-room, tore it from the frame, and dropped it into the fireplace. For a short time, he thought he could hear a scream; but then it was curling up and burning.

The last part to ignite was the lower corner that bore the artist's signature – *A. Hitler* – then it, too, was gone.

Freud wiped his face, then took his pill-box from his waistcoat pocket.

Out in the hallway, the maid was saying the Lord's Prayer, over and over.

FIFTEEN

FULGOR, 2603 AD

Throughout the tutorial, Roger tried not to think of this morning's message from his parents.

'We've arranged everything with the department administrators,' Dad had said. *'You're cleared to take a five-day break from studies.'*

The semester had only just started, so Admin could not have been happy – but so what? Besides, it wasn't just the thought of a holiday that thrummed inside him.

'Your offworld trip is already logged,' Dad had added.

Offworld! That could mean anything, but perhaps what he really intended was—

'So, Roger Blackstone.' Dr Helsen was focusing on him, dragging his attention back to the tutorial, here and now. 'I'd like to say something about your model of entropy flow in the Calabi-Yau dimensions.'

'Er, yes, Dr Helsen?'

'Nice work. Very well done.'

He blinked several times, while Rick raised an eyebrow. Praise from Helsen, for anyone other than Alisha – this was a new phenomenon.

'So.' Helsen turned to Alisha and smiled. 'I'm wondering whether you could assist me in something.'

'Uh, sure, Doctor.'

'We like to bring in extracurricular guests to give lectures, and Mr Blackstone's work has given me an idea. There's someone I'd like you to invite, all right? It's not her speciality, but I believe she would do a fine job.'

'Of course.'

'Good. In that case' – Helsen looked around the group – 'very well done, and I'll see you all tomorrow. And Alisha, here are the details.'

She gestured; Alisha nodded to confirm receiving the data.

'Have a good day, all.'

Dr Helsen left first, smiling. Everyone else looked at each other before getting up. They remained in place as the quickglass chairs melted back into the floor.

'Holy crap,' said Rick. 'Is old Hatchet Face actually in a good mood for once?'

'Looks that way.' Trudi raised her hands. 'Do we mind? I don't.'

'Serotonin. A relaxed brain.' Stef looked serious, then: 'Maybe she's had sex.'

Everyone laughed or snorted, apart from Alisha. As the group broke up and began to drift out of the room, Roger drew closer, and touched her arm.

'Are you all right?'

'She wants me to deal with a Luculenta.'

'Oh.'

They waited until everyone else had left.

'The thing is,' said Alisha, 'she pretends she wants to help me, but there's something . . . I don't know. She has her own agenda.'

Roger nearly said: *Doesn't everybody?* But glibness was uncalled for.

'And so soon before my—Before I go to the Institute,' added Alisha.

'The—? Oh, the Via Lucis Institute.'

'For upraise, yes. At the end of semester.'

'So . . . Will you be coming back?'

There couldn't be much for a Luculenta here.

'I don't know. After upraise, everything is self-guided, with the help of whatever friends and allies you make. That's why making contacts like this Stargonier woman is so important.'

'Stargonier?'

'The Luculenta that Helsen wants me to cajole into being a guest speaker. So look . . . If I can meet her in person, will you come with me?'

He felt as if the floor were tipping.

'You want my company?'

'Aren't you the expert on realspace hyperdimensions?'

'Is that why you want me along?'

Her smile was a mystery.

'What other reason can you think of, Roger?'

She was still smiling as she walked away.

Bloody hell.

Roger was in awe.

A huge orange column rose into the sky – all the way up. It was formed of twisted quickglass braids, hence its name: Barleysugar Spiral. From the ground, as you tilted your head to stare upward, the column narrowed to a geometric point; but that was an illusion, for it continued past the atmosphere. Down at the base of the great shaft were separate areas for departures and arrivals. Lozenge-shaped flowdrones followed travellers as they walked to or from the lounges.

Mum and Dad were already waiting when Roger arrived.

Will they find a way to tell me?

All night he had kept popping out of sleep, wondering where they were going, not daring to accept what he hoped was true. There had been so much temptation to call an aircab and fly home, where they could talk safely, unsurveilled. But he was an ordinary human student, or supposed to be, so it was more convincing to act insouciant, unmoved – or pretending to be unmoved – by the prospect of a family holiday.

'This is pretty exciting,' said Dad.

'*I'm* excited.' Mum squeezed his arm.

It had been a while since Roger had seen her this relaxed. It was startling, this notion that his parents had been leading stressful lives while he had failed to notice.

'Me too,' he said. 'Excited.'

'You're a good boy.'

'Yes, Mum.'

He smiled, with a feeling of indulgence, flavoured with a soupçon of sadness.

'Well.' Dad looked down at an angle, then at him. 'I guess someone's grown up.'

Presumably because Roger no longer acted resentful at being addressed like a kid.

'It had to happen,' he said, 'sooner or later.'

'Better late than never,' said Mum.

All three of them hugged.

So where are we going?

He was going to ask – that was natural behaviour – but in such a public area, Dad's answer might not be the true one.

'And our destination is . . . ?'

'The place where we're going,' said Dad. 'Don't they teach you nuthin at this here multiversity?'

'Loads of it.'

'Someone your father knows.' Mum was the voice of reason. 'He's got spare bedrooms. Well, spare rooms, but no actual beds.'

'No beds?'

'Also no gravity.'

'Ah.'

In the departures lounge, a human staff member greeted each traveller or group and escorted them to a chamber were they awaited a bubble-capsule. Dad chatted with the uniformed man, pleasantries concerning tax reforms and speedball league results. Roger used to be impatient with conversations about nothing; now he envied his father's easy touch with strangers.

An ellipsoidal capsule arrived, empty. An opening melted in place, and Dad led the way inside. As they sat, the capsule was already sealed and beginning to rise.

'Nice to get away from it all,' said Dad.

Roger nodded, hoping he understood correctly, wondering what had changed Dad's mind.

'You could sit on your father's lap,' said Mum. 'Just as you used to.'

'Technically, that's a correct statement.' Dad winked at him. 'So long as you don't want to, that's fine.'

'Uh-huh. *I'm* disadvantaged because of my upbringing,' said Roger, 'but what's your excuse?'

'A difficult childhood.'

'Oh.'

'Yours, in point of fact.'

According to the status display, they were five hundred metres above ground, rising ever faster in viscous orange quickglass, spiralling upward from the world.

At the apex, Barleysugar Spiral mushroomed into a large complex of observation lounges, restaurants, boutiques and souvenir shops. Consistent with their cover as a family on holiday, the Blackstones dined beside a view window showing black space and the great glow of Fulgor below, creamy-gold with clouds.

Then they returned to their waiting bubble-capsule, and awaited the moment to eject.

When the planet's rotation had taken them to the correct relative position, their bubble popped free of Barleysugar Spiral and drifted away, its initial orbit at the same distance from Fulgor's surface. Then impellers drove it upward, increasing their orbital radius gently.

Inside the capsule, they looked out, saying little.

'Frequent travellers grow jaded by the view,' said Dad at last. 'That's a mistake.'

'Yes, it is,' said Roger.

For another twenty minutes they watched the changing stars – changing relative to them – while soft music played, almost beyond awareness. Then they were approaching a spiky white-and-silver orbital habitat.

'So what's this guy's name?' asked Roger.

'Varlan Trelayne, and his wife is Helena. You've met them, but you were five years old.'

'Ah. Okay.'

'*Contact in one minute,*' announced the capsule.

They said nothing more until quickglass kissed against quickglass: they had docked.

Inside the habitat's first chamber, a large man was floating. He looked pleased.

'You haven't changed a bit, Miranda.'

'Neither have you, Varl.'

'If only that was a compliment, eh? Hey, Carl.'

They touched fists, nodding.

'And this is Roger.'

'How do you do, Mr Trelayne.'

'Good to meet you.'

Roger was prepared for *You've grown since I last saw you,* but there was none of that. He was prepared to like the man already.

'So, everyone,' Varlan went on. 'Let me show you around.'

As they drifted through the chamber, Mum asked: 'How's Helena?'

'A little ... under the weather. She might stay in her cabin.'

The atmosphere changed.

So what's that about?

Tension lines deepened on everyone's face. Caused by something in the past? Or whatever they were up to now?

Then they were in a larger spherical chamber, and the inner doors were sealing.

'All right,' said Varlan. 'We can speak freely in here.'

'We should visit you more often.' Mum raised a hand, rotating in midair. 'Does Helena miss company?'

'In general, yes. But something like this ... She worries.'

Dad said: 'I don't like using you for cover.'

'Uh-huh. Is anything happening that I should know about?'

'Only one thing.' Dad tapped his tu-ring, transmitting data. 'There's a trader called Xavier Spalding, who may know what we are. Or at least suspect.'

Roger stared at him, fully alert.

Spalding?

That was Alisha's family name.

'All right,' said Varlan, checking his own tu-ring. 'I'll get my people to take a look, and we'll catch up when you return.'

'Good. Roger's just started at multiversity, so continuing a normal life is one desirable option.'

Varlan was fetching a collection of drink-bulbs.

'Normal life, eh? I'll drink to that.'

He offered the bulbs. Mum and Dad chose tangwine. For a change, Roger did likewise.

'It's Helena's own concoction,' added Varlan.

'We're really sorry,' said Mum. 'About being here, I mean. The wine's terrific.'

'All right. So when did you want to do it?'

Dad regarded his drink-bulb.

'Just as soon as we've finished this.'

Ten minutes later, they were drifting outside in vacuum, nothingness in all directions.

It's unbelievable.

Scared and amazed, Roger tumbled slowly, conscious of the quickglass suit enclosing him, such a thin layer, wholly responsible for generating his oxygen, for protecting him from space. Mum and Dad floated nearby, their expressions invisible.

Peaceful and vast, the universe was all around.

Isn't it always?

Everyday life was such an illusion.

But part of him was thinking of Varlan's whispered words, back at the habitat. Mum and Dad's suits had sealed up first. He had followed, letting a quickglass blob spread around his waist like a rope. Then it began expanding to cover his skin; but his head was still bare when Varlan leaned close.

'Your dad and I have been friends a long time. His job is important.'

'Yes.'

'So was my own father's. He was a good person, but his problems got in the way of his priorities. Or do I mean that the other way round?'

'I don't—'

'Be your own man,' Varlan had said. 'They should have taken you long before.'

Then Varlan had withdrawn to another chamber, while an outer wall puckered then opened. All three Blackstones tumbled into space.

Drifting.

And then it happened.

There was a burst of darkness against the stars, then a sharp-edged shape was hanging before them: black, dart-shaped and edged with scarlet.

I didn't realize.

It looked dangerous.

My God.

And powerful.

Oh, my God.

And it was Dad's.

Once they were aboard – Dad in the control couch, Roger and Mum behind and to either side: this ship had no passenger hold – their quickglass suits melted off. All three of them removed their smartlenses, revealing their jet, black-on-black eyes.

Then acceleration was pressing them comfortably back; the holoview was a crescent hanging before them in the cabin.

'Son?' Mum asked. 'Are you ready for this?'

Dad looked intent.

'I don't think so.' Roger looked at her. 'Mum?'
'You'll be all—'
Transition.
Golden light was everywhere.

SIXTEEN

EARTH, 1927 AD

Gavriela breezed into the hallway, shopping bags in hand, and pushed the front door shut. From the back, Frau Pflügers called: 'Is that you, Gavi, dear?'

'It's me. How are you doing today?'

'Did you find nice shoes?'

'On Bahnhofstrasse, yes.'

'Then come in the back and show me, while I make tea.'

Frau Pflügers had not answered Gavriela's query about how she was doing. That meant either the arthritis or the fluttering in her chest was back.

'I'm going to the girls' place later.' Gavriela meant Inge, Petra and Elke. 'Oh. What's this? A letter for me?'

'From Berlin.' Frau Pflügers placed the kettle on the stove. 'Isn't it your mother's handwriting?'

'Actually, no.'

She picked up the envelope, then noticed the way Frau Pflügers was wincing as she fetched down the tea caddy.

'Wouldn't you like me to do that?'

'Please, Gavi. An old girl like me needs to keep busy, didn't you know?'

'You're not old.'

'Ha.'

Domestic ritual settled them: three dark spoonfuls of tea into the pot; the pouring of water; tugging the tea-cosy into place; waiting for the tea to draw; and then the pouring. Chatting about nothing very much while they drank. Afterwards, Gavriela rose and headed for the sink, but Frau Pflügers stopped her.

'I'll do the washing up. You've got a letter to read.'

'But I want to—'

'Go on now.'

So Gavriela took the letter upstairs to her room, settled in the small chair by the window table, and opened the letter. It was nicely handwritten on creamy paper.

Dear Fräulein Wolf,

I am sorry we have not met in person, for Erik has told me so many stories of you. He is often laughing about

Gavriela blinked.

Her brother was telling someone stories about her?

I am sorry we have not met in person, for Erik has told me so many stories of you. He is often laughing about the games of chess you played with your own rules, and how the pieces are called the Baker, the Housemaid and so on. And how castling is performed by – but I apologize, because of course you know all this, but you do not know me. My name is Ilse Heckler, and I care for Erik very much.

In fact I love him! There, I've said so in writing. My Christian family would not approve, but I very much hope your wonderful parents do. We have met, and they have been so very kind to me.

And no one had told her.

Only last week, there had been a letter from Mother, with no mention of a Fräulein Ilse Heckler. And these words implied a relationship that had been going on for some time.

So they might not approve of what I need to tell you. I know they have not informed you of poor Erik's state since the

For a moment she had to stop reading.

So they might not approve of what I need to tell you. I know they have not informed you of poor Erik's state since the attack. The doctors fear he will lose his left eye. Certainly his sight on that side is gone forever, though I pray for a miracle.

Several weeks ago, he was set upon by thugs, of which there are too many these days. The family do not wish to worry you, but I feel you would want to know. I'm so very sorry to make your acquaintance in this way, and hope that we can be friends.

Please do write back, so I can keep you informed of Erik's progress, for I know that he is dear to you as he is to me, though of course in a different way. And I write my feelings so boldly! I am neither so confident nor unconventional in everyday life.

Yours truly,
Ilse Heckler

Gavriela set the letter aside.

For the past few weeks, since seeing Herr Doktor Freud, she had been feeling wonderful; and now it appeared that Erik had been suffering, terribly injured, all this while; and with no one to tell her otherwise. Until this Ilse had thought to do so.

She wanted to go downstairs and talk this over, but Frau Pflügers was not well. Or was that an example of mistaken thinking, just as her own parents had held back this awful news?

The only thing to do was catch a train to Berlin.

Rubbing her face, she got up, walked in a small circle, and stopped. Then she went to the dressing-table, took a small amber brooch from a drawer, and carried it back to the window table. There, she placed the brooch in sunlight, sat down, and focused on the glowing amber.

Somewhere inside herself, she remembered Herr Doktor Freud's voice, the odd intonation and tidal cadence; and her eyelids were flickering, then closing; and her chin dipped.

She slid deep inside a dream.

She is floating in space, in golden space. There are stars, black and intricate, obsidian snowflakes. Nebulae are crimson: streaks of blood on gold.

A black dart edged with scarlet is moving through this shining void.

And then she is inside, or seems to be. Three people sit in the control cabin, and their eyes are of jet, lacking surrounding whites. In here, the perspective is not quite right; while outside, the effect is stronger: everything is insane, and all she can perceive is a simplified projection.

She has no idea how she knows this.

In the cabin, the older man in the centre, forward of the others, appears to control the ship. Neither he nor the woman are aware of her. But the younger man—

He turns to stare at her.

'Have I dreamed of—? This is impossible.'

Strange washes of energy overlay the sounds, words in an unknown language she somehow comprehends; and she wishes she could answer, but the world is dragging her back, and she reaches out, trying to hang on, but invisible hooks take hold of her and pull.

The world slammed into being all around her, then seemed to shrink and grow steady. This was her room in Frau Pflügers' house, with its dark wooden furniture, white lace doilies everywhere. Solid, yet not as comforting as it should be.

Because the letter in her hands was real, whether it told the truth or lied.

SEVENTEEN

LABYRINTH, 2603 AD (REALSPACE-EQUIVALENT)

Golden space, the odd perspectives burning new paths in Roger's brain. The ship protected them from the worst effects of fractal time, but even inside the cabin there was amber light, and the certain knowledge this was another universe.

And off to one side was a wraith-like figure, sharpening in focus – a young woman he did not recognize yet felt he knew – and he spoke without thinking.

'Have I dreamed of—? This is impossible.'

Beside him, Mum was staring – at him, not the apparition. Could she not see it?

Then the young woman flung her hands out, as if trying to hold on to some support, while an unknown force grabbed her and whisked her out through the bulkhead; and then she was gone.

Mum smiled as the ship slowed, and the forward view filled the cabin.

Home.

Labyrinth, finally.

This was how she appeared from the outside, the fabled Labyrinth: stellate and complex, bristling with shining towers in all directions, fractal and grand, with a core that curved beyond the hyperspherical. It was a cathedral, a sculpture, a maze. It – she – was a living city-world in the ur-continuum of mu-space, a place that grew and evolved in mysterious ways even during the early days, when Pilots were her supposed architects and builders. Now her relationship to the citizens who lived within was more complex but closer than ever.

She was rooted in the spacetime geometry of this continuum, the only universe whose dimensionality was not an integer, the ur-continuum beneath and beyond all others: mu-space.

And she was the Pilots' home.

No reception committee waited for them.

Dad-and-ship as one threaded their way among the flock of vessels outside the city – all the ships bigger than this, none of them looking half as powerful – and entered a tunnel that was wider than a building, a canyon with sapphire sides sprawling with constructs that might have been architecture or machinery or art: there was no way to tell.

They flew into a huge hollow space where dozens of ships were floating: bronze or silver, decorated with lustrous cobalt, shimmering indigo, deep swirling green.

Roger wondered what Alisha would make of this – if she were able to retain her sanity in this universe.

'See?' said Mum. 'It's not impossible.'

'What do you mean?'

'That's what you said earlier, as we flew.'

She did not understand, obviously. He was about to ask whether it was normal to see apparitions as one voyaged through mu-space; then he realized the answer was no.

Gavriela.

The mirage had a name. Or was this some delusion created by the shock of entering the continuum after so long away? Yet his body was almost vibrating with energy, filled with a sense of rightness and supreme capability; and this place was the opposite of shocking: it was where he belonged.

Perhaps there were neurocognitive effects all the same, so the rational choice was not between talking and keeping silent, it was between confiding in his parents or in a medic, here in Labyrinth.

=No, that is not necessary.=

He looked all around.

=Only you can hear me at this time.=

About to speak, he closed his mouth, deliberately touching the tip of his tongue to the roof of his mouth, quelling the desire.

=You are most welcome here, Roger Blackstone.=

A powerful sense of humility descended through him. He bowed his head.

Then Dad said something unsettling.

'On Fulgor, you're used to keeping everything a secret, son. Realize that it's not so different here.'

'Excuse me?' Roger pointed to his own eyes. 'Do I usually walk around like this?'

In fact it was refreshing to see his parents with their natural, glittering, obsidian eyes revealed.

'Your true nature is a matter of course. My job is not.'

'I . . . understand.'

'We're not under surveillance, but this is a complex place and ... Not all our operations are carried out on human worlds.'

'You mean, you spy on other Pilots?'

'Not me personally, and that description is too crude. Think of peacekeeper intelligence officers on Fulgor, how they monitor their own as well as strangers.'

'All I know is *Fighting Shadows.*'

He meant the holodrama saga that was as much soap opera as action thriller.

'Good enough.' Dad smiled. 'I find the series quite addictive myself.'

'So we maintain your cover?'

Mum smiled at the spy jargon.

'Yes.' Dad looked at her, but his own smile dissipated. 'Okay, Roger. I'm still a consultant and trainer on Fulgor, big corporate and political negotiations a speciality. The additional tweak is that I'm a Pilot living incognito because of personal failure. And I don't have a ship.'

'But—'

'We'll disembark in private. No one will see us.'

They were now gliding into a narrow tunnel, barely wider than the ship, shining blue and purple.

'And if anyone asks,' added Dad, 'we travelled awake in a passenger hold inside a large vessel. You don't know the Pilot's name, and you never saw the ship's exterior.'

'All right.'

Then they were docking, and as Dad had said, when they left the ship it was via a series of halls, empty apart from the Blackstone family. Finally, they came out into a public place, something that might have been a sweeping mall magnified a hundred times, opening out into a vaster space beyond.

On one of a thousand balconies, they stopped.

'Will you be all right sightseeing?' asked Dad.

'Of course, dear.' Mum winked at Roger. 'We'll go shopping.'

'She's joking, son. See you both later.'

At that, Dad turned away, his face hardening in concentration. Then a rectangle of empty air was rotating – somehow – and when Dad stepped inside, his image swirled around an impossible axis, and the enclosing rectangle twisted out of existence.

'There are different levels of, well, reality,' said Mum. 'Including different timeflows, so please don't try to use this technique without training.'

'Technique?'

'Fastpath rotation. Call it a shortcut. A doorway to a tunnel to another doorway.'

Roger looked around. Several hundred people, Pilots all, were going about their unknowable business. Any who knew Dad would consider him a reject from society. How could Dad stand that? How could anyone swallow their pride so much?

But Roger had some education in Pilot history, studies at home – in their Fulgor house – where surveillance could not reach. He had studied the works of Karyn McNamara, the first true Pilot, the first to be born in mu-space. She hadn't been much for the adulation of others.

'They say that people lead lives of quiet desperation – but I prefer to live in quiet triumph. The simplicity of shibumi *in work and family life, that makes us human.'*

He knew the old term for elegant minimalism, an austere aesthetic that he admired but thought he was too weak to follow.

'So where do you want to go, Mum? Is this one of the major sights?'

'This?' Mum looked around the cavernous, vaulted space. 'It's just a minor place, tucked out of the way.'

'Uh . . . Right.'

'Let's start with Borges Boulevard,' she said. 'But we won't travel its full length.'

'Why not? Is it too long?'

'You could say that. It's infinite, in fact.'

'That's not poss—'

But of course it *was* possible, in this place.

Finally, they stood at the top of a slender ramp that arced down to a magnificent white gleaming road. It shone and flowed, a white river sparkling as though with diamonds, carrying people and goods on its surface, in a myriad intricate currents. And its length, supported on silver spans, arced across vast spaces whose far ends were misty, sweeping forever through Labyrinthine magnificence.

'Welcome to your real home, son.'

'Oh, Mum, Mum. This is so—'

'I know.'

Then Roger said something that came straight from the subconscious.

'I would die to protect this place.'

That caused Mum to frown.

But she said nothing, since a group of Pilots was passing by, conversing in rapid Aeternum. And a few moments later, a female voice called down from an overhead balcony.

'Miranda Blackstone, is that you?'

'Laura?'

Mum's smile was glowing, and Roger could see how she must have looked when younger, say about his age now. She waited for the woman, Laura, to descend on a floating disk.

They hugged, then:

'This is my son, Roger.'

'No! But you're so—Well. I'm pleased to meet you, Roger.'

'Ma'am.'

They shook hands, the ancient ritual strange to Roger.

'We have so much to catch up on,' said Laura. 'There's a new trade hall that I'm heading for right now, and we can have a meal there: lunch, breakfast, dinner, whatever.'

Was there no standard time for the city? Or perhaps it was obvious that the Blackstones were newly arrived from realspace, from some arbitrary timezone on a world with an arbitrary rotation period. He could learn so much just by talking to people – but Mum and Laura looked brimming with words, anecdotes and reminiscences waiting to spill out, tales of people and places that had no relevance to him. And it wasn't that he didn't want to hear; but the best way for old friends to catch up is alone.

'I'm perfectly happy,' he said, 'to wander the city by myself.'

'Are you sure?' asked Laura. 'I mean– Miranda?'

'No, I . . . Is that what you'd prefer, Roger?'

'Definitely. Why don't you two go off and catch up?'

'If you're certain, then.'

'Here.' Laura pointed, and Roger's tu-ring flared orange. 'Directions to where we'll be. Or just ask anyone. We'll be in the Keynes Centre, just off Feigenbaum Flowbridge.'

'I love the names.'

'You'll grow used to them.'

*

There were so many places to stroll. After an hour of dazzling, mind-bending sights, he settled down for a cup of jantrasta in a golden building where he sat on the ceiling – from the perspective of the atrium he had entered by – watching others walk up walls or along landings that turned through paradoxical angles. For a moment he was struck by the sight of a wide-shouldered young woman in a black jumpsuit, with some kind of firearm tagged to her hip. She looked at him, broadcasting a sense of physicality; and they smiled at each other, in a moment of connection that might have led somewhere, if the universe had been different.

Then several other Pilots similarly dressed joined her, she nodded, and they departed together, heading in the direction of Hilbert Hall. A fleeting near-encounter that would never have a follow-on: just one of the many odd things that seemed to happen the more he opened his senses to this place.

'Military,' said a voice behind him.

'Excuse me?'

'Those people in black.' It was a shaven-headed man who was standing there. 'They're military, or the closest thing we have to it.'

'Uh ... Right.'

'You're wondering how I know you're new here.' The man smiled. 'Believe me, it shows. I remember how it was for me.'

He was blocky, his sleeves pushed up to reveal forearms cabled with muscle.

'There's no shame in it,' said Roger.

'My point exactly. My name's Max, Max Gould.'

'Roger Blackstone.'

'So you live on a realspace world? Er, you mind if I join you?'

Max sat down – or up, whatever you called it, since when you craned your head back, there were upside-down people walking above you – and ordered a drink. It rotated into existence in mid-air, just above his outstretched hand, and he grasped it.

Roger had failed to manage the procedure so smoothly.

'I live on Fulgor, if you know of it,' he said.

'Oh, yes. I visited Petrurb, years ago. Love the quickstone buildings.'

'That's in Tarquil,' said Roger. 'I learned to speak Quitalan in school, but not very well.'

'Hmm. So how are you finding Aeternum, using it for real? You sound practised enough.'

'If I stick to Core Aeternum, I get by. So far.'

'Taking on new upgrades gets ever harder.' Max sipped, put the cup down – or up, whichever – on the table. 'Anyone who's been on a high-distortion geodesic knows how it goes, especially a hellflight.'

'Catching up on a century's worth of language changes ... That must be interesting.'

'I've only done it once, to that extent. All I can say is, I'm glad I had the experience, and I'm far too old to repeat it.'

'Wow.' Roger wondered what it would be like, not just to fly a ship, but to follow time-distorting trajectories that took you out of synch with everyone you knew at home. 'I can't imagine.'

He looked inside his cup. Empty. A refill might be nice – except that he was conversing with a stranger who had simply sat down, seemingly open but with enough personal power to mask an ulterior agenda.

Dad had said his cover needed to remain intact. So far, this Max had asked nothing about Roger's family; but it was an obvious way for the conversation to go next.

'Anyway.' With an abrupt wrist-twist, Max caused his drink to rotate from existence. 'It was nice talking to you, but I have a meeting I need to attend.'

He stood up, and held out his hand.

'Er, right.' Not sure of the protocol, Roger stood also. 'Nice to—'

They clasped hands.

Max's grip was unbreakable.

'What—?'

Something, a dislocation in space, revolved around them. *Fastpath rotation*. Then Max released his hold.

They tumbled into a steel-lined vault.

'Steady on,' said Max. 'You're fine.'

'Where the hell have you taken me?'

'You know the meeting I said I have to attend?'

'Huh?'

'This is it.' Max gestured, and a portion of wall melted away. 'Tell me what you see.'

It was a maelstrom of black chaos, a thunderstorm in a cell, a whirlwind of black nothingness: a hypergeometric storm, at whose centre slumped a small figure bound in a flowmetal chair.

'What is all that?' Roger took several steps back. 'What's going on in there?'

The blackness battered against some invisible barrier as if trying to get out.

'So you do see it.'

'What are you talking about?'

'All *I* see,' said Max, gesturing for the wall to reform, 'is an exhausted prisoner, seated in an otherwise empty cell.'

The darkness continued to rage, as the gap dwindled, the wall shutting out the maelstrom once more.

'Who are you? Is Max Gould your real name?'

'More or less, and I'm a friend of your father's. From your reactions, you perceive the threat more easily than he could have. Many times more clearly.'

'Threat?' But he could not help looking at the wall, wondering whether it could hold against the massive forces behind it. 'What threat?'

'It would be best for Carl,' said Max, 'if you didn't go into details of what you've seen.'

'Best for Dad how? How could this cause *him* trouble?'

'There's a possibility it might trigger, well, some odd and dangerous reactions. I cannot explain further, but understand I'm telling the truth.'

'As you have so far?'

'Exactly so. Now, shall we go and see him?'

'See Dad?'

'I'll take that as a yes.'

They swirled into a conference chamber, where Dad leaped from a chair at their appearance.

'Roger! What are you– How did you get here?'

'We had a nice chat,' said Max. 'He's a fine young man.'

'Thank you, Commodore, but I happen to know that.'

Roger noted the rank: *Commodore*.

Perhaps he needed to remain quiet for now.

'Right. So, Roger Blackstone.' Max's eyes were compelling. 'Since you have the makings of a fine Pilot, exactly what purpose are you about to devote your life to?'

'Does everyone have to have a single purpose?'

So much for remaining quiet.

'No, Roger. Some people stumble through their days not knowing what they want, hopeless and dissatisfied. Do you want to turn out that way?'

'No.' He looked at Dad, who was statue-still. 'Is Max – Commodore Gould – trying to recruit me?'

'That's a good idea,' said Max. 'Are you interested?'

Was Roger the only one to see faint glimmers of golden sparks, deep inside Dad's eyes? Did Max understand how much danger he was in?

But of course he did. He was almost certainly Dad's commanding officer, or whatever they called it.

'No, he's not,' said Dad. 'And you don't want me to resign.'

Stone-faced, they stared at each other.

'Very well,' Max responded at last. 'On his next trip here, you'll take Roger to see us officially, and we'll give him the proper tour. Give him enough information to make up his mind. Good enough?'

Dad continued the hard stare; and then he nodded.

'All right.'

'And you'll keep everything to yourself' – Max turned to Roger – 'because that's a basic requirement, and it's for everyone's safety.'

There was a double meaning there: he also wanted Roger to keep quiet about the prisoner, and the storming darkness that dominated the prisoner's cell. How telling that story could damage Dad, well, that was unclear.

'So, both of you, Carl and Roger. It's been wonderful. Have a relaxing stay. Really.'

Max clapped his hands, and reality spun.

Roger and Dad were standing on a platinum-inlaid balcony, amid floating dining-tables, surrounded by chatter and soft chamber music. Mum and Laura looked up from their meal.

'Hello, you two. You found each other.'

'Er, yes,' said Dad.

'And what have you been up to?'

'Sightseeing,' said Roger.

Mum stared at them for an extra second, then turned to Laura, who was frowning.

'The men in my life are back,' said Mum. 'I guess we've a holiday to begin.'

Their farewells were cooler than their greeting, and Roger wondered what had gone wrong. Then he saw momentary disdain on Laura's features – looking at Dad – and believed he understood.

'Interesting city,' Roger said, 'but disappointing people. Some aren't nearly as bright as our friends on Fulgor. Actually, some are pretty dumb.'

Mum and Dad were smiling as they all three turned their backs on Laura. In front of them, beyond the balcony, stretched the infinite length of Borges Boulevard, gleaming with its promise to carry them past wonders; while off to one side was the complex elegance of the Logos Library, housing its endlessly branching stacks and corridors, where polished shelves were filled with infocrystals that glowed, hinting at limitless knowledge strong enough to disperse the shadows of ignorance.

EIGHTEEN

EARTH, 1927 AD

There are no ghosts. Graveyards contain crumbling bones, some mouldering meat, and well-fed beetles. Hallucinations are a brain malfunction caused by false triggering of the circuits that recognize faces, bodies, human and animal movement.

It was only the cold that made her shiver, crouched inside the cemetery at night.

That, and the memory of Erik propped up in bed, his one good eye trained on her, the other side of his face a suppurating purple mess. Perhaps getting out of the family house was more to do with escaping her brother's condition than seeking out the enemy.

From beyond the low stone wall came the sounds of men gathering, their voices a murmur, rising then falling as they went indoors, to a school hall that in the brightness of morning would be filled with children, singing their prayers and taking in the headmaster's instructions, afterwards to create not so much essays and equations as their own coalescing minds. A school should be a place of hope.

It was her third evening back in Berlin; and already things seemed changed. Before she went to Zürich, no one had held political meetings of this type, and certainly not in her old school. But now, when she peeped from behind a headstone, she saw men in military-style shirts that looked grey under moonlight.

Where they ushered the ordinary men in suits inside, illumination fell on them, highlighting the scarlet armbands, like fresh blood against tan soil.

Knowing her way round, she left the cemetery via the far corner, and came to the school buildings from the rear, crossing the playground – it seemed so much smaller now – to reach the canteen. She used slow pressure on the doorknob, checking it was locked. No way in.

The windows were latticed with handles, unlike the casement windows in houses. Inside were catches, used to hold the window in place when open, and as locks when shut. But despite moonlight shining solidly on the glass, she could see that one of the catches inside was raised.

And when she tried it, the window opened far more quietly than expected.

Wishing she had paid more attention to athletic endeavours, she dragged herself up over the sill, catching her knee and possibly cutting it, biting back the pain in silence. From out in the corridor, she heard men's voices passing.

'Is he here?'

'In the building, yes. Can't you tell?'

'Well I can feel the—'

Then they were gone, distance muffling the words.

Moving in a half crouch, she reached the inner door, turned the knob with constant tension, and slipped out into the corridor. Her shoes were quiet on the parquet flooring as she moved to the old staircase, paused to get her balance, and then went up, keeping to the outer edge of the tread where it was unlikely to creak.

Up and up she went, until she reached the old music room. Here she had expected potential trouble; but again the door was unlocked. Inside, music stands were like skeletons at attention, and she moved slowly to avoid clashing against them.

The sounds of murmuring seemed to come through the floor now.

At the end of the room, the other door was standing open, leading to darkness, to the old loft used for props and costumes. Inside would be clutter she could not see; but if she tripped over, then in the hall below several hundred pairs of eyes would turn to the ceiling, wondering at the noise.

She remembered *The Barber of Seville*, everyone speaking their lines in hard-accented French; and Goethe's *Faust*, the school's shining triumph, at least in the period of her last few years in this place. And she remembered how privileged she had been to arrange the stage lighting, playing with filters and rheostats during rehearsals until she had the timing and the atmosphere just right.

But tonight, even through the floorboards, she could tell the ambience was very different.

There were several tiny gaps between the boards, one of the reasons that the loft remained in darkness during performances. Now, on hands and knees, she edged toward a sliver of light.

Near another such gap, she imagined a momentary reflection, a glittering eye – but then it was gone; and even if there was a rat, it could not be as big as her. Then there was only shadow once more.

As she lowered her face to the hole, she could see a portion of the stage, and a small figure from above: combed-over hair, brush moustache, and an aura she could feel from here.

Words were once magic, Herr Doktor Freud had written, *giving them power.*

Since her encounter with the man she had sought out his books. They formed a strange counterpoint to her studies of electromagnetism, optics and mechanics: so definite in their tone, so lacking in mathematical structure or empirical proof; and yet insightful, at least in parts.

It took a few moments to tune in to the speech rising from below, and to understand why her unconscious mind had delivered up those words from Freud.

'—those times, the true folk were warriors in misty forests, gathered up by the Death Choosers, Odinn's Valkyries, if we fell in battle.' His words held a thrumming resonance, an unexpected power. 'Since then, our magnificence and bravery have ebbed away beneath the deceptions of secret Jewry, the illusions created by bourgeois curs who fail to understand the subhuman nature of their unnatural masters, the Jesus-killers who—'

The voice rose and fell like oceanic waves, like the feelings of the crowd, washing back and forth, rushing, compelling. And through the gap she could see—

Impossible.

—twisting shards of black light, of shining darkness that—

Some hysterical illusion.

—writhed and revolved around the pasty, sweat-soaked man gesticulating below.

She shifted, pushing her eye socket against the hole, careless of splinters, trying to see more. And then she did.

A mirage could not occur inside a school hall. An hallucination could manifest only in the mind's eye, not in reality. There was no explanation for this vision.

'—will advance along Bifrost, the Rainbow Bridge, in triumph. When the homeland is cleansed of bipedal vermin who differ from humans by their stink, then we grasp our—'

His words conjured up dark forest and mist, hard warriors with cloaks and spears, a bridge of shining light; and the vision was *there*, in moving colour below her, floating above the heads of a spellbound audience.

While the man onstage walked amid rotating darkness, inherently unnatural, revolting and malevolent. None of this was rational. All of it was real.

What can I do?

She pulled back, and again she noticed the glittering of an eye across the loft; but this time she also made out a kneeling figure, thin and sharp-chinned, holding forefinger to lips.

From below came: '—till we have wiped them out, scoured the world of Jews, and through strength, gained freedom once more!'

A great roar ascended from the enthralled mob, for that was what they were.

*

It was another hour before the frenzy dissipated, the speaker disappearing first amid a phalanx of brown-shirt-clad men, and finally the others leaving, their words buzzing, no doubt continuing to see some remembered resonance of the vision that had been conjured above their heads, without their conscious knowledge, laid down inside their unconscious minds.

Her limbs felt like fluttering moths, her body vibrating beyond her control.

There was a different kind of dark movement, a shadow within shadow that meant the other watcher was crawling towards her. She started to back away, but her foot touched something, a box, and she stopped.

'Wait,' came a man's whisper. 'Just another minute.'

'They'll lock up everywhere when they leave.'

'Not everywhere.'

So the unlocked window had not been random convenience, but part of a deliberate plan, considerably more organized than her attempt. If the world was filled with good people – those who would be appalled by tonight's meeting – then perhaps this man was one of them.

He drew closer, a thin man wrapped in a heavy, too-big overcoat.

'I'm Dmitri Shtemenko,' he whispered. 'Who are you?'

'Gavriela Wolf.'

'So, come on.'

He led the way along a route she probably knew far better: music room, staircase, the downstairs corridor. Yet he must have prepared, for he navigated through dark areas without hesitation. They exited via the canteen window, Dmitri moving well but without athleticism.

Then he stopped, for there was a group of men around the corner where he was intending to go. Gavriela pinched his sleeve, tugged, and pointed towards the graveyard. She headed for the low wall, followed by Dmitri.

As they slipped through the opening in the wall, they straightened up – and stopped.

Two men were pissing on a grave; another was buttoning up, already finished. He was the one who noticed first Gavriela, then Dmitri, and gave a sonorous burp.

'You're skulking like Jews,' he called out.

'Who are you calling a—?' One of the two men paused in urinating. 'Oh.'

'Are they really Jews?' said the other.

'They look like it to me.'

Finished, the two men shook themselves off, still facing her. A part of Gavriela noted with interest what she was seeing; an unimportant part for now.

'No,' she said. 'He's my . . . husband. We just wanted some time alone, not in my mother's house, you know?'

'Ah.'

'Right. We should have some of that, shouldn't we? Pretty, pretty.'

Dmitri moved beside her, shifting inside the overcoat. Perhaps he had urinated or soiled himself. Maybe Gavriela would do the same, as soon as the fear hit home. Right now she was struggling with the concept that this was real, even more than the insane visions earlier.

I'm going to die here.

Somehow it was all wrong, an aberration, a crack in the rules of reality. The three men were advancing, two not bothering to button their flies, all the easier for what they had in mind. The first man, big and bulky, had picked up a spade from somewhere.

Help me!

In her mind it was a scream, filled with the energy of horror, not to the God she did not believe in, but to someone else.

Roger, help me!

And then the night became strange.

'What? Where in realspace is this?'

The figure was translucent, clad in black with eyes to match, and she knew the face, remembered him from dreams; but she was not the only one to see him now.

'Help us,' Gavriela said to him.

'How?'

But he already had, causing the three attackers to stop, the big man tripping on something – a pile of soil beside an empty grave – and then Dmitri leaped forward, hands flashing downward then cutting curves through the air, making figure-eights; and then the second man was done as well, before Gavriela had processed what was happening.

The last attacker stopped, half turned, and began to run; but silver moonlight flowed through the air and then there was a *thunk,* a sound straight from the butcher's shop when a housewife orders a prime cut; and then the man crumbled.

Dmitri walked forward, stood on the corpse's back, and yanked his blade free from the neck. He wiped the blade, along with its twin in his other hand, on the dead man's coat; then he tucked his hands inside his overcoat and the weapons were gone.

The jet-eyed apparition looked appalled.

'You're one of—'

Then he rippled apart and was gone.

All she could do was take this Dmitri home: whether for his protection or her own, she could not tell. Outside the front door, he took her sleeve as she had taken his earlier.

'Do me a favour, Fräulein Wolf. Call me Jürgen, all right? Jürgen Schäffer-Braun.'

'You said your name was Dmitri.'

'It is in fact, but I've no idea why I told you.' His voice slowed, his Hochdeutsch becoming crisper. 'The truth and my identification papers have little in common.'

At that point she realized that his voice had evinced a trace accent earlier, under stress.

'You're a Bolshevik?'

'I'm no friend of bastards like the Sturmabteilung, for sure.'

'The who?'

'Never mind. Are you going to knock? Or do you have a key?'

'Tell me.'

'You met three of their about-to-be recruits in the graveyard. The SA. Once they join up they get those stylish brown shirts.'

'Oh. Them.'

'What I don't know is why they stopped dead.'

'You didn't see the—'

'See what?'

'I mean, you didn't see anything either. I thought they caught sight of a ghost. That is, from the way they acted.'

'Hmm. Well, are you going to knock, Fräulein?'

'As it happens, I do have a key.'

They went inside. She did not trust him; but he should not be wandering the streets alone, not tonight.

But after what he did ... With the knives ...

His overcoat should have been spattered with arterial blood, but it appeared unmarked save for an ordinary grease stain near the hem. Had she imagined the knife fight, too?

No. It happened.

She had witnessed murder, but it seemed unreal.

'Father, this is, er, Jürgen. He helped me earlier.'

'Helped you?'

'It is not entirely safe, sir,' said Dmitri. 'But she was only a little lost.'

'Come in.' Father's gaze slid towards Mother, then to the ceiling, in the direction of Erik's room where he still lay injured. 'We'll have some cognac.'

If he had his own opinion about how likely Gavriela was to be lost in her hometown, he would voice it later, not now.

'That would be marvellous, sir.'

In the front parlour, everyone gathered, including the lovely Ilse, Erik's fiancée who seemed perfect for him. Gavriela felt she had gained a sister.

Tonight's discussion was comfortingly domestic – about the current prosperity, which Dmitri (still calling himself Jürgen) claimed was due to Anglo-American loans propping up the German economy, loans which could always be called in; while Father agreed about the international agreements but not about the likelihood of their ever failing.

None of it seemed to have anything to do with a world of graveyards and apparitions, orators surrounded by impossible darkness, reified visions taking root in men's minds, or three dead bodies lying in the night.

'Everyone,' said Dmitri finally, 'I'm so very pleased to make your acquaintance, but I must be gone. Thank you so very much.'

As he stood up, Ilse cocked her head, and looked from him to Gavriela and back.

'You know, Jürgen, never mind Erik. *You* and Gavriela could be brother and sister.'

Dmitri stared at Gavriela; she stared at him.

'I fear that's no compliment,' said Dmitri finally.

'But she has a point.' Father smiled at Ilse. 'You have a good eye, my dear.'

It was nice that he approved of her.

Mother said to him: 'It's your father that Gavi follows in looks, don't you think?'

'Are you Jewish, Jürgen?' asked Ilse. 'It's all right if you're not, because unfortunately I'm Gentile myself.'

'Not as far as I know.'

'My ancestors,' said Father, 'were Vikings, I'll have you know. Some of them, anyhow.'

'I don't see how mine could have been.' Dmitri laughed. 'But we'll never know what our forebears got up to, will we?'

Mother frowned, disapproving of risqué humour, or the hint of it.

'Excuse me, Frau Wolf.' Dmitri gave a Prussian bow. 'I'm fatigued after a long day, as I'm sure you must be. Goodnight, everyone.'

'Goodnight.'

Gavriela escorted him to the door. He went out, checked the street, and nodded.

'I'll be safe, I think.'

For a second, dark flecks seemed to move through his eyes; then they looked normal.

'What are you going to do about tonight?' she asked.

'Perhaps a little counter-agitation. Their movement is not powerful, not yet.'

She had been thinking of the men he had killed; but there was the other thing as well.

'The speaker tonight was persuasive.'

'Ach, yes. Have you heard of Gustav Lebon? He theorized that a mob thinks with a single mind. I never quite believed it before.'

'But the vision that he—that he created overhead. I mean, um, in their minds.'

Dmitri sucked in a breath.

'So you did see it, Gavriela Wolf. I wondered if you did.'

'The visions are real?'

'Yes, but only some of us can. . . . No. Excuse me, I've made a mistake.'

His expression, half lit by the nearest streetlamp, half in shadow, was shutting down.

'What kind of mistake?'

'We're different.'

'What does that—?'

But his coat, undone, whirled around him like a cloak as he turned. Then he was striding into darkness, and for a moment he seemed to have vanished before reaching the street corner; but she was tired and in some kind of shock, her eyes barely able to focus, so who knew what she had seen?

She went back inside to the comfort of her family home, a comfort that once felt eternally stable, but now seemed a cracked stone fortress built on shifting ground, deep inside an earthquake zone.

NINETEEN

LABYRINTH, 2603 AD (REALSPACE-EQUIVALENT)

This was how Roger's dream went.

First there was the calling, her sweet voice reaching for him.

'Help me. Roger, help me!'

And the dark cemetery all around, like some nightmare from history, prompting his panicked question: 'What? Where in realspace is this?'

But *she* was there, the one whose name he knew, somewhere in his mind.

'Help us,' she said.

'How?'

Then the ghostly figures were in shock – because of him? – and suddenly everything changed as a cloaked figure – no, a man in a billowing overcoat – leaped *through* Roger – *am I dead?* – and his hands flashed silver with reflected moonlight, like the martial-dance motions Roger drilled over and over but had never used for real; because these were knife-blades and those were flesh-and-blood men; and in a few seconds they were dead.

One of them died with a thrown blade piercing his cervical vertebrae. Roger had some idea how difficult it was to hurl a weapon at a moving target; he could not have done it even if the man had been still.

The knifeman had saved the girl, or woman, whatever, and whatever her name was. Then he turned.

Blackness rotated in his eyes.

'You're one of them!' Roger yelled, but halfway through the words something yanked the night away, the cemetery spiralled into nothingness, and he popped out of nightmare, fully awake and wondering at the content of his own exclamation.

His room was a marvel of silver and gold, lined with panels whose infinitely recursive designs could not be painted in realspace; and it was furnished with every convenience: food and infocrystals available through fist-sized portals in the air. By Labyrinthine standards it was economy class; for him it was luxury.

Against it, the memory of Lucis City and its quickglass towers became ordinary. Or perhaps all humans, including the Pilot variety, were ingrates, forgetting that most generations scrabbled in poverty and died young, that the ancestor species foraged in undergrowth and ran or climbed from predators, everything raw and immediate and simple.

Dazed by a change of universe and the weird philosophical notions spinning in his head, he scarcely noticed the fading memory of dream, and those awful graveyard surroundings, cooked up perhaps by his work on the Zürich simulation for Dr Helsen, the simulation that he knew with too much accuracy – for he had worked on coding characters, not historic streets and buildings – for Dr Helsen, she of the darkness, the strangeness . . .

When he slipped back into sleep, it was dreamless.

TWENTY

EARTH, 777 AD

Nine days before they left for the chieftains' gathering, Chief Folkvar ordered Ulfr to meet him at dawn on Heimdall's Rock, a promontory that overlooked not just the settlement but the whole valley. Using a willow-twig to clean his teeth as he walked, Ulfr wondered what was going on. Beside him, Brandr walked with his tail wagging, unconcerned.

Perhaps Ulfr could learn some lessons from his warhound.

Early though he was, Chief Folkvar was already at Heimdall's Rock, fur-cloaked and bear-like. It was not a comparison that would have found favour, for a bear was no warrior spirit.

Unlike me.

But whoever named Ulfr could not have known his fate or character in advance. No one could anticipate the Norns.

'The men are practising,' said Folkvar. 'I told them to.'

'But not me, chief?'

'I mostly practise alone, with stones and against the post.'

Folkvar meant small boulders for lifting and hurling, the upright oak post for straining against and striking. The post was a wrestler that could not be thrown, a warrior that could not be knocked down.

'And I practise later than the others,' Folkvar went on. 'Do you know why?'

Ulfr looked down at Brandr, whose tongue lolled.

Because you like being alone, Chief?

He held back his answer, uncertainty like a half-clenched hand inside his guts, then spoke. 'Chief, you are not the youngest among us—'

'No. Nice of you to remind me.'

'—but you don't work alone to hide your weaknesses. So I believe it's to let you watch the others at *their* practice, without distraction.'

'Hmm. Perhaps. So, Ulfr.'

'Chief?'

'Come watch with me, and tell me what you see.'

From Heimdall's Rock they could see down into the practice square. Some two dozen men were hard at it, some with training weapons bound with hemp sacking for safety. One twirled twin hammers solo, his opponents only in his mind's eye.

'Tell me of Hallsteinn,' said Folkvar.

'He is the strongest.' Ulfr stared down, considering how intimidating the warrior would be up close. 'His eyes become blank stone when he works hard.'

'Losing himself in the fight?'

'Yes. Brave as Thórr, but injuring others when he doesn't mean to.'

'All right.' Big fists on his hips, Folkvarr mused, then gestured with his chin. 'Tell me of Ormr.'

The man in question was using fast footwork to keep his opponent out of range and unbalanced.

'Devious.' Ulfr grinned as Ormr scooped his opponent's ankle with one hand and whipped him to the ground. 'Like that. Focused.'

'So what would be their weaknesses leading *other* men into battle?'

Ulfr tried to read Folkvar's expression.

Why is he asking me such questions?

But those grey warrior eyes gave away nothing besides proud certainty.

'Hallsteinn might overcommit,' Ulfr said finally. 'Go berserker, and take everyone down with him. Honourable, but an honourable defeat, not victory, against a clever enemy.'

'And Ormr?'

'The opposite. He would be like the clever enemy, but—'

'Tell me the truth of your thoughts, Ulfr the Wolf. I require this.'

'Ah, he might hold back, unwilling to take the losses, so losing the chance for victory. But that's only my thought, Chief.'

'Which is what I asked for.'

Ulfr looked down at the practice area.

'They could do with Kormr's skills.' He pointed at a smiling man who was making corrections to his partner's technique. 'People bond to him because he cares.'

'And his weakness as a leader?'

'I've never seen him, well, act ruthless.'

'Is that part of being a leader?'

'Yes,' said Ulfr. 'Especially if you act that way only when necessary.'

'Hmm.'

'If you could bind all their skills into one warrior, he'd be the man to follow.'

'Good.' Folkvar's hand clamped on his shoulder. 'Think on that. A chieftain is always alone, but has Kormr's ready way with the clan.'

'Er—'

'Meanwhile, we could do with meat for our travels, while those remaining here would appreciate the same.'

Ulfr smiled.

'Then Brandr and I will hunt.'

'And in the silent moments, you might have time to think.'

'I don't—'

'Begone now, young Ulfr.'

So Ulfr climbed down from Heimdall's Rock, Brandr beside him, and when they reached level ground he began to jog, Brandr loping at his ankle, scanning the terrain by sight and feel, while a part of him tried to puzzle out the conversation that had just occurred, to decipher the implications.

Two weeks later, they were in a landscape of sweeping ice and rock, of lakes that looked like steel, surrounded by swirls of tough heather, brown-green and purple. Spectacular crimson streaked the wide sky. A distant column of steam rose from broken earth.

There were eight men and two hounds in the party, each warrior carrying a pack of supplies over his cloak, even Chief Folkvar.

'So, the gathering,' said Steinn, a lean warrior with a mis-shapen nose. 'There'll be drinking and contests, I take it? And maybe a few women?'

The others laughed.

'And plenty of Sigurd's hair to be won,' said Folkvarr.

Ulfr smiled and the others chuckled, appreciating the chief's quick comeback. At one level, *Sigurd's hair* was a simple kenning, a two-word allusion, which in this case meant gold. But there were overtones, evoking images of blonde maidens, and the wordplay and poetry contests whose winners might well impress those very maidens.

He remembered what Folkvar had said in private: a chieftain needs to be alone, yet have an easy way with clan members.

But then, with the notion of maidens, his thoughts returned to the settlement where Eira lived alone in the *volva*'s hut, beautiful and gifted, still grieving for her brother, dead at Ulfr's hand in an act of mercy. When he returned from this journey, would things be different? Or had she sundered him from her thoughts forever?

Two shapes came running through the grass: Brandr and Grigg, Steinn's hound.

'All's well,' said Steinn, and Ulfr nodded.

Both men understood their hounds, could read the nuances of gait and stance. Brandr and Grigg had been having fun but also working, sweeping the surroundings and finding neither enemy nor prey.

Hallsteinn was making the sign of the fist, hand pressed against the small Thórr's hammer he wore on a leather cord. In the distance was a raven, a reminder of Óthinn.

'I think there's another band of folk travelling,' he said. 'See? Beyond that lake.'

Ulfr tried to work out where he was looking, then gave up. The others shrugged.

'What do we do, Chief?' asked Skári.

His voice still caused Ulfr to tighten up, to imagine himself cutting the bastard down. But Skári had been ensorcelled, just like the others; he would not have killed Jarl otherwise – merely outlawed him. That was what he had said afterwards.

'We walk and keep watch.'

Their pace had been a warrior's distance-eating lope; now they slowed, letting the rhythm of motion recharge their limbs. Ulfr kept scanning the distant ground; finally he saw movement.

'There are others ahead. Hallsteinn is right.'

'You have the eyes of Heimdall,' Chief Folkvar told Hallsteinn. 'We have our own Watcher of the Gods.'

'Unfortunately, I have the ears as well.'

'You can hear the grass growing?'

'Aye, and Ulfr's farting while he sleeps.'

'No,' said Steinn. 'That doesn't make you Heimdall, my friend. They can hear Ulfr all the way down in Niflheim.'

'You cooked the rabbits that Snorri killed,' said Ulfr. 'I blame the food.'

'It's all right, lad. You were just snoring like Thórr.'

'Thank you, Vermundr.'

'From both ends, mind you—'

'Quiet now,' said Folkvar.

They walked on, checking their weapons could be drawn or unslung as needed, becoming watchful now.

By a frozen river with steep banks, they drew near to the other party, who had stopped but kept their swords sheathed. Their cloaks were browns and greens, blending with the landscape.

'Twelve folk,' said Hallsteinn. 'Three of them women.'

Most of them, in Ulfr's estimation, stood like hardened warriors.

'How can you tell from here?' asked Snorri.

'My godlike attributes.'

'That wasn't how it looked when we bathed in the lake.'

'The water was cold.'

'Isn't that what they all—'

Folkvar cleared his throat. Everyone stopped, shrugged off their packs and lowered them to the heather. Then they moved their shoulders, getting rid of the ache.

'We move forward now,' he said. 'Slowly.'

In the river bank were hollows, not quite caves; farther along was a tumbledown wooden bridge; here and there lay boulders and thickets of heather. All were potential hiding-places, so the men kept watch in all directions as they advanced.

The other party had also laid down their packs. One of their number, a hefty man with a braided beard, advanced.

'Hail,' he called out. 'I am Gulbrandr, chieftain of these good folk.'

'And I am Folkvar, likewise chieftain.'

'Fellow travellers for the gathering?'

'That we are.'

Men in both parties relaxed a little as they leaned on their spears.

'So if we are peacefully bound for the same destination, good Folkvar, perhaps we should—'

'Look out!' yelled someone.

'Troll!'

'It's attacking—'

With a grinding screech, the thing came running from beneath the bridge: formed of moving boulders and stones, roughly man-shaped but twice as big. From gaps between stones came flashes of scarlet light.

By the Gods, it's real.

Then the troll was on the other party, crushing two men. Blood spurted.

'By Thórr!' roared Hallsteinn.

'Attack!' yelled Folkvar.

They spread out as they ran, Hallsteinn hurling his spear. It stuck alongside several spears thrown by the other party. Two pierced gaps between the moving stones; then they were splintered as the troll's limbs brushed them away.

Beside Ulfr, Steinn's face was deathly white. Big Vermundr unslung his great hammer as he lumbered on, and began swinging it.

We can't kill it.

Brandr and Griggr were racing ahead. They were going to die. But the troll was moving away, swinging at the other warriors who were backing away in fear.

No, not in fear. To draw the troll away from a woman lying on the ground, her leg glistening with blood and badly bent.

Ulfr's run was taking him past her, very close.

'No, warrior!'

Her hand caught his ankle and he stopped, hand rising as he looked down, ready to strike although she was not the enemy. From up ahead came barking, shouts, and a scream as someone fell.

The woman's face glistened with pain.

'Use ... this.'

What she held was a staff tipped with crystal, black runes on the shaft and a single red rune *inside* the crystal. How that could be, Ulfr had no idea.

Nor could he understand how the rune appeared to glow as if on fire.

'Strike ... inside ...'

Something about her was similar to Eira – *she's a* volva, *has to be* – and in an instant he had already decided, snatching the staff and running forward with it, raising it to his shoulder – *I'm going to die* – as the troll turned, its massive hard presence dominating the world, and the stone appeared to look at him as a boulder-fist rose to crush him – *now* – and then he was twisting, both hands on the staff as he rammed it forward –

Valkyries, take my spirit – and the crystal tip blazed for an instant before he slammed it between stones, into the creature's body.

The world blew apart.

Like a volcano whose incandescent fire-river heart runs all the way from Surturheim, home of Fire Giants, the troll exploded stones in all directions, revealing crimson fire.

Then it was uncovered, a complex lattice of naked red light glowing in the air, while simultaneous words sounded inside everyone's head.

<<Beware it, children of men.>>

<<Do you not see the darkness?>>

<<They are not of you, yet among you.>>

<<Foolish creatures, regard your danger.>>

Above the ground, it twisted, perhaps wounded. Then it floated north, moving faster than a man could run; and after a moment it turned in a way that was impossible, into itself, and then it was gone like a dream in the brightness of morning.

Leaving behind strewn boulders, whimpering wounded, and several crushed corpses.

After several moments, warriors from both parties began to move, converging on the fallen. From behind a large tussock rose a narrow man with a wide-brimmed hat. Clearly he had been hiding.

'Good poet,' called the other party's chief, Gulbrandr, 'are you intact?'

'I am, sir.'

'Then we shall pay more heed to your songs of dread, Stígr.'

The poet's one eye shone as his gaze fastened on Ulfr.

'You carried out a brave deed, warrior.'

Ulfr said nothing, disquieted by the twists of shadow above this Stígr's shoulders, a darkness that Gulbrandr seemed not to see.

Then Folkvar was clasping first Gulbrandr's arm, then Stígr's.

Can no one tell what he is?

Perhaps killing the troll – if that was what Ulfr had done –

had not been for the best. Something about the poet made his skin crawl.

What if the troll had been after Stígr alone?

Then Steinn called out to Griggr, and Ulfr felt sick, remembering. Breaking eye contact, he went to Brandr.

'Good boy. Good boy.'

The warhound licked his face.

'How is he?' called Steinn.

'Minor cuts only,' he said. 'Unbelievable.'

'Likewise my Griggr. She was lucky.'

'We all were.'

'And you were amazing, Ulfr.'

'I don't think so.'

That night, after burying the dead beneath stone cairns, the conjoined bands talked together, getting to know each other. When Stígr rose to declaim a poem, Ulfr left the circle and went to where the wounded *volva*, Heithrún, was resting. Her injured leg was bound with leather straps; and her face was clear of pain.

If it had been Ulfr with the wound, he would be moaning in agony; Heithrún's control of her spirit was tremendous.

'What is it that haunts you, son of the wolf?'

'I don't know.' Ulfr looked back towards the fire. 'What is our purpose? Why are the chieftains gathering?'

'That's not what troubles you.'

'No, I—'

'Stígr is a strange one, but I think you see something more.'

'Why only me?'

'That I cannot understand. Please hand me my staff.'

'Here.'

The crystal seemed clear. What had happened to the embedded rune glowing so strongly earlier?

'We both need to spend time in dreamworld, Ulfr. I to heal, you to explore questions.'

'Yes . . .'

'And we can begin our journey together as you cannot help but blink your eyes now, yes, and my verse will accompany our descent' – the world flickered, then his eyelids closed, and Heithrún's singsong chant carried him, his spirit, into trance – 'as it doesn't matter whether you cannot see the things that are not invisible or let go the things you cannot grasp or grasp what you cannot let go here as we drift deeper and deeper into dreamworld now . . .'

He sank very deep.

This was a hall unlike any he had seen before, though its glass-and-sapphire walls were hung with shields that looked familiar. Around a table stood chairs carved with tiny runes, difficult to make out; and it was when he reached to the nearest chair that the full impact shook him, because his hand looked transparent, like living ice, or rather crystal.

As was his entire body, beneath a clear tunic that draped and fell like fabric, yet could not be such.

—Welcome, good Ulfr.

A regal woman stood at the table's head, and she was of crystal too.

—Who are you?

—My name, good warrior, is Kenna.

—Are you a Soul-Fetcher? But I am not dead.

She gestured to the table.

—We form a war council, Ulfr. Soon we will meet together, the first of us.

—What war?

—I believe you know, inside yourself.

This was impossible, even for dreamworld.

—No. I need to wake up.

—You will awaken later. For now, just wait.

He stared around, looking for a weapon. Then it came to him that he was not under attack, not truly. And finally he realized that he had not taken a breath since this place had appeared.

When he tried, there was nothing to breathe; yet his body did not panic.

—*So we wait. What for?*

—*Two of our comrades.*

He nodded, composing himself.

—*There is no hurry.*

The crystalline woman smiled.

TWENTY-ONE

FULGOR, 2603 AD

Rafaella exulted. Inside her cache was the fragmented self of Daniel Deighton, or more precisely the quantum state of his plexweb at the instant of his death. Soon she would loose it from the cache, letting it flood through her; but first she would sink deeply into code-trance, performing the trickiest of mindhacks as she cleared space inside her own brain-plus-plexweb, a psychocomputational feat impossible to explain to a non-Luculentus.

Soon, though, she would face the problems that had doomed her predecessor, Rafael – extending her neurocognitive capacity to handle her enlarged mind. In his case, there had been a network of distributed plexcores buried in many locations; and the need to avoid lightspeed delays had been the proximate cause of his death, for he had relied on comms relays using processors in mu-space, controlled by Pilots.

I have more resources than you ever had, sweet teacher.

She settled down in lotus position, on the median strip of carpet that ran along the south wing's main corridor. It pleased her to command the carpet to flow, bearing her along as she closed her eyes and sank deep inside her awareness.

A faint *ting* at the edge of consciousness indicated a comms request. So soon after Daniel Deighton's death? She would need to answer.

'Hello, ma'am,' said a pretty young woman in Skein.

'Your ident says you're Alisha Spalding.' Rafaella spoke, but only in Skein; in reality, her lips did not move. 'You're a student . . . and soon to be upraised.'

'Yes, ma'am. That's why I hoped I could prevail on you for a favour,

if you're the kind of person who likes lecturing to interested audiences.'

'I presume you already know that I am. And you'd like to engage me as a guest speaker?'

'With expenses reimbursed, of course.'

Rafaella considered the young woman's soft, ripe mind and the ease with which she could plunge inside her plexnodes. But there were two problems: one was the use of in-Skein protocols instead of direct person-to-person tightcode, leaving data that might be traced by forensic specialists; the other was the lack of a true plexweb – because the girl was not yet a Luculenta – rendering her a delicious short-term snack that would in the aftermath feel empty.

'Of course. And do you have a subject in mind?'

'Perhaps the hyperdimensionality of realspace would interest you enough to—'

'I don't think so.'

'But some of your past research in architectural frames used n-dimensional techniques that included Calabi-Yau perspectives for the transfer of load. At the sub-femtoscopic it matters because—'

'In fact I do recall my own work, but it's no longer of interest.'

'Oh. I was so hoping to see a true Luculenta not just demonstrating in-depth understanding, but presenting it in a way that simpler minds could grasp.'

'You say that with a straight face, Ms Spalding. So, all right.' She had decided: this morsel was for later, not now. 'Give me some interesting analysis of your own, some original work on the topic, and share it with me.'

'But it's your thoughts we'd—'

'And I'll explicitly acknowledge your contribution as a collaborator. That's my condition.'

'Well . . . Thank you.'

'Call me when you've got something. Endit.'

The virtual holo disappeared from Rafaella's awareness.

Now I'm alone.

'House, give me privacy for one hour.'

In lotus, she sank her chin and closed her eyes, deep into trance. She felt like a miner excavating the caverns of her own mind, chipping and picking away at internal walls, rearranging her geometry of self. And then she was ready.

To enjoy!

Her internal buffer screamed.

Come to me, Daniel Deighton.

And he burst out, flooding into her; she yelled in ecstasy.

You're mine!

A tsunami of pleasure, orders of magnitude beyond anything before, crashed through her.

You're the first.

She cried out again as cognitive patterns and raw emotions swirled and tore inside her.

The first of so very many.

It was profoundly satisfying. Yet she remained so hungry.

I could eat the world.

And soon perhaps she would.

Behind the study hall was a bluegrass park bordered with indigo trees. Alisha stepped out of the building and onto the grass, and considered kicking off her shoes, or commanding them to dissolve into her other garments. Whether her conversation with Luculenta Rafaella Stargonier had been success or failure, she was not sure; but the outcome was certainly a challenge

New research. For a guest speaker's talk.

It was not as if Alisha was aiming to get a doctorate in the subject. On the other hand, if she managed to impress such a Luculenta, there would be tangible advantages.

Across the park, she could see Dr Helsen talking to a burly man. Thinking back, Alisha recalled her first sight of Helsen from the saucer-balcony, and the way that Roger had stared at both her and – yes, this same man.

Blinking her smartlenses to magnify, Alisha lipread Helsen's words.

'—to make the call, Greg. Now we wait to ... Look, there she is.'

Shit.

Alisha double-blinked back to normal vision. Helsen was waving at her.

They were talking about me.

She advanced toward them. Helsen came to meet her, while the man – Greg, presumably – stayed where he was.

So she won't have to introduce you?

'Alisha. I was wondering if you'd been able to contact Rashella Stargonier.'

'Yes, although that's not her name.'

'Excuse me?'

'She's Luculenta Rafaella Stargonier now. A recent change.'

Trained to notice minutiae, Alisha noted the dilation of Helsen's irises, a fifth of a second before she looked down to her right.

Surprised pleasure?

It was an odd reaction.

'But you've talked to her,' said Helsen. 'Did she say yes?'

Now her tonality was lower and slower, as if fighting hesitation. As if puzzled by something.

'No, but she didn't turn me down outright. I've got to do some work to impress her.'

'Well ...'

'And I'd like to do it. In fact I'm determined to, Dr Helsen.'

'Good for you, Alisha. Let me ... Let me know how you get on.'

'Of course, Doctor.'

'Then I'll let you go. See you tomorrow.'

Helsen turned and walked away. The man, Greg, was already gone. Maybe waiting to meet up with Helsen out of sight?

Why would he do that?

But it was strange, the disappointment in Helsen's voice, as if she had expected more from Alisha's call to the Luculenta.

I wish Roger was here.

Speaking of strange, why had he seemed so withdrawn and jumpy the night before leaving on holiday? And on a sudden offworld trip with his parents, so soon after the semester's start.

Until he returned, she would have to do the research by herself, which she was surely equipped to do. A lifetime of hothoused education, in her father's clanking steel house with little else to do but study, had left her capable of speeding up her thoughts for extended periods, just as an athlete will effectively slow down time under stressful conditions.

Her old schoolfriends – her few friends – had thought her a genius; but the truth was, her primary talent consisted of working hard.

So it was time to prove herself yet again.

Rafaella let him loose inside her, the memory of Daniel, and she arched back on her flowing carpet, screaming with ecstasy, shuddering, and finally laughing as the absorption took hold, an opened dam releasing the flood into a large, welcoming lake: turbulent at first, then a deep sense of changes in the dark spaces where sunlight did not reach.

Part of her contained a memory of flying the quickglass glider, staring down at the Rafaella-figure from altitude, and wondering not so about her so much as her ecologist-gardener, Greg Ranulph.

Did Greg plant the plexcore?

Or were his suspicious actions related to something else? And if so, were they in fact innocent? She remembered, as Daniel, devising the new query algorithms, knowing they were not yet proven.

That was something to determine fast. She created some netSprites – with even more ease than before – and set them loose in Skein to find out what they could about Greg Ranulph.

Her forebear, Rafael, had hesitated before striking in Skein; but she felt so much more confident, particularly with Daniel's knowledge of the peacekeeper instruction sets, and besides . . .

the hunger was inside her, and she could handle more minds, maybe three or four.

Maybe more.

She laughed at her own greed.

From among all the Luculenti she had dealt with in the past, she chose the top eight, ranked according to another algorithm devised on the spot. All of them were highly ranked, successful in business and in learning; all lived in Lucis City or the environs; and all were here on Fulgor right now.

Yes. Do it.

Rafaella loosed her code.

In Lucis City, Chen Hu-Seng stopped what he was doing to gape at the shocking intrusion in his mind. Two kilometres away, Dianne O'Mara dropped five simultaneous corporate takeovers in mid-transaction, then severed all links in Skein – all save the one she could not close, the ultra-high-bandwidth channel linking her to Rafaella Stargonier.

Arne Svenson suddenly fell as he was demonstrating a somersault to his gymnastics class. Typically he composed poetry in three simultaneous languages while he taught them tumbling skills. His attention was already engaged fully; when Rafaella snapped her link into him, he was done for.

Stephanie Argentum and Yukiko Kaku were in the same physical room, checking over the suborbital flyer Yukiko had designed for aurora research over the south pole. They jerked, stared at each other, then fell, their plexwebs already overwhelmed by vampire code.

Dev Boaz was arching back in orgasm when the code struck. His non-Luculenta partner whimpered at the unexpected strength of her own climax. But Dev continued to shudder and moan before giving a final exhalation, then slumping.

And then the woman was screaming, as her world turned awful.

Scott Talwin was in contemplation, kneeling in *seiza*, buttocks on heels. His consciousness roamed through abstract mathematical spaces, exploring theorems in social topopsychology, the emergent laws that governed thinking driven by the spatial relationships of real and virtual cultural settings.

His model predicted increasing behavioural flexibility from a certain segment of the population who were most comfortable with the latest morphing architecture, driven by the quickglass floating cities of Molsin, now increasingly popular on Fulgor. So far the data matched his predictive model.

At the edge of his awareness was a hint of—

No!

—darkness, pain and chaos magnifying to total agony.

Then death.

While all this was happening, Hailey Recht, the final chosen victim, was fighting back.

She was a Skein designer, an associate of the Via Lucis Institute who knew the LuxPrime protocols – even the ultra-secure financial interface, the bedrock of all transactions, each amount a vector in multidimensional space. All parts of her conscious, subconscious and superconscious minds were in alignment, like a fully committed athlete with exact technique. She braced herself against the attack, holding back the ravening code.

Furiously, she worked in Skein. The virtual world depended on a physical substrate of a trillion billion processors across the face of Fulgor: inlaid in quickglass walls and quickstone floors, every smart artefact sharing its power. If Skein was an ocean of computation, then Hailey Recht was a dolphin, a virtuoso.

Suddenly she was blinded. Rafaella's code – already Hailey knew the identity of her attacker – slammed through every plexweb portal, cutting her off from Skein. This was devastating, but not the end. She was still a code designer extraordinaire; and she retained the computational arena that was her own mind.

Milliseconds passed.

Still she fought, for an entire tenth of a second. And kept on fighting.

Half a second elapsed.

By now she had pushed back the advance but the bulwarks were straining, and it was hard to keep shoring up the barriers. The vampire code grew stronger and smarter by the pico-second. She was going to die. Reaching out in the physical world, desperate to write Rafaella Stargonier's name, she trembled and—

Two seconds.

—fell back, eyes rolling up, and her corpse slumped.

Now, on the floor in Mansion Stargonier, Rafaella truly writhed and howled, filled with painful joy, the torture of ecstasy, memories and awareness of eight more minds – such superb minds – torn apart and blended with her own dark core, her intentions strengthening with every second, her evolving self faster and more powerful.

Call her Rafaella; call her human. These are approximately true. Labels attach to referents more complex than the words.

Reality changes.

The part of her that was Rafael flowed like howling blood throughout her; the part that had been Rashella added pitiless ambition; while the part that once was Hailey Recht remembered expertise the others never dreamed of, a mastery of Skein.

Powerful and different, vastly complex, there was only one simple categorisation that applied to the emergent gestalt.

She/it was a predator.

TWENTY-TWO

LUNA, 502013 AD

Gavriela slept, and stared at her surroundings: a high-sided hall, a glistening table surrounded by high-backed chairs ... and two beings of living crystal, a woman and a man, watching her.

—I've dreamed of you before.

The woman's smile was a gleam of fluid transparency.

—Welcome back, Gavriela.

—And your name is Kenna. I recall.

Then she re-examined the hall, while tuning in to the feelings of her own crystalline body, noting the lack of breathing.

—We're in a vacuum?

—On your Earth's moon. Of course.

The other being was a man, lean and muscular, a scar along one crystal cheek.

—I don't recall you, I'm sorry. I'm Gavriela.

—My name is Ulfr, good lady. So you are a warrior?

—I hardly think so.

She was asleep somewhere, and yet this was real.

—Not somewhere, somewhen. Half a million years ago.

Could Kenna read her mind?

—No, but I understand what you need me to understand.

All of this was impossible; yet all of it contained an immediacy, a heightening of every sensation that told her it was happening.

—I'd forgotten my previous time here. Will I remember this one?

—Perhaps, but the part of your mind engaging in this conversation is not the part that controls your most conscious waking thoughts.

—Could you explain that more fully?

—Wait. We're not all here yet. Ah . . .

The vacuum shimmered as if refracting light, rainbow spectra washed and flowed, and for a second Gavriela thought she saw two outlines, one of them odd – *antlers?* – then the other solidified into a crystalline man while the first was gone.

—Roger?

—Gavriela?

Kenna stepped between them, reflections sliding across her body, looking from one to the other.

—You've interacted directly already? This is a good sign, my friends. And our comrade here is Ulfr, a warrior.

Roger held out his fist; Ulfr grasped his crystal forearm. Roger understood, and returned the clasp. Then he turned to Kenna.

—How can we be here now, and yet alive in the past?

To Gavriela this was impossible, despite her acceptance of the situation.

—Can our timelines criss-cross without paradox? I can't see how.

It seemed obvious that if they communicated across time and remembered in the past, any number of paradoxes became enabled.

—Our meetings here will always occur in the same sequential order, as experienced by each of us individually. Call it a form of temporal tensegrity.

Roger was nodding, but Gavriela did not quite understand.

—I don't . . .

—It's a concept that will make sense in your personal future, else the thought would not have resonated at all.

That sounded like a paradox, except that their communication was not via sound; but Gavriela noticed how Ulfr had made a sign with his fist. Suddenly it came to her that Ulfr understood the words via his own frame of reference, using concepts that she would consider superstitious – because that gesture was to ward off evil, she was sure of it.

None of her own reactions were making sense. Why wasn't she panicking, filled with hysteria?

Then Kenna added:

—*No one in your lifetime will discover a basic equation that distinguishes future from past. Only the qualified generalisation you call the second law of thermodynamics even attempts the task, and it is not fundamental. There is no such thing as a closed system.*

Gavriela blinked her transparent eyelids. For sure, if you described a particle's motion via an equation, whether in mechanics or electromagnetism – such as a billiard ball floating through space – and then replaced *t* with minus *t*, you now had a picture of the same thing moving backwards, with time (or maybe just electric charge) reversed. The new situation would not appear to violate any physical laws; it would just run *backwards*. So the basic equations did not explain why you cannot unbreak an egg or grow younger by the day.

Roger touched Gavriela's shoulder, and there was a spark of light, perhaps some odd reflection of the hall's illumination.

—*Don't worry, I don't understand either. And I'm alive much later than . . . Kenna, how can I know this? My life is centuries later than Gavi's.*

—*You have good intuition.*

—*Is that an answer?*

—*It's deeper than you think.*

Gavriela looked at Ulfr. Clearly the warrior was content to stand apart from the conversation for now. Perhaps he considered it the realm of wizardry.

—*Our brains are centuries in the past, yet we're interacting with here and now. Is that what you're saying?*

—*Partly, for sure.*

—*Therefore information is propagating backwards in time.*

Kenna smiled at her and Roger.

—*In terms that are common to both of you . . . If you stare at a star that is a hundred lightyears away, how long has that photon been travelling?*

—*A century, of course.*

—*And how much time has elapsed as far as the photon is concerned?*

Gavriela checked for Roger's reaction, but it was no more

than a raised transparent eyebrow. Perhaps the new relativity of her time remained intact for Roger's generation.

—No time at all.

—All that energy in the universe, more than the so-called matter, and it comprises splinters of timeless space. A photon is born and dies, travels perhaps across the universe, yet the duration of its life is zero.

That was what the equations said. Gavriela did not expect to understand the concepts intuitively, for she was a human being exploring realms beyond the macroscopic world, beyond the environment humanity evolved to cope with.

—How does that account for what we're experiencing?

—It doesn't, but symmetry is one of the most powerful concepts of all. Consider this possibility: splinters of spaceless time, orthogonal to photons. Call them orthons for now.

Gavriela shook her head, trying to incorporate the concept in her understanding.

—I need to think about it.

—That's one way of formulating our interaction. At least part of it. Enough to work with for the time being.

Roger smiled. Perhaps there was more subtle humour here than Gavriela recognized. Or perhaps it was his different knowledge of physics that made his comprehension more sophisticated. If only she could learn from him!

Then her fear of paradox returned.

—We're doing something dangerous here, aren't we?

—Yes.

This seemed to be what Ulfr was waiting for.

—So what is our plan of battle, Lady Kenna?

—We devise a campaign, a war, not a single conflict . . . whatever it may boil down to in the final days. Have you identified the enemy?

Gavriela shared glances with Roger and Ulfr.

—Those touched by darkness?

—That's part of it.

Kenna waved towards the table, but it was not an invitation to sit.

—We will share knowledge and strength, remembering some

consciously. Our first task is to observe, to identify the enemy truly.

Ulfr was looking at the spears upon the walls.

—*And then we fight.*

This was scaring Gavriela. However much she accepted what was occurring, she was no fighter, and talk of warfare made her sick. Then she realized that Roger must feel the same way, as he asked:

—*How? And what for?*

But Kenna's answer was directed more towards Ulfr.

—*First we observe, then we deduce the enemy's intentions.*

Ulfr bowed his head.

—*You speak wisdom, Lady Kenna.*

Roger was looking at Gavriela, and she felt sure his thoughts followed hers. Of the three of them, it was this Ulfr who most closely accepted what Kenna was saying, and was most closely in tune with her intentions. Gavriela and Roger's sophisticated understanding counted for little.

Perhaps Kenna sensed the same thing.

—*We are all important. Every one of us.*

—*Are we?*

—*Immensely more than you think, good Gavriela. Immensely more.*

Roger raised his crystal hands.

—*So what do we do now?*

—*Why . . .*

Kenna's smile was a rainbow sculpture.

—*You wake up, of course.*

It was ended.

TWENTY-THREE

FULGOR, 2603 AD

In their quickglass bubble-capsule, they moved along a low Fulgor orbit – the planet fat and full, creamy-looking below them – heading for the apex of Barleysugar Spiral. Roger was lost in strange recollections of dreaming in Labyrinth, wondering whether the shock of being in another universe had done strange things to his brain, to his subconscious mind.

Mum kept her voice low as she talked to Dad.

'Varlan didn't want us to hang around, did he?'

'Probably Helena was giving him a hard time.'

'So when you and Varlan talked in private ... Was there anything Roger and I should know?'

'No. Maybe.'

He looked bereft. For a moment, Roger came out of his reverie, wondering how Dad could bear to part from his ship and return to his quotidian existence down below, to his life that was one long acting performance.

After leaving the ship wearing quickglass suits as before, they had jetted to Varlan Trelayne's orbital, where Varlan was quiet and his wife Helena once more did not appear. Meanwhile Dad's ship returned to mu-space, to do whatever it did while waiting for his call.

'Xavier Spalding is an interesting character,' said Dad finally. 'And some of his merchandise could be classified as weapon systems, in the right context on the right world.'

Roger pulled himself into the conversation.

'You're saying Alisha's father is an arms dealer?'

'That's exaggerating Varlan's findings. Let's say he has more clout and more connections with interesting parts of society than you'd expect, given his respectability.'

Then Dad's expression compressed with concentration, his gaze defocusing. An incoming private call. His throat moved with subvocalized speech. Then he spoke aloud.

'Since this affects my family, I want them in on this.'

A real-image holo sharpened before them: the shaven head of Xavier Spalding.

'That's fine. If Alisha were at risk, I'd forgo all other considerations.'

'I'm not clear what you're offering, or the price.'

'Future friendship is enough.'

'That's not specific, but anyway, in return for what?'

'There have been certain serious crimes among Luculenti recently. Nothing made public.'

'And you think I'm involved?'

'If you were, Carl, I wouldn't be warning you.'

'Warning me about what?'

'All arrivals at Barleysugar Spiral are being deepscanned by peace-keepers.'

Mum sucked in air, then bit her lip.

'That's perfectly all right with me,' said Dad.

'If you've nothing to hide.'

'I don't, in fact.'

'I mean absolutely nothing at any level, no subterfuge of any kind. Nothing to show up using the new scanners they're deploying in public for the first time.'

Dad looked very calm.

'Designed to counteract all known subversion and shielding methods,' Xavier Spalding went on. *'And since my folk had some involvement with the design, I'm rather proud of it.'*

'So why tell me?'

'Well . . . Hello over there, Roger. Alisha seems fond of you.'

'Er, hello, sir.'

'Call me Xavier. And allow me to present you with a gift, Carl. And my respects to you, Mrs Blackstone.'

Dad blinked.

'Received. Thank—'

'Endit.'

Mum said: 'What has he sent you, Carl?'

'Full schematics and in-house control codes for developers.'

'The scanner design,' said Roger, 'but not the shieldware?'

'Perhaps they never coded any.'

'So do we go back to Varlan's place?'

'No. Let's not compromise him further.'

'But if they deepscan us for real' – Mum glanced up to her right, envisioning consequences – 'they'll suspect Varlan too.'

'No, it's okay.' A complex three-dimensional tangle of arcs and nodes glowed above Dad's tu-ring. 'Our current shieldware can upgrade itself to cope.'

'Are you sure?'

'No. But I'll let you know.'

Mum and Roger stared at each other.

This is nuts.

But in a few seconds, Dad was chuckling.

'We got it, folks. The developers' control codes swung it for us.'

'So—?'

'So let me deploy the deltas to your tu-rings, and we'll be ready for them.'

Part of one wall was transparent, revealing black space and the growing orange splendour of Barleysugar Spiral.

Roger's tu-ring chimed, acknowledging the upgrade.

'Got it,' he said, as Mum nodded.

'And now we work on staying calm,' said Dad.

They continued to drift towards Barleysugar Spiral.

Among the uniformed officers was a Luculentus in civilian clothes. His hair was coppery, intertwined with bronze wires, and he introduced himself as Superintendent Sunadomari.

'Pleased to meet you,' said Dad. 'Is there something going on?'

'We're just performing extra checks.' Sunadomari looked at

one of the officers, who nodded. 'And of course you're fine.'

Other arrivals, newly disembarked from spaceborne bubble-capsules, were walking through checkpoints as they entered the apex lounge. Some headed for the bars or restaurants, to enjoy the view from space for a while longer; others streamed for the central column, and lined up to wait for a free descent capsule.

'You're not checking departures?' asked Dad.

'Actually, we are. Down at the surface, before they enter.'

'Ah. That makes sense, Superintendent.'

Roger wondered where the new scanners were. From the body language of the officers, the tightening of their muscles when passengers passed through certain locations, he thought the scanners were looped in arches through the quickglass walls and ceiling. Insinuating the scanners inside the architecture was discreet – a smartmiasma would have been more obvious, though only to a minority: those with extended turing functions, and Luculenti.

'You've a successful career, Mr Blackstone. I don't suppose you've ever met Dianne O'Mara or Yukiko Kaku?'

'No, I don't believe so. What's their line?'

'Lab equipment, mainly, for offworld export.'

'I'll look out for them.'

'Or Stephanie Argentum?'

'Head of the Silver House?'

'That's right.'

'Um, I talked to her deputy twice for short periods, a couple of years back. I can send you logs of our meetings, if it's official. One of their subsidiaries hired me for a short project.'

'No need.' Sunadomari's eyelid gave the faintest of flickers. 'Just wondering if we had mutual acquaintances. Please have a pleasant trip home.'

'Thank you.'

Roger followed his parents, knowing they would have seen what he had: Sunadomari accessing private logs while talking to Dad, using peacekeeper privileges. Checking Dad's story, and fast-viewing the meeting logs.

This might have been worrying, but as they walked on he could hear the superintendent having a similar conversation with a newly arrived couple, asking about some other acquaintance they might have in common. At certain levels of commerce and society, connected-world thinking applied: on Fulgor, you were rarely more than three 'handshakes' removed from any chosen person.

Their descent through the shaft of Barleysugar Spiral was slow and steady: the capsule lightly scented with roses and playing soft baroque music; their conversation apparently free – wondering what the peacekeepers were up to, and whether there had been a reason for Sunadomari's particular questions. But their choice of words and tonality – and visual expression – formed an elegant masterpiece of subterfuge, every nuance designed to convince watchers of their innocence.

Roger's inward preoccupation would appear natural, he hoped; but no one would guess what he was thinking of: strange half-seen dreams, soundbites from odd conversations, all involving people he knew closely, yet whose names were lost to him.

Maybe I'm turning psychotic.

It could happen, though he was careful in his choice of study methods. On Earth, Dad had told him, research on 'logotropes', a kind of viral alternative to Luculentus plexwebs, had caused disaster. Their most able designers had fled to the world of Nulapeiron, adopting new identities among the founding colonists, hoping to continue their work. It was one of the few pieces of covert intelligence Dad had shared – dated, but still secret – and it had been to discourage Roger from trying out certain new thoughtware for Fulgidi who were desperate to enhance their minds.

'Mindhacks are dangerous,' Dad had said. 'Especially one designed for a different kind of neurophysiology.'

'Meaning an ordinary human.'

'You're human enough for me, son.'

Now, in the descending capsule, they were chatting like normal folk; but it was an act, therefore underlining the difference between Roger and his college friends. They would be worrying about academic assignments, granting them an importance that seemed nonsensical to him. Even Alisha, who should find everything easy, seemed tense about her studies.

His tu-ring chimed, and he accepted the incoming call.

'Hello, Alisha,' he said.

Dad raised an eyebrow, clearly visible beyond the virtual head-and-shoulders image of Alisha in Roger's smartlenses. So Roger had just been thinking of her. It wasn't as though he thought about her all the time, was it?

Was it?

'*Roger, did you have a nice holiday?*'

'It was, um, relaxing. I guess.' He switched to subvocalizing, as his parents smiled. 'Is everything all right with you?'

'*I guess. I talked to the Luculenta woman, Rafaella Stargonier.*'

'Er ... Right, the one Helsen needs as a guest speaker. How did that go?'

'*A bit weird. Wants me to demonstrate my knowledge of the subject. Show her some original research, which she'll incorporate in the talk with full acknowledgement.*'

'That *is* weird.'

'*Actually, it's the sort of mindgame Luculenti like to play, and it's her real fee for making the effort to come visit in person.*'

'You so don't need my help in researching anything.'

'*I do, even if it's just someone to talk to. And it's not just that. My father's been acting odd, even asked about you. Er ... I didn't mean to say that, actually.*'

'So you don't plan everything you say?'

'*Hardly. So, do you want to just go for a walk or something when you get back?*'

In his mind's eye, nothing to do with virtual holos, he saw himself holding hands with her.

'Yes. Let's do that.'

A feeling of lightness meant the capsule was slowing; or perhaps it was something to do with the promise of Alisha's company.

'And if you *have any original thoughts on realspace hyperdimensions'* – her image smiled – *'I'll make sure you get a mention, too.'*

'All right. Deal. Um ... We're just reaching ground level now.'

'Then I'll see you soon?'

'Sure.'

'Good.'

Her holo faded. Roger blinked at Dad.

'Just someone I know,' he said.

'Right.' Dad glanced at Mum. 'You know my expertise is in diplomacy, don't you?'

'Er, sure, Dad.'

'So just how *is* your love life, son?'

'I—'

Mum laughed, and in a second so did Roger.

'I'll get back to you on that,' he said.

Once on solid ground beneath a clear green sky, they called for separate aircabs: one for Mum and Dad to go straight home, the other for Roger to return directly to Lucis City. They hugged and made smart remarks before climbing into their respective vehicles.

Then Roger's aircab ascended, giving him a nice view of the great braided quickglass mass of Barleysugar Spiral reaching straight up through the atmosphere. Seconds later, he was at altitude, speeding towards the city.

Original thoughts on hyperdimensions?

He pondered this.

Is that the way to your heart, Alisha Spalding?

If it was, then he, Roger Blackstone, had insights other people lacked. Because it was not only Pilots who traversed mu-space – there was one other realspace species who had that capability ... plus they could manipulate realspace in a way impossible for Pilots. They were part of the reason that Pilots maintained an intelligence service.

There was a resource right here in Lucis City that could help Alisha, a research institute that was theoretically not secret, but whose lack of public interfaces meant it was hidden away as if invisible. It was only because Dad kept an occasional watch on the place that Roger knew of its existence, dedicated to studying the aliens who no longer kept an embassy on Fulgor, though they once had. At some point they simply stopped coming – removing trade competition for Pilots – for no reason that anyone knew. Well, perhaps intelligence services had secret information, but one thing that was public knowledge was the impenetrability of the aliens' motives.

Zajinets were strange.

TWENTY-FOUR

EARTH, 2146 AD

There were going to be repercussions for bringing Sharp back to Earth. Rekka had known that since she first had the idea. In orbit around EM-0036, when the so-called *pre*-contact team assembled in the passenger hold, her colleagues were eager to meet Sharp – Mary Stelanko, as team leader, was the first to converse with him – but their raised eyebrows and wry faces were a clear signal. Everyone was used to interpreting dry regulations on the ground, in the messiness of real situations. They might be envious of Rekka's work with Sharp; but they were glad they would not be facing the same bureaucratic grilling.

Luckily, this ship carried the new delta-bands instead of injecting anaesthetics. It took a few minutes to reconfigure a band for Sharp's use. His neurology, while not even DNA-based, had emergent structural similarities to Terran evolution; and his species slept after a fashion: more like dolphins than humans, shutting down different parts of the brain at different times. It was Rekka who placed the band on his forehead beneath his antlers, as he lay back on a morphed couch big enough to hold him. His amber eyes narrowed to horizontal slits, then closed.

Then the team lay on their own couches, activated their delta-bands – and woke up in Earth orbit, beginning a gliding descent to Desert One, some thirty kilometres from Tucson Crater. Within minutes they were on the ground, settling before a collection of geodesic buildings. Several vehicles were advancing: big TAVs in UNSA white-and-blue, their thermoacoustic engines whispering.

One TAV was designated to go straight to the xeno facility. Rekka got in with Sharp, and no one objected. Inside the vehicle, Piotr Poliakov nodded to Rekka while staring at Sharp. Poliakov scarcely glanced at Rekka for the duration of the drive, or their walk – surrounded by UNSA scientists and security – through the air-conditioned corridors, heading for the lab suite they had activated with only minutes' notice, since the Pilot had informed them from orbit of the extra passenger.

But not all xenos were new species to be investigated; some familiar entities used the facility as a place to stay when visiting the base, since rooms could be altered to create chemically comfortable environments. Now, two lumpy shapes far bigger than humans were lumbering this way: one formed of red Arizona sandstone, all pebbles and boulders; the other more amorphous, formed of rubbery yellow sulphur (an allotrope, bearing the same relation to the more common powdery form as ozone bears to oxygen), but glistening with inserted quartz, or maybe diamonds.

Rekka had never seen a Zajinet before, not for real. Of course these two individuals – big, roughly humanoid, but only in outline – were clothed in Terran substances; their naked forms would be glowing lattices of light, usually of one pure frequency: often crimson, the colour of burning strontium; or the green of igniting copper; or occasionally an odd shade of sapphire blue.

The sulphurous individual clomped past Rekka, Sharp and the others, as if it had not noticed them. But the sandstone figure stopped.

<<No ending, though we have met.>>

<<Electric taste, they can not.>>

<<You are unlike, so good.>>

<<No beginning, though we have not met.>>

Sharp sniffed, his eyes widening. Perhaps he was going to attempt a reply, but with a grinding noise the Zajinet recommenced its motion and lumbered off, following its sulphurous companion.

'They are strange creatures,' Rekka said.

'No,' came the reply from Sharp's chest speaker.

Poliakov raised his eyebrows.

'Their cognitive structures,' he said, 'evince macroscopic quantum superposition. All known sentients from any world are composite minds, multiple overlapping personalities; but the Zajinets embody the concept in a more literal way. They rarely broadcast anything other than four simultaneous messages, hardly ever comprehensible.'

Poliakov could work on speaking more clearly himself, in Rekka's opinion. Sharp did not reply.

Then Rekka's infostrand-bracelet beeped.

'McStuart here. Please come to conference room 21-A, Rekka.'

'Shit.'

Beside her, Sharp emitted a peppermint odour, his analogue of a human chuckle.

'Right away.' She thumbed her bracelet, ending comms. 'Sorry, Sharp. Dr Poliakov, you'll look after my friend, won't you?'

'Of course. Sharp, I am very pleased to meet you.'

'You smell sincere,' said Sharp. 'Thank you.'

Poliakov's smile was open-mouthed, his eyes wide and shining.

Rekka grinned, clapped Sharp on the arm, then went off to face the bureaucrats.

After the debriefing, Rekka went to the refectory. It was a long, low-ceilinged canteen bouncing with the energy of conversation from some two hundred engineers, scientists and support staff. A thin man came loping towards her, smiling wide, opening his arms.

'Hey, you.'

'Simon. My God, Simon.'

They kissed to applause from nearby tables.

'Get a room,' called someone. 'Oh, you already have.'

Rekka pulled back. 'Is that Gwillem?'

'Am I my brother's keeper?'

'Someone should be.'

Gwillem was heavier than Simon, bearded and with thicker hair on top, but you could tell they were brothers. He came up and clasped his bearish arms around both Rekka and Simon, just for a second.

'You, dear Rekka, are the talk of Desert One right now.'

'Uh-huh,' said Simon. 'On account of the confidential mission she's just completed.'

'It's not confidential, it's just not been made public yet.' Gwillem gestured at a table. 'Come and sit with us, both of you.'

Mary Stelanko was there, but no sign of her partner Amber.

'I'll get you some food.' Simon held out a chair for Rekka. 'The usual preferences?'

'Sure.' Rekka settled on the chair.

'You okay?' Mary asked.

'The debrief went as well as expected. Unfortunately.'

'So are you grounded?' Gwillem raised his fork. 'Excuse me while I carry on stuffing my face. Got to make sure my food's digested by sixteen hundred.'

'Probably, and what's at sixteen hundred?'

'Aiki demo.' Gwillem nodded to Mary. 'Kinda thing your sweetheart does, right?'

'Did. A long time ago.'

'Well, I kinda gather it's out of fashion.'

Both aikido and Feldenkrais movement had been part of Pilot training since the first voyages into mu-space; but in the early days, things had been different, the sacrifices awful. Some seventeen per cent of Pilots now were natural born, their eyes black-on-black, requiring no surgery to survive in that other continuum; and that percentage kept increasing. Pilots like Mary's partner would eventually retire – three or four decades hence, in Amber's case.

The current training curriculum was under critical review.

'So,' said Mary. 'You're *probably* grounded?'

'McStuart was ambiguous about the future.'

'But clear about his present mood?'

'You got it, exactly. How was *your* debriefing, anyway? They can't blame you for my actions.'

'They can try, but it'll backfire on them if they do.'

'Son of a bitch,' said Gwillem.

'Excuse me?'

'Top table. Look who's here.'

Rekka and Mary looked past Simon, who was approaching with a tray, to the far table where men and women in business suits were sat. And one white-haired man in particular.

'Professor Jiang-Shen,' said Mary. 'That bastard.'

Rekka shook her head.

'What?' asked Gwillem.

'You know about my biological parents.'

'Er, yes. I remember the story, not that *you* can remember that far back, since you were a baby.'

'It was the Changeling Plague that got my father. That's why my mother tried to kill me in the Suttee Pavilion. Along with herself.'

'I forgot that part. Sorry.'

'What part?' Simon put a veggie biryani in front of Rekka, the same in his own place, and sat. 'Am I missing something good?'

'Something bad.' Gwillem nodded to the top table.

'Ah. No one ever proved it was his biotech that got loose.'

'Nor will they, while he's so useful to us.'

'Good point.'

Mary had been eating with her eyes closed, slowly.

'The food's so good,' she said. 'So where's Professor–? Ah, I see him. And the two special guests.'

'You're up to date on the gossip already?' Rekka looked at her infostrand-bracelet, considered going online, then shrugged. 'So who are the special guests?'

'Those two.' Simon pointed. 'With the near-identical features.'

A man and a woman, aged somewhere between twenty and forty, with flawless skin and black hair, the man wearing a goatee. They smiled with charisma, the centre of everyone's focus.

'Brother and sister?'

'Cousins, in fact. The Higashionnas, Japanese-Brazilian, from Rio. UN senators, and real superstars.'

'Hence my dramatic and exciting aiki demo for the VIPs,' said Gwillem. 'Which you'll all be attending?'

'Haven't you got a lab to work in?' asked Simon.

'And haven't you got a management cubicle to do no work in at all?'

'Huh. Sixteen hundred hours?'

'Right.'

'I'll be there. Rekka?'

'If I can't get in to see my special friend,' said Rekka, 'then I might come along.'

'Special?' said Gwillem.

'Handsomely endowed.' Mary spread her arms wide. 'I mean like *this* big.'

Simon held his fork underhand, and waved it back and forth between Mary and Rekka.

'You better be talking about antlers.'

'What else is there?' asked Rekka.

'You don't remember?'

'Certainly not.'

At four p.m., Rekka was sitting on a bleacher seat with Sharp on her right, Simon to her left. Poliakov sat the other side of Sharp. On blue mats in the sports hall centre, some thirty people in white pyjama-like jackets and what looked like black ankle-length skirts were rolling and rehearsing footwork, warming up. Some carried blunt wooden daggers.

'Where's Gwillem?' said Rekka.

'There.' Simon's arm encircled her. 'See?'

'Oh, yeah. How come you never took up this kind of stuff?'

'I wasn't the one who got bullied in school.'

'You're kidding.'

'His growth spurt came late, and there was something about his middle name that got people taunting him, once they learned it.'

'Guillaume?'

'Which you can pronounce two ways, one of which the kids found funny.'

'Strange thing to latch on to.'

'Yeah . . . He turned out all right though, didn't he?'

Rekka leaned her weight into him, feeling the slender muscles beneath, so different from the massive fur-covered alien on her right. Then she noticed two things: Sharp was very still, nostrils wide; and Poliakov was leaning backwards, avoiding Sharp's bulk, so he could talk to her across Sharp's back.

'You are a bad person, Rekka Chandri.'

'Excuse me?'

'You spent considerable time with our friend, and he does *not* make you whimper with desire at his will, does he? Unlike poor Claudia and Justine in the lab.'

Now it was Simon who said: 'Excuse *me?*'

A giggle rose inside her.

'You might want to check my biofact logs.'

'I did. You made nose filters.'

'Of course.'

'But you forgot to mention that.'

'Oh, McStuart was so kind to me in debriefing that the joy overwhelmed me.'

'Rekka, Rekka.' Simon's hug tightened. 'Bad girl.'

Sharp's attention was not on the aikido people down on the mats, but on the VIP seating, where the Japanese-Brazilian cousins, the UN senators, were taking their places. Rekka stared, about to ask what was wrong, then realized she was too used to being alone with him. Any reply he made would come straight out of his chest speaker, loud and clear to everyone.

I never thought about private conversation.

Later she would have to ask Poliakov's advice.

'You're not annoyed too much, are you?' she said to him.

'Our friend's ability to fine-tune his synthesized emissions is incredible. He exactly matched the energy resonance of an alien species, meaning us. And in so little time.'

'He emits human pheromones?' asked Simon. 'How is that possible?'

'Sharp fine-tunes his output molecules, but they're not human pheromones. Unless you think that humans smell molecules according to their shape, you'll realize it's very possible.'

'Er—'

'Simon's expertise lies outside bio sciences,' said Rekka.

'Scent receptors respond to patterned electrical resonance – to put it simply, the receptor resonates with the molecule – which is *related* to molecular shape but is not the same thing. In particular, two different configurations can smell identical, so long as the energy levels are correct.'

'Oh,' said Simon.

Rekka snuggled back against him. Down below, a thin Japanese man, also in white jacket and long black skirt – actually it was a split skirt, she realized – walked to the centre of the mats, knelt down and sat back on his heels. The others, Gwillem included, followed suit. The Japanese man clapped his hands several times, in a careful way that denoted ritual, and everybody bowed, forehead to mat.

Someone announced the man as Akazawa-sensei, and then the demonstration began, with fifteen pairs of aggressors and defenders. Attackers threw graceful punches or knife-thrusts, then cartwheeled to the ground as defenders became an axis of rotation, using angular momentum to put their attacker down.

Rekka remembered Sharp's people, huge bannermen rushing toward her campsite, and thought that perhaps real violence was something messier and more brutal than the nice display below.

On the other hand, Akazawa-sensei had enormous presence, and a centred composure that perhaps he could maintain under any pressure. Sharp looked at him, then at Rekka, then gave a nod: a learned human gesture.

He smells the charisma.

Part of what the Chinese called *chi*, the part relating to aura or charisma, must be simply pheromonal emissions. Rekka had never thought of it before. The rest was balanced muscular tensegrity – her years of yoga taught her that. Aiki discipline for Pilots was to enhance their spatial awareness, to open up their proprioreceptive senses.

Gwillem attacked Akazawa-sensei with a wooden knife, but there was a blur of motion, and Gwillem lay on the mat, while Akazawa-sensei raised the knife in the air. Rekka had not seen the weapon changing hands.

The demo concluded with what looked like a free-for-all, Akazawa-sensei the calm, moving centre of the storm while attackers flew in all directions. Afterwards, Rekka clapped as hard as anyone, calling out approval, though she could not match the volume of Simon's cheers.

Afterwards, as they walked outdoors – Poliakov sure that Sharp would be fine in the bright Arizona sunshine, monitoring his blood chemistry nonetheless – they saw the Higashionna cousins, the UN senators, climbing into a TAV on the tarmac.

Sharp slowed, and so did Rekka, while Poliakov and Simon walked on.

'Only you can hear me?' The voice from Sharp's speaker was slightly muted, corresponding to subtle scent emission, but louder than a whisper. 'Is that right?'

'Only me, for the moment.'

It was hard for Sharp to calculate hearing distance.

'Why do you not fear them, those two?'

'Simon and Poliakov?'

'No. In the device.'

It took her a moment to understand the mistranslation. She pointed towards the TAV, which was starting to move off with the Higashionnas on board.

'Yes, Rekka. Do you not taste their evil?'

'Evil?'

'Can you not smell dark nothing?'

'I don't think so. No.'

Sharp turned and stopped. Rekka realized what he was looking at. Around the corner of one building, there was a hint of sandstone that moved, perhaps sulphurous yellow beyond.

The Zajinets.

Then they were not there.

What—?

It wasn't fast movement; it was something else. But then the aiki demo had seemed like magic.

'I can't believe it.'

The Zajinets had been standing there; now they were not.

TWENTY-FIVE

LABYRINTH, 2603 AD (REALSPACE-EQUIVALENT)

In the language called Aeternum, the word for *office* still existed, but it was marked as deprecated, meaning that at some point, in some future upgrade, the word would be dropped from the core vocabulary. Language affected thought, and change was necessary – in this trivial case, because people had long been able to work anywhere – but the Logos Academy was careful with semantic evolution. Pilots occasionally followed extreme-geodesic emergency flightpaths, including hellflights, and might return centuries later than departure, relative to Labyrinthine mean-geodesic time. Catching up with the language, through prepared upgrade paths, was a key part of arrival procedures.

Still, Max considered this golden room to be his office.

'I need to be sure,' he said out loud. 'I need to know what's there.'

=You know what Carl Blackstone saw.=

'Twenty-five years ago.'

=An insignificant duration, on these timescales.=

'I still need corroboration.'

=And will you tell the Council?=

'Why do you mention them?'

But now the golden walls were silent. Max ran a hand over his shaven scalp, then folded his massive forearms, revealed by his pushed-up sleeves. When people called Labyrinth a mysterious city, they had no idea how true that was.

He rubbed his face, then gestured a small holospace into being, and said: 'Will you fetch Avril Tarquelle now, please?'

'Sir,' said the Pilot in the image.

The holo winked out.

He strode to the doorway, where the wall melted open, then stood with arms folded, beneath the archway, observing the outer chamber. At first it was empty. Then slabs of nothingness rotated through the air, and a young red-headed female Pilot stepped out of the disturbance.

'How's it going, boss?'

'Very good, Avril. How's your ship?'

'Beautiful, as always.'

'Good. Come in.'

The inner office – what word would he use when the language eventually changed? – was shielded against direct geometric shortcuts. If an enemy appeared in the outer chamber, Max could wall himself off. Not that such a thing had ever happened. This was Ascension Annexe, and well protected, inside a city-world that itself was safe.

Call it professional paranoia. In the field, such habits saved lives.

'Relax.' Seats morphed into place. 'You've been feeling all right?'

Avril did not sit.

'If you're talking about Powell, sir, then I'm well over that bastard. Begging the commodore's pardon.'

Max laughed.

'Granted. So sit down, will you?'

'Sir.'

He gestured a holovolume into being. Avril examined the data, checking the trajectory figures, then sucked in a breath.

'The galactic core?'

'You see why I need a good Pilot.'

'I'll say.'

Few ordinary humans appreciated the complexity and risk associated with moving between universes. Scarcely anyone understood how the presence of great mass or energy made either continuum more difficult to leave or enter accurately. It was the difference between parachuting on to a playing-field-sized mattress versus a jagged mountain peak, all razor-edged outcrops and fatal precipices, buffeted by storms.

'All right.' Avril finally closed the holovolume down. 'I know where I'm going. What do I when I get there?'

'Take a peek, and come straight back.'

'Is that all?'

'Full stealth. Observe, record, bug out.'

'And no one the wiser?'

'Right.'

'Then I'm gone.'

Max walked her to the door. In the outer chamber, she summoned a fastpath rotation, stepped inside, and departed the way she arrived.

For a long time, Max just stared. Then he slammed a hammer-fist against the wall.

'Fuck.'

He went back in and sat.

=She has no family, no current relationships.=

'Avril's a terrific Pilot, and her ship is fast.'

=Is that the only reason you chose her?=

Max lowered his chin and clasped one hand across his face, fingertips pressing hard into his own skin. Then he let go and looked up.

He might have been about to speak, but a low chime sounded, and a holovolume opened.

'Hello, Max.'

It was a woman with white cropped hair, her face deeply lined, but her expression strong.

'Admiral Kaltberg.'

'Are you free at the moment?'

'Yes, ma'am.'

'The Admiralty Council is about to convene. We've had a last minute thought, and we'd like you to attend.'

'I'll be right there.'

She nodded, and the holo was gone.

'Last minute thought, indeed. I wonder what's going on.'

Max looked at the ceiling. 'You knew, of course.'

Labyrinth did not reply.

The Admiralty Council was in session when Max arrived in an outer chamber. Three Pilots, wearing black, gold-trimmed capes over their jumpsuits, saluted.

'We're to show you straight in, Commodore.'

'Go ahead.'

The big doors curled back, and Max entered with his escort. Once inside, the trio saluted, turned on their heels, and marched out. The doors folded into place without a sound.

At the head of the long table was Rear-Admiral Schenck. To his left was Admiral Kaltberg, her expression like stone. To Schenck's right was Admiral Turnbull, his face relaxed and smiling, which meant nothing.

Six other admirals sat at the table, all of them with their-eyes-only holovolumes open – Max could tell from their eye movements and the faintest glitter of reflection.

Turnbull said: 'We have some news for you, Max. A change of membership among us.'

Max raised an eyebrow. If Turnbull meant this Council, then he was talking about a group whose faces remained the same for decades.

'I'm standing down,' said Admiral Kaltberg. 'It's finally time.'

'Surely not, ma'am.'

Was she being forced out? Perhaps she was frailer than she had been. Perhaps it was simply age and the natural order of things.

'Kind of you to say so Max, but I'm retiring fully.'

'It's been my honour, Admiral.' He meant it. 'And it's been the service's privilege.'

'Then you'll ask Dr Sapherson to treat me gently?'

'Like one of the family, ma'am. The procedure grows more exact every year.'

'Good, because I'd like to hang on to what I can.'

There were chuckles from all but the youngest admirals,

some perhaps uncertain. At least two others were old enough to have mulled over the treatment, contemplating their own retirement.

Max still could not tell whether Admiral Kaltberg was retiring voluntarily or because she had lost some political game. Either way, there would be furious covert deals playing out right now, as cliques sought to put their own candidate in place, taking Kaltberg's seat.

This would be interesting.

'We decided to tell you in person' – at the head of the table, Schenck gestured around his colleagues – 'since you deserve to know. I can't exaggerate how important you are to this Council.'

The statement was ambiguous, causing Max to smile. Schenck was a consummate game-player, and rarely spoke without thought.

'Thank you for the compliment, sir.'

On one side of the table, two of the younger admirals, Whitwell and Asai, echoed Max's smile. They were supporters of Kaltberg; and Max thought it might be worthwhile to spend some time with each of them in private, over the next few days.

'So, that's probably all we need you for.' Schenck looked around the table. 'Unless there's anything else for Max?'

'Not really,' said Turnbull. 'Oh, I saw you had an old friend visiting, Max.'

Admiral Kaltberg tilted her head. It might have meant nothing; Max took it for a warning.

'Who was that, sir?'

'Carl Blackstone and his family. We noted that you took the son – Roger, is it? – on a quick informal tour.'

'That's right.' Max controlled his breathing, aligning all his mental resources. 'It seemed like a good idea, given his father's previous capabilities.'

'You're not saying you showed him the prisoner?'

There was no need to ask which one; but Turnbull would

expect him to deny everything about the trip inside the Annexe.

'I did in fact, sir. For several minutes.'

So Turnbull's people – or more likely Schenck's – had observed him meeting Roger on Borges Boulevard. But they could not have had surveillance inside the cell complex: he had triple-checked.

'And what happened?'

'Not a trace of the father's former ability, I'm afraid.'

'You're sure?'

'I kept him there for long enough. Carl would have started to grow uneasy after about two minutes. By four minutes, his intuition would have told him that something was wrong.'

'And Roger showed no reaction?'

'None, sir.'

The admirals were great psychological tacticians. Max had to be better.

'Disappointing,' said Admiral Zajac finally, and nodded towards Schenck. 'Time to press on, Boris, don't you think?'

'Yes.' Schenck raised a hand. 'Thanks for your time, Max.'

'Sirs.'

Max nodded, turned to the doors as they curled back, and stepped through, careful to maintain full control of his body language as he walked out.

Then the doors were shut behind him.

Bastards.

On the other hand, how could they possibly be worse than him?

Avril. You'd better come back.

Her ship burst into glorious realspace, amid blazing stars: the heart of the galaxy. All passive sensors were on maximum gain; all active scanning was off. She was in full stealth mode, hanging in the void, surrounding by a billion glorious suns, and the galactic fire produced by the vast black hole that tore stars into incandescence. This was as magnificent as realspace could get.

She continued to float, scanning in all directions, awed by what she saw.

And then, the anomalous data.

'A jet?'

Was this what Commodore Gould meant by observe, record, bug out? Or should she carry on taking—?

Starlight shimmered, rippling with refraction.

'That can't—Ship, *let's go!*'

But invisible hooks were through her poor ship, holding her in place.

'Damn you. Damn you.'

She was sobbing as she made the cutting gesture. It was called the *seppuku* command.

Ship, I love you.

I love you, too.

Nova brightness enveloped them, as they blew themselves to oblivion.

In his office, Max waited, hoping for Avril's return, praying for it, knowing that if she did not come back, he would still have learned what he needed to know.

For that, he hated himself.

TWENTY-SIX

EARTH, 2146 AD

They met at a restaurant specializing in nouveau Nihonjin, though Rekka and Simon planned to stick with traditional fare, perhaps mizo soup and vegetable tempura. Leonora and Alwyn were a couple, Hussein and Peter were colleagues, and they were waiting for Mary Stelanko and her partner Amber Hawke to arrive.

'It's good to be back,' Rekka told them.

After the initial drinks, Alwyn – an artist from the Welsh Republic – restarted his ongoing debate with Simon.

'See, every one of us is unique—'

'Especially you,' murmured Leonora.

'—so there's no such thing as numbers. They're not real, because no two things are identical.'

'So if you prepared lunch for us, expecting two people,' said Simon, 'and we turned up with four hundred of our best friends, it wouldn't matter that we're all different. Only that there's four hundred and two of us.'

'You're wilfully missing the—'

And so on, harmlessly and without conclusion.

'Shall we call them?' asked Hussein finally. 'I'm getting hungry, so I think we should—'

But at that moment the hubbub around them died, conversation attenuating to murmurs. This was New Phoenix (the city motto: *We Rise From The Ashes*) with plenty of UNSA personnel resident here, but still the sight of a Pilot caught everyone's attention.

Amber walked with her arm lightly on Mary's. UNSA provided guide dogs for Pilots, both for long-term companionship and for short durations; but Amber was not unusual in refusing them.

Highlights glinted off the steel sockets where her eyes had been.

'Hi everyone,' said Amber, sitting down. 'Nice to see you all.'

The words were ordinary conversation, not ordinary. Everyone knew she would never see again, not in this universe. They also knew she experienced wonders in mu-space that they were literally incapable of imagining – or imaging – because their occipital and parietal lobes had not been virally rewired for fractal dimensions.

'Good to see you, too,' said Rekka.

'Hey, congratulations. You bagged yourself a first contact.'

'Uh-huh. Tell McStuart and the rest how good that was. He asked me what the *pre* in pre-contact might possibly mean, but he supposed they didn't teach Latin where I come from.'

'Bastard.'

'I told him it derived from the preposition *prae*, as in *pretentious*.'

'Good for you,' said Hussein. 'A toast. Congratulations to Rekka.'

'Congratulations.'

'Cheers.'

But Simon was looking at Mary.

'What is it?' he said. 'What's that smile all about?'

Rekka remembered why she had fallen for him. He understood the unspoken in every conversation.

'I was maybe going to mention it later—'

'Come on, Mary. Tell us.'

'But Amber and I are pregnant. Well, she's the one doing the hard work.'

'Wow.'

'Well done, you two.'

Rekka was first in line to hug and kiss them both. There were excited embraces for the next couple of minutes.

Simon asked, 'Are we hoping for Mary's beauty and Amber's brains, or the other way round?'

'Don't answer that,' said Rekka. 'I'll punish him later.'

Finally, when the meal was underway, the conversation moved on to topical areas, and Pilots' education came up. The Higashionnas – Robert and Luisa – were pushing for a new curriculum that emphasised UNSA control and discipline. Since all the youngsters now were natural-born Pilots, carrying the organelles nicknamed fractolons in every cell, their potential for self-determined lives was worrying conservatives.

Rekka noticed how quiet Amber was during the discussion.

After the meal, they said their farewells in the car park behind the restaurant. The night was warm, the desert palms were spiky shadows against dark sky, and the ever-present cicadas sang their insect song.

Mary saw Amber into their car, then walked back to where Rekka was standing. Simon was bantering with Hussein, Peter and Alwyn, while Leonora was trying to get them to call it a night. For the moment, Mary and Rekka were alone.

'Is everything all right?' asked Rekka.

'Sort of. We—We want Amber's son, our son, to be a Pilot.'

'It's a boy?'

'Yes. But management said no to the treatment.'

'They can be real bastards.'

Without fractolon insertion and related procedures, the child would be born fully human. Only natural-born Pilots gave birth to their own kind – and even then, the later stages of development had to take place in mu-space.

'So we went ahead anyway. Don't ask me how.'

'Mary! My God.'

'Exactly.'

'But how will you—?'

'That's going to be the real trick, isn't it?'

With Amber pregnant, and her an old-school Pilot rather than natural-born, she would be grounded for the duration.

'What's the cut-off?'

'Six months, latest.'

Meaning that the last three months of foetal development, at a minimum, had to take place in mu-space, along with the birth itself.

'You'll never manage it.'

'Some of the younger Pilots are real renegades, you know. Ro herself is.'

Ro McNamara had been the first Pilot born in mu-space. She was maybe twenty-three, twenty-four years old – Rekka wasn't sure. The others of her kind, all bearing fractolons derived from hers, started to be born about two years after her.

Giving a twenty-year-old Pilot responsibility for a massively expensive spacecraft was a risk. No wonder UNSA were so concerned with education and training.

'Let me know if I can help,' said Rekka.

'Do you really mean that?'

'Yes. But if McStuart has anything to do with it, I'm grounded forever.'

'Don't count on it. Kilborn runs the schedules, and he hates McStuart.'

'Are you sure?'

'Uh-huh. Plus, your friend Sharp will be flying home in a few months, and you're to go with him. He wants it, Poliakov recommended it, and Kilborn's insisting on it.'

'You're kidding.'

'You did good, girl.' Mary hugged her. 'A lot of us know it.'

'Thank you.'

Later, as they drove across desert beneath a spectacular night sky, Simon asked what the private conversation with Mary had been about.

'Girl talk,' said Rekka.

Three months later, just past four a.m. on a Friday, a Pilot with glittering black eyes walked along an unlit corridor in Desert

One. Then he paused before a locked door to which he did not have the code.

In his eyes, tiny golden sparks danced like fireflies. They faded as the door clicked open.

'Hello,' he said.

Inside, seated on a large couch, Sharp turned to see his visitor, his antlers looking hard and massive in the half-light.

'You are the Pilot.' The words came from his chest speaker. 'It is good to meet you.'

'Yes, Sharp. My name is Luís Delgado, and I'm honoured to be taking you home later.'

'I will not see you during the voyage?'

'No, that's why I'm here now.'

'Do you know Rekka?'

'Oh, yes.' Luís smiled. 'And I like her very much.'

'So do I.'

'I'm glad I talked to you. Farewell, Sharp.'

'Farewell, Luís Delgado.'

Luís nodded, and then walked out. The door automatically locked behind him.

Continuing through the xeno complex, he came to a door leading to an equipment bay. No automatic lights, as he walked the corridors, had activated. Now, the door failed to scan the person standing before it.

Once more, golden sparks glimmered in his eyes. The door slid open.

Big TAV cranes looked like giant silver scorpions, their tails capable of lifting enormous loads. In six hours, they would be loading equipment aboard Luís's vessel. He looked around for the stacked white crates, and found them.

He walked closer.

One of the crates came up to his chest. After a few seconds, he pressed his fingertips against it and closed his eyes. Then he smiled slowly.

Then he walked back among the shadows, slipped out of the bay, and into the night.

*

At 9:38, Mary Stelanko was standing next to Simon in the control tower, staring down at the gleaming white-and-silver delta-winged ship that shone on the runway.

The TAV cranes were moving out of sight, their cargo already aboard the ship. Then a smaller vehicle rolled slowly across the tarmac, and came to a halt beneath a massive wing.

Sharp and Rekka alighted.

The ship's own carry-arm extended from the hold, providing a small platform for them to step on to. Then it carried them up, and they disappeared inside.

Simon turned to a holodisplay on one of the controllers' consoles. It showed Rekka checking Sharp was on his couch, then pressing the tailored delta-band across his forehead and activating it. She watched the status displays for a while – they were reproduced on the console, and Simon could see they were normal for Sharp – then she climbed onto her own couch, put delta-band to forehead, and pressed it.

Her hand dropped to the couch. She was deep in sleep.

Neither Mary nor Simon said anything as the remaining minutes elapsed. At exactly ten o'clock, one of the controllers said, 'It's a go,' and blue flame brightened at the ship's rear. Then it began to roll.

'And . . . *now,*' said the controller.

The craft blasted along the runway, pulled impossibly fast up into the sky, and disappeared in a blaze of whiteness.

'Godspeed,' said Mary.

'Come back safe,' said Simon.

Above Desert One, the sapphire sky was empty.

TWENTY-SEVEN

FULGOR, 2603 AD

So how was he supposed to pretend everything was normal? Roger commanded his bedroom window to swell outwards and open down, forming a balcony; then he stepped out on to the quickglass. He stared across campus, remembering golden space and the endless elegance of Labyrinth. Not to mention strange, dark dreams that kept popping into his head.

Gavriela. You're only in my mind.

From above, a voice called: 'You okay down there?'

'Huh? Sure.'

'So, do I need to open Skein comms?' It was Stef, leaning from her own balcony. 'Or shall I come down in person?'

It wasn't like her to be friendly.

'If you want to,' he said. 'Would you like a cup of daistral?'

'You bet. See you in a second.'

He half-expected her to morph her balcony into a ramp, leading down to his own. Instead she disappeared inside, presumably to descend indoors like a civilized person. He requested drinks from the house system, and he had a cup in each hand by the time the door melted open and Stef came in.

'Here you are.'

'Thank you, Mr Blackstone. So, did I catch you staring into space, thinking of your girlfriend?'

For a moment he thought she meant Gavriela, which was insane.

'Are you talking about Alisha? Because she's not—'

'That's who I'm talking about, and I've been pretty snotty with her, haven't I?'

'Well . . .'

'Can we sit down?' Stef gestured for chairs to sprout from the floor. 'Maybe I've been a bit short with everyone.'

They both sat.

'Everyone has their own mannerisms,' said Roger.

'You're very polite. Truth is, I've been a bit mixed up. I had an older boyfriend, you see. Long-term, and we split up as part of my coming here.'

'Oh.'

'The bust-up was ... I don't know. He told me I was only something because of him. Without him, I was useless.'

'He was wrong.'

'Thank you. I think I know that. But without him, I'd never have dragged myself out of the mess I—Look, I was mixed up since I was ten, starting when—'

What she related was the story of a childhood formed by self-involved parents who never noticed their daughter sampling amphetamist and booze left over from their frequent parties. At school, she had become a bully, a nasty piece of work – in her own words – and the kind of subversive pupil every teacher hated: intelligent and nuts.

Accidental pregnancy was so primitive and stupid a mistake that it wasn't even a cliché. There was some legal trouble that she skated over, a succession of boyfriends, then the one stable relationship that pulled her out of chaos.

'Not that anyone else approved, you understand.'

'But you came out if it,' said Roger. 'You've been through the mill, and come out a stronger person.'

'Maybe.' Her smile was sad. 'You're sweet.'

'Not really.'

'You are.' She leaned over, and pressed her palm against his cheek. 'You understand why I can't be with you, don't you?'

'Er—'

'So, look.' She stood up. 'I want to see you going out on a date with Alisha Spalding, or you're in big trouble. Understand me?'

'I guess.'

'Good. Then I'm off.' She walked to the opening door, blew him a kiss, and left. 'Ciao.'

The quickglass flowed back into place.

What was that all about?

He remembered a conversation with Dad, perhaps a year ago.

'Son, no matter how much cognosemantics and neurocoding you learn, women are a mystery. And some of them are strange attractors.'

'Isn't that some kind of archaic gender stereotyping?'

'It certainly is.'

Obviously Dad hadn't told him half of it.

In the sports hall, he stared down at the wrestling area, watching people roll on the mats, wishing he could join them. His solo exercises might have combat applications, but without practising live, he was never going to feel confident. The problem was the additional deepscanning that athletes went through – both for health and to prevent cheating – and the danger of revealing his true nature.

Being here was like picking at a scab. What he ought to do was call Alisha, as Stef had pretty much commanded, or else put her out of his mind. He felt about as decisive as Hamlet, the protagonist of the most boring holodrama he had seen. According to Alisha, it was all in the poor translation; but English was about as accessible as Sanskrit. To be fair, among old Earth languages it had some nice characteristics – more verb tenses than some, more subtly different verbs, so reducing the need for qualifying adverbs – but it lacked the tonality or symbolic resonance that made allusions and multiple meanings so easy. Other ancestral usage, from Old Norse kennings to Mandarin numerology, allowed subtle simultaneous messages to be delivered in a single—

He forced the tip of his tongue against the roof of his mouth, shutting himself up.

Then his tu-ring chimed. It was Alisha.

'Got a moment?'

'Sure.'

'You know Lupus Festival starts tomorrow, right?'

'I guess so.'

'So we're building a mannequin for the parade. Our gang, plus some friends of Stef's.'

'Did she ask you to call me?'

'Not directly. Why–? Never mind. We've all got studies today, so we're pulling an all-nighter in the labs to do the construction.'

'You mean, no sleep?'

'Sure, unless you can sleepwalk. It's Rick's design, and he's done a good job.'

'That's nuts.'

'Part of the fun. Oh, and ... the parade's tomorrow afternoon, so it'll be a long haul.'

'Also, totally insane.'

'Hope you make it. Endit.'

The holo shrank to a point, was gone.

Mannequins. Carnival parades. First day of Lupus.

What am I doing here?

This was supposed to be the centre of learning, of leading intellectual activity. Instead, Alisha wanted him to hang around with a bunch of giggling people, working through the night to achieve nothing serious, just for the hell of it.

It's stupid.

Or maybe he was the stupid one, brooding by himself about things that mattered only to him, while the world continued to flow around him, and people could enjoy or be miserable as they wished, none of it making a difference to anyone but themselves.

They worked in a bay designed to receive large transport vehicles. Roger turned up when the project was well under-way, his friends hanging off a half-constructed silver skeleton, or dangling from the scaffolding around it. The mannequin's joints were complex cogs. Once finished, it would be four times taller than a person.

'Where does the engine go?' asked Roger.

'Hey, Rog,' Stef called down from a precarious position five metres up. 'Couldn't stay away, then?'

Rick tapped Roger's shoulder.

'Glad you made it, my friend. And there's no engine.'

'With those joints and cable-inserts ... isn't it meant to walk?'

'It certainly is.'

'But—'

'We're using no artificial power. That's the fun of it.'

'So it *is* going to walk in the parade.'

'Sure.'

'And it doesn't have an engine.'

'Uh-huh.'

'So you dangle it from a hovering flyer and work it like a puppet?'

'That would be cheating.'

'I give up. I can't imagine—'

'Sure you can.' Rick turned him. 'There's your clue.'

Alisha and two people he didn't know were assembling some hardware involving narrow chains and gears. Roger stared at them, then shook his head.

'You have to be kidding. *Pedals?*'

'There, you've got it.'

Roger tilted his head back, examining the shining skeleton, estimating its mass.

'Sorry, Rick. It can't be done. Are you sure you've done the calculations right?'

'Feel those metal bones, my friend. They're only half as dense as you think – rather like myself, ha, ha – and just because there's no artificial power, that doesn't stop us using superfluid bearings and a bit of smartmaterial.'

'If you say so. Just don't ask me to get inside that contraption.'

'I wouldn't dream of it.' Rick looked up into the scaffolding.

'Stef, would you order this boy to get inside the mannequin and get to work?'

'Hoy,' shouted Stef. 'Blackstone, get your arse up here and make yourself useful.'

'You tell him, Stef,' called Alisha.

Roger laughed. He wanted to talk to Alisha, but she had already turned back to the others. They were loosening a chain loop, trying to slip it off a cog; and one of them was swearing, a streak of blood on his finger.

'We're all nuts,' Roger said.

'Finally, the boy understands.'

'Totally insane.'

He grabbed the scaffolding and swung himself up.

By lunchtime, a headless giant clothed mannequin with hands was ready to go. Cables and chains were its ligaments and muscles, counterbalanced tension holding it upright. When they took the scaffolding away, it swayed – Stef and Rick were inside the thing – but stayed upright. Then several others, Roger included, pulled back the diaphanous 'skin' and clambered into the skeleton, finding their saddles.

'Mad, mad, mad.'

'We know that, Roger.'

'Everyone get ready,' called Stef. 'And . . . Now.'

They got to work, Stef giving orders, while Rick kept himself busy on levers, switching gears and touching brakes – and the whole thing lurched into motion. The first footfall rocked Roger, then the next, but soon they had the knack of it. The mannequin was walking.

'Time to get a head,' said Rick.

None of them had authorization to command the roof to open. Roger would have designed a mannequin that actually fitted inside the building – but that would have been too easy, clearly. Instead, they pedalled and Rick steered, and they clomped out through the big exit, made a quick left turn –

almost on the spot – and came to a halt, standing next to the wall.

Up on the roof, some more of Stef's friends – she had obviously been socializing outside the study group – were manoeuvring a large head into position.

'Careful.'

A magnetic bolt dropped through the hollow interior, and bounced off some part of the skeleton with a clang.

'Sorry.'

'Not just mad,' muttered Roger. 'Suicidal.'

His eyes were sore and his muscles felt detached from his body; yet he seemed to have passed beyond the need for sleep.

'Okay, people. Pedal and step. Here we go.'

That was the beginning of an hour-long session of pedalling inside the mannequin, not seeing where they were going. From outside there was the occasional cheer, but it was not until they reached the main parade that the volume grew, indicating that they were in fact part of Lupus Festival.

Alisha was one of the team walking outside, guiding Rick by constant comms. All Roger could do was concentrate on the pedalling, far harder than he had thought it would be. High up inside the mannequin, Stef working a secondary set of pedals, her buttocks moving inside tight trousers, and it was a while before Roger pulled his attention away.

In his tired head, he seemed to hear a voice.

—Will they really leave Berlin for Amsterdam? Oh, please . . .

It took a moment to decide that he was experiencing a neural resonance of words originally uttered in another language.

—Gavi, is that you?

But Rick called down: 'Roger, sorry pal, but can you increase power?'

'Got it.'

The auditory hallucination was gone.

I really need to sleep.

For now, he concentrated on the physical work.

Rick projected small holos down to Roger and the others:

views from external public surveillance showing their own clanking progress amid a line of morphballoons, animated dancing flames (Roger kept changing his mind about how they did that), and hundreds of students in bright costumes and masks. Among the crowds on either side of the wide avenue, many wore half-masks around eyes and nose, some like butterflies and other exotica, many like wolves.

It made the pedalling easier, feeling they were part of something. But it was hard to focus on the holos when your eyes felt like dust-filled slits, and your stomach was bubbling with acid.

Finally, they stopped somewhere on Nexus Heptagon, a wide plaza where pink snow was falling among a hundred food vendors, musicians and jugglers. Crowds milled on all sides. Some of them offered congratulations as Roger and the others limped out of the mannequin. Rick and Stef were the last to exit, after double-checking the clamps and brakes, ensuring the abandoned mannequin would remain upright.

He looked for Alisha, but she was standing with her eyes focused on some virtual image, deep in conversation.

'Let's party,' said Rick. 'Everyone, meet back here in an hour.'

'You're kidding.'

'What happens if we don't pedal it back?'

'The festival authorities will take it away to dismantle.'

'And that's bad because—?'

'Look, if we're all back and we want to pedal it home, fine. If not, that's fine too. The main thing was to do it.'

Roger said: 'Was that sentence semantically null, or was he just babbling?'

'Babbling,' said Stef. 'Come on, everyone. Let's find some drinks.'

She grabbed Rick and the others, pulling them into the crowd, with a wink at Roger to indicate that she was manoeuvring them deliberately, leaving Roger and Alisha behind.

But Alisha was nodding, and she moved off among the

people without looking back. Not knowing whether he should, Roger followed.

Passing beneath a golden archway, he took a free glass of warm wine from a table and sipped as he walked. Real food would be better, but he did not want to lose Alisha. Nor did he want to interrupt her. He walked on, past flowsteel helical ramps leading to a temporary piazza on stilts where hundreds of revellers were dancing, the music a complex rock-baroque symphony that suddenly went discordant with an underlying *da, da-dum, da-da-da-dum, da-da.*

But the stamping feet of dancers continued, as if only he could hear the new theme.

He was among revellers who were dressed in beautifully expensive silk clothes, real fabric rather than smartmaterial, some with masks made from synthetic feathers, others with holomasks, rendering animal snouts and eyes with exquisite exactness. He bumped into one by accident – a man wearing a canine head and Egyptian robes: dressed as Horus or Osiris, or whatever – and apologized. It had distracted him, and for a few seconds he had no idea where she was, but then he saw.

Alisha was talking to a Luculenta.

The woman was tall, dressed in black and silver. No wonder Alisha had ignored her friends; even from here, in a crowd of thousands, Roger could sense the woman's charisma.

All around was distraction: holoflames and fireworks, a thousand illuminations and—

There. Darkness, moving in impossible ways. Then gone.

I'm hallucinating.

But it seemed he was not. Just for a moment, in a gap between revellers, he spotted a pale-faced woman he knew for certain – Dr Helsen – and beside her a stocky man, who might be the friend he had seen her with before. Then the crowd moved like one massive creature, shifting position, hiding Helsen and the other man from view.

Alisha was leaving the plaza, walking with the Luculenta. Roger was tired and going crazy, so the sensible thing would be to find food and a place to sit down, maybe sleep. But his feet moved by themselves, and he continued to follow.

In this crowd, no one would notice his behaviour.

The reveller dressed as Anubis took an ice-cream from a vendor. As he licked it, the cone seemed to disappear inside his jackal's head, the Horus holomask. After a moment, he made a gesture, and the mask faded.

Now he could eat his ice-cream more naturally. As he did so, he watched two pairs of figures leave the plaza in opposite directions: Helsen and Ranulph one way, the Spalding girl and Rafaella Stargonier in the other. Young Roger Blackstone chose to follow the latter.

The question for Superintendent Keinosuke Sunadomari was, who should *he* be watching?

TWENTY-EIGHT

EARTH, 777 AD

From the camp came the sound of drumming and the cheers of dancing warriors. Tall carved poles were hung with shields. Orange light blazed from massive fires. For a temporary location, there was a lot of organization involved in setting up this place.

There was no point in asking whether anyone else heard disturbing music among the drums – Ulfr knew it was only him. His mood disquieted Brandr, the warhound occasionally growling.

It was not just that Ulfr felt no sense of celebration, either at the troll's defeat or at the way several dozen chieftains had managed to come together in peace. For he was used to slipping in and out of dreamworld, often guided by sweet Eira back home. Since Heithrún had led him into trance the previous night, strange dreams kept recurring: of himself among warriors whose bodies did not appear like normal flesh, looking more like the crystal that topped Heithrún's staff, with which he had driven the troll's spirit out of its stony body.

'If they are elves of the light,' he said to the hound, 'then we could do with their presence. For we have an elf of the dark among us.'

Brandr growled at the mention of Stígr. They had spent all day hunting, mostly to be alone, away from the poet's growing tale of the travellers' battle against the troll – the battle that, as far as Ulfr could tell, Stígr had observed while cowering beneath his cloak, tucked face-down behind a small outcrop.

During the hunt, Ulfr had surprised a young fawn who had strayed from her mother. She was within an easy spear's throw, and Ulfr was downwind; but her legs were slender and fragile, and her big dark eyes – when she finally saw him – held a surprised awareness that reminded him of Jarl. In earlier life, not meeting his end bound to a doorpost, cut apart by axes and hammers.

'You should grow older,' Ulfr had said, 'and make deerlings of your own, before sacrificing yourself to men.'

The fawn had skittered, then galloped away.

After a moment, he pulled himself out of memory. The drumming had stopped at some point, and the only sounds were the crackling of fires and a lone voice, speaking.

There was a hillock to one side of the camp's centre, and two figures stood on it. The man speaking was Gulbrandr, chief of the party that Stígr had travelled with. The other figure, wide hat low over his face, was Stígr himself.

Were Stígr's lips moving? From this distance, and because of the shapeless hat, it was hard to tell. Besides, it was Chief Gulbrandr whose words boomed across the warriors, and everyone's attention was on him.

And on the misty visions growing in the air above them.

Sorcery!

Could no one else see it?

'By Mjǫlnir, they are ensorcelled.'

Brandr was silent, a warhound ready to attack.

'—to south and west and east,' Gulbrandr was saying, 'where the folk are rich and soft, no longer warriors. Their ancestors' strength is gone.'

Ulfr was not sure of that. But the entranced warriors had no doubts.

'A-viking, a-viking,' they chanted. 'A-viking! *A-viking!*'

Their dreams were visible above their heads: the glory of battle, golden spoils, and Valkyrie, the soul-choosers, swooping down to fetch the shades of the slain.

It was real; and it was wrong: turning honourable courage to something dark. But there were so many warriors between him and the two men on the hillock.

'We take from the weak,' roared Gulbrandr.

'A-viking! A-viking!'

'We take from the cowards.'

'A-viking! A-viking!'

'We take their women and their gold!'

'A-viking! A—'

Ulfr grabbed a warrior's head and twisted.

'—viking!'

'Because together we are greater—'

He forced another two men aside, used his elbow, kicked another in the back of the knee, creating space.

'—than those who hide inside—'

Brandr bit a man on the calf, allowing Ulfr to push past.

'—city walls like rats!'

A huge warrior swung at Ulfr but he moved inside, cycling punches and slaps to knock the man down, and then he was into a clear space. Gulbrandr's eyes widened. The nearer warriors grew silent, though the others continued to chant.

'A-viking! A-viking!'

Twisting curtains of black light fell on him, but he was faster, sprinting across the gap, leaping high – *stay back!* – as ravens from nowhere clawed at his eyes, but too late – *bastards* – and his elbow smacked into Gulbrandr's forehead, splitting the skin.

But he was not aiming to put the chief down – he was going through him. Stígr's arms were raised high, about to call down some dark magic, but Ulfr's kick scythed across his legs, he hammered with the side of his fist, then Stígr was down.

Ulfr dropped knees-first on to Stígr's chest, feeling the crunch of ribs breaking; but the man was already unconscious, and the dream-images overhead were evaporating. The ravens screamed, wheeled through the air, and were gone.

Gulbrandr looked puzzled. Then he stared at Ulfr.

'You have killed the poet.'

'He lives, Chief.'

'Violating the peace oath in a gathering.' Gulbrandr's mind was returning. 'Warriors, bind this man and—'

'No,' called a woman. 'He saved us all, when I could not.'

'Heithrún, is that you? Hold, warriors.'

The young *volva* limped forward, her leg still splinted from yesterday's injury, supported by a white-haired woman, surely another *volva*.

'Some of you know me,' said the older woman. 'I am Eydís, one-time teacher to Heithrún, and she has the right of it.'

'Sorcery?'

'Aye, Chief. And neither I nor Heithrún could move against the spell.'

At that, Stígr's one eyelid moved, and his groan was loud.

'Don't let him speak,' said Heithrún.

'Warriors.'

Two men grabbed Stígr, while a third undid a leather cord from around one calf – the man that Brandr had bit: he grinned at Ulfr, then at the warhound – and wound it around Strígr's head, deep into his mouth.

Finally, Stígr came awake, his one eye shining as he focused on Ulfr.

A normal man would have wriggled and moaned, testing his bonds, cursing or trying to persuade. But he just lay there, staring.

'He's just a poet,' said Gulbrandr.

But then shadows twisted in a way only Ulfr could see, discordant notes sounded while ravens cawed, and the air shivered.

Stígr was gone.

'Thórr's blood!' Gulbrandr made the sign of the hammer. 'He is a dark one, in truth.'

The man who had gagged Stígr now clapped Ulfr on the shoulder.

'Well done, warrior.'

'Yes,' said Gulbrandr. 'You have saved us. Warriors, I show you a hero!'

Cheers became a crescendo of relief and celebration. Against the noise, only Ulfr could hear Eydís's words.

'You have an enemy in the darkness now.'

Then he patted Brandr and raised a victory fist. Tonight he would carouse with these warriors – among them he could see Chief Folkvar nodding and grinning – and let the dawn deal with whatever evil the Norns would throw at him next.

For now, he lived!

TWENTY-NINE

FULGOR, 2603 AD

Superintendent Keinosuke Sunadomari smiled as he trailed his suspects through the festival crowds. He was a Luculentus peacekeeper; to be keeping a Luculenta under surveillance was a worthwhile challenge. But then his smile attenuated to nothing.

Daniel, if she was responsible, she's going down.

This had started with his suspicion of the Blackstones, a family with a secret he had not deciphered yet. And now, following the son – as the son in turn trailed Alisha Spalding and Rafaella Stargonier – it became obvious that Roger Blackstone had received some basic training in surveillance. But a part of Sunadomari's awareness, in Skein, despatched an investigative netSprite that came back in milliseconds with an answer: the lad enjoyed espionage holodramas, particularly *Fighting Shadows*. Perhaps he had picked up tips that way.

The irony was that, several years back, poor dead Daniel Deighton had himself written several episodes for the series, under a pseudonym and without revealing any current operational procedures that villains would not know already.

But was there a different connection here? Because Daniel had been one of nine Luculenti to die strangely, and he had been in his glider at the time. Naturally, investigators backtracked the flightpath, but found nothing. Yet Sunadomari had no need to access the logs in Skein – he remembered that the glider had passed over Mansion Stargonier.

His friend Daniel had been more analyst than frontline operative; but he was a peacekeeper and a Luculentus, therefore not easy to kill. Young Roger Blackstone could not have done it; but perhaps Rafaella Stargonier could.

He sent off another flurry of netSprites and netAngels in Skein.

Meanwhile, in reality, he walked along a ribbon-spiral path, through colonnades where bubblefish swam in the air, finally coming out at the top of a wide custard-yellow ramp that led down to Parallaville. The crowds were thin here, and down in Parallaville there were few pedestrians at all.

The city quarter was a jumble of trompe-l'oeil illusions, mixing holo with physical architecture in ways that beguiled the eye. This was the first day of Lupus; by the end of the festival, Parallaville would be teeming with revellers out of their heads with hallucinogens, looking to freak themselves even further among impossible polygons, trick staircases and doorways leading nowhere.

Some fifty paces beyond the foot of the ramp, Rafaella Stargonier stopped. She turned, but Roger Blackstone had sunk out of sight, apparently inside a solid wall. It was a nice use of holo cover.

Luculenta Rafaella Stargonier walked on, into the heart of Parallaville, with Alisha Spalding beside her.

If the Stargonier woman could illegally access building systems – or even SatScan – she would probably have spotted Sunadomari already. But her behaviour indicated awareness of something: probably the Blackstone boy, not him. Still, Sunadomari did not want to take the risk of surveilling in Skein and having his data compromised – it had not escaped him that one of the other murder victims was a Skein designer, Hailey Recht, who should have been able to stop any kind of physical or psychological attack and call for help, for she had knowledge and capabilities far beyond those of an ordinary Luculenta.

Besides, Sunadomari had his own tricks, and he rarely got to deploy them for real.

The bracelets on his wrists were quickglass, which was not unusual. But any watchers – there were none – would be surprised to see the quickglass morph into six floating teardrop shapes, each half the size of a fist. Mini flying cameras were decidedly old school and low tech, but the quickglass used chameleoware to be invisible to SatScan from above – and sent back data using protocols that were entirely his own, all they way down to the core trinary, bearing no relationship to anything used in Skein.

'Fly now,' he murmured.

All six spydrops rose into the air.

Once more Roger had to duck out of sight. This time he commanded a quickglass wall to form an alcove, using commands that would not set off alarms – not here in Parallaville, where the public were encouraged to tweak the architecture at their whim – but would be perfectly open to official scrutiny of the building's memory.

Several laughing, drunken festival-goers staggered past without detecting him.

Why am I doing this?

It was Helsen who set off all his alarms – she of the darkness, she and her creepy friend – but it was Alisha he cared about.

So why should I mess up her chance of upraise?

If she was supposed to be networking with the Luculenti élite, that was fine. But he remembered that it was Helsen who had told Alisha to make contact with someone called Stargonier. He had no way of knowing for sure – if he tried an image search in Skein, he might attract peacekeeper attention – but his intuition was that this Luculenta was Rafaella Stargonier. For one thing, he thought that Alisha did not know many Luculenti.

Then he saw the Luculenta in clear, and the back of his neck felt cold.

'Trust your intuition,' Dad had told him more than once. *'Civilized people disregard the wisdom of four billion years of evolution, and step inside a room or vehicle with someone who makes them uneasy, or let someone help them carry things for them out of politeness,*

while their reptile brain is screaming alarm signals. Becoming a victim out of embarrassment is stupid.'

Predators and psychopaths have unusual biochemistry – neither cause nor effect, for behaviour changes hormonal balance, while hormones alter behaviour, in a feedback loop that can be benign (optimism produces health produces optimism) or deadly. The reptilean part of every human brain can smell danger.

Roger knew this because he had consciously learned it, with the civilized part of his mind. When he looked at the Luculenta, his intellectual understanding reinforced the automatic emotion.

She scared him.

Up ahead, Alisha nodded to the Luculenta, touched fists and walked away. She headed through a maze of vertical levitated flanges that formed a smiling human face or a scowling tiger, or merely a jumble of shapes, depending on the angle.

And was that a hungry look on the Luculenta's face, as she watched Alisha leave?

His tu-ring chimed.

Shit.

But he accepted the incoming comms request, perhaps because of his unease, in case there was something wrong.

'Hey,' said Stef in a virtual holo. *'I just talked to Alisha.'*

'In reality?'

'No, she's not with us, and neither are you. But you're not together, either.'

'Was that semantically null, or are you just babbling?'

'You've used that line before. Don't you play double-bind games with me, Roger Blackstone.'

'Tell me you're sober.'

'I'm sober. Just don't expect me to tell the truth. Except we want you back here now.'

'Maybe—'

Beyond the virtual Stef he could see the real Luculenta, the presumed Rafaella Stargonier. A masked man was approaching her – he wore a holo fox's head, a yellow cape – and he was staggering a bit, laughing. Propositioning her?

The man fell back, hand clutching his forehead as his fox mask disappeared.

A Luculentus, playing with altered mental states for recreation – he could have sobered with a single well-formed thought – but now he stood there, swaying. The Luculenta stared at him, trembling, then she pulled back, turned, and stalked away, heading for a mirror-bright ramp that led into the heart of Parallaville.

'—I'll see you soon, Stef. Endit.'

The virtual holo snapped out of existence just as Stef had been about to say something.

Stargonier wanted to kill him. Or something.

But she stopped herself. Because this was a public place? Or for some other reason?

Not believing his own actions – this was a kind of social daring that was new to him – Roger hurried down the yellow ramp to the Luculentus, who was rubbing his face but looking much better.

'Sir? Are you all right?'

'Absolutely. Thank you for asking, young man. The ability to tailor one's own neurocognitive states for recreation is not for the unskilled.'

'Does that mean you can make yourself feel well again?'

Normal colour was returning to the man's face.

'It does indeed. As you can see.'

'Er, may I ask what you talked to the Luculenta about?'

'Which Luculenta in particular?'

'Just now.' Roger pointed. 'Standing there a few moments ago.'

'I think you're mistaken. Perhaps I'm not the only one who needs to take care with altered states.'

'I—Maybe.' Roger smiled, remembering the effect of the warm wine, and exaggerating it in his mind to deflect suspicion. 'That could be the case.'

'You weren't looking for company during the Festival?'

'Er, no, sir. I've friends waiting for me.'

'Then enjoy the rest of the week.'

'And you, sir.'

Roger walked away, heading for the mirror ramp. Clearly the Luculenta was dangerous, but perhaps mostly to her own kind. Still he would need to stay well back in case she—

Danger.

Overhead were three distant itches – that was how he felt them – and when he looked, he could just make out the hovering teardrop outlines. Belonging to the Luculenta?

Regardless, the devices were complex, not legal, and too powerful for him to waste time deciding whether they were armed.

Beneath his smartlenses, golden fire grew.

Then he commanded the lenses to clear as he let loose. The release of energy felt wonderful.

And when it was done, he made a move – not to follow the Luculenta, but to get out of Parallaville as fast as possible.

Sunadomari crouched over his smoking, fallen spydrops. The case had just become more complex. If there had not been one of his friends among the murder victims, this would have made him smile, enjoying the challenge.

Now what?

He could access the surrounding buildings' memories using peacekeeper privileges, and he could try for SatScan, although there were so many smartmiasmas and holos in the sky for Festival, there was no guarantee of clear data. But he was aware that Hailey Recht, Skein designer, had fallen. Perhaps the normal methods of tracking were insufficient. If the enemy, whoever it was, could monitor Skein enquiries, then interrogating the buildings would send a clear warning; and if the enemy could alter Skein data without logging it, then whatever surveillance logs he found would be worthless.

His spydrops were not strictly legal. Given that, there was

no point in keeping them as forensic samples. He stood up and commanded the quickstone ground to swallow up the destroyed devices, dissolving them.

When they were gone, he looked up into the sky, requesting SatScan access, not specifying a person to search for, just an aerial view of Lucis City. Then he changed his mind, realizing that even this much could be dangerous if the enemy was as capable as he suspected. He closed the link down.

But his spydrops had not perished because of someone with Skein mastery. Their design was proprietary all the way down, so the attack had been more basic and generic than tricky code. There was only one kind of person he knew capable of inducing destructive resonance in any kind of device.

And if young Roger Blackstone was an undercover Pilot, what were the chances that his parents were, as well?

There was no sign of Stef, Rick or the others near the mannequin; but Alisha was there, holding a jantrasta-coated apple from which she had taken a single bite.

'Hey,' said Roger.

'You're not with the guys?'

'No. What have you been up to?'

Merrymakers swirled around them. Music played, cheerful and loud, with none of the discordant tones that seemed linked to danger.

'Talking to Rafaella Stargonier, in actual person.'

'The Luculenta? She's here for Festival?'

'Sure. She was asking about Dr Helsen, but if she's researched in Skein then she already knows more than I do, because I've never bothered.'

'So you're still trying to get this Stargonier person to come and give a talk?'

'Her precondition still applies. I mean, about me having to produce some original work just to tempt her.'

'And when's the talk due to take place? If it happens, I mean.'

'The day after Festival.'

That would give him time to get home and tell Dad everything. There was something dangerous about the Luculenta, and he did not want Alisha to be at risk. Not only was she his friend – her father Xavier had done Dad a favour, allowing him to shield against the new peacekeeper scanners.

There was a way to guarantee that Rafaella Stargonier would deliver that talk, provided she was serious about doing it if Alisha produced original research. Perhaps it was a way to pin the Luculenta down to a known place and time.

'My Dad knows some people, sort of.' He tapped his turing, then pointed at Alisha. 'I'm not sure if mentioning his name will do any good, but at least you now know they exist.'

'A research institute?' Alisha blinked, scanning virtual holos: the data he had just sent, plus more. 'I see what you mean. They're legitimate, but you wouldn't find them easily. Makes you wonder how they get their funding.'

Roger wished he had thought of that. Perhaps he should have talked to Dad before offering this much – but he had done it now.

Alisha was blinking fast, her eyes focused on a point one metre in front of her. Her throat and lips moved, and then she nodded.

Finally, she said aloud: 'Thank you, Ms Weissmann. We'll be right there.'

After a final blink, she focused on Roger and smiled.

'There's someone in the building, despite the time. Obviously not the kind to celebrate Festival.'

'You just talked to the institute?'

'Sure. Shall we walk to someplace an aircab can land?'

'Uh—'

'You are coming with me, right?'

'I . . .' What he wanted was to sleep. 'Sure.'

Alisha looked down at the jantrasta apple she was still holding. She dropped it, watched the ground swallow it, licked her fingertips, then returned her attention to Roger.

'And while we fly, you can explain to me what Zajinets have to do with realspace hyperdimensions.'

'Um. Right. Okay.'

They alighted from the aircab, in a pedestrian precinct that was otherwise deserted. Then the aircab whispered up into the air, and disappeared behind a tall quickglass tower at the precinct's far end. Roger turned to the ochre building in front of them: quickstone pillars with motile scrollwork, ceramic doors that resembled antique wood, floating brass glowglobes. Old, discreet, well-financed.

'No name sign,' said Alisha.

The main doors curled open.

'Hello,' said a white-haired woman. 'I'm Stella Weissmann. Do come in, you two.'

Her eyes were bright, her stance erect. Her forehead and scalp held no hint of wires or studs, but for a non-Luculenta she broadcast a lot of charisma.

'Thank you,' said Alisha. 'We won't take up much of your time.'

'A chat would be very welcome, in fact. This way.'

There was a foyer of marble quickstone, then a corridor containing display cases, and finally Ms Weissmann's office, with a faux wooden desk and chairs. Everyone sat.

'So you're interested in our alien friends?'

'Yes, ma'am,' said Alisha. 'Certainly in their reputed ability to teleport.'

'Well, this *is* the Zajinet Research Institute, so you're in the right place.'

'I think we are.' Alisha smiled at her. 'Can I ask, is Zajinet teleportation a real phenomenon, or is it something else?'

'What other kinds of thing were you thinking of, Alisha? Is it okay if I call you Alisha?'

'Of course, ma'am. Uh, confabulation among witnesses, maybe caused by neurochemical imbalance. Aliens able to mess with human biochemistry are more likely than those with an ability to manipulate spacetime.'

'That's true, but the Zajinets' *known* abilities mean they're rather different from the average, don't you think?'

'There is that. Do you think that they can make short hops through mu-space without using ships? Is that it?'

'We've researched that possibility among all known sightings,' said Weissmann. 'Some of the translocation events – that's our term – have taken place amid smart buildings, leaving full surveillance data, and not just here on Fulgor. There has been no indication of the energy spillage one would expect from a mu-space transition.'

'Then it's just a coincidence, that they can teleport in realspace and fly mu-space ships?'

'No, my dear.' Weissmann's eyes were wonderfully intelligent. 'I think they grasp spacetime physics in a way none of us has, not even Pilots.'

Roger did not like the glance she gave him.

She can't suspect.

'Pilots can't teleport,' said Alisha. 'If they could, there'd be at least a rumour of it by now.'

'Which implies, my dear, that an ability to function in mu-space is not sufficient. But you're aware of the macroscopic superposition of Zajinet mentality. Parallel identities in every individual.'

'Um, sure.' Alisha's eyelids flickered as she accessed data. 'Very . . . different.'

'If Pilots had minds like that' – Weissmann smiled at Roger – 'perhaps they could do the same. Or perhaps they couldn't. We truly don't know.'

'But the Zajinets transport themselves among the Calabi-Yau dimensions?'

'It's the only hypothesis that remains. They don't leave our universe, they don't travel through the four dimensions we perceive, so it's only the hyperdimensions that are left to them.'

'If we could do the same—'

'Wouldn't that be wonderful? But there's no hope of that, not for many centuries. The research is far beyond us.'

'Well ... Thank you for your time, ma'am. Thank you so much.'

'Just a moment. Here.' Weissmann gestured, and Alisha's eyes widened. 'Those are monographs that we've written here in the Institute. Feel free to quote from them. With attribution, naturally.'

'Oh, gosh. Ms Weissmann, this is far more than I expected.'

'Well, I like you.' She stood up behind her desk. 'Let me know how you get on.'

'Sure.'

'Thank you,' said Roger.

'I'll see you both out.'

Partway along the corridor, Weissmann paused before a display case.

'Fragments of a mu-space ship. Part of the hull.'

'A Zajinet ship?' asked Alisha.

Roger already knew the answer – to him, the material clearly did not come from a Pilots' vessel.

'Absolutely,' said Weissmann. 'The poor thing crash-landed in a hypozone, nearly twenty years ago, just after it departed from the Zajinet embassy.'

'Of course. Was that when they withdrew their delegation?'

'Embarrassing, but yes. They thought we could not guarantee their safety, which perhaps the accident demonstrated, but it was their ship that malfunctioned. It's also why our little institute is such a quiet backwater. Since their species stopped visiting Fulgor, people's interest has waned.'

Roger pointed to the next display case.

'Is that from the same ship? It looks different.'

'Ah, you have sharp eyes.' Weissmann smiled at him for a little too long. 'This is a much older sample, from Earth.'

'How old?' asked Alisha.

'Let me just say ... Rather older than you might think. But we're still working on that.'

Alisha touched Weissmann's fist, all very formal.

'That's our cue to leave. Thank you so much again.'

'You're welcome.' Weissmann looked at Roger. 'Do come back, whenever you like.'

Roger followed Alisha out of the building.

I need to talk to Dad.

Then he half-tripped, managing to right himself.

'You look exhausted, Roger.'

'Only because I am.'

'So here's an aircab.' Alisha pointed at a descending vehicle. 'Let's get straight back to the house.'

Sleep would be good. He could talk to Dad in the morning.

'Let's do that.'

They climbed inside, the aircab ascended, and Roger closed his eyes.

Alisha had to wake him when they reached the student house.

THIRTY

FULGOR, 2603 AD

Stella Weissmann, seated behind her desk, looked at the four holo images surrounding her in Skein. Their communication was realtime, using ordinary speech – enciphered, but able to be replayed to non-Luculenti should the need arise.

Superintendent Sunadomari said: '*You agree Roger Blackstone is a Pilot?*'

'From his reaction to my words,' Weissmann replied, 'I give it a ninety-seven per cent near certainty. He recognized the Siberian fragment was different from the other.'

The building's memory contained full recordings. If necessary, anyone with sufficient authority could browse them to check her conclusions.

Commander Maria Petrova said: '*I'm checking the father's activities right now. He's been in place for such a long time. If he's a Pilot, he's no ordinary one.*'

'A sleeper agent?'

'*No, a fully active agent-in-place, in my opinion.*'

'*So what we're conducting is a counterintelligence operation.*' Sunadomari was frowning. '*How does this fit with the murders?*'

'Perhaps they compromised Blackstone's cover.'

'*Unlikely.*' This was Luculentus Harvey Bashir. '*It's a rather noticeable way of maintaining a low profile.*'

'The deaths are almost unreported in Skein' – Weissmann nodded towards Sunadomari – 'thanks to Keinosuke here.'

'*Agreed,*' said Bashir. '*But the killers could not have counted on that.*'

'*You still think it's a group?*' asked Sunadomari.

'*Eight of the victims died at the same instant, pretty much,*' said

Colonel Keller. *'Think how much more capability that implies, taking them down at the same time, compared to eight or more killers working in coordination.'*

'The thought of eight people able to strike through Skein is pretty awful.'

'We don't ignore a scenario just because we don't like it.'

'True. So what happens next?'

Bashir's image turned towards Sunadomari's.

'You've got full surveillance on the boy?'

'SatScan, building systems, and watch teams on the whole family.'

'And this Rafaella Stargonier?' asked Weissmann.

Commander Maria Petrova was frowning.

'We don't know where she is.'

'Excuse me?'

'She's dropped out of surveillance entirely.'

'How can she do that?'

'If we knew, maybe we could find her.'

'Damn it. So, everyone, presumably we're done for now. When do we hook up again?'

All eyes, real and holo, turned towards Colonel Keller's image.

'Oh-nine-hundred, or when something significant happens. Agreed?'

There were four nods.

'Then out.'

Stella Weissmann was alone in her office. She lowered her chin, closed her eyes, and relaxed into trance, letting herself go deep, allowing the submerged parts of her extended mind to integrate all her perceptions, to allow new insights to arise.

Five minutes later, she looked up.

'Hello, Stella Weissmann. Or should I say—'

A tall Luculenta with black hair was standing on the threshold.

'—*Luculenta* Stella Weissmann?'

The stranger was Rafaella Stargonier.

No!

Weissmann tried to form the trigger thought activating defenceware inside her plexweb and the room's inbuilt weaponry. But it was too late, as vampire code burst through her interfaces, ravened through her nervous system, and heisenberged her mind to destruction.

Her universe was set to null.

Rafaella knelt down beside the corpse and turned the head. No trace remained of studs or wires, the normal signs of upraise. Either someone had performed excellent surgery, or Weissmann had been upraised with this appearance all along, meaning she had planned a career in the intelligence services even then, with the collusion of the Via Lucis Institute.

The woman's torn, fragmented memories would tell everything; but for now, Rafaella needed to keep them brimming inside her internal cache, sandboxed from the rest of her mind, because for several seconds during integration with another persona, she was vulnerable to attack.

Soon, even that limitation would be gone.

But at least she had newness waiting to suck into her. She had been so hungry, after relinquishing her opportunity in Parallaville, knowing her current configuration was almost full. She needed more plexnodes, to increase her capacity to absorb new minds.

Preferably without the limitations that had led to her predecessor's demise.

'Stella Weissmann, you were a *bad* girl. Keeping secrets.'

During the transfer, she had picked up that much.

'Let's see where you've kept it, the poor thing.'

She went out to the corridor, looked at the flagstones one by one, then formed a command. The floor swirled like a whirlpool, and she stepped into the disturbance.

'Clever.'

Closing her eyes, she let the quickstone take her down – three metres, five, an estimated ten metres before it lowered her into clear space. The material sucked back into the ceiling.

She was in a subterranean chamber, far larger than she had expected. But then half of it was walled off, divided by a massive transparent barrier. And beyond it—

'Well, look at you.'

—floated a lattice of crimson light, darkened here and there by two decades of torture, interrogation that had failed to yield anything about the matter she was interested in.

'Weissmann and her little pals understood enough to cripple you, didn't they? To keep you from teleporting out?'

The Zajinet prisoner twisted and roiled, backing away in its cell.

'That's right. I'm interested in Calabi-Yau dimensions, and how to send energy along them.'

Now, the Zajinet was blazing with desperate light.

'Twenty years of torture, and they got nothing from you.'

The alien's spilled light turned Rafaella's face the colour of blood.

'Amateurs,' she said.

THIRTY-ONE

EARTH, 1927–1930 A.D.

Gavriela immersed herself in studying. By the time she graduated, her brother Erik had married Ilse and moved to Amsterdam; but Father and Mother resisted her cajoling, and remained in Berlin. She could stare at the complex dots and smears of an X-ray diffraction image, and from it deduce a crystal's structure without working through the maths. But deciphering her parents' thoughts and motivation were of another order of difficulty, and far beyond her.

You would think that the older a person was, the more they would recognize that the world could change, and sometimes very fast.

She began to teach students privately, as she worked for her doctorate. The atomic theory that owed so much to Einstein – who remained her hero – was one of the great intellectual achievements of humanity. What she wanted was to learn the secrets of the universe.

It was something to remember when she shopped carefully, counting every centime, and wondered what it would be like to have a career that brought in steady earnings. Still, she found enough funds, leading up to the summer break, to buy a railway ticket for Amsterdam, so she could visit Erik and Ilse.

Finally, it was the end of July, and she rode in a warm train carriage whose rocking motion lulled her, despite the jagged white Alpine magnificence on view outside; and she drifted, remembering last week. Professor Hartmann was her supervisor now, and she was glad for his support.

'I would like you to deliver a few lectures next year,' Professor Hartmann had told her, a big smile on his leonine face, his mane of white hair glistening. 'And once you are Frau Doktor Wolf, we can make it more regular.'

'Why, yes, Herr Professor!'

'There is only one thing. My name will have to appear on the lecture notices, and you will be announced as the assistant.'

'Oh. Well, I understand.'

'Without Herr Professor Möller's support, the faculty board would not have agreed at all, but there is one good thing.'

'Herr Professor?'

'This is the start of the 1930s, telegraph lines run beneath the Atlantic, aeroplanes fly the skies, and more books are being published than ever before. German culture – I don't just mean within that country's borders – remains unparalleled, from philosophy to music, and now in science.'

'Perhaps the twentieth century is when we finally become civilized. Have you read Korzybski, Herr Professor?'

'Ah, *Manhood of Humanity*, and his dedication to Gantt and scientific management of commerce. The Great War taught us that rational thinking is the only way to maintain peace, so Korzybski has that much right, at least.'

Moments like that made her realize how lucky she was, to be in a place where human understanding advanced, where learning was taken seriously.

But now, as the train carriage rattled over a junction, she recalled some different stories coming from Bavaria, from the pretty gingerbread town of Munich that she had lived in as a girl, taking ice-cream in a café on the cobbled Marienplatz and staring up at the mediaeval town hall, walking to the river, stopping on the way to giggle at the stern statue of Maximilian on his horse.

Professor Hartmann's optimism was a comfort when she thought of Bavaria.

There were others in the carriage: a young Belgian man who perhaps tried to catch her eye, but then hid himself behind his *Süddeutsche Zeitung*, bought from a news-vendor on the station concourse. An older man was asleep. An elegant woman whose blond hair shone with careful grooming sat with a basket on her lap, staring straight ahead.

She wore a feathered hat and a coat that was surely too warm, but seemed not to notice.

Gavriela sneezed – stray summer dust – and the woman looked at her.

'Bless you.'

'Thank you.'

After a time, Gavriela took out the book she had been reading, holding it so her fellow travellers could not make out the title or author. There were those who would consider Herr Doktor Freud's works unsuitable for a feminine readership, however many of his patients were women. Part of her was afraid to find a reference to a Fräulein W, meaning herself – but her own case had been nothing interesting, not then. Doktor Freud's mesmerism had relaxed her, making her life so much better, but it had been simple tiredness from overwork, no more ... at that time.

Until those events later in Berlin, the apparition in the churchyard, the visions that hung above the entranced men's heads in the school hall—

She floated in a golden space, near a city-world that bristled with towers and complex structures, where vessels swarmed amid futuristic splendour ...

'—my dear?' It was the glamorous woman.

'Oh, I'm sorry.' Gavriela came awake, and smiled around the carriage. 'My apologies.'

The two men, smoking – the older had also woken – told her it was nothing. The younger man glanced at the book on Gavriela's lap. Face growing warm, she closed the book and tucked it away beside her.

'Although the gentlemen are not hungry,' said the woman, 'perhaps you could snack with me? So I'm not alone.'

'I'm not—Actually, yes, thank you. You're very kind.'

'So what did that lazy maid of mine pack for us? I let her get away with too much. My husband always says, Magda, you're too soft with that girl.' She opened the basket. 'So. Good enough. We have bread and sausage and all sorts. Does that sound good to you?'

'Absolutely.'

They shared the food mostly in silence, the two men declining another offer to join them. It was only afterwards, as the woman was packing the remains back in the basket, that the food Gavriela had eaten petrified in her stomach.

'At least,' the woman said, 'it proves you're not one of them.'

She nodded towards the newspaper, and a small article entitled *Bankers Are Predominantly Jewish.*

'Excuse me?'

'The pork sausage you enjoyed so much. It means you're one of the *Volk*, doesn't it?'

The word meant so much more than *people*.

Folding up his newspaper, the young Belgian shook his head, saying nothing. The beautiful woman paid no attention, retaining a faint smile for the remainder of her journey.

Steam billowed and whistles sounded, as Gavriela carried her suitcase along the platform. Ilse was waiting for her, smiling and waving her glove. She put the glove back on once Gavriela had spotted her.

'Would you like to take a taxi?' asked Ilse after they hugged. 'Or shall we walk?'

'My case—'

'Oh, I can carry that.'

So they walked, following clean streets, alongside canals where possible. Gavriela liked being in new places; but she was equally impressed – almost intimidated – by her sister-in-law. She had not realized how physically strong Ilse could be. She herself could not have lugged the case far – it was small but heavy – yet Ilse carried it as easily as a handbag.

Ilse quickened the pace as they passed along a narrow passageway. Women with reptilean eyes were waiting in the doorways, their gazes flicking away from Gavriela and Ilse, fastening on the few men who walked here.

'Sorry,' muttered Ilse. 'But it's much quicker this way.'

'All right,' said Gavriela, not understanding.

It was ten minutes later, at the corner of a well-kept road, that she paused and said: 'Oh.'

'What is it?'

'Those women—'

'Exactly.' Ilse raised her eyebrows. 'You think Berlin is any different?'

Indoors, the rooms were high-ceilinged and smelled of wax polish, everything spotless. Being a housewife was hard work, but Ilse was more than that.

'How is the book-keeping going?'

'The tobacco shop's owner, Herr van Rijk, is alternately mortified at having a woman keep his figures and overjoyed at the job I'm doing. I nearly asked him if I could serve in the shop for a while, but I didn't want to overtax his heart.'

'My dear,' said Gavriela. 'That would hardly be seemly in a gentlemen's tobacconist.'

They giggled.

'And that brother of mine,' Gavriela continued. 'How is he?'

'He walks very well. His employers at the Census Bureau work him hard, but he enjoys it. We're doing all right.'

'You deserve it.'

It was evening by the time Erik arrived home – he used a silver-tipped walking-cane with the straightforwardness of long practice – and hugged Gavriela. Her day had passed quickly, gossiping with Ilse, comparing their lives and cities: Ilse's Amsterdam, Gavriela's Zürich, and the Berlin they both knew.

Now her beloved brother was here. His leather eye-patch was clean, his face somehow harder than before, and he looked very handsome.

'I've got something to show you,' he said as they sat down for supper. 'Take a look at this.'

Reaching inside his suit jacket, he withdrew a card bearing broken rows of tiny square holes.

'What is this?' Gavriela took hold of it. 'I've not seen anything like it.'

'It's a Hollerith card,' said Ilse. 'If you hang around Erik long enough, you learn these things.'

Erik smiled at her, an expression that told Gavriela everything she needed to know about their marriage. She grinned at them both, then returned her attention to the punched card.

'They're used to control mechanized looms,' Erik said. 'The pattern of holes effectively forms instructions for weaving.'

'Very good.' Gavriela caught on immediately. 'If you change the pattern of holes, you obtain a different weave.'

She might not recognize prostitutes when she saw them on the street, but logical principles were clear to her, whether in theory or in mechanical devices.

'So you've been visiting a clothing factory?' she added. 'Or is it carpets?'

'Neither one. We're using them now at the Bureau.'

Ilse passed plates around the table.

'The Bureau has realized that taking census figures is boring,' she said. 'So they're branching out into dressmaking.'

'That would be one explanation.' Erik smiled at her again. 'Or there's another use, storing information about people. One card, one citizen.'

'You could decide what pieces of information you need to hold,' said Gavriela. 'And you could change the encoding accordingly. That's interesting.'

'Or one might write the information' – Ilse pointed to a sideboard where a closed notebook lay with a fountain-pen on top – 'on paper, in a manner comprehensible to actual living people.'

Erik spread his hands.

'Try searching through millions of pages for the information you need. Machinery can do it so much better.'

'It'll never catch on, dear,' said Ilse.

'Whatever you say,' answered Erik.

All was well. They ate their supper, chatting about trivia, enjoying their time together.

Later, Erik smoked and drank brandy – the latter a new habit – while Ilse did the washing up in the kitchen. Gavriela, at Ilse's insistence, remained sitting opposite Erik.

'Mother and Father,' he said, 'think you're soft in the head, trying to get them to leave Berlin. But I'm glad Ilse and I made the move.'

'She's the best.'

'Yes, she is.' Warmth filled his good eye. 'I am so very lucky.'

Gavriela thought that other people in his position would count their misfortunes; but Erik was better than that.

'I think perhaps Ilse is lucky also, dear brother.'

'Ha. I hope so. But it wasn't only you that persuaded me, it was your friend Jürgen that night in Berlin, the night you never talked about.'

Gavriela's happiness seeped away.

'You never saw him. You were up in your room. And he wasn't a friend, though he helped me.'

And his real name had been Dmitri Shtemenko.

'Was that the only time you ever saw him?'

'Yes. Absolutely. Erik, why does that matter to you?'

For several moments, he toyed with the Hollerith card, staring at it as if he were alone in the parlour. Then he looked up at her.

'I'm a rationalist, you know that. Not to mention an atheist like yourself, good sister.'

'A Jewish atheist, you mean.'

She remembered the awful woman in the train carriage. Eating pork was fine by Gavriela; it was the realization that she had passed a test by eating the sausage, showing herself to be a real person in the woman's eyes – that was what had sickened her stomach.

'It could be worse.' Erik's smile lightened the moment. 'We

could be *Catholic* atheists, and how guilty would we feel then?'

'Right. So Comrade Dmitri Shtemenko, who called himself Jürgen . . . What about him?'

'A Bolshevik? And Shtemenko was his real name?'

'That's what he said.'

'He—' Erik stopped, lit another cigarette, and took two deep pulls. 'He walks in darkness. I don't know how else to say it.'

'How did you—?'

'It's insane perhaps, but black – things – floated around him as he walked down the street, leaving the house. I was watching from my window.'

'I don't believe it.'

'They were very faint, and I know it was only weeks after this' – he pointed to his eye-patch, then his bad leg – 'so I could have hallucinated. But my mind had knitted itself together by then, thanks to Ilse. I'm sure of it.'

Gavriela let out a long breath.

'I don't believe,' she said, 'that you can see the darkness too.'

'*What?*'

'I thought' – she began to cry – 'I thought I was the only one.'

Perhaps she could see it more easily, for the darkness that she detected was always hard-edged and strong, curling and revolving in impossible ways; but at least he perceived something.

Erik stared at her for a long time. Then he said: 'There's at least one other that we know.'

'Who's that?' Gavriela dabbed at her eyes, recovering. 'Who do you mean?'

'Comrade Dmitri Shtemenko. He was aware of the shadows around him. He tried to shrug them off and walk away, but they moved with him. It looked as if he was used to doing it.'

'*Oy vay.*'

'*Oy oy,* indeed. He looked as if he was used to failing, too. To get away from the shadows.'

Gavriela stared into her own memory.

'I saw something strange in the old school hall,' she said after a time. 'Not to mention the graveyard afterwards.'

Then she related all she remembered of the darkness-haunted orator, the real-seeming visions he conjured above the crowd, and later the apparition that appeared in the cemetery, distracting the thugs who were advancing on her and Dmitri, allowing the Russian time to use his blades, killing all three of them.

When Ilse returned, teapot in hand, she looked from one to the other.

'Are you two all right?'

'Talking about . . . dark things,' said Erik. 'Sorry, dear.'

'Well, there is evil in the world, I know that much.' Ilse put the teapot down. 'But there are good things too.'

'And you're one of them, Frau Wolf.'

'Thank you, Herr Wolf.'

Gavriela blinked.

'I love you both,' she said.

THIRTY-TWO

LABYRINTH, 2603 AD (REALSPACE-EQUIVALENT)

Max gave it seven days, mean-geodesic time, before talking to the ancient Pilot whose title was Head of Records. His name was Kelvin Stanier, and they met in his office – that deprecated word again – because this was something that deserved to be done in person.

'I'm here for a bad reason, Kelvin. Sorry.'

'An operative deceased?'

Max nodded.

'My condolences. Will there be a body?'

'No.'

'And the ship?'

Max looked down to his right, then straight at Kelvin. 'Nothing.'

'Okay.' Kelvin gestured a holospace into being. 'The officer's name?'

'Avril Tarquelle.'

'Shit.' Kelvin lowered his hands. 'She's so— She was a bright one.'

'Not to mention young.'

'Have we notified the family?'

'There isn't—She had no relatives. Or close relationships.'

Kelvin said nothing for a time.

'It was that kind of mission, was it?'

'Yes.'

'Do you have confirmation, or was it just that she never came back?'

'The latter.'

'So. Very well.' Kelvin made the control gestures in a fine, exact manner, like sacramental ritual. 'It's done.'

No trace of Avril Tarquelle's existence remained in the official data.

Kelvin added: 'How are you doing, Max? Are you sleeping all right?'

'I feel fucking awful.'

Old eyes glittering, Kelvin looked at him for several seconds.

'That's exactly how you *should* feel, old friend.'

Max used fastpath rotation, stepping out into the antechamber of his office. Just as he reached the threshold, more panes of nothingness began to rotate behind him.

Waiting in the open doorway, he watched as a familiar white-haired figure stepped through, her movements lithe despite her years.

'Admiral Kaltberg. Please come in.'

He went inside, and gestured for drinks. A selection of decanters and crystal glasses rose on a table from the floor. Old-fashioned but stylish: that was the way to conduct this meeting.

But something in the admiral's manner, as she took a seat and crossed her legs, told him that this was not going to proceed in a predictable manner.

'Brandy ma'am? Or something different?'

'I don't—Sorry, Max. What am I here for?'

'Admiral?'

'My retirement, was that it?'

Max moved behind his desk and sat, every sense on full alert.

'You wanted to check that Dr Sapherson was going to give you very selective amnesia, ma'am. I believe that was your concern.'

'I—Yes, that must be it. Why I'm . . . here.'

'Only the most confidential data will disappear from your mind,' he said. 'A team of watchmen did a survey of retired operatives just last year. Practically zero memory disappearance beyond the desired data. And they reported a *strengthening* of cognitive functions, as the majority of memories were repotentiated during the procedure.'

Beneath his desk, his hands formed a control gesture.

Shit.

In the admiral's old eyes, golden sparks were forming.

'Admiral, I need to warn you—'

'M-Max ...'

He admired her so much. The idea of harming her was awful.

'What's going on, ma'am?'

'G-uh ...'

'Ma'am?'

'G-uh ...'

There two choices. He looked up at the ceiling.

'Medical emergency,' he said. 'Open up—'

'Get ... out ... Max.'

Her left hand was trembling.

Oh fuck.

The hand that was holding the graser pistol, pointed at him.

'Stop this.'

It was an antique weapon, which was why it got past scanners – if it was carried by an admiral – but coherent gamma rays could kill as easily as smartmist.

And her eyes were brightening, golden sparks whirling in black orbs.

'Flee ... Max. My ... friend.'

Her left hand was shaking, but the graser would still get him, and it took just a tiny movement to squeeze the firing-stud.

'I'm not leaving you, Admiral.'

'Must ...'

Finger, about to tighten.

Everything dropped from his perception except that knuckle, about to squeeze.

'Aaah! Fuck!' she cried out.

A golden explosion took place *inside* her eyes, yet no energy burst forth. Max had never heard of such a thing. His last new experience before dying?

Still she had not fired.

'Max.' Smoke rose from her eyeballs. 'I'm neurally wired. Get the fuck out of here.'

'I can't.'

'Now. It's an order. Whether I fire the graser or not' – her eyes were opaque grey, burned out, but she could still target him – 'it's going to explode. You've ten seconds at most.'

He made the emergency control gesture.

'Drop the weapon. We'll both go.'

Behind him, a whirlpool of yellow nothingness grew: his escape.

'I can't control the hand, Max.'

'No—'

'Quick. *Go!*'

She fired as he leapt into the yellow.

He fell through layers of reality.

Someone will pay.

Max accepted the danger of his job. But someone had used Admiral Adrienne Kaltberg as an assassination tool, and that deserved punishment. In a city-world with fractal time, pain could be made to last forever.

She would be dead by now. Clearly part of her mind – part of her brain – understood what had been done to her. It was easy to set a graser for self-destruction, and the explosion would be devastating – would have *been* devastating, for it had surely occurred.

Bastards.

Whoever they were, he would find them and bring punishment on their heads.

Admiral, you were the best.

Ironically, his office was thoroughly shielded and armoured. It would have served to contain the explosion; but everything and everyone inside would have been annihilated. He wondered how long it would take Internal Security to break in.

And whether they would think that he had perished along with Admiral Kaltberg.

That would be a help.

He came out into a long cavernous space that looked as if it stretched forever – which was geometrically true. Bulbous pillars in all directions, glowing, illuminated the soft, endless, grey-blue floor and ceiling.

There were food stashes all over – he had planned his emergency routes with care, over many years – but no devices existed here to help him. That was part of what kept this entire infinite subspace off the grid, undetectable from the rest of Labyrinth.

And that was why the only way to reach any of his exit points was on foot. None was closer than a three-day walk from here.

The Med Centre. That would be a good one.

By exiting outside Ascension Annexe, he would be into public areas where enemies might hesitate to move; but the Med Centre would have access to emergency systems. He could mobilize people he trusted.

Because the enemy, whoever they were, clearly included people with the highest level of security clearance, able to plan a killing inside the heart of the intelligence service.

So, the Med Centre it was.

'Here we go,' he said aloud, to an entire reality inhabited only by him. 'Might as well start now.'

It would take seven, maybe eight days to reach the exit point he had decided on.

Reading subtle rune-like markings on the pillars – his own secret code – he headed in the chosen direction. Perhaps twenty minutes into the journey, he stopped.

'My God, Admiral. How did you do it?'

For he had worked out the meaning behind her actions, and

could not imagine doing it himself. Such discipline and courage were beyond him.

The neural wiring had been active and adaptive, reinforcing itself as it worked, predominantly inside the right hemisphere of her brain. Thinking back, it was obvious.

Every intelligence officer learned to read minutiae. In everyday conversation, often a person's left hand will make subtle gestures that either reinforce or give the lie to the words that the person is speaking. It happens all the time, yet so few people notice.

But, though the admiral's left hemisphere could utter words, it had not been enough to quell the cross-brain compulsion from the implanted neural 'wiring' – a femtoviral targetted infection.

Not until she had directed her inductive energy inwards, burning out the corpus callosum in her own brain, severing the bridge that linked her two cerebral hemispheres.

And then she had fought, herself against herself inside her mind, giving him time to escape.

Admiral Kaltberg. She deserved to be remembered with honour; just as her enemies deserved to experience eternal pain.

Now he had two reasons to keep on going.

THIRTY-THREE

EARTH, 1930–1939 A.D.

One afternoon on Bahnhofstrasse, Gavriela was walking with Florian Horst, the big ex-soldier who had been in her class that first day, helping Herr Professor Möller use the big wire basket as a Faraday cage. Like Gavriela, he was working on his doctorate; and they were deep into discussion of the new Rutherford results when someone called Gavriela's name.

'Oh,' she said. 'Florian, these are old friends of mine.'

Petra, Elke and Inge were smiling, waiting to be introduced. Elke blushed when she shook Florian's hand.

'You've known Gavriela for a long time?' asked Florian.

'Since her first week here.'

'Well, that's how long I've known her.'

'So,' said Petra, 'do you know any juicy scandal about Fräulein Wolf that we don't?'

'I don't think so.'

'Then we'll just have to tell you all her secrets.'

'Oh, please.' Gavriela was smiling.

'You're not the one who's going to Denmark, are you?' asked Elke.

'Ah, no.' Florian shrugged his heavy shoulders. 'That would be Lucas Krause.'

'I see,' said Elke, smiling.

Petra, Inge and Gavriela exchanged looks. Lucas was the one with the offer to join the Bohr Institute; he was also the one whose eyes captivated Gavriela, but who shied away from any hint of intimate conversation.

'I believe I know you, sir,' said Elke.

'Fräulein?'

'There was a strongman competition in a beer hall, during the autumn festival. Lifting the stones and anvils.'

'Ah.' Florian grinned. 'That could be.'

'Herr Horst used to be a soldier,' Gavriela said.

'I adore the military,' said Elke.

'But I'm only a physicist now.'

'So you can explain to me how big the solar system is?'

'And the entire universe, which we call the Milky Way.'

'Gavriela was talking about the galaxy, but I didn't understand.'

'Galaxy and universe are the same thing,' said Florian. 'The Milky Way is just our perspective on the rest of the galaxy-universe. We're right out on the edge, you know.'

'Near the end of everything?'

'That's exactly right.'

Elke shivered.

'And it's also the reason,' Florian went on, 'that we need careful management of the peace, because we're a fragile species on the only known inhabited world, orbiting around the only star that is known to have planets.'

The awe on Elke's face bore little relation to the mild interest she showed in Gavriela's physics. Among themselves, the others would later decide this marked the moment Elke fell in love.

'We were about to go to a café,' said Petra, for Elke's sake. 'Please join us.'

'I'd be delighted.'

Once installed at a table, they chose cakes and ordered coffee. While they were waiting, Petra put a tiny silver box on the table.

'Anybody need a pick-me-up?'

'What is it?'

'Something that Sigmund Freud recommends' – Petra nodded towards Gavriela – 'as a way of clearing the mind of neurotic malaise, a positivity tonic.'

'You mean cocaine,' said Florian. 'I hear it has some unfortunate drawbacks.'

'Nonsense. Does no one else want to try some?'

'No, thanks.'

'Not for me.'

Petra opened the little box.

'Suit yourselves.'

Later, Gavriela would pinpoint that day as a turning-point, when their old friendships changed course. For Elke, it would be the commencement of a swift romance, a delirious marriage, and eventually emigration, as Florian too gained a post in Copenhagen.

For Petra it was the beginning of a different kind of tale.

Over the coming months and years, Gavriela sometimes met a lover – but only in her dreams, and though she sometimes woke with Roger's name upon her lips, by the time she came to full wakefulness, the shards of remembered fantasy had sunk into amnesia.

It continued that way until the decade's end, when nightmare rushed into the waking world, as German tanks began to mobilize and the warlike mood strengthened, after the horror known as Kristallnacht descended out of nowhere.

Even after Kristallnacht, there had been letters from Berlin. But as the year slipped from '38 to '39, the news became worse. Many of those imprisoned at first were released – save for the two thousand beaten to death during their incarceration; but then the true intention of the Nazi state revealed itself. News became darker, whispered rumours and the things that were not stated in the newspapers; and eventually, no more letters from Berlin, none at all.

Switzerland, determined to maintain neutrality, continued to run train services, though no one pretended these were normal times. It was possible, if you chose to risk it, to travel into Germany.

One morning in September, nearly a full year after Kristallnacht, Gavriela walked to the Hauptbahnhof without luggage and bought three return tickets to Berlin. As she boarded alone, she could only hope – or delude herself – that her parents would be with her on the journey back.

Dmitri awoke to the sight of pert buttocks – four cheeks, two nice little arses – bare to the air in his bed. Piotr and Ludmilla were brother and sister, and very willing. To do anything, for so little payment, but never for free.

They were in his bed, but he was alone, and always would be.

He rolled out, bare feet on the cold floor, and found the greatcoat he used as a dressing-gown. Then he pulled it on, slid open the wooden door to the hallway, and grabbed his towel and soap from the table inside the apartment's front door. He could have washed with the pitcher and bowl in his room, but he preferred the communal bathroom.

Also, it was a test. If any of his belongings were disturbed on his return, he would take it out on Ludmilla first, then her lovely brother. And the valuable stuff was beneath floorboards, at the back of the pantry, and underneath the wardrobe, in hiding-places that amateurs were unlikely to discover.

Back in his bedroom after getting washed, his hair slicked down and tightly combed, he dressed quickly, using double knots on his shoelaces as always, because the ability to run could be a lifesaver. His twin stilettos went into their usual hidden sheaths – on his left forearm and left calf – because they could be deathbringers.

He adjusted collar studs and cuff-links, checked his reflection, ran the comb through his beard, then turned to the two naked teenagers on his bed.

'Be out of here by nine. Take your present from the table by the door.'

Pulling on his overcoat and fur hat, he left.

The street was cold in the early morning, wide and deserted – like Paris but free of traffic, for only a few official cars ever passed along the wide boulevards. Few Muscovites would know what Paris looked like; but Dmitri was no ordinary citizen, and the comparison seemed natural to him.

There was a large M over the station entrance, and whether you pronounced it *mye-tra* or *mé-tro*, it was still the same thing, another similarity. Dmitri descended into the depths of Dobrininskya Station with his fellow commuters.

Here, the similarity to Paris ended. The walls were a yellow neo-Renaissance splendour, with a mosaic whose nearest Parisian counterpart was inside the Louvre, not an underground railway station. But Moscow's Metro stations were palaces of the future, with crystal chandeliers and the most expensive marble, each station unique in its artistic architecture.

In a secular state, the proletariat's faith was restricted to their descendants' hopes for prosperity; the stations were a reminder that such mundane paradise was possible.

At Park Kultury, sometimes called Gorky Park but never officially, he alighted from the Circle Line. Coffee-coloured swirls in marble surrounded gleaming white panels; and again the chandeliers shone.

He made two interruptions to his journey, both short stops to meet informants, and finally reached Dzerzhninsky Square, where Beria's fearsome statue frowned down upon the citizens who dared not look upon his face.

Inside Headquarters, a young lieutenant saluted and said: 'Sir, Colonel Yavorski would like to see you now.'

'Thank you.'

There was a samovar in the canteen full of the dark tea he needed to get his brain functional. But if the colonel said now, he expected instant compliance. Dmitri's shoes clicked along the parquet flooring, then he knocked on the colonel's door and slid it open.

'Sit down,' said Yavorski, 'so I can thank you properly for another job well done.'

'Sir?'

Dmitri closed the door and crossed to the hardbacked chair, while Yavorski took his place behind the heavy desk, beneath which was slung a holstered Stechkin pistol that was supposed to be a secret.

So what kind of thanks do I get today?

Inside, he smiled, though his face remained blank. He had dark impulses, betraying what he thought was right; and he had *twisty* impulses, driving him to betray the darkness inside him, to trick the Trickster. It gave him a love of gambling, though he despised money.

He preferred more interesting stakes.

'I'm referring,' said Yavorski, 'to one of your perspicacious reports from several years back.'

There was a folder on his desk. A vindication or proof of incompetence?

Here it comes.

Yavorski tapped the folder.

'The Nationalist Socialist movement in Germany has risen from obscurity to power, as you predicted. Although how you could guess that Hindenberg would offer the Reichs-chancellorship to Hitler, I have no idea. Luckily, your report was my defence.'

'Thank you, sir. I knew that Hitler has . . . persuasive powers.'

'Well, good. Without your report . . . I'm just glad we're not in the regular army. Do you have any idea how many officers have been shot by our Great Leader's order?'

'Not exactly, sir.'

But he knew that thanks to Josef Stalin's actions, the military was almost headless, leaving only ordinary troops who would do whatever the Great Leader said, but without the strategic and tactical experience to wage any kind of true warfare.

'Only the British have been yelping about German rearmament, and that's stirring things up in an interesting way, because the Great Leader despises the British above all.'

'They *are* reactionary imperialists, sir.'

'True, and this little Bavarian corporal heads the National *Socialist* party, but they're the natural enemies of Bolshevism, not our allies.'

'Allies?'

'Premier Stalin will do the opposite of whatever the British want. That, I'm sure of.'

'That's . . . very interesting, Colonel.'

'But you think the Germans will turn on us later, even if they sign a treaty of alliance?'

This was the kind of question that could make the difference between promotion and the firing-squad.

'I do.'

'Privately, Dmitri, I agree with you. But I'd like you to be far away from here, just in case someone disagrees with your assessment.'

So this was to be an assignment. Every nerve thrummed with alertness.

'The west is a known quantity, at least to me,' Yavorski continued. 'What I need is a linguist with a devious mind to work on the east.'

'Within the USSR, sir?'

He knew that western Europeans woefully underestimated the vastness of the Soviet empire, far larger than the United States of America, and the mix of peoples from Aryan types to Mongol, all united by the common tongue of Russia, just as Latin once united Europe.

'You'll spend a few weeks in the Kueriles,' said Yavorski. 'But only to acclimatize and equip yourself. There's a ship arriving with your assistant aboard, an experienced man called Sergei Alegeev, who's quite a wrestler.'

Dmitri blinked, then asked the question Yavorski was clearly expecting.

'A wrestler, sir?'

'Once you're in Tokyo, he'll use his contacts at the judo headquarters, the Kodokan, to help you. It's not the sportsmen we're interested in, it's their military connections.'

The Kuerile Islands had long been disputed territory. The Japanese claimed they belonged to the emperor, not to Mother Russia.

'I did the usual sambo course in training,' said Dmitri. 'Is it similar?'

Yavorski looked left and right, an indication that whatever he was about to say, he would deny later.

'Sambo actually *is* judo, but we've erased the story of its origins for the usual reasons. So now it's a purely Soviet discipline, not a Japanese art with a few add-ons from our territories' native wrestling.'

Dmitri remembered hearing about a top judo man being executed, and had dismissed the case as unimportant.

'You want me to observe the Japanese military, sir?'

'The Great Leader is terrified – or would be if he weren't so courageous – of the Japanese intentions. So, by the way, are the few surviving generals who are giving thought to the current situation.'

Rubbing his face, Dmitri thought it might be allowable to reveal his ignorance at this point.

'I'm no expert on the Orient. Not yet.'

'Trust me, Dmitri, neither am I, but I'm clear on one thing.' Yavorksi tapped the folder again. Perhaps it wasn't Dmitri's work, but a different dossier. 'The Japanese have held Manchuria even longer than the other new territories, from Burma to the Philippines. Think of it – Vladivostok is surrounded by the bastards. Either they'll go all out into central China at some point, or they'll turn their attention to us. But they don't have the resources for both.'

'Ah.' Dmitri thought about the geography, and the Chinese 'magnetic warfare' strategy that had drawn the invaders so far inland already, at huge cost. 'They might decide we're the easier target. '

'Precisely. However murky and complex your job gets out there, that's the simple heart of it. Do they intend to attack us? Answer that question, and your mission is fulfilled.'

Dmitri nodded. This was more clarity than he often had before a long-term assignment. Now he could assimilate the details against a background of understanding, a logical context.

'We have the force of dialectical materialism on our side, Colonel. Our victory is inevitable.'

Yavorski smiled, reached beneath his desk – *going for the pistol?* – then pulled open a drawer and extracted a large bottle of Stolichnaya, the lemon vodka that he loved and Dmitri detested, but had never said.

'Let's drink to that, Dmitri.'

In Amsterdam, Ilse Wolf was working at home, poring over a ledger on the kitchen table, when the brass knocker rapped twice on the front door – surely not Erik, having forgotten something – then a third time. A stranger's knock.

She capped her fountain pen, used blotting paper on the figures she had written, then went to answer the door.

'Ah, Frau Wolf. You remember me, I trust? Hans t'Hooft, from the Census Bureau?'

He smelled of hair tonic, his blond hair slick, his parting made with razor precision.

'Um, yes. Of course. Erik's already left for the office.'

'That is good, because it is you I would like to see. Shall we go inside?'

Ilse was already inside, and every instinct warned her to slam the door shut. But this was one of Erik's colleagues, and the job was important. Or perhaps it was the disquieting news from Germany that made her feel the need for conversation with someone she recognized, even if she disliked them.

'I was just going to make some tea.'

'That would be very nice, Ilse. It's all right if I call you Ilse?'

'Um . . .' She shook her head, then headed for the kitchen. 'Please sit yourself in the front parlour, Herr t'Hooft.'

But he followed her into the kitchen, and stood too close as she filled the kettle, popped the whistle over the spout, and put it on the range.

His tongue was like a snake's as it flickered across his lips.

Ilse said: 'May I ask what you wanted to talk about?'

'You may.' From his inside pocket, he withdrew a punched card. 'You know what this is?'

Ilse wiped her hands on a tea-towel, although they were clean.

'It's a Hollerith card.'

'An impressive answer, but quite incorrect, dear beautiful Ilse. You *are* very beautiful, did you know that?'

She backed away, cloth held before her.

'I'm a married woman, Herr t'Hooft.'

'Plainly, but you haven't identified this, not clearly.' He held the card out to her, then gave a smile, and slipped it back inside his jacket. 'It's your death sentence.'

Ilse's ears filled with a sound like rushing surf.

'I don't understand.'

'Erik Wolf is a Jew. His card marks him as such. Plainly.'

A sick greenish phosphorescence seemed to slide across her vision.

'No . . .'

'Surely you knew you were marrying a Jew.'

She shook her head.

'For certain' – again the flickering lick – 'favours, it might be possible to alter incriminating information. Certain *intimate* favours.'

'Incriminating? There's nothing criminal about—'

'Surely you follow the news. Wehrmacht tanks will be rolling along Amsterdam streets in a matter of months, and we've already had certain – well, private visitors – who have indicated how useful it will be to use machine searches for vermin.'

From the range, a whistle sounded, steam flowing through the kettle's spout: a touch of domesticity amid the monstrous.

'No.' She let her hands drop, the tea-towel dangling to the floor. 'Please . . . the kettle.'

'By all means take it off the boil. But let's not pretend it's tea I'm interested in.'

Her hand was shaking as she reached for the kettle—

Dear God. Dear God.

—and swung it backhand, pivoting fast, smacking its weight into t'Hooft's temple. There was a soft crunch, and scalding water splashed on her hand. She yelled, then put the kettle down.

'Oh, no. Oh, no.'

Blood so dark it was almost purple was welling from the supine man's head. The slick hair was splayed like wires, or the limbs of a daddy-long-legs.

'Oh, no.'

Then she crouched down, reached inside the corpse's jacket with her unburned hand, and extracted what she needed.

So much evil, contained in a rectangle of innocuous card.

THIRTY-FOUR

FULGOR, 2603 AD

A nightmare tipped Roger into wakefulness before dawn. Grey images of heading on a train into a city filled with danger were evaporating, scarlet banners marked with a hooked cross, and then the real world coming into focus. In seconds, he had forgotten why he woke, remembering that he had gone two days without sleep prior to last night; and his body needed more.

But he had screwed up – possibly – by taking Alisha to the Zajinet Research Institute. There was something very sharp about the Weissmann woman – that came back to him now – and he did not like the way she had looked at him.

Had he betrayed himself and his family?

'If we ever get tripped up,' Dad told him when he was young, 'it will be through something trivial, something utterly harmless. So we treat each everyday action as *non*-routine. We focus on the moment, always. And lead better lives as a result.'

Later, when Roger was older, Dad had explained it differently: a streetwise fighter learns to put his or her attention out in the world, always aware of the current threat level – and in doing so, adopts a form of mindfulness that both mystic and psychological disciplines have aimed at for millennia.

'It's why Zen and killing are linked,' he said, 'when they ought to be opposites.'

In the context of holodramas like Roger's favourite, *Fighting Shadows*, there was something exciting in such discussions. But in the reality of everyday life, the likelihood of prison sentences arising from careless words delivered when exhausted ... it was just too stupid.

I've got to talk to Dad.

He had ways of establishing enciphered comms in emergency, using codes that not even Luculenti could break – or so Dad claimed. But although the signals might not be decipherable, they were detectable, and such high-encryption traffic was suspicious in itself.

Starting here on campus, he could possibly make the journey home undetected, using every trick he knew; but it would take many hours. Or he could simply call an aircab and fly home to see his parents: overt, perhaps a little unexpected, but surely nothing to raise suspicion in any watching peacekeepers.

So he washed with smartgel, and pulled on his clothing, refactoring it to jumpsuit shape, tuning it to dark blue. He could have done with breakfast, but he no longer thought he had time to waste. He used the fast route to exit his room – using the window as an extending quickglass slide that carried him to the house forecourt.

Walking clear, he summoned an aircab, and within a minute one was descending. Its interior was dark as the classic gull-wing door lifted. He slipped inside, the door came down, and as the aircab ascended he realized he had company.

The interior brightened to reveal a blond-haired man with bronze forehead studs smiling at him.

'Who the hell are you?'

'You don't know me?'

'No . . .' Roger blinked, then reached out. 'But I know *what* you are.'

His fingertips disappeared inside the man's arm.

'Well, part of it, at least.'

The holo changed.

'You.'

'Yes.' Now the virtual man next to Roger was familiar: pale oriental features, subtle bronze wires like highlights in his hair. 'You're not under arrest.'

'Superintendent Sunadomari.'

'You remember. Good. Would you like to know *why* you're not under arrest?'

There was no reason for an ordinary aircab to have ultra-res lasing capability, to project holos inside its cabin that were so realistic you needed senses other than sight to tell the difference.

'Is this a peacekeeper vehicle?'

'You're fast, Roger Blackstone. That's good.'

Mild acceleration pressed Roger back in his seat.

'Where are we going?'

'To your parents' house. That's where you want to go, isn't it?'

'I—'

He stopped. Sleep deprivation had fallen away, as the hormones of fear washed through his body: the ultimate stimulant.

'You didn't recognize this person.' For a moment, the holo Sunadomari became the holo blond Luculentus; then it snapped back to Sunadomari's actual appearance. 'Did you, Mr Blackstone?'

'No, Superintendent.'

'That's why you're not under arrest, despite what you are.'

Roger tried to swallow, but it felt as if murderous thumbs had fastened on his throat.

'Not only that,' Sunadomari went on, 'but you passed as ordinary human at Barleysugar Spiral, where we had new scanners in place. And I see you were well aware of that.'

All of this could be bluff, and a Luculentus peacekeeper would have enormous acuity and psych training; but the aircab was no civilian vehicle, and it could be filled with biotelemetry, scanning Roger's entire neurophysiology, with realtime results and analyses in Sunadomari's full awareness.

It was as close to mind-reading as you got in reality.

Dad, I'm sorry.

He got ready to transmit one last tu-ring signal, the bug-out burst that would tell his parents to flee now.

'Don't bother,' said Sunadomari. 'We're shielded in here.'

Defeat.

Half a kilometre from the house, at altitude, a peacekeeper flyer took up position alongside the aircab; and the holo Sunadomari disappeared. Roger said nothing as both vehicles descended and touched down.

Dad was waiting in the open doorway.

'I'm sorry,' said Roger.

'Everything's fine.' Dad's smile was gentle. 'So, Superintendent. Nice to see you again.'

Sunadomari was beside Roger.

'Shall we go inside?'

'You trust me that much?' said Dad.

With an upward glance, then a nod towards the landed flyer, Sunadomari said: 'I'll be expected to reappear intact.'

'No doubt.'

Indoors, they sat in the lounge with Mum, and a goblet of citrola daistral rose from the arm of each chair. Sunadomari hesitated over his for a moment – there was a flicker of light, perhaps some form of spectroscopic analysis – and then he sipped.

'Very nice. It's good to have a civilized confrontation, don't you think?'

'Is that what we're doing?' asked Dad.

'It could be. Thank you for allowing my signal to continue getting through.'

'You're welcome.' Dad glanced at Mum, then Roger. 'Deadman transmission. If we block it, the interruption is the danger signal.'

It showed Dad's awareness of a threat; but it was also a reminder of the power he held in this place, in a house whose full capabilities remained unknown even to Roger. This was not a stalemate – Sunadomari had the full peacekeeper force behind him – but neither were the Blackstones helpless.

'You've never visited the Pilots Sanctuary in the city,' said

Sunadomari. 'An ordinary man in your position, with the amount of offworld commerce you facilitate, might have been curious enough to attempt a meeting there.'

'So you've trawled through years of surveillance logs.' Dad crossed his legs, looking even calmer. 'But that's not the evidence that swung it for you.'

Roger wanted to speak up about Barleysugar Spiral and getting past the scanners, but he had done enough damage. He was out of his depth.

Then Dad did something surprising.

'Carl—' Mum started from her seat, then sat back.

With two quick dabs, Dad had removed his smartlenses. He gazed at Sunadomari with eyes of shining jet, pure polished black, and smiled.

Sunadomari smiled back.

'Pleased to meet you, Pilot Blackstone. If that's your real name.'

'It is.'

'Good. So, Pilot. Have you ever had dealings with—'

'Call me Carl.'

Sunadomari paused, then: 'Call me Keinosuke.'

It gave up a psychological advantage; but it was a sign of his confidence. Roger looked from Sunadomari to Dad and back.

'Tell me,' Sunadomari went on, 'about Luculenta Rafaella, previously Rashella, Stargonier.'

'I'd have to search in Skein,' said Dad. 'I've had no dealings with her, not directly.'

'May I access your house system to display an image?'

'Go ahead.'

Standing beside Sunadomari's chair was the image of a blond Luculentus, the same man he had manifested in the aircab.

'This was Luculentus Daniel Deighton,' said Sunadomari. 'And he was a friend.'

All three Blackstones looked at each other, understanding the implications: the man was dead, and probably not of natural causes.

'Who do you think killed him?' asked Dad.

Talk about getting to the heart of the matter. Roger focused on Sunadomari, wondering what he was going to say or do next.

Sunadomari looked straight at him.

'What did you notice about Rafaella Stargonier's behaviour?'

'I—' How could just speaking be so hard? 'She did something to a Luculentus in Parallaville. He rocked back, and ... and afterwards, when I talked to him, he had no memory of her.'

Dad's eyebrow was raised.

'Sorry,' Roger added. 'It's part of why I was coming here.'

'Tell me' – Sunadomari's voice became a shade deeper – 'about Drs Helsen and Ranulph.'

'Sir? Um ... Helsen is my tutor. I don't know the other person.'

Sunadomari gestured, and a small holo appeared on his palm, an image of a stocky man.

'Oh,' said Roger. 'He's a friend of Helsen's. I've seen him at a distance.'

He looked at Dad.

Should I tell all the rest?

After a moment, Dad gave a half smile.

'I suggest you come clean, son.'

'There's—' Roger rubbed his face. It felt as if he had a dirty secret habit about to be made public. 'In the past, I ... Look, I thought I was stressed out. I get weird dreams and ...'

Mum spoke for the first time since Sunadomari sat down.

'Let's stop here. This is my son, Superintendent.'

'No, Mum, it's all right. I thought I was hallucinating, that Helsen is a' – he shrugged – 'a creature of darkness. But that's not really what I mean.'

'Tell us,' said Sunadomari.

'Sometimes she's surrounded by – things. Twists of darkness. Black fragments of, of – *nothing*. And they twist in odd ways, I mean geometrically odd ways.'

Now Sunadomari was blinking. So it was possible to surprise

a Luculentus. The superintendent stared at Dad, eyes widening, then returned his attention to Roger.

'You thought these were visual hallucinations, is that it?'

Roger wanted to sob with the relief of confession.

'Yes. No one else sees them. No one.'

Except in my dreams.

He pushed that aside.

'And Greg Ranulph, Helsen's friend. Does this darkness surround him too?'

Roger nodded.

'I'm curious about something,' Sunadomari continued. 'Why were you following Rafaella Stargonier?'

'I ... she was suspicious. I mean, I was suspicious of her.'

'But why did you even see her?'

'She was meeting with Alisha, my friend ... Oh, shit.'

'What is it?'

'It was Dr Helsen that put Alisha in touch with the Luculenta, er, with Rafaella Stargonier.'

The atmosphere was already charged; now it stepped up a notch.

'Why would she do that?'

'To get her to talk about Calabi-Yau, about realspace hyperdimensions. That's why I took Alisha to the Zajinet place, the research institute.'

He bit his lip, and looked at Dad.

'All right, son.'

But Sunadomari was looking pale, his eyelids flickering as he immersed himself in Skein.

'There's no reply from the institute,' he said. 'Did you talk to Luculenta Weissmann?'

'Luculenta? But she had no—' Roger thought about her intellectual sharpness, the sense of charisma despite her lack of forehead studs or scalp wires. 'I should have realized.'

'So you did speak to her?'

'Yes. But if she's not answering—'

'She should always answer. One moment.' Sunadomari sank

deep inside himself, then came back out of it and looked around the room. 'I'm despatching full forces, but I expect the worst. And that is the *quid*, Carl, in a *quid pro quo*.'

Dad inclined his head.

'We had our suspicions about the institute, Superintendent. You had the Zajinet prisoner, I take it? The one whose ship crashed nearly twenty years ago?'

'Yes. Clearly you'll not speak about this outside this room.'

'Not in this universe, at least.'

'Touché. So tell me about the darkness.'

Dad twitched.

'I don't—'

Mum reached over and held the back of his hand, which was tightening on the arm of his chair.

'Carl, relax. Whatever it is ...' She looked at Sunadomari. 'What have you done to him?'

'Not me. Carl, breathe. Just breathe.'

Roger was scared.

'Dad?'

'Breathe, Carl,' said Sunadomari.

After thirty long seconds, Dad's chest stopped heaving, and his respiration returned to normal. He wiped sweat from his face.

'I have no idea what happened,' he said.

Sunadomari regarded him for a moment.

'Would you like me to tell you? Perhaps it will be a lesson in whom to trust.'

'I ... I don't know.'

'Think about it. Now, Roger, it's clear that Alisha's father enabled you to pass through the scanners in Barleysugar Spiral. He was the only one with relevant access.'

Roger tried to show nothing.

'What's this about a dead person?' Mum, still looking concerned over Dad, spoke up. 'Is there a connection, Superintendent, between Xavier Spalding and your murdered friend?'

But Dad was breathing easily now.

'Was your friend,' he asked, 'one of the eight Luculenti who died at the same time?'

'You know of that? Impressive, Carl.' Sunadomari blinked. 'In fact no, Daniel died earlier, but it's likely the same killer or killers did it. Do you have any suspects?'

'Sorry. My monitoring picked up the news of their deaths, nothing more. Except for a hint they might have been killed through Skein. Is that what happened?'

Dad was treating Sunadomari as an ally. Roger hoped it turned out to be true.

'Almost certainly.'

'So this Rafaella Stargonier must now be your prime suspect.'

'Perhaps.'

'Roger said she manipulated a Luculentus, causing ... amnesia.'

'That's right.' Sunadomari looked at Roger. 'It's Dr Helsen's role I find interesting.'

The paleness was returning to Dad's face.

'In the light of what we've shared,' Sunadomari went on, 'is there any data you can give me, of any kind? Additional speculations?'

'No,' said Dad. 'None I can think of.'

'I believe you.'

'So—'

'So I suggest the three of you leave however you can, as fast as possible. I take it there are faster ways offplanet than through Barleysugar Spiral?'

'In emergency, yes.'

Roger felt as if the room had tipped sideways. They were fleeing to mu-space? After all his indecision about where he belonged, there was suddenly no choice?

Sunadomari was shaking his head.

'What is it?' asked Dad.

'The institute. My people had to break in.' Sunadomari looked at the floor, then at the Blackstones. 'Stella Weissmann is dead, killed in the same way as the other Luculenti. And the basement level is destroyed. A tac team has secured the place.'

'You mean the cell where you kept the Zajinet prisoner?'

'Difficult circumstances make for difficult—Never mind. Whether we tortured the Zajinet or not, someone certainly did. There's nothing left of it.'

'Why were you *interrogating* the prisoner, Superintendent? There are other ways to learn about mu-space.'

'We were more interested in realspace' – with a glance at Roger – 'and teleportation through the hyperdimensions. Can't you imagine how useful that would—?'

Sunadomari stopped, held up a hand, then lowered his chin to his chest and closed his eyes. Five seconds later – surely an age for a Luculentus in the full flow of Skein – he looked up, eyes widening.

'Thank you for your assistance.'

He stood up.

What the hell?

'You've been very helpful, and I keep my promises, both implied and explicit. You're free to go.'

Dad also stood.

'Thank you, Superintendent.' He held out a formal fist. 'We'll be gone within ten minutes.'

Sunadomari touched his fist to Dad's.

'Then I'll share the information I offered,' he said, 'because it might inform your decision of where to fly to.'

Surely there was no decision. Or perhaps Sunadomari did not know of Labyrinth – it wasn't something Pilots talked about.

'What information?'

'You know all about the darkness, if we label the phenomenon that way.'

Dad's face dampened once more.

'I . . . What?'

'At least you *did* know, in the past. Whatever Roger saw, it has a deep resonance inside your unconscious mind.'

There was a flickering in Dad's eyes; then a tightening of his facial muscles as he brought the reaction under control.

'Amnesia.'

'Deliberate, targetted and induced. And it happened a long time ago, perhaps before you came to Fulgor.'

Mum was looking scared.

'What do you mean?'

'He means' – Dad's voice was shaky – 'it was our own people that carried out the procedure. Probably.'

Sunadomari smiled, an adequate comment on the likelihood of a trained Pilot intelligence officer undergoing amnesia at enemy hands and there being no trace of it.

Roger felt as he were about to vomit. Nothing could be this bad.

'Good luck,' said Sunadomari.

With a fingertip salute to Roger, he turned and left. A kind of tangible absence remained, a psychological vibration that told of everything changing.

Then Dad blew out a breath.

'Time to bug out,' he said.

THIRTY-FIVE

FULGOR, 2603 AD

In their lounge, they looked around for the last time. Dad appeared bigger and more muscular than usual, his face stronger. Perhaps this was the kind of situation he lived for.

Roger suddenly realized the impossibility of ever knowing his father's mind.

Concentrate.

'All right,' Dad said. 'Miranda, Roger, let's make our departure nine minutes from now, outside.'

They nodded. Dad closed his eyes, and his lips moved. The words might have been: *Come, my love. Come get us.* Or Roger might have been mistaken.

'Good.' Dad's eyes opened. 'She'll be here. Now, let's check our understanding. The superintendent's offer is genuine, but it's not official. If it were, he'd have said so.'

'What does that mean?' Roger did not understand. 'We're *not* free to go?'

'It means he's told the ordinary peacekeepers nothing. We're not under suspicion. But once a mu-space ship bursts into the open right before our house, there'll be SatScan alarms screaming everywhere. They'll try to disable the ship via grasers from orbit, so we're talking only seconds. And maybe five minutes before armoured flyers make an appearance.'

Roger looked at the quickglass walls.

'Can they subvert the house system remotely?'

'Huh.' Dad smiled. 'Good tactical thinking, and the answer's no. We're well protected.'

Mum glanced at the rear wall, which was glistening in a way Roger had not noticed.

'I thought we were going to have to use the tunnel.'

'Me too,' said Dad. 'But I wasn't sure we'd make it without Sunadomari stopping us.'

'He's all right, though, isn't he?'

'Yes. He's a good man.' Dad glanced at the wall. 'But he wouldn't break through that shielding. Not after twenty years of improvements.'

The glistening surface meant the wall was currently permeable, a viscous liquid, ready to allow three fugitives to run through: to reach the safety chamber that lay beyond, and the entrance to their shielded escape tunnel.

'All right,' continued Dad. 'One last thing, and I'd better do it in here, unsurveilled.'

He gestured a holovolume into existence.

'Yes?' Xavier Spalding's image regarded them. *'Carl. Have you seen Alisha?'*

For the second time this morning, a vomit reflex threatened Roger's stomach.

Alisha's missing?

'I'm sorry, no. But the peacekeepers know what you did for us. A Superintendent Sunadomari, a Luculentus, worked out everything.'

'That doesn't matter now.'

Dad looked at him.

'Good luck. You won't see us again.'

Xavier Spalding nodded, and his image disappeared.

'All right,' said Dad. 'Both of you, get ready to move.'

'I'm ready.' Mum clasped his arm. 'It'll be fun, right?'

Roger was backing away.

'And I'm . . . ready.'

Alisha is missing.

She was gone, her father was a criminal, Luculenti were dead . . . and he was running away, never to see this world again?

'Roger . . . ?'

'No!'

He leaped back.

'Sorry—'

And fell through the permeable wall, quickglass sliding over his skin. Then he tumbled into the chamber and yelled: 'Seal up!'

The wall shimmered and hardened, just as Dad's fist struck it on the other side.

'I'm sorry,' Roger said.

In the final minute, they were shadows, barely visible to each other through metre-thick armoured quickglass. There was no way to undo Roger's command, no way to make the wall permeable once more. No way for his parents to reach him, or him to get back to them.

And Dad's ship was a matter of seconds away from appearing outside the house.

'I love you,' Roger said.

He kissed his own fingertips, then pressed them against the quickglass. On the other side, after a moment, Mum did the same, followed by Dad.

Then Dad grabbed hold of her, and they moved fast, heading for the front door.

They're gone.

He waited until thunder crashed outside. Then he counted fifty seconds more, just in case.

'Really gone,' he said aloud.

He formed the control gesture Dad had drilled him in so many times.

'Shit.'

And closed his eyes as the floor became a liquefying whirlpool, dragging him down to the tunnel below.

There were two last things Carl could do for his son. As he ran outdoors with Miranda, he worked his tu-ring at a speed beyond thought. Behind him, a smartmiasma trailed, and the image it broadcast upwards was his first gift: to SatScan, it would appear that Roger Blackstone was fleeing the house behind his parents.

The second gift was easier: a tightbeam from his tu-ring to Roger's, zipblipping copies of all the espionageware he possessed.

'Be careful,' he muttered. 'It's dangerous stuff.'

'What—?' asked Miranda.

'Nothing.'

Then his ship burst into being overhead: a curved dart, black and powerful, edged with scarlet, ready for anything.

He was grinning, dreadful though that was, as she hauled him and Miranda on board with a fast black tendril. Within four seconds of her appearance in realspace, he was in her control couch.

And go.

Yes, my love.

Fulgor slammed out of existence around them.

Finally ...

Replaced by golden void, a sprinkling of black fractal stars, and a distant crimson nebula.

'What have we done?' said Miranda.

'The best we could,' answered Carl.

Then he immersed himself in the joy of flying hard for Labyrinth, aware that despite the elation of being with his ship, there were hard issues to deal with: Roger, alone on Fulgor; Miranda's distress; and the truth Sunadomari had revealed to him: the tampering with his mind by his own people.

Max Gould would have the answers.

'Oh, Carl.'

'I know, my love.'

He increased the severity of their trajectory, following a geodesic that would add to Miranda's strain, but should be manageable. It was less than he wanted, more than he should aim for.

A hellflight was out of question.

*

After a time, Miranda was able to ask: 'Will we live in Labyrinth now?'

'Do you want to?'

She thought, then: 'Yes, I believe I do.'

'Then so do I. Continuously.'

Miranda blinked her obsidian eyes.

'You mean you're giving up field work?'

'Don't you think it's time I did?'

They were both thinking of Roger.

'Way past time,' said Miranda.

'Yes.'

They flew on a short way.

'Miranda?'

'Darling?'

'There's—' Carl's face tightened. 'We have someone chasing us.'

A crescent of golden display showed a tiny shape moving. Then another, and another.

'Three of them,' said Carl.

They're fast, my love.

I'll bet we're faster.

They swung into a new trajectory.

'Who are they, Carl? Zajinets?'

'Our own kind.'

Miranda looked puzzled.

'Shouldn't we make contact?'

'They're using targetting systems.'

Carl frowned, and the ship took a hard turn. The trio followed.

Enemies.

It was a short time later that the pursuers closed the range, their weapon-nodes beginning to sparkle. The only escape was a hellflight, something he had not wanted to put Miranda through. But neither did he want to fight.

Twist now.

Carl-and-ship tumbled through a gut-wrenching geodesic jump, and then a series of shifts to different scales of reality; and Miranda might have cried out but he could no longer tell, because he was the ship and the ship was himself, and all that mattered was the flying.

Cascades of energy whirled past them.

Shit.

Ship-and-Carl flung themselves through a helical descent into fractal magnification, the hull coruscating with spillover from the weapons fire, as they corkscrewed away from the enemy trio.

Energy slammed past them again.

Faster.

Judge the moment right, and they could slip onto a geodesic that no one could—

It burns.

Energy touched her hull and Carl's voice cried out and then they were one again, into a howling turn, and as they came out their resonance chambers hummed; and the first of the ships was right in front of them, no longer pursuer but target, then ship-and-Carl let loose.

He yelled at the release.

Then he-and-ship were twisting away as the enemy exploded, a nova burst of detonation leaving a storm of dazzling fragments; and then the remains were behind them.

But the remaining two were closer now.

Nebula.

I see it.

They plunged though crimson, arced hard, burst back into golden void. One of the enemy was side-on as Carl-and-ship fired.

Its delta wing blew apart, but only as the last ship cut loose with every weapon.

Another cry filled the cabin, then he-and-ship were twisting away – *geodesic, there* – trying to find the path – *got it* – and then they were pouring on the acceleration – *do it* – putting everything they had into forward power – *do it now* – as they howled into the only way out, the most extreme of flightpaths that few survived.

Hellflight.

And finally, the calm.

They came out into peaceful golden space, Carl's mind separating from the ship as he slumped back in the cabin. Inside was—

Red.

—not the crimson of nebulae, more like the hull's scarlet trim, glistening with oxidation.

'No. Please . . .'

He pulled himself from his seat.

'Oh, Miranda.'

THIRTY-SIX

EARTH, 1939 AD

The Wolf house was broken. The yellow star – runnels of yellow ran toward the ground: they had been careless with the paint – marked a front door whose lock was smashed. Only a few triangular fragments of glass remained in the windows. Inside was darkness.

Gavriela did not dare to stand on the street gaping.

It's not possible.

She lowered her head as forced herself to walk on, trying to work out how she might circle around to the back. But a low voice said: 'Get away.'

A bent-backed man was in front of her.

'They took your parents. I'm sorry.'

'Herr . . . Herr *Schäffer?*'

'Yes, and you're little Gavi Wolf. Do you need money?'

'No—'

'All you can do is get away. Survive. Here.' He pressed a book into her hands. 'Carry this.'

It was battered from much reading.

'I can't.'

The title was stark: *Mein Kampf.*

'Carry it, read it on the bus or train, nod as if you're agreeing with it. You have papers that declare you're Aryan?'

'Sort of.'

Her Swiss cantonal ID showed her religion as *None*. But the German passport, in an inner pocket of her coat, could kill her.

'Go.'

Herr Schäffer walked on. She wanted to call him back, but knew it was dangerous for both of them. If he could recognize her after all this time, what about the other neighbours?

Without destination, she forced herself into motion.

It was some unknown time later when a guttural male voice said something. She looked up, saw the elegant length of Unter den Linden stretching before her, the eponymous trees making twin perspective lines; and she saw the grey-uniformed soldier with his hand out. Behind him, two more soldiers stood, watching the subdued passers-by.

'I'm sorry?'

'Your papers, Fräulein.'

The ID shook as she produced it.

'Swiss?'

'Yes.'

'You don't sound Swiss to me.'

'My family moved—'

Her brain swirled with the effort of trying to construct a convincing fiction. She was dead, and nothing could save her. That knowledge seeped through her, and her shoulders slumped.

Suddenly a beautiful blonde woman was standing there, smiling above her red-fox collar. A small dog was at her heel.

'Soldier, this lady is a good Aryan. I have travelled with her in person.'

'And you are—?'

But she was already showing her papers.

'Ma'am?' His eyes widened, then he slammed his bootheels together. '*Sieg Heil!*'

'Likewise.' She returned the salute. 'Be vigilant.'

'Yes, Frau Göbbels.'

'Nice to see one of our own,' she said to Gavriela. 'You have a husband?'

'A . . . a fiancée, Lucas.' It was the first name she thought of. 'He's serving in, er, I think he's in Poland right now.'

'Ah. Good.' Magda Göbbels tugged her dog's lead. 'Come along, Rufus.'

Then she continued along Unter den Linden without looking back.

'Thank you.' Gavriela looked down once more as she shuffled away. 'Thanks.'

Earlier, during the train journey, she had been heartened by how easy it was to cross the border. Now she understood what she had failed to register: it was getting out that was impossible.

Mother. Father.

And for the sake of survival, there were things she should not think of, could not allow herself to dwell on.

I love you . . .

Her Swiss ID was correct in that she had no religion, therefore no belief in heaven.

But there was a hell, and proof was all around her.

At the same moment, several hundred kilometres to the east, Dmitri Shtemenko stood on a broad grey plaza. In front of him stood the forbidding pile of Moscow University, its spire rearing towards a secular heaven, its red star dull in daylight, requiring darkness for its full glory, when its internal lights would transform it into the state's blood-red eye staring down upon the grateful proletariat.

But Dmitri would not be here to see it, not tonight. In his coat pocket he carried the train ticket that would take him away from the city that he had – somehow – grown to feel part of. He also had a gift, from his former tutor, Dr Lande: a Japanese-Russian dictionary, which would see much use in his new assignment.

He nodded, then turned away. Things would be different in Tokyo.

Don't think about the food.

That brought back not just memories of the village, of the shame they shared, but also a more recent event: burying the human fingers he could not bring himself to eat or destroy, his little trophies that he kept either because of or in spite of the darkness – he never knew which.

Just don't think.

Now he faced the round sweep of the city, while below him, at the bottom of the arcing slope, rolled the turgid grey waters of the Moscow River. He took a deep breath of chill air, then made his way down to the stately bridge, and began the long walk across.

Moscow was Paris writ large, its grand boulevards laid out in a spiderweb configuration, while the intelligence services headquarters were the watchful spider, lurking off-centre in her web. It was a strong city, an impregnable city, in a country whose vastness remained unrecognized by so much of the world.

But suddenly, Dmitri was glad to be leaving.

The train station was heaving with a mass of people, thousands crushed together, refugees whose eyes were wide with the only thought a civilized person could produce: *It's a mistake, and someone will work it out, and fix it.*

Because the real world could not produce this crowd who were paying for the privilege of travelling in cattle-cars, their yellow cloth stars granting them the right to climb aboard, and Gavriela did not wait around to hear the platform guard's whistle, nor the chuff of steam and piston as the engine got underway.

She stumbled back towards the city streets.

But it was behind the station that everything fell apart.

'You're one of them.'

'No—'

'And you know the penalties for not wearing the star.'

There were three of them, dressed in suits and overcoat, one with a truncheon, another with brass gleaming across his gloved knuckles, while the third was already unbuttoning his flies as they pulled her into an alleyway.

'Might as well get some use out of it,' he said.

'It better not squeal.' One of the others was pulling a cloth from his pocket. 'Put this in your mouth, darling.'

'I've something else to put in its mouth.'

'Ach, Mannfred. All right.'

'Who gets first dip?'

A punch exploded against her eye socket, and suddenly she was lying on her back, knees akimbo and her skirt up, hard paving beneath her. Someone's hand hooked deeply into her face and twisted, torqueing her nose and cheekbone hard against stone, the pain immense, her head about to fracture, while strong hands tore her panties away with a distant ripping sound.

No.

There was nothing she could do to prevent what was happening.

Help me.

She yelled, but only in her mind.

Help me!

Roger pauses in the escape tunnel, his skin layered in greasy sweat, his stomach sick, needing to get away before peacekeepers investigate beneath the house, knowing that Alisha could be in danger, but the voice he hears is not hers, not Alisha's, but another from the distant past and dreams, calling across centuries—

'Help me!'

The thoughts are of violence and this is madness. He's eaten nothing and his world has lurched into awfulness. Call it delusion.

'I . . . I can't.'

He drops to his knees and finally throws up.

There was pain inside her, incredible waves of sickening intrusion, and she cried out yet again.

HELP ME!

Ulfr snaps awake. Beside him, Brandr does likewise, the warhound alert as his master.

All around are snoring warriors, deep in drunken slumber, for the carousing lasted many—

'HELP ME!'
His lips pull back.
'So kill . . .'
Man and war-hound snarl together.

And then it came, the rage.

So kill . . .

Kicking and wriggling, and then her nails were claws – a distant yell as she raked hard – and her teeth were fangs and everything was rage, the world a redness of blood-lust, and the snarls were hers as she tore and ripped, thrust and pulled, over and over like cycling pistons, tearing and hitting and ripping again and again and again.

And finally she staggered back.

Victory, by Thórr.

Away from the three torn corpses.

May Niflheim take your souls.

She pulled her ragged coat around her as she stumbled from the alley.

Ulfr looks up at the stars, and laughs.

'Óthinn's blood, girl.'

Beside him, Brandr barks.

THIRTY-SEVEN

FULGOR, 2603 AD

Roger staggered into the open.

He was at the top of a scree. Across his face was a respmask, which he had picked up inside the escape tunnel's exit. This was the border of a hypozone – at the foot of the slope, two lozenge-shaped creatures moved by laminar flow, their flesh looping like caterpillar tracks, along the rocky ground.

His mouth, inside the mask, tasted like vomit; and he was still not sure what had happened inside the tunnel. Whatever delusions he might have, some had enough relation to reality for a peacekeeper superintendent to take seriously. He wondered whether Sunadomari was hunting Rafaella Stargonier or Dr Helsen, or both.

Mum. Dad.

They would be safe. Dad's ship was the most powerful, amazing thing he had ever seen. So for now he could concentrate on finding Alisha; later he would think again about the meaning of his dreams.

Stones crunched beneath him, each step another fall corrected just in time, as he stumbled downslope. At the bottom, he followed the native creatures, then jogged to overtake them, keeping the pace as he entered a tall ravine, its floor sandy, and continued to the end.

Before him glowed an orange transit station.

From here he could get back to Lucis City, and transfer to anywhere on Fulgor. While following the escape tunnel, he had browsed his tu-ring's upgrades, courtesy of Dad; he knew there was a great deal he could do to hide from surveillance.

But, as he watched a tribe of Shadow People herd

slimebellies past the station, it occurred to him that there was another place he could go, and he might not even have to leave the hypozone to do it.

There was a great deal of Dad's illegal ware that he could not use, not without many days training; but he could see how to form an anonymous query in Skein. He tapped the turing, subvocalized commands, and saw several representations, lased into his smartlenses, of the routes he might take.

One, overlaid across his vision, was a gleaming silver line that tracked along the broken ground. It resembled the path left by moving slimebellies, but it represented the ground-level option. From here to his destination, he could travel on the surface entirely within the hypozone, where the peacekeepers would not expect him to feel at home.

The transit station led to subterranean tunnels; but here up top were slickbikes for hire.

'Fog,' called one of the Shadow People.

'We see it,' a station worker answered.

That made up Roger's mind for him.

Banks of tiger-striped fog, violet and grey, rolled silently across the landscape. Bi-coloured fog, its Turing pattern emergent from simple chemical reactions, as if nature wanted to cloak itself from SatScan.

He inched through the fog towards the slickbike stand.

Sunadomari's flyer touched down on a blue-and-white patio of Mansion Stargonier. En route from the Blackstone house, he had immersed himself in a sea of surveillance data. There were sightings of Rafaella Stargonier dating back less than two seconds; but the images were all in Skein, all from surveillance logs he could no longer trust. The last verified sighting might have been yesterday, when Roger Blackstone saw her in reality.

Twenty-five armoured officers were already waiting in the grounds, while two specialists from Domestics Division, both top-class Luculenti, worked through Skein, sitting safely back at Peacekeeper HQ. As soon as the DD men cracked the mansion's security, the tac team poured inside through doors and windows.

Sunadomari waited outside.

'Anything?' he asked.

The tac team commander, Helen Eisberg, responded in Skein, via tu-ring.

'Sorry, sir,' she said. *'No one openly in the rooms. Deepscan shows no one hiding inside the architecture.'*

Simultaneously, he talked in Skein to the DD Luculenti.

<<audio: Any luck with the house logs?>>

Their reply took a millisecond to arrive.

<<video: Rafaella Stargonier boarding a flyer.>>

<<image: A large red question mark icon.>>

One of the Luculenti had a sense of intellectual irony, using a symbol from the archaic Latin alphabet to comment on a Luculenta with the Latinate name of Rafaella. Sunadomari thought it puerile, remembered the origins of *that* word, then shook distracting thoughts away.

What was clear that the woman had left yesterday and at some point simply disappeared inside Lucis City. Then:

<<audio: Shit!>>

<<audio: The house memory is reinitializing.>>

Sunadomari closed the in-Skein link and sighed.

'Lieutenant Eisberg?'

'Sir?'

'Leave two people in situ, and let's find someone we can arrest. Protocol zero.'

Eisberg checked her weaponry status.

'I take it they're maximally dangerous, sir.'

'They may be. Their names are Helsen and Ranulph.' He concentrated, sending data through Skein to Eisberg, while making the arrest request to JusticePlex in Skein. 'JP is issuing warrants now.'

NetSprites tore through Skein, questing through video data, trying to match search arguments to moving-image objects via their *heuristicEquals( )* functions: a low-level, brute force approach that could succeed where sophisticated strategies might fail.

Nothing.

'Shit.'

'Sir?'

'When our global, ubiquitous and all-seeing surveillance actually manages to find who we're looking for, I'll let you know their locations. Until then, remain on stand-by.'

Helen Eisberg's face remained almost blank.

'Yes, sir.'

'*Shit.*'

He had let three known spies escape from Fulgor because they weren't the particular criminals he sought. Now all the remaining suspects were gone as well. He knew less than he had two days ago.

Except that Stella Weissmann's name had been added to the list of the dead, her corpse lying close to the remains of the Zajinet prisoner they had kept for so long – and failed to extract information from.

He gathered himself.

'Helen,' he said to Lieutenant Eisberg.

'Yes, Keinosuke?'

'Ignore my mood. Have you two good people you could spare?'

'To go with you?'

'Right. To the Via Lucis Institute.'

'What's there? I mean, besides all the Skein experts and plexweb designers and shit.' For the first time, she almost smiled. 'Is there anything actually *useful?*'

'A history lesson.' He gazed around the grounds. 'I need to find out what happened a hundred years ago.'

'Talk about tracing root causes.'

'Tell me about it.'

Alisha had been set up. Roger, dear Roger, had told her about the Zajinet Research Institute – without him, she probably would not have found it. Rafaella Stargonier, had she been sufficiently interested, almost certainly *would* have discovered the place – and probably obtained more useful data from the Weissmann woman.

This was a strange place.

'Another glass of daistral, miss?' It was a pliable, smooth humanoid shape that gestured with its caricature hand and spoke. 'She shouldn't be too long.'

'No, thank you.'

Alisha was sitting on soft quickglass, in a cylindrical quick-glass chamber whose walls were translucent, predominantly ice-green, and filled with complex shapes of blue and violet, along with continuously rising bubbles. The roughly humanoid shape was a quickglass extrusion, part of the surrounding system. Call it an exotic accessory; but Alisha did not like it.

Am I even in the same building?

Having taken part in that mannequin thing, pedalling the construct through the parade, she had been exhausted. Had it not been for Stef's persuasion beforehand, she would never have agreed. It was only when they were struggling en route that she put together all the hints: Stef had subtly (or not so subtly) made sure that Roger was taking part.

Matchmaking. That was a set-up, but not one she minded. Roger was sweet and she herself was too uncertain to make the first move – she might be only weeks away from upraise, a reward for hard work and capability, but that did not help. The countdown to upraise was terrifying; and the thought of how different she would be afterwards ... that was a barrier to friendship, never mind romance.

For a few seconds, when everyone climbed from the man-nequin, sweaty and tired, there had been an opportunity to speak to Roger. But she had walked away, wanting to think things through, knowing she was too tired to make reasonable decisions. And then, she had caught sight of Luculenta Rafaella Stargonier, who had smiled and seemed eager to talk, though not for long.

Far too eager. Why didn't I spot it?

She looked at the quickglass person-shape, and changed her mind.

'I *will* have that daistral, thank you.'

'Coming up, miss.'

Rafaella – she had insisted Alisha use her first name – arranged this meeting to 'catch up on your findings,' and allegedly so Alisha could see what a successful Luculenta could achieve by way of commercial sidelines. Twenty minutes ago, she had entered the foyer of Aleph Tower, where a human employee had led her to a conference room to wait. What had been unexpected was the way the room descended, a bubble through quickglass, and opened into this waiting area, some ten metres (she estimated) below ground.

But it wasn't the location, it was the decor that was strange: weird geometric shapes and rising bubbles within the wall, the person-shaped extrusion that offered drinks ... and now handed her a goblet morphed from its own hand. Alisha snapped the goblet free, looked at the daistral inside, then set it on the floor.

'Is everything all right, miss?'

'Fine. Thanks.'

For a soon-to-be Luculenta, she had been slow on the uptake. It wasn't just Rafaella, it was creepy Dr Helsen playing games. Realspace hyperdimensions weren't some academic topic chosen at random: there was something going on.

Why would Helsen want Rafaella to be thinking about hyperdimensions?

Something to do with Zajinets?

The woman at the Institute, Ms Weissmann, had raised the subject of teleportation, then ruled out Roger's hypotheses about the mechanism, leaving only one: the Zajinets could project themselves along the Calabi-Yau hyperdimensions of realspace.

But she had also said that teleportation was beyond the reach of current knowledge. Surely Rafaella could not think it was possible to discover the Zajinets' technique?

Maybe that's it.

It would explain her . . . shiftiness. She would want to patent the concepts and bring a first application to market before anyone else got hold of the knowledge, or even knew of its existence. That made commercial sense.

She looked down at her untouched daistral.

'Shit.'

'Miss?'

'Nothing.'

I really am *slow on the uptake.*

Missing a night's sleep and doing that crazy mannequin thing might be contributing factors, but not a good excuse. She should have realized last night, not now.

Weissmann's a Luculenta.

All the signs of it had been there. How could anyone miss the way she—?

Something moved.

'Hello, Alisha.'

It was Rafaella Stargonier, her long black hair twisting as if in wind, though the chamber's air was still. She reached out a fist, and Alisha touched it with hers.

So Rafaella was real. She had risen up through the quickglass floor so fast, Alisha had thought she might be holo.

'Rafaella, good morning. I'm glad to be here.'

'Did you come alone? You were welcome to take a friend.'

'I—I decided not to disturb anyone else.'

She had called Roger in Skein, receiving no response. Her disappointment was mitigated by how exhausted he had looked last night. He was surely off Skein by intent, catching up on sleep.

'So, my little place here is somewhat exotic, don't you think?'

'Er, yes, ma'am.'

'We're on first-name terms, remember? And I want to give you the tour.'

'The tour?'

'There's so much in the world that people ignore. So much wonder they could experience, but they distract themselves with trivia instead.'

'Um . . .'

Rafaella raised both hands, and her eyes were shining as her voice become resonant.

'Let me show you the world beneath.'

All around them, the room began to change: flowing and morphing, the person-shape melting back into the floor, the concave space reconfiguring to something like the inside of a hollow tear-drop. Alisha's seat budded a twin, and Rafaella sat down next to her.

'Here we go.' Rafaella patted Alisha's hand. 'You'll love this.'

Essentially they were in a sophisticated bubble, but it felt like a craft, and the illusion strengthened as they moved forwards, like a clear submarine through green waters. Then their direction dipped, as they began a forty-five degree descent.

'Where is this?'

'My little Alisha. Did you never ask what exists below the towers and marvels of Lucis City?'

All around, within the translucent depths, were straight-edged shapes and rippling streamers, a complexity of organic and geometric structures she found hard to look at – there was so much of it, all around their pseudo-vessel, like a vast biological abstract sculpture, like a giant technological organism, deep inside the organs, the lymph nodes and capillaries, the microstructures within the cells, the complex molecules of life.

It was like a fantasy of being shrunk to tiny size and floating through a great living body; but it was real.

'There's so much of it,' Alisha said. 'So . . . beautiful.'

'Ah. That's why I wanted another person to see it.'

'To—?'

'So I know it's not just me. This place *is* a marvel.'

Alisha stared around as they continued to sink deep among nameless structures.

'I still don't understand.'

'Welcome,' said Rafaella, 'to The Marrows.'

They popped into an enormous vault – perhaps containing air – their 'vessel' a true bubble now, lowering on a quickglass thread in a space big enough to contain several buildings, each a quickglass tower. In the distance were ranged other vaults, equally huge.

'It's like a different world.'

'This is where we grow the city.'

'Oh.' The meaning of what Alisha saw became clearer. 'It's just so . . . Oh.'

'Isn't it?'

The descent stopped. Rafaella stood, and the craft-bubble's walls shivered apart, leaving only the floor. They were now on an exposed quickglass platform suspended by a hundred-metre thread from the vault ceiling, at the centre of this huge space, far below the surface city.

'The architecture above is just the tip of everything,' said Rafaella. 'People would know this, if they bothered to look.'

Alisha stood, her legs wobbly.

'I . . . Can we go back up now?'

'In a moment. See over there? You gave me the idea.'

'I'm sorry?'

A row of long, silver-scaled dragons hung in place, their wings diaphanous red, their crystal eyes bulbous. Quickglass dragons. Huge.

'For Last Lupus,' said Rafaella. 'I thought we might end Festival with something spectacular. Your little mannequin inspired me.'

Alisha's bottom lip hurt. She realized she was biting it.

'And you gave me the Zajinet,' Rafaella added. 'You have no idea how helpful that was.'

'I don't—'

'My capacity for expansion is now effectively infinite. Isn't that something wonderful?'

Shaking her head, Alisha found the surrounding marvels blurring as tears filled her eyes.

'You're going to kill me, aren't you? I don't know why, but you are.'

'Oh, no. You're thinking of the old me.' Rafaella's mouth turned up at the corners, but the expression was not a smile. 'I do things differently now.'

Her eyes appeared to expand.

Oh, God. Oh, no.

Vampire code poured through Alisha's plexnodes.

THIRTY-EIGHT

EARTH, 1939–1940 AD

The Bohr Institute, home of startling ideas, was everything it should be: stone walls, an atmosphere of grandeur, the great man's coat of arms upon the wall: heraldic icons around a yin-yang. When Bohr had been knighted, he had chosen a superposition of classical and new, of west and east.

It was all very appropriate; but Gavriela found it hard to care.

'Florian Horst.' Her Danish was almost non-existent. 'Please.'

In German, such abruptness was rude enough for insolence. She did not know if Danish was as formal. Perhaps her accent might mitigate offence.

'You're from Berlin?' asked the woman behind the desk, in fluent German.

'Oh, thank God. Yes, originally. You can recognize regional accents?'

'Not much, but it's hard to mistake a Berliner for anything else.'

There was an old joke about the difference between someone from Berlin and a doughnut – nothing, they're both Berliners – but she pushed it aside. Danish bakeries probably didn't even make Berliners, though Swiss bakeries did.

She had eaten so little food for the past fifteen days. At least, she thought it was fifteen days.

The trek across wild countryside had been long, and she survived only because it was not her – she had no other way of thinking about it. Her body had lived off the land, trapping small animals in ways she should not have known, slipping past troops and civilians, always afraid.

As for what she had done to the three Gestapo men, if that was what they were—

'Fräulein?'

'I'm sorry. You were saying, about Florian Horst?'

'He left for—Ah, Fräulein. Are you Frau Horst's friend?'

'You mean Elke. Oh, yes. In fact I introduced them, Elke and Florian. I'm Gavriela Wolf.'

'Could you wait a moment?'

The woman slipped from behind the desk, and went down a corridor to the rear, high heels clicking. There were sounds of two men talking, a knocking – someone tapping his pipe free of old tobacco – and then a rustle of paper. Then the woman came back, carrying a large envelope.

'For you, Frau Doktor.'

'Thank you.' Gavriela took it. 'But what's inside?'

'There are so many ... They're trying to help as many as possible. Professor Bohr is a marvel.'

She opened the envelope, finding several typed sheets, a small box and some banknotes: various denominations of Kroner.

'What—?'

'I'll take you through to meet the Professor,' said the woman. 'Your ... friend made certain arrangements.'

'Florian?'

'Not Doktor Horst. He's ... He went missing, along with Frau Horst.'

'Missing?'

'Perhaps they returned home.'

'To Zürich?'

'I understand Doktor Horst was from Stuttgart originally.'

Now Gavriela understood the woman's reaction.

'Oh. I can't believe he's ... one of them.'

'It was Herr Doktor Krause who made the work arrangements for you, before he left for England.'

Lucas is in England?

The woman tapped the envelope in Gavriela's hand.

'Save as much as you can,' she said. 'You might need it later.'

'What do you mean?'

'My cousin captains a fishing-trawler. But he never works for free.'

Six months later, Gavriela was throwing up over the side of that exact fishing-trawler, into the North Sea. In between bouts of paroxysm, she huddled inside the small wheelhouse with captain and crew, straining to make sense of reports broadcast by the BBC.

The woman at the Bohr Institute was Helga, and her forecast had been correct. April had been the beginning of spring – and of Nazi occupation. As grey-uniformed soldiers swarmed the streets, few citizens were anything but cold to them; but neither did they have illusions about their ability to fight back.

Not just Helga, but a whole string of friends helped Gavriela and others escape the country. When Gavriela asked why Helga stayed, Helga's eyes had been fjord-grey, as unreadable as wild sea.

'I have work here,' she said.

Now the trawler captain, Helga's cousin, spat through the open wheelhouse hatchway, and turned up the volume on the radio.

Far south of here, in France, from an obscure seaside town called Dunquerque, an incredible evacuation was taking place: a flotilla of military and private boats alike, thousands of them, taking the defeated British troops to safety, to their island fortress where they might regroup.

Nazi forces were sweeping like a riptide through Europe; the commentators were casting the story of Dunquerque as some kind of victory.

While on every side of the tiny boat, the massive ocean swelled and simply existed, huge and persisting, possessing a greatness no tiny, short-lived creature could enjoy.

THIRTY-NINE

THE WORLD, 5563 AD

Harij sat on the rough ledge, watching dawn come up over the canyon. Liquid highlights rippled on his silver skin, where his short tunic left his shining limbs bare. He was too hot already, while the rest of the townfolk would be sensibly asleep, deep in the cavern system behind him.

Below, the canyon was in shadow, almost hiding a mating-flight of dartbirds, the tri-winged creatures swooping as they swiftly joined in triplets before breaking apart, and soaring onwards.

The black-and-silver moon of Magnus was high to the east.

What's that?

Surely he was the only one mad enough to be out in daylight. None of his classmates could imagine such a thing. But across the canyon, on the purplish mesa, a tiny figure was moving.

A Seeker?

Could it be? Distant, tiny, and robed against the heat. It had been so long since such a one had visited, but Harij remembered, and dreamed.

Then the tiny figure disappeared into a dip, was gone.

If only he could . . .

Something was in the void, just beyond the edge.

A spin-glass Hamiltonian is analogous to an allele-suitability matrix in a context of fitness-suitability space provided gene mutations are epistatically interdependent in every—

It drifted away, accelerating, for the flux was strong here.

But to be so close to an Idea!

He pulled himself to his feet, and moved along the ledge, wondering if he could yet reach out and grasp it before—

Too late.

For a second he was in danger of toppling over, but he caught himself.

So close.

He called out, unable not to.

Come back, please.

But the Idea tumbled on, in the air above the canyon, propelled by flux that paid no heed to one unhappy youth, however desperate his need for knowledge.

FORTY

EARTH-CLASS EXPLORATORY EM-0036, 2146 AD

Rekka and Sharp stood within the microward boundary, looking around their old campsite, now renewed. There were three equipment cases standing open, although four cases had been designated for the mission. But she could not think of that, not now, because Sharp's future was her main concern.

'I'm willing to come with you,' she said.

'I know.' The voice from his chest unit was soft, reflecting the subdued scent. 'But they will believe me in the city.'

'If you're sure—All right, dear Sharp.'

'I love you, Rekka.'

'And I love you.'

His massive arms enclosed her, as she pressed her face sideways against his chest, inhaling the scent of his fur. She had no idea how his people would greet him on his return; she only hoped they were more open-minded than humans.

In fact, she thought they probably were.

'You'll walk to Mint City?' she asked, drawing back.

'It will give me time to . . . remember.'

After months on Earth, he needed to reacclimatize. She smiled at her friend's wisdom.

'Go well, Sharp.'

'Go well, Rekka.'

Then he walked from the camp, his gait erect, his antlers wide and proud. Rekka stood watching until he was no longer in sight.

You'd better be safe.

But there were ways to help, still. Bending down at her biofact, she got to work, executing the pre-designed procedures. Within minutes, the first of her bees took wing.

She despatched them after Sharp.

FORTY-ONE

LABYRINTH, 2603 AD (REALSPACE-EQUIVALENT)

Carl-and-ship hurtled through Auric Void, howled past the edge of Mandelbrot Nebula, and a long time later burst into clear golden space near Labyrinth. Their distress signal gave them priority, and they tore along a docking tunnel into a wide space adjoining Med Centre.

It was his first public appearance flying a ship, destroying a false identity established decades ago. That counted for nothing.

Not with Miranda like this ...

He disengaged his mind from his ship as they touched against the dock. Med-drones were waiting, along with medics, and as soon as his control cabin formed an entrance gap, a drone floated inside.

Panes of nothingness rotated, and three green-clothed medics stepped into the cabin.

'It's my wife ...'

But the medics worked in silence, sealing Miranda, limp and bloody, inside the drone. Then the drone floated out, towards more waiting medics. Two of the medics in here backed off, summoned fastpath rotations, and twisted out of this reality-layer.

'Can't you rotate the drone through to—?'

'Pilot Blackstone, your wife's condition won't allow it. A transition to another level would cause a trauma she's not strong enough to cope with.'

'Is she ... Is she dying?'

'We're going to do our best to make her live.'

'I—'

'Excuse me, I must go.' As the medic summoned the rotation, he added: 'The staff on the platform will take you to her.'

Then he stepped into the twisting fastpath and was gone.

Carl rubbed his eyes, trying to get his bearings, swaying after the effort of wild flight. Then he noticed a lev-platform touching against the hull opening. Two Pilots stepped inside, neither of them dressed in medic green. One wore a goatee, the other was shaven; both were wide-shouldered and hard-faced.

'I'm Clayton,' said the clean-shaven one, 'and this is Boyle.'

'You're not from Med Centre.'

'Not exactly. More like the same place you're from.'

Boyle had gestured a privacy shield into place, covering the entrance gap, turning the sight of the dock outside into a sparkling haze.

'You work for Max?'

'We're with the service. And you need to debrief.'

'Gentlemen, I strictly don't care. That's my wife, and you've just seen—'

'We also heard' – Clayton's voice was softer than Boyle's – 'the medic say she needs to remain on this level of reality.'

Carl stared at him, trying to work out what was going on, and why these idiots could not understand that Miranda was—

'We'll fastpath through to Ascension Annexe,' Clayton continued, 'but remain at a slower timeflow. All right?'

Carl shook his head, not processing the words.

'He means' – Boyle was already summoning the fastpath – 'we'll debrief you at a normal rate for us, then bring you back to mean-geodesic time inside Med Centre within ten seconds.'

'Ten seconds?'

'Guaranteed,' said Clayton. 'Your wife will have experienced ten seconds, and you'll be able to concentrate on helping her. All right?'

Everything was awful. He could no longer think.

'All right,' he said.

The fastpath twisted, expanding, and surrounded him.

I shouldn't be doing this.

And expelled him into new surroundings: plain dark walls, and a single chair morphed from quickstone.

'You fuckers.'

An interrogation cell.

When Carl woke up, Clayton and Boyle were staring at him. They looked angry.

'Welcome back, Blackstone.'

He swayed in the chair, but its shape remained static, not morphing to help him.

'Trance-tell?' Closing his eyes then pulling them wide open, he tried to speed up the process of dragging the world into focus. 'You used trance-tell?'

Clayton said: 'Blackstone, you arsehole. Why didn't you stay away?'

Recent memory seemed vague.

'Away from where?'

'He means, away from Labyrinth,' said Boyle. 'For his convenience, not yours.'

'And you really want a trip to Dr Sapherson's fun-lab, do you?' asked Clayton.

'What are you talking about?' Carl had to use one hand to push himself upright, his hips wobbling, then growing steady. 'Tell me.'

'You were under amnesia conditioning.' Boyle raised his eyebrows at Clayton. 'Pity you didn't stay that way.'

Carl tried to focus.

'Sunadomari ... Superintendent Sunadomari told me I'd been treated. Given amnesia. So why's that a problem? You're saying someone else did it? An enemy?'

'Oh, no, they did it here,' said Clayton. 'Whoever was in charge of psych security before Sapherson.'

'That was before our time.' Boyle gave a nearly-grin.

'Then ... what? I told you all I knew, did I?'

'Yeah, but you didn't know anything fucking useful.'

Clayton slammed a palm-heel against the wall. 'For fuck's sake, Boyle and I are going to lose the assignment for *nothing.'*

Carl slumped back down in the chair. Was he taking too long to recover, or were these two actually talking nonsense?

'He hasn't caught up yet,' said Boyle. 'Look, Blackstone. Carl. We . . . We didn't find what we were looking for, all right? But you did relate your buried memories that are supposed to be inaccessible. Cosmic fucking conspiracies and all.'

'I'm sorry, but I don't—'

'They'll come back to you, over the next few days. Unless Dr Sapherson does the rewipe first. The techniques are better these days– the way Sapherson does it, there's nothing left to resurface, not even under trance-tell.'

It took three deep breaths, and a deliberate command to himself to relax, but finally Carl got it.

'You mean . . .' Then he chuckled. 'You mean, I've spilled things *you're* not authorized to know, is that it?'

'Fuck,' said Clayton.

'That's just his way of saying yes,' said Boyle. 'He's a sweetie, really.'

'So now you two are going to get the amnesia treatment too?'

'Uh-huh.'

'And you don't think that's funny?'

'No, I—'

'Come on.' Boyle smiled. 'Man's got a point.'

'It's not funny.'

'Yes, it is,' said Boyle and Carl together.

They laughed, and after a moment, Clayton said: 'Oh, fuck it,' and joined in the laughter. Soon, all three of them were hysterical, the sound bouncing back off the walls; and just when it seemed to die away, Boyle made a sound like blowing a raspberry, and set them off again.

Finally, the humour sank away, leaving a kind of amused tiredness.

'So what were you after?' Carl asked finally.

'Ah, well.' Clayton wiped his eyes. 'Bad news, actually. Just like—Shit, man. I'm sorry. With your wife . . .'

Boyle said: 'We're both sorry. We'll keep our promise.'

'Promise?'

'Getting you to Med Centre within– You remember now.'

Carl's world fell away.

'Miranda.'

The truth-tell had messed with his mind so much. Now everything slammed into him.

'Let's get Carl on his way,' said Clayton.

'Yeah.' Boyle summoned a fastpath. 'Here we are.'

More to distract himself than because he wanted to know, Carl said: 'So why were you questioning me?'

'It's about . . . Admiral Kaltberg's dead.'

'Oh. I'm sorry.'

'She died in an explosion in Commodore Gould's office.'

'You mean Max—?'

'We don't know. He might have escaped.'

This was too much. Only Miranda mattered.

'Maybe he's all right.'

'I hope not,' muttered Clayton.

Boyle shook his head.

'What do you mean?' Carl asked.

'Because if he slipped away unharmed, he's the murderer, isn't he?'

'Murder?'

But the fastpath rotation was in place, and Med Centre was where he had to be.

'Let's go,' said Boyle.

They stepped out into Med Centre, right beside the drone housing Miranda. Medics were immersed in holodisplays. The man who had talked to Carl before said: 'It's not the best of—'

Red icons flared as the drone screeched.

'What's happening?' Carl felt as if something had clawed open his chest. 'What does it mean?'

But the medic's hands worked flickering control gestures, and panes of nothingness whirled.

'I thought you said a fastpath was too dangerous to—'

'It's the only chance now.'

Medics and drone – with his beautiful Miranda inside – were gone.

'You've got to be all right,' he whispered. 'You've got to.'

Somebody put a hand on his shoulder, either Clayton or Boyle, keeping him steady.

You have to pull through. For me, for Roger.

Had he told her enough that it was her he lived for? That everything was in the end for her?

You have to, my love—

Rotation again, and they were back.

Perhaps hours had passed on the other timeflow, wherever they had been. Maybe it had been days – Labyrinthine time could be that crazy.

The medic's face was haggard.

'I'm sorry, Pilot Blackstone. We did everything we—'

'No . . .'

Carl pressed his hands against the drone's carapace.

Please no.

The drone that was now Miranda's coffin.

FORTY-TWO

FULGOR, 2603 AD

Amid grey-and-purple fog, Roger rode the hired slickbike up a jagged, stippled ascent and came into the open. Behind him, the top of the fog glistened in sunlight; in front of him, a steel monstrosity clanked and thumped its great piston-legs, following the ridgetop.

The Spalding residence would look squat from a distance, but up close it was a huge armoured presence, tangled with pipes and funnels, complex and ugly, ringed with piledriver legs that hissed and clanged and thumped, crunching the ground.

Alisha. You grew up in that?

Up here, he still needed his respmask. Xavier Spalding preferred to keep his peregrinating house inside the hypozone. How best to signal the man?

But steel maws clanged open, and a curled-up rampway unfurled, like an unrolled carpet constructed of clanking iron. Roger directed the slickbike upwards, and it slid up the metal on its flowbelly, and squelched to a halt inside an entrance hall.

Steel decking, copper-and-steel chandeliers encrusted with spikes, and a floating glass arrow that trembled when he looked at it: that was all he saw.

'I understand.' He dismounted from the slickbike. 'Carry on.'

The arrow moved and he followed, along a metal corridor ending in a door that split into a thousand razor-edged leaves and drew apart. Beyond, a silver door shivered into a mass of interlocking penrose tiles that folded back, like a snowdrift in strong wind.

Inside, the massive lounge was black and grey, touched with metallic purple. A shaven-headed man – Xavier Spalding – sat on a silver couch. Three steel eagles watched from perches, their heads turning to track Roger's advance. One of them clashed its metal feathers; another opened and closed its angular steel beak.

'They won't attack,' said Xavier.

'But they could.'

'If it were necessary. Clearly, we're on the same side, Roger.'

'What makes you say that?'

'I may not be a Luculentus, but I have a measure of success, and many friends. You know how social networking follows an inverse-power relationship, I presume.'

'There are many people with few acquaintances, and few people with many acquaintances, and it's a straight-line relationship.' Roger decided this was a test. 'Like the first internet, if you know your Terran history.'

The test was not to get annoyed at being asked what every child should know. If there are a million servers with a certain number of connections, then there might be *half* a million servers with *double* that number of connections, in a scale-free network. Or some similar inverse relationship.

'A small number of nodes with a vast number of links,' said Xavier. 'Just so.'

'Mathematically, you can't define a meaningful average. Strategically, such networks are robust against random attacks, vulnerable to directed assaults. The original internet took twenty minutes to die, and it's surprising it lasted that long.'

Xavier stared, picking up the implication: he was a vulnerable target.

'I can see why my daughter likes you. Sit down, Mr Blackstone.'

'Thank you. So you're a primary node in a social network, are you, sir?'

'Call me Xavier. So yes, Roger, I have a lot of friends.'

'Or allies?' The metal chair he selected was hard-looking, but felt comfortable. 'Business acquaintances?'

'Some of them are true friends. So I know, because of my *acquaintances*, that a mu-space ship burst into the open just above ground level, right in front of a house occupied by the Blackstone family. So where is it now?'

'Where's what?'

'Your father's ship. I'm assuming it's your father's, since he was clearly the major spy. Or have I got that wrong?'

This was not what Roger was here for.

'It's in another universe and they're not coming back, that's all, sir. Xavier.'

'Ah.' Xavier glanced at one of his steel eagles. 'I see.'

'Look, it's Alisha I came to—'

'Your parents fled, while SatScan thinks all three of you did. I'm guessing a smartmiasma was involved. So the peacekeepers think you're offplanet for good, I take it.'

'I don't know.'

'But you made your way here without problems.'

'Not without—' Roger thought about it. 'If they were actively hunting me, I wouldn't have got here as I did.'

Thanks, Dad.

Still looking out for his son, even as he ran for his ship – that was Dad.

'Superintendent Sunadomari,' he added, 'knows you warned Dad, and gave him what he needed to shield against the scanners.'

'Yes, and no one's brought charges yet. Either Sunadomari is busy with more urgent affairs, or he intends to keep this knowledge as leverage. A primary social node is a useful asset for him to obtain, don't you think?'

'Er, yes.'

'But then to protect me, to keep me useful, he has to be my friend also. Isn't it interesting how that works out?'

Roger wanted to yell, but he made his voice soften.

'It's Alisha we need to be—'

But one of the steel eagles turned its head, and its eyes flashed yellow.

'Interesting.' Xavier's smartlenses shone for a second. 'You have access to the house. The student house on campus.'

'I live there. Er . . .'

He used to. Where he lived now, that was undefined. Everyday life was in suspension.

'Quite. So between your authorization and my resources, we can poll the system and trawl the logs. Alisha was in the house last night – she called me late – but this morning she's gone.'

'And she's off Skein.'

'My . . . friends . . . have been looking, unofficially. No sign in public.'

'What if you make it official?'

'A young woman is off Skein for a few hours. You think that will launch a high-priority surveillance sweep?'

'I . . .' Roger forced an exhalation. 'You should talk to Superintendent Sunadomari.'

'That's right, and I will. But after you've gone.'

'What do you mean?'

'You're a Pilot, and that comes with certain abilities. And you care about Alisha.'

'So?'

'My friends here' – Xavier nodded, and three steel eagles rattled their wings – 'can maintain line-of-sight tightbeam. You access the house from somewhere on campus, and they'll relay the whole session via here.'

'I don't—'

'This room will appear to be the point of origin for the signal.'

'Oh.'

'So if our peacekeeper friends are surprised by your continued presence on Fulgor, and decide they'd like to chat, they'll think you're with me, not in the city.'

'And Sunadomari?'

'Take one of my flyers, get to campus, interrogate the student house. Then I'll call Sunadomari.'

'While other peacekeepers are maybe already descending on this place?' Roger gestured around the black-and-grey room. 'Are you going to hold them off by force?'

'I could, but that isn't the way.'

A vertical steel cylinder was rotating to reveal an opening.

'Lift-tube,' Xavier went on. 'It'll take you to the flyer bay. The white flyer is ready to go.'

'What if we're already under full surveillance?'

'Then it doesn't matter what we do.'

'I'm not sure we're doing the—'

'Get going, son. We need to find Alisha.'

Roger felt light-headed as he pushed himself up from the chair, realized he had eaten nothing, then pushed the feeling away. The lift-tube was waiting for him.

Sunadomari, in his flyer with two of Helen Eisberg's tac troopers, could not wait to reach the Via Lucis Institute in reality. There were things he did not want to say, even in Skein, not until he was deep inside the physical as well as Skeinware barriers available to LuxPrime's senior people. But he needed to talk to someone now.

In Skein, a Luculentus with golden headgear smiled at him.

'Keinosuke Sunadomari, and you're on your way here in person.'

'Hsiu Li-Cheng, I certainly am.'

They used in-Skein audio, zipblips of sound, compressing sentences to millisecond-duration.

'This can't wait. Can you ensure we're not being eavesdropped on?'

'Excuse me, this *is* Skein.'

'Assume you had a rogue Skein designer, with full knowledge.'

'That's not—All right, we're secured.'

Neither of them made any attempt to create in-Skein images

of themselves matching the spoken words; but Li-Cheng caused his visual representation to raise one eyebrow – a thousand times faster than reality.

'Tell me,' said Sunadomari, 'about the worst rogue Luculentus of all. Rafael de la Vega.'

'Problems with the soul-father transfer caused it . . . a long time ago. Come off it, Keinosuke, we don't even do that any more.'

'Soul-fathers.'

'Right.'

Gradually during the past century, the practice had, well, died out. In the past, a Luculenta chose a soul-daughter, a psychological successor; while a Luculentus chose a soul-son. When the elder was nearing a natural death, he or she would transfer chosen fragments of their selves into their chosen successor. Passing on the best to another generation.

It was a form of continuation; it was a form of suicide. For the scanware to work so deeply, it had to deconstruct the neural quantum states. Like smashing an object to see how hard it is, quantum scan destroys the very state it records. The Luculenti minds were heisenberged to random oblivion.

But fragments of their minds survived, incorporated in the next generation, who might or might not be genetic descendants.

'De la Vega's mind was screwed up during the procedure? When he received from his soul-father?'

'That was the finding of forensic examination a century ago. Modern methods might reveal more.'

'I don't think that matters,' said Sunadomari. 'When I learned the story, it called him a mind-plunderer. Ah . . . He used similar ware?'

'Exactly. His vampire code – that's how forensics named it – derived from the old soul-successor transfer systems.'

'Have you always known this, my friend? Or are you retrieving it from knowledge archives as we speak?'

'From archive. I'm no historian.'

'So tell me more about his demise.'

'He was defeated by—' Li-Cheng's eyes widened. 'Are you playing a clever game, old friend? Or do you truly not know who the Judas goat was?'

'Judas goat?'

'A newly upraised adult of mature years – newly arrived on Fulgor – with plexcores embedded purely to tempt de la Vega to attack her. So you didn't know. But the whole case was classified, obviously.'

'Tell me.'

'The person who acted as bait was called Yoshiko Sunadomari.'

'But—'

'Bravery clearly runs across the generations.'

'Coincidence.'

'Of course. Or subtle causality, for how many of us' – Li-Cheng meant Luculenti – 'have any interest in being a peacekeeper?'

Sunadomari could dive into his childhood reflections for influences, but for now it was irrelevant.

'So my ancestor was the bait, and peacekeepers trapped de la Vega?'

'Not exactly.'

'I don't—'

'Perhaps this should wait until you get here.'

'If anyone is eavesdropping now, despite your monitoring, will they guess what it is you want to tell me?'

Li-Cheng's image, in Skein, gave a thousand-times-accelerated smile.

'If they already possess the knowledge, then they'll know what I'm referring to. If they have no idea, then I'll be providing them with classified information.'

'They know already.'

'You're sure?'

'I take responsibility for the decision.'

'I'm sure your great-great-grandmother would have

approved. So. De la Vega expanded his plexcore array, to increase the capacity. He was attempting to plunder dozens of minds.'

'That would tip his neural systems through phase transitions, wouldn't it?'

'If you mean the new mind would no longer think like a human being, you're right. Yet it would still be a coherent entity, provided the plexcore array functioned correctly. But you can't scale them up.'

'Surely you can. The topology is—'

'Lightspeed delays across synaptic interfaces. The farther apart the processors are, the more—'

'Understood. I hadn't realized. He was spreading his mind across physically distant plexcores.'

'In the end, yes. We have the whole collection in our museum here, the old plexcores. Or nearly the whole collection, at the moment.'

'What do you mean?'

'One's on loan to the multiversity for study. It's a long-term thing.'

For an entire second, Sunadomari withdrew from Skein, sucked in a breath, glanced at the two peacekeepers in his flyer's cabin with him, then immersed himself in Skein once more.

'Let me guess,' he said. 'You lent it to a Dr Greg Ranulph.'

'No, it's a team effort, but he's not on the list.'

'Then Dr Petra Helsen.'

'She's on the team. But ... tell me you don't think there's another de la Vega.'

'There is.'

'Helsen's an ordinary human, my friend.'

'I wonder about that, but she's no Luculenta. I do know someone who fits the description well, however.'

'So are you hunting for this person?'

'SatScan and full surveillance on the ground, but it's not helping. On the other hand, I don't think it matters where she is physically.'

'She's attacking through Skein?'
'Exactly.'
'Then that's how we'll find her.'
'See you in reality, soon.'
The flyer cabin came back into awareness. His conversation with Hsiu Li-Cheng had lasted less than two seconds. Neither of the peacekeepers showed any awareness that there had even been a discussion taking place. It was the kind of thing one grew used to as a Luculentus, the ability to move things along at the speed of thought.
But Rafaella Stargonier was just as fast.

FORTY-THREE

FULGOR, 2603 AD

A steel eagle circled overhead, while Roger stood on the quickstone forecourt, stared at the student house he theoretically still lived in, and used his tu-ring to open up a small holospace. Thanks to the eagle, this enquiry would appear to originate from the Spalding home, where it clanked along inside the hypozone. But not everything depended on Xavier – the tu-ring had spyware functions he had never used before, his last gift from Dad.

'Got it.' It was quicker to use control gestures and abbreviated subvocalizations. 'And show.'

He now had access to the logs from Alisha's room. Her nipples were so pink on soft white breasts, as she climbed from the bed where she had slept naked—

'Shit.'

Face burning, he fast-forwarded through to where she made a call, then zoomed in. She had not spoken in clear, but her lips moved as she subvocalized. A second holospace opened above the tu-ring, showing the ware's analysis of her words.

'Roger,' she was saying. *'I have to be at Aleph Tower at nine. I'm meeting Rafaella Stargonier. She owns the building, I think.*

'If you get this before I leave, you could come along. If you like, I mean. It would be good to . . . Never mind.

'See you later.'

He shut the display down.

'Shit. Shit.'

If he had only dared to log on to Skein. She had left a message for him. For *him.* No need to spy inside her room's memory. All he had needed to do was check his own bastard messages. How many hours he had wasted from cowardice?

He looked up at the steel eagle, wondering what Xavier made of this.

'Maybe I should—'

'Hey, Roger!' From an upper balcony, Stef was leaning over. 'How did you guys get on last night?'

'I'm sorry?'

'You know what I'm ... Oh, a gentleman never tells, huh?'

'We didn't—'

'See you in class. You can tell me then.' She blew him a kiss. 'Later.'

Then she went inside.

Crap.

He re-opened the hololog at the same point, scanned forward until Alisha appeared to be making another call. He zoomed in once more. This time she was calling for an aircab to take her to Aleph Tower. Speeding the log forward, she did nothing significant until leaving the room two minutes before the aircab was due.

Not caring now whether he was tracked, he called down an aircab of his own, and told it to take him to Aleph Tower. The steel eagle flew overhead – the call would still appear to have originated from the Spalding home – but surveillance might realize that a physical human being had boarded from the multiversity campus, and wonder who it was.

Once at the tower, he requested that the aircab remain hovering while he alighted.

'Roger.' The shaven head of Xavier appeared in holo. *'Open up a query to the building system. I'll piggyback from here.'*

'But the people inside—'

'We can scan a system a lot faster than we can persuade a person.'

'All right.'

He pointed his tu-ring at the quickglass wall, and waited. In ten seconds – a long time in computation – a shaky moving holo appeared next to his hand. Alisha, staggering from Aleph Tower, almost falling into an aircab.

'One moment, Roger. Shit.'

'What is it?'

'The aircab was commanded to take her to Killian's Dive in Quarter Moon. But it wasn't one of mine, damn it.'

'Sir?'

'I mean the aircab. I own—Ah, you are *using one of mine. Good. Get back in, and you're off the grid.'*

'But I don't know what—'

'Roger, there are two peacekeeper flyers over my roof. I'm going to try to contact Superintendent Sunadomari before they get inside, but I have to shut this down now.'

The holo was gone.

Overhead, the steel eagle was flying away. All Roger could do was climb into the aircab and tell it where to go.

'Killian's Dive. Quarter Moon District.'

The aircab soared upward.

Perhaps there were shabbier districts in Lucis City; perhaps there were more dangerous; but none could match old Quarter Moon for sleaze. Roger walked away from the ascending aircab, feeling dirty already. From a doorway, a small man beckoned.

'Hey, you like girls?'

'No. I mean yes, but—Sorry.'

Dark buildings, bright holos. Perhaps night could add a veneer of glamour; in daylight, the streaks on walls that ought to self-clean were evident, while beneath the warm scents of cooking that floated from cheap eateries, pungent undertones were lurking.

The entrance to Killian's Dive was a vertical oval, ringed with long-fibred matting. The fibres curled, and it took him a moment to understand the pubic symbolism. He wanted to puke.

Inside, he took in the silver bar set diagonally across the half-lit space, the customers that sat or stood, tired or morose or stunned-looking, drinking whatever morning drinkers took. None of the customers was Alisha.

Behind the bar was a large man with motile purple tattoos crawling across his scalp. His thick-muscled arms were bare, except for steel rings set around wrists and biceps that appeared to be set into the flesh.

Usually, a human bartender added a touch of class, since any quickglass room could provide service. Here, the big man provided visual intimidation – and probably backed it up with violence as needed.

How am I supposed to question him?

This was stupid.

I can't threaten someone like that.

He turned and walked out on to the street.

'Lovely, luscious girls,' said a dark-skinned woman in front of him, her low-scooped top displaying large, soft cleavage. 'They're sitting around in their underwear at the house right now.'

'I don't—'

'And you can choose any you want.'

Blood pulsed in his groin.

Oh, God.

'For you, lover, there's a discount. It will be—Oh.'

A tall man was extending his fist, his tu-ring flashing a holo sigil directly into Roger's eyes.

'Peacekeeper,' he said. 'We're watching this area, just so you know.'

Roger nearly fell to the ground, as if the ligaments in his knees had detached.

'You look like a nice lad,' he continued. 'What do you do for work? *Her*, we know.'

'I'm a, er, student. At the multiversity.'

'Good for you.'

'I . . . Thank you, officer. Thank you.'

He backed away, waves of sickness washing through every internal organ, nodded to the officer, then strode to the corner, turned and carried on walking to the end of the block. There, he leaned back against the wall, not caring about the faint scent of ancient urine, just rubbing his eyes and trying to bring his mind together.

'Hey, lover.' It was the woman again. 'Don't pay any mind to him. The girls are still there waiting, and you know they'd just love to meet you.'

'No. Just ... No.'

'Are you sure?' When she wiggled, waves of motion rippled up her cleavage. 'Really, really sure?'

'Go away.'

Something seemed to snap out of existence inside her eyes, and she simply turned and walked away. Once at the corner of the main street, her gait changed, becoming a saunter once more.

Roger turned away, and realized he was at the head of an alleyway that ran behind Killian's Dive. One step at a time, while an internal voice complained, he made his way to the rear wall, then stopped.

The wall was black quickglass, worn and crusty outside, its interior still malleable. He stared at it for a moment, then pulled up a menu in his tu-ring, checking the expanded list of commands available to him now: the maintenance services and engineering aspects normally hidden beneath security.

He formed the instructions, pressed his forearms against the wall, and waited. It took some twenty seconds for the inner layers to respond and seep through the hardened parts like liquid tar. First several drops, then runnels of black quickglass twisted around his forearms.

When he backed off, the quickglass came free with squelches and popping. He gave it another two minutes, allowing it to merge with the smartmaterial sleeves of his clothing, and begin to creep downwards. While the integration continued, he set up several shortcut commands, and kept them in the tu-ring's execution space, ready to initiate.

Earlier, fear had made him want to throw up. Now he felt like a sick patient in the euphoria when the vomiting was past, able to move and not care. He was almost lightheaded as he walked back on to the side street, then turned again and found himself at Killian's Dive; and then he went in.

The huge bartender was still there.

'Excuse me,' Roger said.

But the bartender pointed to one of the other customers, then at the man's empty glass.

'You want I should get you another purple stripe?'

'Uh-huh.'

Big fingers, his hands like crushing machines, tapped a control sequence on the metal countertop. An iris opened before the drinker, and a glass rose up, its contents a Turing pattern that reminded Roger of fog in the hypozone.

'So whaddyou want?'

'Um, one of those, please. Purple stripe.'

'Huh.'

The command was a single tap against the countertop. The bartender was already starting to turn away when Roger held up his fist, a small holo image floating above his tu-ring.

'Have you seen her?'

The man's eyes flickered to his left.

'No, pal. I serve drinks.' He raised his massive shoulders then pulled them down, causing them to widen. 'You drink 'em. That's it.'

'Please, I think she's in trouble.'

'Huh. Girl like that in here' – when he sneered, an old scar twisted the bartender's pale lips – 'she's past caring, pal.'

'Tell me.'

'Fuck off.'

The bartender walked to the far end of the bar, and folded his massive arms.

Now what?

All his years of schooling, and there had been nothing to cover situations like this. Teachers lived in a world where clever words were everything, including weapons; but here was reality.

Oh, shit. Here I go.

As Roger walked behind the bar, his sleeves stirred and began to flow downwards, covering his hands like slick gloves.

'Hey.'

'Sorry. ' Roger held one hand up, palm forward, not threatening. 'I just wanted to ask about the woman.'

The bartender unfolded his arms, and grabbed Roger's shoulder with painful force.

'Go back around the—'

Roger's palm slapped against the muscular slab of the guy's chest.

'I don't—'

And when the big hands pushed him back, strands of quickglass hooking inside the bartender's flesh pulled the skin outward.

'—think so.'

'The fuck is this?' The big man took hold of Roger, squeezing and hauling him off the ground. 'Get this off me or I'll snap you now.'

Roger's bones felt about to give way.

'No,' he said.

His free hand slapped against the back of the man's neck.

'You lose.'

Quickglass tendrils infiltrated the cervical vertebrae, a narrow filament targetting a ventral junction of the spinal cord. The big man shuddered, then collapsed.

Roger fell on top of him.

'You saw her.'

'No, I—'

A stench grew in pungency.

'You just shat yourself,' said Roger. 'I keep this in your neck much longer, the paralysis is permanent. Or you can tell me where she is.'

I really can't believe I'm—

'Not . . . here.'

—doing this.

'Tell me.'

'At . . . Ingram's Corner, man. You know.'

'What's that?'

'No . . . Uh. Drone Dollies. Garber picked her up.'

'Who's Garber?'

'Pro-procurer.'

'What does he procure?'

The bartender was beginning to cry.

'Come on,' said Roger. 'What does he procure?'

'Girls, man. Drones.'

'Are you talking mindwipe here?'

'They're far gone when they come here.' A sob. 'Like, almost drones already.'

'Drones.'

But he was not going to get anything more from the paralysed bartender. He formed the command, and the quickglass sucked free from the man's body.

When Roger stood, only one of the drinkers was looking in his direction, raising a purple stripe in toast.

Roger looked at his own untouched drink, and considered knocking it across the counter or throwing it at the supine, sniffling bartender. But he carried on walking.

Did I just do that?

Whatever had happened to Alisha was more terrible than he had thought. And he realized, as he came out on to the bright, sleazy street, that he himself was capable of so much more, and so much worse, than his comfortable life had taught him.

His quickglass gloves glistened on his hands.

FORTY-FOUR

LABYRINTH, 2603 AD (REALSPACE-EQUIVALENT)

They tried to stop Carl; but they could not.

His former interrogators, Clayton and Boyle, were perhaps overwhelmed by the thought of their own impending amnesia treatment, Carl's innocence in the matter they were investigating – Admiral Kaltberg's murder – and their genuine sympathy at Miranda Blackstone's death.

Still, they attempted restraint holds when Carl pushed himself away from the med-drone containing his wife's body and started to run. But he moved in a torrent of sorrow, a whirlpool of rage, spinning and twisting so Clayton and Boyle and grasping medics were flung aside; and then he was sprinting into the open, summoning a fastpath rotation dead ahead.

'Stop that—'

Hands reached but he was past them, and then he was into the fastpath and the others had no chance.

He spun back into reality inside his ship. She reacted immediately, sealing her entranceway and gathering power, her hull reactivating its protective event membrane, sealing it off from fastpath intrusion; and she was already backing away from the dock, turning inside the great vault where other ships floated. Now she gunned for the exit tunnel.

Only Labyrinth itself could stop them now.

But the city chose not to act, and within seconds Carl-and-ship burst free into golden mu-space, their minds unitary once more as they flew hard, getting separation from the mass of Labyrinth, before shifting with precision to a chosen geodesic; and then they were gone.

It was a tough trajectory they followed, to appear in realspace in a short elapsed time, while the onboard duration would be long, a relativistic dilation they both needed, Carl and ship: one to think, the other to cope with her Pilot's grief, both to make their preparations.

They flew on.

FORTY-FIVE

EARTH, 1940 AD

Three weeks after her journey across the North Sea – the memory a montage of seasickness, waves and fish-stink – Gavriela was sitting in a snug Oxford pub, a small pressed-cardboard suitcase at her feet, trying to understand how she had come here. Some kind of process had been set in motion, and now she was waiting, scared and happy to be meeting someone she didn't just know but cared about.

Will he even remember me?

In Zürich he had never responded – but she had been too young; now she was a woman who could act when she had to, because opportunities were temporary, and fragile.

If he doesn't take the initiative, I will.

In front of her was a glass of sherry, which she did not like but knew Englishwomen drank, if they entered pubs at all. All around were chattering voices, the sounds bouncing and washing around the dark bar, a sea of accents and too-fast words from which she plucked occasional minnows of meaning.

In a corner near the fireplace, an intent man was writing in a notebook. While ordering her drink, Gavriela had seen the runes he was inscribing in the middle of dense English prose. Now, from her small round table, she could hear – but not quite follow – conversations about shear forces in Gothic arches, lepidoptera speciation, the difference between polycentric hologenesis and polyphyletism, and Shakespeare's unspeakable relationship with the Earl of Southampton. Not to mention the paucity of butter rations, the difficulty of obtaining a decent pipe tobacco, and the desirability quotient of Vera Lynn's legs.

Two young men in RAF uniform were drinking at the bar. A much older man, from a corner table, watched them, his eyes bereft, perhaps remembering a lost son.

She adjusted the other chair at her table, and realized that someone had left a book on it. The title was *Mesmerism: History and Techniques*, by D.A.R. Greene, and it opened naturally at a page where someone had underlined a passage in pencil.

One may utilize extended fixation of the eyesight upon an object, the text said, *such as the traditional fob watch, or indeed any bright object, to induce mesmeric trance. As a dramatic alternative, the patient may be induced to plunge into an altered state almost instantaneously, by interrupting an ingrained, automatic behaviour. This latter requires skill and timing, and has as much in common with a sporting practice, such as lawn tennis, as normal psychological technique.*

It is useful for the practitioner to recognize the exterior signals of trance, viz. rapid fluttering of the eyelids, defocused eyes, and altered skin lividity. In addition, limb catalepsy is a both an indicator and a convincing—

She read on, lost in the book.

'You can keep it if you like, dear.' It was the barmaid, clutching more empty beer glasses than seemed possible. 'I know the gentleman who left it. He's off to the Army, so he won't be coming b—I mean, it'll be a good while before he's back.'

'Oh. Thank you. Let's hope he's all right.'

'Yeah. You Polish, is that it?'

'Um, sort of.'

'Thought so. Got an ear for an accent, I have.'

Gavriela tried to smile, but the barmaid was already moving on to swap a cheeky comment with the men at the next table – the ones enamoured of Vera Lynn – and remove their empties.

What if I said I'm German?

She remembered Professor Hartmann talking about the splendour of German culture, but here Germany was the fount of bloody barbarism spilling through the world.

'Gavi!'

It was the same intelligent eyes, though the face was older and the curly hair had receded a little.

'Lucas. Oh, Lucas.' She stood, let her hand be taken in both of his, and reminded herself to speak in English. 'It's so good to see you.'

'Yes, it is. Good to see you, I mean.' He grinned, plunging her memory back to that first day in Zürich. 'And this is my friend Rupert. Rupert Forrester, meet Gavriela Wolf.'

'Good to meet you, Dr Wolf.'

'Um, thank you.' They shook hands.

'So you'll have another sherry? No? And Luke, the usual for you.' Rupert smiled at them both. 'Why don't you catch up, and I'll take my time chatting to Susie.'

That would be the barmaid.

'Let's sit down,' Gavriela said.

Lucas looked at the book and raised his eyebrows.

'Interesting,' he said. 'I do hear neurotic people can be helped with such techniques. But how are you, dear Gavi? It's been a frightfully long time.'

To her inexpert ears, his English accent was perfect.

'It's been—Oh, it is so different back there.'

'I was in Denmark when it all fell apart.' He reached inside his jacket, and withdrew an ID card. 'This is who I am now.'

The name read *Luke Cross*. But he was still the same Lucas Krause who had captivated her attention so long ago.

'You remember my first day at the ETH?' She pronounced it *eh-teh-ha,* then caught herself, remembering the English. 'I mean the *ee-tee-aitch*. Professor Möller with the wire basket.'

'And Florian Horst the trusted assistant. Did you see him in Copenhagen?'

'No, he and Elke were gone.'

She did not want to say the rest: that no one knew whether they were in hiding or had returned to Germany. She had thought that Florian detested the Wehrmacht; but she might be wrong. So many beliefs had turned to twisted rubble.

'Oh. Well.'

'Well.'

There was so much to say between them. Gavriela stared at his face, and no words came to her, none at all. When Rupert returned, they both looked at him.

'So, Luke,' he said, setting down pint glasses. 'Have you shared your good news?'

'Oh, no.' Lucas raised his left hand, smiling. 'Look. At last.'

It took Gavriela a moment to notice the gold.

'That's a wedding-ring.'

'It certainly is.'

'He's on his honeymoon, strictly speaking,' said Rupert. 'So we don't expect you to hang around very long, do we, Dr Wolf?'

'Er, no. Congratulations, Lucas. Well done.'

'And they'll be gone by the end of the week.' Rupert tipped an invisible hat in salute. 'A cross-Atlantic cruise.'

'Not exactly a cruise. And Mary hates the heat.'

Rupert raised an eyebrow.

'Sorry,' added Lucas. 'We're off to the States to live. It'll be . . . interesting.'

The structures of Gavriela's life had been swept away. This was just one more disorienting transition.

'So.' Lucas downed half of the pint very quickly. 'Rupert will show you to your digs. It's a good place.'

'Digs?'

'Your lodgings,' said Rupert. 'It's all arranged.'

'Oh.'

'You told the officers in Edinburgh that you want to help the war effort, didn't you?'

'Yes.' She had disembarked from the trawler there, and been surprised when policemen seemed to know her name already. 'I meant it, very much.'

'Then we've something lined up for you.'

'Oh.' She looked at Lucas, then at Rupert. 'You're not just a friend of Lucas, are you?'

Those same police officers had plied her with sweet tea,

taken her to stay in lodgings – no one called them digs – at a house belonging to the station sergeant's mother. Finally they had told her about Lucas Krause waiting to meet her in Oxford, and the train journey, lasting overnight, had been an epic of anticipation, as she imagined their reunion.

But he was off to live in the United States, with his new wife.

'Not just a friend, no,' said Rupert. 'Call us distant colleagues, and Luke a very impressive boffin.'

'You're too kind.' Lucas took several more swigs of bitter. 'Gavi's brain is bigger than mine, I assure you. Razor sharp.'

'That'll be interesting to see.' Rupert took a tiny sip of his beer. 'We'll find plenty for you to do, Dr Wolf, now our new prime minister's shaking things up.'

Lucas tipped back the last of his drink, and put the glass down. Foam slid inside the glass, the motion catching Gavriela's attention. Bubbles were an interesting phenomenon, caused by—

No wonder he never looked at me. He didn't want a physicist to talk to; he wanted a lover.

Her throat clenched.

'Are you all right, Gavi?'

'Sure, Lucas. Sure.'

'Then . . . I have to go.'

He stood up; Gavriela and Rupert did likewise.

'Good luck,' she said. 'And congratulations once more.'

This time they hugged instead of shaking hands; but there was none of the electric contact that had featured in her imagination.

'Take care, Gavi.'

He went out, carrying his hat and overcoat, squeezing past the regulars, and disappeared through the blackout curtain. A second later, the door to the street clicked shut.

'You don't like sherry, do you, Dr Wolf?'

'I—' Gavriela looked down, then at Rupert. 'Actually, I hate it.'

Rupert laughed.

'Do you want something else?'

'No, thank you.'

'Then I'll show you to your lodgings.'

'If you call me Gavriela, I'd be happy to walk with you.'

'Um . . .'

She swallowed.

'I'm sorry. Your customs are—'

'That's not why I hesitated,' said Rupert. 'I'd prefer to call you Gabby, if that's all right. We thought it sounded similar enough that you'd respond, er, be comfortable with it.'

'Gabby.'

'You're Gabby Woods, and in the morning you'll have the paperwork to prove it. Does that suit you?'

'And if you're a Forrester, what does that make you? My keeper?'

She knew *forest* and *forester* by chance, for they were nothing like the German.

'Luke was right. You *are* sharp. So, are you ready to go?'

'Yes, I am.'

'Let me take your case.'

As they were leaving, she noticed again the man sitting alone with his notebook, the pages dense with words but also some runes. Once they were outside, in the darkness of St Giles, she asked Rupert about it.

'He looked as if he was writing code.'

'Not so you'd know. He's an interesting fellow, but we know who he is.'

'Oh.'

'He writes about habits, or something. And how's that book you're carrying, Gabby?'

It took her two full seconds to respond to her new name.

'Sorry. Er, I've not really read it yet.' She looked at the mesmerism book. 'I think it might be interesting.'

'Hmm. Well, come along. It's a short walk in peacetime,

but making one's way without streetlights tends to slow one down.'

'There's a quarter moon.'

'Luckily, or we'd more than likely be tripping onto our faces.'

Banbury Road was quiet, with only a few souls walking home at this time, in darkness. They passed University Parks – 'Many a rugger match I've played in there,' said Rupert – and then had to explain what he meant by that. Such inconsequential chat sustained them until they reached a big old house, no grander or spookier than its neighbours. Their feet crunched on gravel, and then Rupert was tapping on the front door.

'Hello, Mrs Wilson. We're here.'

It was strange for someone to open their door in darkness.

'Come in, Master Forrester. Come on in.'

Rupert touched Gavriela's arm, and led her inside. Once the front door was closed and a heavy drape pulled across, Mrs Wilson switched on an electric light.

'Into the front room, my dears.' She was white-haired but lively-looking. 'We have chicory coffee or acorn tea, your choice.'

'Whichever's best for you,' said Rupert.

He beckoned Gavriela to a well-stuffed green armchair, and sat in its counterpart.

'You can trust Mrs Wilson,' he added. 'But it's best to make a habit of keeping details to yourself.'

'A habit you have?' asked Gavriela.

'I should hope so. Why?'

'Because you have not told me anything yet.'

'Ah.'

'So besides the fact I'm working in Oxford, I don't—'

'Not really. It's such an obvious target, don't you think?'

'I don't understand.'

'It's not the best place to conduct war work, you see. You'll stay here only until we find you someplace closer to the project. Assuming it works out tomorrow, when you meet the others.'

'I suppose that's—'

But that was when Mrs Wilson appeared, tray in hand.

'A night-time cuppa, and then you, Master Forrester—'

'She's known me since I was young,' said Rupert.

'—can make your way home or sleep on the sofa, your choice, but this tired-looking young lady will be going straight to bed.'

Rupert looked at Gavriela, then at their hostess.

'Yes, Mrs Wilson,' he said.

Gavriela's was an attic bedroom, under the eaves. The bedstead was of polished brass, the floral curtains were reinforced by drapes of rough fabric, and dark-green linoleum lay on the floor. On the small bedside table lay her notebook and writing implements: a fountain pen and revolving pencil in identical mother-of-pearl, a present from Mother and Father, all that she had left of them. Her few clothes hung in the wardrobe. With everything organized, she simply stood there in her cotton nightgown, taking in the domestic solidity of the room.

Then she switched off the electric light, padded on bare feet to the window, and pulled open the curtains, allowing silver moonlight in.

She climbed into bed, then shifted her pillow so she could lie diagonally across the narrow bed and see the quarter-face of the moon. On the day she met Inge, Petra and Elke in Zürich, Inge had talked about a rocket trip to that other world, and its impossibility when there was nothing to push against. She remembered explaining Newton's laws, and still finding it impossible to convince Inge, until she got Inge to close her eyes and imagine she was standing on a frozen lake, wearing ice skates and holding a heavy case. And when she threw the case away from her, what would happen?

'Why, I'd slide backwards and—' Inge's eyes had snapped open. 'Gavriela, you're a genius.'

Gavriela was not sure, but perhaps that evening formed a beginning: the moment she began to understand the relationship between daydreams and equations, imagination and analysis.

She let out a sigh, wondering where her Inge and Elke were now. Not Petra – she was in a cemetery in Brandenburg, courtesy of a downward spiral that no one had been able to pull her out of.

So bright, the moon.

One may utilize extended fixation of the eyesight upon an object, such as the traditional fob watch, or indeed any bright object, to induce mesmeric trance.

She drifted amid echoes of a dream, fragments of hallucination, shards of imagination.

—I am Kenna.

—And you're the leader.

—Yes, Gavriela.

—And the others?

—You're the first.

The moon, so enchanting, so silver, so bright.

She wrote in her notebook, pen-nib and pencil-lead lightly scraping the paper. Although the moon appeared bright against the night-sky backdrop, inside the room it provided poor illumination; but that did not matter.

Beneath her closed eyelids, as she wrote with a pen in one hand and a pencil in the other, Gavriela's eyes flicked from side to side.

FORTY-SIX

FULGOR, 2603 AD

Banners and holosculptures, quickglass birds and persistent fireworks, smartkites and dirigibles, were proliferating over every district of Lucis City – even the exotic parts, like Parallaville, and the sleazy areas, like Quarter Moon – for today was Last Lupus, the final day of Festival, and the last chance for everyone to party.

Ingram's Corner was a crossroads, a juxtaposition of opposing architectural styles, yet an apposite communion of appetites: from the battered building that contained several dozen fifteen-minutes-and-you're-finished brothels and smackjoints, to Ebony Tower, a rearing quickglass monstrosity, home to some two hundred floors of restaurants and stores, and clubs that never closed, not to mention a hard-to-classify establishment called The Church of the Continual Orgasm.

Roger watched from a window on the twentieth floor, staring across the way at the squat building opposite, plotting his entrance to Drone Dollies. Part of him was yelling that this was stupid, that he should call the peacekeepers and damn the consequences; but Roger Blackstone's name, image and voiceprint would be on the detain-immediately list, and there was no telling how long it would take before he could get someone to listen to him.

One option was to take time to create a false ident, using the new utilities in his tu-ring – or he could take direct action, and make somebody pay.

The squat building from above was an eight-storey hollow rectangle. From here he could see how to work it: ascend to roof level, go over the inner edge, get in through a quickglass wall. The building's logs would tell him where she was; but he had no hope of cracking the security without the breach causing alarms to execute. The extraction needed to be fast, and that meant having Superintendent Sunadomari's ident in his call buffer, ready to make contact. Roger could report Alisha's circumstances even if building security took him down.

I still can't believe I'm doing this.

He had a visceral hatred of heights and a civilized horror of violence; but this was going to happen. With a last look at the target building, he turned away, took one of Ebony Tower's flowshafts down to ground level, and went outside.

Overhead, a smiling blimp with cartoon smile was waving stubby arms, chuckling and singing a children's song. On the ground, the number of revellers was growing by the minute, some waving streamers or causing holofountains to sparkle, virtual fireworks to bring on the party mood; while in the distance, a silver dragon stood out among the floating marvels. But Roger was not here for Festival.

Head down and swallowing, he went through the ground floor entrance, not looking at the six hulking men and women who lurked there on guard. But nervous young men were welcome, ideal customers for the trades practised inside.

The more he tried not to think of what might be happening to Alisha, the more his muscles shook.

Access to each floor was by flowramp. He went up them in sequence, trying not to pause overlong at the fifth floor, seeing the Drone Dollies holosign, then continuing up to the top floor. His hands were bare as he pressed his tu-ring against the wall, sending infiltration sprites through the system, their questing algorithms keyed on Alisha's appearance. Leaving them running, he stepped back, looked up at the ceiling, then beamed a command. An oval opening melted, revealing green sky, and the edge of a dirigible passing overhead.

No one saw the quickthread tendril descend then haul him up to the roof. He rolled sideways on to the surface as the tendril slurped back and the opening closed up.

A small holo opened, showing Alisha's location. He transferred a mapping to his smartlenses, and blinked. Now a glowing blue line appeared to cross the roof, leading to the edge and over, with a straight three-storey drop to a highlighted cross-hair target: an innocuous portion of wall. It seemed Drone Dollies' customers did not care to have windows opening on to the rooms where they received their services.

They can't have done anything to her yet.

But he knew where she was. He blinked away the visual overlay, no longer needing it, then dabbed at his eyes and threw away his smartlenses. Damn what people might think if they saw obsidian eyes. For the first time in his life, he knew who he was.

From his sleeves, quickglass slithered over his hands, forming gloves once more.

He closed his eyes, visualizing, remembering his last experience being terrified by heights, knowing he had to watch himself as a detached observer in his mind.

Roger, himself, wobbles and nearly falls, walking along a too-narrow ridge in Quiller Park. No, back up. *He is calm in the moment before he sees the trail, and starts to get afraid.* Then afterwards. *Cursing, rubbing tears from his eyes; and finally laughing, realizing he is safe once more.*

It was an ancient technique but he never had the motivation to use it. He ran the memory backwards in his mind, five times over, concentrating hard, because the amygdala reacts faster than the frontal lobes, and that was where he had to change the unconscious process that the surface of the mind calls fear, making it ridiculous.

There was no time to create a new visualization of confidence, or to check if the partial neurocognitive recoding had worked. Instead, he extruded tendrils from his left glove, hooked into the roof material, then stepped over the edge, and looked down.

And for a moment, grinned.

Alisha.

He lowered himself into the abseil.

Bands of quickglass formed spirals around his torso, reinforcing the left sleeve and spreading the load, taking strain away from his shoulder. Leaning back, he walked down the wall.

It was an open atrium, and other businesses were less shy than Drone Dollies: they had windows overlooking the quadrangle below. He had the peripheral impression of people inside rooms, but whether they saw him or not, he was too busy to care. He counted steps, estimating his descent, and then he was in place.

His tu-ring broadcast its command signal, and the quickglass wall began to soften. Roger closed his eyes for a second – *shit, I* am *scared* – and brought his knees to his chest, torque keeping his soles against the surface so he squatted against the wall.

Oh shit oh shit oh shit.

And he thrust himself away, swinging back, before returning feet-first for the softened area – *fuck I'm insane* – and then he was sliding through – *holy shit* – and he was inside.

What he saw and smelled was awful.

Fat pale buttocks pumping, and then the man was rolling off her – 'Oh God, oh no, I'm sorry' – his hairy belly wobbling, while the stench of semen was awful. Roger's only thought was: *It shouldn't be like this.*

Alisha's eyes were rolled up, her splayed limbs limp, her clothes open.

'I'm ... Sorry. Sorry.' The fat man was backing away, his limp, dripping penis not quite obscured by drooping flesh. 'Don't ... Please.'

Shouts from the corridor outside, and the sound of running feet, told of security heading this way. Roger had disabled the room's inbuilt defences; he had not thought to seal the door.

Shit. Alisha. Shit.

His left hand was still attached to the tendril, but there was slack. He pulled her up to a sitting position, clasped her hard and lifted, then backed out of the room with her, through the window, and jumped.

The wall was hardening in place above them as he and Alisha descended like a spider to the ground.

Five minutes later he was high up, on the roof of Ebony Tower, looking down at the building far below where had rescued Alisha – if it had been a rescue. She lay limp, sprawled inside the parapet, her clothes not quite wrapped around her. Now he had succeeded in what he had planned, he was clueless as to what should happen next.

I've always been shit at planning.

He could not look at her. Not straight on.

I didn't think it would be this bad.

This was Lucis City, the richest city on Fulgor, and this kind of thing should *not* happen here. It should be impossible.

'"Should",' Mum had said once, *'is usually code for "ain't never gonna happen." You* should *bear that in mind.'*

Everything was awful.

No guards had stopped him at ground level, as he walked through a square archway from the unkempt quadrangle to the street outside. They must have all run up indoors, answering the alarms on the fifth floor. But plenty of pedestrians had stopped in their tracks, scarcely able to process the sight of him carrying a near-naked mindless woman in public. Commotion followed as he entered Ebony Tower and took a flowshaft, commanding a fast ascent through two hundred storeys, and coming out on the rooftop observation deck.

There had been maybe a dozen sightseers, but they had backed away, wide-eyed, and gone down inside the building. No doubt peacekeepers would already be on their way.

He activated his tu-ring.

'Superintendent Sunadomari?'

So even a Luculentus could look surprised.

'Roger Blackstone. You're still on Fulgor?'

'I have Alisha Spalding.' He moved his fist, changing the transmitted point of view. 'We need medics.'

'They're en route now. Remain on Ebony Tower.'

The holo winked out.

Overhead the sky was filled with celebration: dirigibles and holofloats, gleaming banners, virtual fireworks, diaphanous smartkites, and now a whole flotilla of glistening silver dragons. On the streets below, revellers thronged, determined to enjoy the final day of Festival, to glory in Last Lupus.

While Roger could only watch, his thoughts hollowed out, in a world filled with absence.

FORTY-SEVEN

EARTH, 1940 AD

The birds in the oak trees knew nothing of totalitarian regimes or the cares of humans; they sang because it was spring, and to ward rivals off their territory, for they had nestlings to care about. To Gavriela, coming awake on her first morning in Oxford, it was the truest of hymns, celebrating life.

And then she saw her open notebook on the floor, the fountain-pen next to it, and the matching pencil beneath the bedside table where it had rolled.

'What's this?'

The pencil script and ink passages were on opposing pages, and their styles differed.

Consciousness, she read on the right page, *is thought observing thought. Freud identifies the majority of thought with unconscious processes.*

Gödel's theorem applies only to logic systems that allow statements about statements. Logics may be self-descriptive like conscious thought, or not, like unconscious mentation.

Night-time jottings could be hints of profound ideas that might be recaptured; or they could be dust from the imagination, blown away by the morning.

Schrödinger's wave equation is deterministic. The behaviour of the probability wave, moving through time, is exactly calculable from the initial conditions. Perhaps a deterministic, predictive psychodynamics of history is possible, provided it restricts itself to the unconscious behaviour of the world's peoples.

And, further down:

The behaviour of the mob?

While the writing on the lefthand page was shakier.

High
Energy
Interstellar
Meson
Detection,
Amplification &
Lensing
Lattice

It seemed like a joke; and if the handwriting had not been hers, it would have been funny.

When she went downstairs, Mrs Wilson was in the kitchen, frying bread in lard, while Rupert Forrester was in the front room, talking to a one-armed man called Brian, who it appeared was also a lodger.

'We're in luck this morning,' Brian said. 'Old Rupert is our bus driver for the day.'

'Don't expect it as a matter of course.' Rupert went to the door and checked that the hall was clear. 'But I'll take you both back again tonight. It's nice to visit here when I can.'

'He went to school with Mrs Wilson's son,' said Brian.

'Oh.'

'Now Gabby' – Rupert gave a microsecond smile – 'you're going to be in Hut 27, but there's something you need to know about that.'

Brian's head tilted, revealing scars on his neck.

'There is no Hut 27.'

'That,' Rupert told Gavriela, 'is the thing you need to know.'

'I'm sorry?'

'We're codes and ciphers.' Brian shrugged his intact shoulder. 'It's not just hush-hush, it's more important than anybody knows.'

'Even more than *you* know,' said Rupert.

'But where are we working?' asked Gavriela.

'You'll see.'

Then Mrs Wilson called them in to eat, and for a short period it was like an ordinary peacetime breakfast, except that there was no butter, only lard; the tea was made from ground-up acorns; and the curtains that stood open were blackout drapes, to avoid light spilling out at night, assisting Luftwaffe bomber crews to navigate.

And Gavriela wondered, as she ate, how far her night-time writing could creep from rational reality before becoming signs of psychotic delusion, a mind finally cracked in a world grown mad and horrible.

FORTY-EIGHT

FULGOR, 2603 AD

Sunadomari stalked through the splendour of the Via Lucis Institute, scarcely seeing the shining kaleidoscope of holos and Skein projections, an avalanche of visual stimuli that would overwhelm an ordinary human. One holovolume that kept pace with him showed the face of Hsiu Li-Cheng, whom he would see in person within seconds; another showed Helen Eisberg with her tac team troopers, inside a flyer en route to Ebony Tower.

'Why's this Alisha Spalding important?' Eisberg was asking. *'I understand she's a victim, but what's it got to do with your case?'*

'It wasn't the slimeball perverts who raped her. It was Luculenta Rafaella Stargonier who tore out her mind.'

'Oh. I was under the impression the murder victims were Luculenti.'

'Spalding is pre-upraise. She has interface nodes without true processors. Maybe that's the difference.'

'And you want me to take her straight there?'

'Yes. Please.'

They stopped talking but kept the hololink open.

'As soon as she's inside the flyer,' said Li-Cheng in the other holovolume, *'I can pass through the emergency med-nodes and start my analysis.'*

'Do you think it will help?'

'Maybe. I'm curious about these other people, Helsen and Ranulph. What are they, some kind of pure-humanity terrorists? Setting a rogue Luculenta loose among her own kind, and serve us right?'

'I'll be very curious myself,' said Sunadomari, 'just as soon as we find them.'

A third holo opened: Roger Blackstone.

'Your people are here, Superintendent. A Lieutenant Eisberg?'

'That's her.'

In Eisberg's holo, the viewpoint shifted, showing her officers carrying the girl on board. Immediately, the medscanners whirled into action, new displays blossoming red and orange all around Sunadomari as he reached the end of one shining corridor, passed beneath a razor-edged archway, and came to a halt. A silver wall rippled open, revealing an immense workspace filled with holo glory – phase spaces and rippling manifolds, network graphs that glimmered and equations that shone, tabular data in swirling ribbons, and a million realtime images floating all around.

Beneath the glory, twelve Skein designers were working, deep in the flow, while at their centre stood Hsiu Li-Cheng, the golden studs gleaming on his forehead, smiling when he saw Sunadomari.

'We should have results in about—Ah. There.'

He was staring at a holospace.

'What is it?' asked Sunadomari.

'Throw her out now!'

'What?'

In the comms holo, Lieutenant Eisberg said: *'Sir, can you repeat that?'*

'Put her out of the flyer.' Sunadomari was staring at his friend, Li-Cheng. 'Do what he said, Helen.'

'All right. Doing it now.'

On Li-Cheng's skin, dots of sweat expanded, while the muscles around his mouth hardened.

'Vampire . . . code. Remnants.'

'Can you fight it? *Hey.*' Sunadomari turned to the twelve designers. 'Help him.'

But they remained in their seats, locked into whatever they were working on Skein.

'Doing. It.' Li-Cheng was wheezing. 'My. Self.'

Sunadomari's fists were tight. Being this helpless, especially with Skein involved, was new to him. But this was happening at such a level that he had neither the expertise nor the authorization that would allow him to follow the processes, much less render help.

Helen Eisberg was asking for further instructions, but he ignored her.

Finally, Li-Cheng shuddered and dropped to one knee.

'Ah . . .'

'Are you all right?'

'Hurt my knee, maybe the anterior cruciate ligament, otherwise' – he smiled at Sunadomari – 'my mind is clear. Finally.'

'The vampire code has evolved, I take it?' Sunadomari helped him up.

'Yes, and I think it might have a different . . . intent. It's hard to tell in Alisha Spalding's case, because she did not have a true plexweb. Probably why she was abandoned.'

'Not to act as an amusing boobytrap for any Luculentus who tried to investigate?'

'Ah, Keinosuke. You have a twisty, paranoid mind.'

'Thank you,' said Sunadomari. 'So how is the code different?'

'I'm not sure it's designed to kill— What's this?'

Li-Cheng stared at the twelve designers, all of them deep in Skein.

'They wouldn't answer me,' began Sunadomari, 'when I tried to—'

'Hush,' said Li-Cheng. 'Let me think.'

That was not something you heard a Luculentus say every day – one's ability to think powerfully and fast was taken for granted. Sunadomari could not understand the multidimensional phantasmagoria of holos; but he could read Li-Cheng's expression as he tried to make sense of the displays.

Then Li-Cheng strode forward and placed one hand on a designer's shoulder.

'Cataleptic,' he said. 'I've never seen a person work so hard, do so much at one time. His effort is incredible, over two thousand simultaneous sessions and each one non-trivial.'

'What is he doing?' said Sunadomari. 'What are they all doing?'

'They're—'

One of the designers screamed, sat upright with sinews tight, toppled back in her chair, and slid to the floor.

'It's Skein,' said Li-Cheng.

'What about Skein?'

'It's attacking through Skein.' His face turned a luminous ash-grey. 'I think we're finished.'

On the edge of the city stood a natural stone house in its own grounds. The property was surrounded by a high wall, and a tall gateway of black iron separated it from the long trail that led to the nearest residential area. But neither its isolation nor its design was the reason for its safety – that rested on reputation, and the very real capabilities of those who sojourned here.

Currently, three Pilots were resident in Sanctuary. The eldest was Jed Goran, the youngest Al Morgan, while Angus Cho was a psychologist and military intelligence specialist, normally based in Labyrinth, who did not have a ship. It was Angus who was deep in holo displays on the patio, while the other two were drinking daistral and talking about the news from the Admiralty Council.

'They can't possibly select Arrowsmith,' Al was saying. 'He's no replacement for Admiral Kaltberg.'

'Never underestimate our superiors' ability,' answered Jed, 'to perpetrate total, utter—'

'Guys,' said Angus. 'Look at this.'

A spiky network of golden lines hung in front of him – a network glistening here and there with a redness that appeared to be spreading.

'Tell me that's not an infiltration,' said Jed.

'It's not.'

'But it looks like—'

'It's going to be genocide.'

*

Last Lupus, the final day of Festival.

Now trompe-l'oeil holoillusions marched across the sky, 'Fanfare for All' resounded from quickglass buildings used as musical instruments, and everywhere were streamers and cloudflakes, sparklemist and twirlywhispers, while vendors dispensed sweetbeer and plasmaberry wine, roast cicaderm and gyle nuts, jantrasta-coated fruit and daistral whips.

Merrymakers laughed or embraced, watched amused or wistful, meeting new lovers or losing old, or staying with their long-term lover, the ongoing growth and renewal of family, or they simply joked with friends, sang stupid, surreal songs, composed poems, played 7-D killchess, drank, belched, ate, pissed, burped, stood on someone's toes, made friends, caused arguments, held hands, smiled, cried, farted, picked their noses, said sorry, drank some more and put the world to rights.

Yet in the midst of swirling, interacting, splendid-yet-mundane humanity, something was changing.

It started with a trio of Luculenti, walking together, tracking the patterns in the aerial displays. The silver dragons were just one more attraction among the smartkites and dirigibles and holoillusions; but now the nearest dragon was catching their attention.

Within the next two seconds, another fifty-nine Luculenti looked up at one or other of the dragons and wondered what was different about it.

Then they all screamed.

Tightbeams rained down from the dragons, pinning the Luculenti in place, broadcasting their locations to the one who waited deep below the city. Now they were hooked and landed fish, awaiting the terminal blow – but the hooks came through the hyperdimensions, and so did the vampire code.

It was the opening salvo of the Skein War.

Deep in The Marrows beneath the city, the body that had been Rafaella Stargonier floated amid translucent green splendour, tiny in her quickglass sea, surrounded by the organic vastness and geometric lattices that were the city's true body, the towers above mere epidermis, the visible exterior of the true marvel that grew and provided everything from food to sanitation, enfolding civilization.

Now she and it could be so much more.

On the surface, her Luculenti still lived, components of herself, while her first body flung out its arms, drifting cruciform in its living, subterranean surroundings. Perhaps her head tilted back and smiled; or perhaps it was a random motion, caught in quickglass current.

Each of her remote Luculenti entered Skein, eyes blazing, searching for prey.

It took no more than seconds for each to subsume another, then another. Geometrically, vampire code spread, as Luculentus minds speared others of their kind, cascading through Skein, all remaining physically alive, their neural topology routed through the Calabi-Yau dimensions, the realspace axes that humans cannot see, hundreds then thousands of bodies and plexwebs forming one continuous substrate for a unitary net of cognition and predation.

The once-Rafaella had transcended.

On the rooftop of Ebony Tower, Roger stood beside Alisha's stretcher – the tac team did not carry med-drones – not understanding why the officers had taken her back out of the flyer. But his tu-ring flared, and a strange Luculentus appeared in holo.

'I'm Hsiu Li-Cheng,' he said. 'Download this code, broadcast through tightbeam at her.'

'What will it do?'

'Disinfect her. Destroy the lingering code.'

'Code?'

Behind him, the tac team commander, Lieutenant Eisberg said: 'Something to do with her being pre-upraise, right?'

Roger did as Li-Cheng said.

'Will we able to use this on Luculenti?' Eisberg asked.

In the holo, Li-Cheng's face was a mask of emptiness.

'No,' he said. 'We're trying to build another Skein, but we'll never manage—'

The holo snapped out of existence.

'Another Skein?' said Roger.

'I don't know.' Eisberg shrugged her muscular shoulders. 'This is bad. And Keino–Superintendent Sunadomari is off Skein.'

'Maybe Luculenti need to disconnect for safety. You're saying there's infectious code in Skein?'

'That wasn't what I—You know, that wasn't how this started, but I think you might be right. One moment.' Her jaw muscles moved, uttering tense subvocalizations. 'I can't reach HQ. The connection pool on every channel is full. Shit.'

If the peacekeepers were flooded with calls, from civilians and officers alike, then whatever was happening, it was widespread.

'Lieutenant?' One of the troopers was pointing into the cityscape. 'You see that?'

In her stretcher, Alisha twitched, but nothing more. Roger looked back up, seeing that all of the tac team were staring in the same direction.

'Holy fuck.'

'That's not possible.'

But Eisberg said: 'Clearly it is.'

With the stress of the day, Roger's vision had blurred or tunnelled to a pinpoint several times over, and for a moment he thought it had recurred, a symptom of adrenal overload. But then he realized that it was no artefact of trauma, but reality that he saw.

The sky was still filled with festive smartkites and illusory holos, dirigibles and dragons; while below still lay an elegant expanse of shining quickglass towers, linked by skyways and viaducts, amid streets and plazas and piazzas filled with city-dwellers out to celebrate Last Lupus; but the city was altering.

With a twitch here and a twist there, quickglass towers began to shrug and shift, to compress and expand, and then to flow. Everything began to move. Suddenly, one skywalk flailed like a tendril, spilling tiny humans to the ground below.

The city was coming to life. Viaducts buckled, tore free. Buildings writhed into motion.

It's impossible.

But still the towers walked.

It began in The Marrows. By the time it reached the surface, affecting the quickglass towers that humans lived in without appreciating the marvel of what surrounded them – nor how small a portion of the true city they inhabited – the process was more than eighty per cent complete, the metamorphosis unstoppable.

While underneath, the subterranean quickglass sea pulsed with complex growth, organs and systems combining to expand and move, to grow new surface structures, to reach out and live.

Even as their old homes buckled – luxurious apartments in city towers, quieter mansions in the outer districts, extravagances shaped like ziggurats or giant sculptures – their Luculenti owners did not care. Ordinary Fulgidi, whether employees or friends, backed away from those who had changed; some perished as the floors twisted apart or walls expanded to envelope them, while others ran outside to chaos.

All Luculenti were becoming one – but more than that. For they were the nervous system, while the quickglass city formed the body they were embedded in. This was beyond transcendence.

A new form of life was being born.

In the Via Lucis Institute, LuxPrime's finest Skein designers were fighting back. The global Skein environment was centuries old, its lineage tracing back to Earth; now, those designers were creating a new version in minutes. In the growing

SkeinTwo, as they brought it into being framework by framework, ecology by ecology, emergent configurations – force-grown at a speed no one would have thought possible – bore parallels to the structures they mirrored in the corrupted, dangerous, original Skein . . . but they were rooted in different protocols and codes at the very lowest level. Meanwhile, a specialist team was working on a single service: the gateway that would allow a Luculentus to switch his mind into the new environment, plunge into SkeinTwo while cleansing himself of the old, losing any traces of the vampire code that was destroying everything.

They were mortally aware that any corruption, if it entered SkeinTwo, would take it apart in seconds. Their only chance was to keep the new environment clean.

Sunadomari watched Li-Cheng and his colleagues performing miracles of computation, hacking complexity, bringing forth designs in milliseconds, a crescendo of intellect and concentration. He could only observe in awe; there was no way he could help.

But there was something he could do.

'To all peacekeepers, to all citizens.' He used his authorization to bump others off the connections in Skein – the original Skein, the only one still working – and spoke in clear, because he needed everyone on Fulgor to understand this message, the remaining free Luculenti and ordinary citizens alike.

'Abandon Lucis City. Quarantine the region.'

He prioritized what he said, while another part of his awareness devoted itself to making sure the message spread, contacting comms controllers, both Luculenti and subsystems, urging them to override all other signals with this one. All of them complied.

'Every Luculentus is in danger. We are attempting to create a haven in Skein, but for now Skein is dangerous. All Luculenti are being attacked. The result, we think, is a gestalt mind, and it's embedded in the city's quickglass architecture. It's Lucis City that has become an organism.'

He watched the designers for another moment, realizing that the longer he himself spent in Skein, the more likely he was to fall prey to the ravening code.

'Skein is global, clearly. I don't know how safe the other cities are. Be prepared to evacuate them all.'

Finally, Li-Cheng turned to him, whispering: 'We're ready. Let them in.'

'You're incredible,' said Sunadomari in reality.

In Skein, he broadcast: 'This, for any Luculenti who can read me, is how you enter SkeinTwo. The invoked code will hurt, but it *will* get you through.

<<cm:dIF::Skein.register(self, 2)>>

And I wish you luck, every—'

It was like invisible hands, strangling him.

'Keinosuke!' yelled Li-Cheng.

But it was too late for Sunadomari. There was only one way that Hsiu Li-Cheng could help his old friend; and he did it now, flicking to command interface with the building's defences and giving the order to activate grasers.

Invisible gamma rays cracked the air, blowing Keinosuke Sunadomari's head to mist, a spray of blood and brain that spattered throughout the room.

Then they turned on his body, destroying the entire plexweb before it could be absorbed.

A full thirty seconds later, Li-Cheng had recovered enough to slip back into monitoring his battling designers, all of them incredible, as they worked to shore up SkeinTwo, strengthening and restrengthening the cleansing routines for transfer. More and more across the globe, Luculenti were shifting into SkeinTwo, fleeing the virtual hell that had been their intellectual home. Status displays showed their geographical coordinates; only a few dozen were in Lucis City – most were in distant regions.

Then a private comms request pinged him. That fact was incredible enough, overriding his shutout barriers; but the ID code accompanying it was nothing he had expected. This was a risk, lowering his barrier, even if he sandboxed a portion of his own mind, ready to destroy it in case of corruption. But the code identified a Pilot, with highest diplomatic authority; and so he opened the link.

'My name is Carl Blackstone.' The Pilot's face was strained. *'Are all Luculenti lost?'*

'We're fighting back.'

'And if you don't succeed?'

'Then we're clearly defeated, Pilot. What are you–? Wait one moment.'

Li-Cheng returned his attention to the room, where one of his designers, Clara Calzonni, had dropped out of computation trance and was staring at him, unaware of twin tear-tracks rippling down her face.

'Oh, no,' said Li-Cheng.

'It's got through,' Clara whispered. 'SkeinTwo is corrupted.'

Li-Cheng bit his lip.

'Activate the suicide protocol. Give me sixty seconds, if you can.'

'There's something—'

'Tell me.'

'The . . . entity . . . links through hyperdimensions, effectively making all the brains and plexwebs contiguous, as though they're physically touching each other.'

Li-Cheng was aware of Pilot Blackstone, waiting for more information.

'I don't know if it's thought of it yet,' continued Clara, 'but soon it will be able to . . . able to . . .'

'What? Just say it, please.'

'It will be able to subsume organic minds. Ordinary, non-Luculenti minds.'

'Oh shit.'

It was the end of the Skein War.

'The world is lost.'

Nodding, Li-Cheng shifted back to comms.

'Pilot Blackstone, our efforts are failing. Soon every Luculentus will be part of a global mind that appears destructive and predatory. The ordinary Fulgidi – ordinary people are unaffected as yet, but at some point, the entity will be able to absorb them as well.'

'Then we need to evacuate before that happens.'

'You can't evacuate an entire— How many mu-space ships are on Fulgor right now?'

'Three,' said Carl Blackstone, *'including mine.'*

'Then how can—?'

'Leave that to me.'

Pain slammed into Li-Cheng's mind and body, severing the link.

'I'm sorry,' said Carla. 'We can't hold it—'

'Suicide. Now.'

'I'm—'

'Now.'

'Yes.'

The Via Lucis Institute, home of LuxPrime, originator of all that had been best in a glittering culture unmatched on any human world, detonated inbuilt plasma bombs and disappeared into blazing vapour, shining nova-bright, a sphere of burning energy.

From orbit, Carl Blackstone saw the explosion as a small white dot.

FORTY-NINE

EARTH, 777 AD

In the morning, Ulfr's head was thick, but he woke up smiling. It was not just the celebrations, but the memory he took with him from dreamworld, of fighting alongside the woman Gavi in some demon realm. Or perhaps *alongside* was not correct. The details were fading as his eyes opened.

Beside him, Brandr came awake, ears twitching. The old *volva,* Eydís, was watching them both.

'Good morning, priestess,' said Ulfr. 'Are you well?'

'I need the help of someone strong.'

'Ah. If you give me a moment—'

'We're camped over there.' She pointed beyond the charcoal remains of a large fire.

'All right, I'll—'

Eydís was already walking off.

'—be right with you. Come, good Brandr.'

The warhound followed him. They used the same bushes downwind of the camp for the same purpose, then drank from the same stream, and made their way to Eydís's bedroll. But it was the young *volva,* Heithrún, who lay there with one leg splinted and encased in poultice, while Eydís knelt to one side, chanting.

Ulfr felt his own eyelids began to descend, and the words were not even meant for him.

'Now, good Ulfr. You need to help reset the leg.'

He had done this before, and knew it to be painful. Ivárr had screamed during the procedure, and he was a tough warrior.

'Here.' Eydís guided his hands. 'And here.'

Heithrún's eyes were closed, her face calm, like a young girl sleeping.

'Now pull and—There. Twist.'

It was hard work. The bone crunched and ground.

'And . . . yes, that's it.'

Heithrún's leg bone was pushed into place. But she had remained calm, her lips almost smiling, throughout the manipulation.

'She felt it, warrior,' said Eydís. 'But just a sensation, nothing more.'

'Now what?'

'You set yourself down over there' – she pointed – 'while I rebind the leg.'

Ulfr moved off and sat on the ground, pulling his cloak around himself and Brandr, who lay close, panting. Ulfr patted Brandr and waited.

Finally, Eydís knelt down facing him.

'Show me your hands.'

Ulfr did that. She held them, then made passes across his chest and shoulder. He felt his own body make small adjustments in reaction, all without his thinking about it. Whether his body moved toward or away from her hands, he could not tell.

She stared at him and breathed, and his eyes defocused.

'My words of power accompany you now, and as you choose to blink – that's right – you can breathe out now and close your eyes as you walk farther and farther down the dreamworld path, because there are things you wish to learn and things you already know how to walk into dreams right now—'

His head was down and his eyes were closed, yet he could see every blade of grass and sprig of heather, he could taste the clouds and feel the deep earth, and he could hear the separate movement of each insect's wing. He drifted, rolled without substance across the land; and finally returned to his body, as it was time to awaken.

'—coming back to me *now*.'

Ulfr's eyes came open.

'I felt like Heimdall,' he said. 'Seeing everything, hearing everything.'

'As Watcher of the Gods' – Eydís pointed at him – 'he will be the one to warn Óthinn by sounding his horn, when the All-Father will go to Valhalla to muster his Soul-Fetchers and their armies for the final battle.'

'I . . . Yes, I know. I didn't mean . . . that.'

'You stride between worlds easily, good warrior. You have had a guide to dreamworld, someone you care for.'

'Eira,' he said. 'She's back home. I care about her.'

'And what else? Your voice holds doubt.'

'I slew her brother. Not by choice.'

'Ah. And she is a *volva*, young and trained like our Heithrún?'

'Yes.'

Eydís shook her head.

'Is something wrong, priestess?'

'You are bound to another, but light or dark, I cannot tell.'

'To Eira?'

'You are both the strongest and the weakest,' she said. 'You face some demons with courage yet fall grovelling before others, those that are most subtle.'

'No . . .'

Then Eydís shook herself, drew her garments close, and said: 'Chief Gulbrandr and your own Chief Folkvar have marked you as a good man, potentially a leader.'

Ulfr shook his head.

'Stay away from Heithrún,' Eydís went on. 'This pains me, warrior . . . But she deserves better than you would give her.'

'But I'm not—I mean, she and I aren't . . . You know.'

Eydís looked up into the sky.

'Do you see war-ravens, Ulfr?'

'The sky is clear.'

But Eydís shook her head, and her eyes shone when she focused on him.

'You are mistaken.'

She got up then and returned to Heithrún's side, leaving Ulfr to wonder what had happened, and to watch as on every side warriors were stirring, the gathered bands of fighters come to meet in peace, some far from their homes, while all around was the vastness of the Middle World, heathland and ice, shining lake and rising mountain, and volcanic plumes climbing into a sky that to him looked serene, its blues and greens of ice mixed with only streaks of gold and glimmers of scarlet that ran like blood through a pierced helm, while in the distance a dark speck moved.

The raven was watching.

FIFTY

FULGOR, 2603 AD

On the patio outside the Pilots Sanctuary, three men stood, each working commands in holovolumes with serious intent. Jed Goran, as the Pilot in charge, was initializing every system of the building inside, with the exception of one. That was Al Morgan's responsibility: arming the destruction net, ensuring they could detonate the building with a simple signal, as soon as they were aloft.

Meanwhile, psychologist Angus Cho was monitoring the ending of a world.

'Two cities in Tarquil Province are coming to life,' he said. 'It's spreading.'

'Shit,' muttered Al, still working. 'Are people getting away?'

'Trying to. Thousands are just getting crushed or sucked inside moving buildings.'

Then a mu-space ship crashed into being overhead: black, trimmed with red, and powerful.

'Who the fuck is—?'

'I'm Carl Blackstone.' His image appeared in the holovolume Angus had been working with. *'I've been agent-in-place here for over twenty years. I'm appending auth codes.'*

Authorization data flared orange in a subsidiary holo.

'Yes, sir,' said Angus. 'How we can help? My colleagues are about to summon their own ships.'

'You need to get clear. I'd like to get as many people as possible offplanet, but know this: at some point, the entity that is absorbing Luculenti will also be able to absorb anyone at all.'

'Holy—'

'Exactly. The only chance is a massed evacuation at once, and your ships—'

'Only two,' said Angus. 'I don't have one.'

'—are not enough. I'm going to get help.'

'But it will take too long.'

At that, Jed Goran stepped back from his display and stared at Carl Blackstone's image.

'You have my respect, sir. It's an honour.'

'Likewise, Pilot.' Carl smiled. *'Will you do me a favour? My son Roger is here, probably in Lucis City.'*

'I'll fetch him out.'

'Here's the code for his tu-ring.' More data shone. *'Bypassing Skein, so it ought to stand out.'*

'Got it. Good—'

'And I've something for him. Could you give him this?'

A small gap melted open in the black ship's hull, and a thin black tendril extruded, bearing a rounded triangle of black, webbed with red and gold, about the size of a young child. It descended; and Jed took it in his forearms.

'I have it, sir.'

'Thank you.'

The tendril detached and sucked back up inside the ship; then its hull resealed.

Al said: 'We're not supposed to—'

'Shut up,' whispered Angus.

'I'll find your son,' promised Jed. 'And I'll give him this.'

'You have my thanks, Pilot.'

'And you have my admiration, sir. Godspeed.'

'Blackstone out.'

The black dart ascended in a horizontal attitude; then it crashed forward and was gone.

'That's one hell of a ship,' said Angus. 'Not to mention its Pilot.'

'I don't understand.' Al shut down his own display. 'What's he planning to do?'

'Hellflight.' Angus looked at Jed, who was still holding the convex triangle entrusted to him. 'The kind you don't survive.'

'Oh.'

'Exactly.'

The peacekeeper flyer hovered, its main hatch still open, just above the roof of Ebony Tower. All around, the buildings of Quarter Moon had been among the last to begin moving, perhaps because so many were old, solid stone. But the quick-glass towers among them were beginning to writhe now; and the black roof beneath Roger's feet was starting to soften and glisten. The building shifted, then stopped.

'All right,' said Helen Eisberg. 'Whatever threat your girlfriend was presenting to Skein, I think we're all agreed. It's too far gone now to make a difference.'

'Luculentus Li-Cheng said she was clear of infecting code.'

'Do we trust him? I don't know, but it doesn't matter.' She and one of her officers were still on the rooftop, along with Roger plus Alisha in her stretcher. 'Let's lift her inside and get the fuck out of here.'

They took hold, Eisberg at Alisha's head, the other officer at her feet. Roger looked at them, then at the devastation across the city, the city that lived and moved and killed its former citizens. He had no idea what to do, besides get clear if he could.

Overhead, thunder crashed, audible above the horrific clamour; then a silver-and-bronze ship with shining delta wings was gliding down.

'Mu-space ship,' said Roger.

'No shit,' said Eisberg.

It was Roger's tu-ring that chimed, then formed a holovolume.

'I'm Pilot Jed Goran, and I think you need a lift.'

The huge ship continued to descend.

'Is that a general offer?' asked Eisberg. 'Because I think this city has had it.'

'For anyone who wants to come.'

Now it floated exactly level with the roof, holding steady, one wingtip only centimetres from the parapet. In its hull, a wide opening melted.

'There are delta-bands enough for everyone.'

Eisberg bit her lip. Then she turned to the peacekeeper flyer, to the troopers sat inside.

'Anyone who wants to get offworld, come out here now and get aboard.'

Roger stared at her.

'You all have to come with us,' he said.

'Thanks, pal. But I've got family.'

'I—'

'Go, and take the girl with you.'

Two troopers came out; the others remained in their flyer, and gave Eisberg a hand to climb inside.

Three troopers and Roger lifted the stretcher with ease. The tricky part was getting it over the parapet as Ebony Tower stirred once more. But then they were moving along the smooth wing – too smooth, a strong gust of wind would send them sliding off – and finally they were at the opening, and climbing inside.

The ship slipped away from the building just as the quickglass began to thrash. It whipped up an extrusion towards the peacekeeper flyer, but its pilot flicked it hard to starboard, into a fast short dive while its hatch was still sealing, then the flyer's nose went up and it started its ascent.

'Nice work,' came Jed Goran's voice. *'Let's see if I can do as well. Delta-bands on, everyone.'*

In the passenger hold, someone had already put a band on Alisha's forehead and activated it. The three troopers had their own bands fastened; one of them held out a band to Roger.

'I don't really need it,' Roger said.

'Oh. Er . . . Right.'

The troopers lay down on couches – there were plenty to spare – and pressed thumbs to delta-bands, sending themselves to sleep. The hull had already flowed shut, intact once more.

'You can come forward.'

'Thank you, Pilot.'

'Call me Jed.'

'I'm Roger.'

'That, I already know.'

'How—?'

'Let's leave it till later.'

Transit.

Golden light was all around as Roger made his way forward, knowing nothing could touch them here, for this was home where everything would be all right, now and always.

Mu-space.

Four thousand seven hundred and seventy-three ships burst into realspace over Fulgor. Two hours and thirteen minutes had elapsed since the fall of Skein; millions of ordinary Fulgidi had poured out of the cities and into the countryside. In the hypozone, tribes of Shadow People had either set up armed perimeters or welcomed refugees, depending on how the clans voted.

One Pilot, Davey Golwyn, took double the capacity his ship was rated for, risking his life to take an entire small clan on board, along with their cats. A few Pilots had to persuade people to come on board, while in dozens of sites, adults pushed their children on board while remaining to fight off the enemy, whatever it was.

Two ships hovering over Lucis City were taken down by quickglass tendrils snapped around by moving towers. One blasted clear, amid shrivelling, melting quickglass; the other blew itself up. Another ship was destroyed outside Sylbam Minor on the south coast, as it hovered in place to lay down covering fire while refugees streamed from the rampaging city.

Five ships numbered Luculenti among their passengers. In every case, tiny pinpoint grasers inside their passenger holds picked out the former elite and killed them. Whether the dead had been infected by vampire code was not always possible to tell; regardless, they died, and Pilots conscripted passengers to throw the bodies out through hatches, before they would depart from Fulgor.

Among the planet's inhabitants were a hundred thousand tales of selfless courage and sacrifice that would never be recorded; while others scrabbled at any chance, at any shameful cost, to get on board one of the too-few vessels attempting to spirit an entire planet's population away from danger.

Young Davey Golwyn took his ship down to land seven times, daring more than most. On the last landing, as the crush of people pressed against each other outside, one man on the ground stared up, and seemed to stare straight at Davey, despite the solid hull that separated them.

Then the man's eyes glowed an odd sapphire blue.

'Bug out,' Davey sent. Every ship was linked to every other ship, awaiting this signal. *'It's taking down ordinary people. Bug out now.'*

He flung his ship upwards; and so did every other Pilot. Three Pilots observed passengers undergoing the same transition, transforming into components of the entity below. Two made the jump into mu-space, then calmly went back to the holds and ejected the passengers into the hearts of stars; the third Pilot flew straight into Fulgor's sun.

The remainder of the flight streamed upwards into orbit. A multi-hued cloud of shining vessels, they moved farther away, checking and rechecking among themselves. No infection. They accelerated, still in realspace, lengthening the separation from Fulgor, passing the limit to Calabi-Yau transportation of energy, at least to the extent they understood Zajinet technology, taking themselves beyond the entity's reach.

Every human passenger seemed clear; and finally, every one of them was in delta-coma.

A final check confirmed that the remaining four thousand seven hundred and sixty-eight Pilots were as normal, unaffected by the entity engulfing Fulgor. What percentage of the planet's population they had managed to save, they were not yet sure. Their first job was to get home – home for the Pilots, not their passengers, who would need to remain in coma for however long they remained in mu-space.

One by one, the ships left the realspace universe.

In golden mu-space, some of the rescue vessels took near-hellflight geodesics back to Labyrinth; but most of the fleet soared at a gentler pace, their mission accomplished, as much as anyone could have hoped for.

At one level, there was no hurry. For the event that was to unite them in Labyrinth, to commemorate the evacuation of Fulgor, would not take place until the fleet's return, whenever that was. The ceremony would be a reminder of victory in sacrifice, of the extent to which a single Pilot could make a difference, a celebration of what Pilotkind could achieve when united.

Carl Blackstone's funeral was to be an affair of state.

FIFTY-ONE

EARTH-CLASS EXPLORATORY EM-0036, 2147 AD

Their fur smelled musty. All around Rekka stood a phalanx of muscular males, dressed in the white-and-gold of city guards in full ceremonial gear. She was hidden from general view by awnings, and her alien scent was absorbed by hangings of porous fibre. But she could see the stadium below, while holo views from her beeswarm hung over the infostrand on her wrist.

Banners of scarlet and gold, set all around the stadium, cracked in the breeze. On white stone terraces, row upon row of Elders sat, with much variety in their fur coloration – they had travelled far, some from other continents – but almost all with stately antlers. There were seats for the general public, too – all of them high up, but already filled. Outside, great crowds thronged the streets. They, like the folk inside the stadium, held small flat crystal rectangles, handed out by the city proctors.

The sights were stunning for Rekka; for the locals, the scents must be overwhelming.

From one entrance, sweet-scented carpet (she knew from her bees' analysis) led across the open area to the white throne forming the place of honour. Excitement swirled through the air, strong enough for Rekka to smell. Then something moved in the entranceway.

It was a bronze cart drawn by maidens. Inside, two adults and a young female sat, looking around in what Rekka read as bewilderment. The cart halted, and gloved attendants helped the three special guests dismount, and led them to a nearby bench of marble. They sat and looked around, while the maidens took the cart away.

Now the tension was ozone-sharp in Rekka's nostrils.

Finally, proctors and bannermen marched into the stadium in twin columns, preceding the person in whose honour the proceedings had been arranged. Rekka's vision blurred. Today was so important for her friend and his family.

Sharp entered, his eyes wide but his gait steady, his antlers level as he walked, his fear hidden from all but those who loved him.

As the proceedings began, Sharp took in the scents, nodding to Father. There would be no mention of the family shame; and after today, their name would be honoured. For Sharp had brought back knowledge of another world, and more.

A Chief Librarian held up a device, like the one he had worn around his chest for so long, and Sharp controlled himself before emitting the rehearsed scents.

~I have visited a city beyond the sky, and returned to tell you of it.

The crystal plates, held by every member of the vast crowd, reproduced his fragrant message, and embellished it with the visual script, known only by the Librarians' caste until now.

~I have so much to share with you.

He looked up at the beeswarm, and bowed in the direction of the awnings that hid Rekka, though he could neither see nor smell her from here. All around was a multitude of people that he could never have imagined gathered in one place, and certainly not because of him.

~I'm afraid.

But that was a private scent, to keep to himself.

From her vantage point, Rekka saw the advancing Librarians before she understood what they meant. And then, once their intent became clear, she ordered her beeswarm to gather overhead, ready to drop and deliver their neurotoxin load.

'Sharp. Oh, Sharp.'

She had to choose.

'Why didn't you tell me?'

For the sake of friendship, there was only one choice to make.

My dear, sweet friend.

She held the beeswarm aloft, and did nothing.

The Librarians drew near, each reaching inside his robe and drawing forth a golden scythe. Meanwhile, acolytes walked at stately pace, bearing the golden plates that would be passed around the gathered Elders and the general crowd. Behind them trailed robed maidens, scattering flower petals from baskets in all directions, the heady fragrance designed to coat the scents of agony.

There were thousands of people here, and more outside, and every one of them deserved to know of this other world and the dark things loose within it. They needed to know, and they would thank his memory for it. This was his vindication for Father's shame, for the slice that had been taken and rejected, the gobbet that was tasted and spat upon the floor.

Today, no matter how bitter, they would swallow the truth and absorb it, for its importance was overwhelming. There was no way for them to escape their obligation.

But no mere single slice of flesh would suffice. Not for all these folk.

Sharp closed his eyes and lowered his head.

One by one, they came.

The next day, the automatic shuttle picked her up from the campsite, and took her to the mu-space ship that waited in orbit. Once inside the hold, she heard the Pilot speak.

'Rekka Chandri?'

'Yes, Pilot.'

A needle in her couch jabbed her arm. Anaesthesia, for the voyage.

'EM-0036 is an official xeno sentient homeworld now. You're the de facto *delegation.'*

'That's nice.'

'So you get to name the world. First contact privilege.'

Privilege. It had been a privilege to know Sharp, so courageous, so intelligent.

'I don't . . .'

'Please don't leave it for the bureaucrats to name.'

'I—*Vijaya.*' Her voice was beginning to slur. 'Means . . . victory.'

'Good name.'

She was asleep in coma as the vessel made a single orbit of Vijaya's blue-and-ochre sphere, hung in space like an eagle about to swoop, then flashed out of realspace existence, to the fractal universe Rekka would never see.

FIFTY-TWO

LABYRINTH, 2603 AD (REALSPACE-EQUIVALENT)

From a balcony on Ascension Annexe, Roger watched the proceedings. He wore black and gold, with brocade and formal cape, while members of the Admiralty Council stood on either side. There were floating tiers of seats from which thousands of Pilots watched, as his parents' joint coffin floated through the great vault before the Annexe, normally filled with ships, now cleared for the ceremony.

A giant holovolume off to one side showed the honour flight waiting outside the city: two squadrons of gold-and-silver ships ready to escort two of their own – Carl and Miranda Blackstone – on their final voyage. Music filled the titanic vault, the mournful chords of *Kian's Lament* echoing and seeping into bones and blood, a skirl of grief with an undertone of triumph, marking the other meaning of today: the difference that one man's choice, one Pilot's courage, could make to a world.

Call it a point gained by humanity, in the quest to bring meaning out of formlessness, enlightenment from non-sentience.

Dad. Mum. I love you.

He could never be the person his father was, that either of them was.

Rear-Admiral Schenck put a hand on his shoulder. Perhaps the gesture was meant to signify something to the crowd of mourners; to Roger it meant nothing. He did not like the man.

The coffin reached an exit tunnel, and began to move out.

I can't watch this.

But he had to. Stiff and formal in ceremonial clothes, he had to, because that was how humanity honours the dead, the only way that we know how.

Now the coffin, as shown in the massive holo, exited into mu-space proper, into golden void, while the squadrons formed twin formations and began to fly, surrounding the coffin, using inductive forces to drag it with them as they accelerated faster and faster towards the distant, spiky black star called Nullpoint. They flew with grace and exact precision, holding their complex configuration with the coffin at their centre—

Dad! Mum!

—and then broke apart, the ships screaming on perfect arcing trajectories away from the deadly sun as the coffin sped onwards, hurtling into the heart of the black star, and then they were gone.

Forever.

As the main part of the ceremony came to an end, Pilots on the floating tiers began to rise from their seats. On the balcony, some of the admirals were already turning to go inside where a formal buffet waited. Down on Borges Boulevard, sudden movement occurred, a fastpath rotation, and a shaven-headed man with rolled-up sleeves stepped out. Within seconds, Pilots in black jumpsuits had descended on the man, surrounding him, then led him away.

'What was—?'

'Nothing, Roger.' Rear-Admiral Schenck took his arm. 'Let's not allow anything to spoil today, shall we?'

It's already spoiled. My parents are dead.

But he said nothing, and allowed Schenck to lead him into the tall elegant chamber where buffet tables offered food and drink he could not even look at. Senior Pilots dressed in black and gold were everywhere. Off to one side, he could see several groups of grey-haired men and women deep in serious discussion, and he realized that for them, today was an opportunity for political wheeling and dealing, with so many gathered in one place.

'Excuse me,' said Schenck. 'There's someone I must talk to.'

'Yes, of course.'

Finally, amid the crowd, Roger saw someone he knew, and slipped past people who did not even notice him, until he was standing in front of Pilot Jed Goran.

'Jed.'

'Roger.'

They clasped hands in the Labyrinthine fashion.

'I'm sorry, my friend,' added Jed. 'You'll survive today, because you have to.'

'Yes. I will.'

'But no one will miss you for a while. Come with me.'

'I shouldn't—'

'Come.'

They walked together, through giant gold-and-sapphire doors into a high ornate corridor. There, Jed summoned a fastpath rotation.

'Trust me,' he said.

Roger followed him through.

They came out into a vast blue chamber. At its geometric centre, a small convex triangle was floating: black, webbed with red and gold.

'What is this?' asked Roger.

But it was not Jed who answered.

=Your father's legacy, young Pilot.=

Jed's hand clasped Roger's shoulder. From him, it was a gesture of support.

'I don't understand.'

'There'll be time. But I thought you should see it now.'

Panes of nothingness rotated, and they stepped inside.